HAWK

THE WILL SLATER SERIES BOOK SIX

MATT ROGERS

D1616915

Join the Reader's Group and get a free 200-page book by Matt Rogers!

Sign up for a free copy of '**HARD IMPACT**'.
Meet Jason King — another member of Black Force.

Experience King's most dangerous mission — action-packed insanity in the heart of the Amazon Rainforest.

No spam guaranteed.

Just click here.

BOOKS BY MATT ROGERS

THE JASON KING SERIES

Isolated (Book 1)

Imprisoned (Book 2)

Reloaded (Book 3)

Betrayed (Book 4)

Corrupted (Book 5)

Hunted (Book 6)

THE JASON KING FILES

Cartel (Book 1)

Warrior (Book 2)

Savages (Book 3)

THE WILL SLATER SERIES

Wolf (Book 1)

Lion (Book 2)

Bear (Book 3)

Lynx (Book 4)

Bull (Book 5)

Hawk (Book 6)

BLACK FORCE SHORTS

The Victor (Book 1)

PROLOGUE

Koh Tao
Thailand
Two months ago...

I t was hot, but it didn't faze them.

They were professionals.

The two men had arrived on the ferry three days ago, barely resembling how they looked now. Just in case there were security measures in place. Systems set up to search for new arrivals with sinister intentions.

As far as they were concerned, the changes in appearance were unnecessary. No-one would be looking for them. And if anyone happened to be, there was nothing to see. But they'd received explicit instructions, so they went through with it all anyway.

For reassurance.

They'd looked like any pair of pasty white men, maybe fresh out of college, here to drink and party and fornicate for a few days or weeks until the money ran out and they crawled back to their tiny apartments in the First World with a headache and an absence of hope for their future. They'd half-heartedly smuggled a couple of oversized glass beer bottles in brown paper bags onto the ferry for the journey across, and made sure to get caught sipping from their stash on a number of occasions by crew and passengers alike, complete with wide eyes and mumbled apologies and sly smirks in equal measure.

By all accounts, they were a couple of harmless fun-loving miscreants.

But then the pair touched down on land, and as soon as they stepped out onto the pier and shuffled through the hordes of tourists and locals, they sauntered into town and found a quiet alleyway tucked between a motorised scooter rental agency and a dive bar. The skin pigmentation cream rubbed off and the faux beer bellies they'd added around their waistlines peeled away and their contacts came out and their wigs slipped off, and suddenly they were lean and chiselled and tanned with eyes that were dull and soulless and short military-style buzzcuts. They looked absolutely nothing like the bumbling idiots they'd portrayed on the journey over. They left the accessories at the bottom of a fetid trash can halfway down the alley, covered in flies and muck and shit, and stepped back out with brand new demeanours.

Looking different, but still putting on a pair of impeccable performances.

Because they'd been told not to reveal their hard, cruel natures at any point in the public realm.

They didn't know who was watching.

Now, three days later, they sat at a carefully selected position in one of the Italian joints catering exclusively to the island's tourists. The owner had made a half-hearted attempt to pass the venue off as legitimate, but it was mostly an exaggerated caricature of an expensive restaurant with cheap beer flowing like water and half-decent pizzas and pastas to boot.

The two men weren't there for the food.

Outside, it was devilishly hot. They each had a thin sheen of sweat coating their foreheads and damp patches under their armpits, but that wasn't anything to be suspicious about in a climate like this. The sun was well on its way to disappearing below the horizon, and a blood-orange glow hung over the dirt road. The entire community near the pier was positioned on steep terrain, and the restaurant jutted out at an odd angle to counteract the way the dusty track sloped down toward the boats on the water.

Past the terracotta patio, a woman in her late twenties with blond hair and an eye-catching physique strolled past. She wore a simple floral dress, and she stared straight ahead. She was Scandinavian.

The two men looked at each other.

Mutual interest.

But not of the lustful kind.

'Should we do it tonight?' the first man said.

The second man glanced at his watch, sat back in his chair, and fingered the five-day-old stubble coating his jawline. It was the colour of salt and pepper. He had many, many years experience in this field. Relatively young on a standard timeline, but practically a wizened veteran in a business like this. He thought it over, and said, 'Why not?'

'There's the unpredictability factor, though.'

'We can deal with that.'

'Did you read the briefing? I don't know if we can.'

'We won't run into *him*.'

'Where is he?'

'Out. Not here.'

'We can't do it here,' the first man said, his gaze drifting to follow the woman. 'Too many variables.'

'No shit. We do it when she gets back home.'

'What if he's there?'

'He won't be.'

'We know he's out. But we're not tracking him. That leaves room for all sorts of problems. I don't like it.'

'You're a young man in this game. You haven't run into problems yet. You fear them like they're insurmountable. They're a part of the world we operate in, and we deal with them as they come. We'll be fine.'

'If there's a problem?'

'I'll handle it.'

'I hope you can.'

The second man sipped at his water and then nodded. 'Okay. Noted. Let's go.'

They slipped out of their seats like panthers in the jungle, with the efficiency of movement of men who had spent their entire lives training for moments like this. There was none of the lackadaisical sauntering they'd been util-ising for most of their time on the island. There was no longer a need for the facade.

The "unpredictable threat" had been spotted leaving the house an hour earlier, as he did the same time every evening. They'd trailed him up to the Muay Thai gym at the peak of one of Koh Tao's hills, and then retreated to the pier to lay in wait for their unsuspecting victim.

On cue, she'd showed up.

So now they paid their bill and left the restaurant as quickly as they'd arrived, disappearing into the vibrant bustle of a tropical island gripped by the tendrils of a gorgeous sunset.

Following a woman who had no idea she was in danger.

~

THE PAIR MADE it to the edge of the target's property just as the sun disappeared from view.

It melted below the horizon and a dull blue hue settled over the trail. The air hung thick and hot and heavy, but it had been the same for all three days they'd spent here. Hot perspiration pooled around their underarms and in the smalls of their backs.

They'd planned this to perfection. All the hypotheticals. Every possibility. They kept their gazes trained on the narrow opening in the trail a few dozen feet ahead.

They were well concealed on the other side of the dirt track. They'd employed all their old military training to reach the bungalow undetected. Not that the Scandinavian knew she was being followed. But it was the same philosophy they'd held on the ferry.

No harm in being cautious.

Both of them had expected more of a fortress when they'd first laid eyes on the property. They'd heard it was a bungalow — that was the intel provided — but neither of them had expected it to match that description in the slightest.

What they found was true to their superior's word. It was a fenceless unguarded trail spiralling into the outskirts of the jungle, opening into a small clearing with a low wooden hut. They could just make out the silhouette of the building inside the tree line. No guards manning the entrance. No cameras fixed to nearby tree trunks. No trip-wires installed to alert the occupants of approaching combatants. Just a normal dwelling in a quiet stretch of a tropical island.

But it made sense, when they put themselves in the

heads of their target and her partner. The pair had been through a whirlwind of chaos for a substantial stretch of their lives. It would be instinctive to avoid anything resembling formality. They both wanted a normal existence. And they thought no-one could find them here.

But they were gravely wrong.

The pair let the trail turn murky. The shadows deepened and elongated, and the buzz of insects seemed to amplify in the quiet. An overhead light inside the hut went out, just leaving the weak glow of a bedside lamp. The pair used night optics coupled with a magnification lens to observe the slim figure curled up on the bed. They had a direct line of sight through the open hut window. It was a close call — there was only a narrow sliver of view through the trees, but they were both confident they could make the shot.

That wasn't what their employer wanted, though.

He wanted it up close and personal.

So they rose out of the darkness and drew compact 9mm pistols from appendix holsters and ghosted across the trail. One man watched her through the lens, and the other watched their surroundings. Nothing passed them by. If the threat was en route, they'd know. But the woman's partner was nowhere to be found. They were alone on the trail.

They headed toward the hut.

The first man — the more experienced of the two — tried the door, not making a sound.

Locked.

No matter.

He took a deep breath, signalled to his partner, and then vaulted in over the open windowsill. He clattered to the floor inside the hut in an explosion of noise, landing on both feet. His partner followed him inside.

The woman's eyes came open in an instant and she

moved like lightning for a small object underneath her pillow. Just as she'd drilled over and over again, no doubt. Preparing for any encounter. Staying ready.

What a waste of time, the first man thought.

He was by the bed in a heartbeat, and he slammed an open palm down on the pillow and pinned her small hand under it with vicious grip strength. She struggled and squirmed and writhed, but she couldn't get the gun free. He kept his hand over the pillow, pinning her in place, and used his other hand to wrench hers out by the wrist. It almost came out with the gun, but he was prepared for that. He planted his palm down harder, trapping the weapon against the mattress, and she rolled off the bed, unarmed and vulnerable.

The second man seized her around the waist and held her in place.

She slashed an elbow behind her, and connected with his jaw, nearly dislocating it. He reeled away, but the size difference was enough to maintain control of the situation. He threw her into the wall and she crumpled to the floor in a heap, her breath rattling in her throat.

You have *been trained well,* the first man thought.

He approached with the 9mm pistol in his grip and crouched down by her. He kept a keen eye on the door, but it remained locked. He made sure to lower his frame below the window's line of sight, preventing him from succumbing to a last-ditch effort to seize back control of the situation. There was always room for that. He pictured her partner storming in at the last second, rescuing her from her attackers.

How valiant that would be, he thought.

It's a shame that's not how the world works.

He took her chin in his palm and lifted it so their eyes

met. The impact with the wall had busted her nose, and the pain had caused her eyes to well with tears. She was beautiful. Drop-dead gorgeous. She could have graced the cover of an international magazine. She could have been a star.

Instead, she'd decided to pledge allegiance to a bad, bad man.

The first man, in a voice barely above a whisper, said, 'Are you Klara?'

She nodded. 'My husband will be back any minute. You don't want to be here for that.'

'We won't be.'

Her face turned white.

Fear.

Raw fear.

There wasn't a sight in the world quite like it.

The first man said, 'He's at the gym. That's a shame. He could have been here. He could have helped you.'

The second guy made some kind of guttural noise, and the first man turned to see him clutching his jaw, shaking his head from side to side in disbelief.

'You need an ice-pack?' the first guy said.

The second guy shot him a glare.

'She's had some training,' he muttered, the lower half of his face already starting to swell.

The first guy shrugged. 'Didn't seem to help her.'

He turned back, and saw something close to hope in her eyes.

It almost made him laugh.

'Are you counting your blessings?' he said. 'You think you're managing to stall us?'

She didn't say anything.

He leant in close and whispered, 'I was letting you think

that. Just to give you hope. But life doesn't work that way. There's no last minute rescue.'

She turned pale again.

He said, 'This isn't a fairytale, Klara. There's no happy ending.'

He raised the 9mm pistol and shot her in the head.

THE BODY WAS HEAVIER than they expected.

The first man took her by the arms, and the second by the legs. They lifted her up and dumped her down on the mattress, in roughly the same position she'd been dozing. Blood welled across the pillow, soaking in. The first man breathed out, put his hands on his hips, and admired his handiwork.

A smile creased his thin lips.

He was savouring the thrill.

The second guy could tell his colleague was high off the adrenalin. He'd been the one to fire the kill shot, and he didn't seem to be treating the situation with the urgency it required. They'd both been briefed about the woman's partner. They knew a rough outline of his operational history. Rumours and whispers of the details that hadn't been blacked out in the records.

As much as their superior could divulge, apparently.

But the second man had a bad feeling about the whole goddamn thing.

It seemed like their employer had been holding back certain details.

The second man said, 'Let's go.'

But he wasn't able to mask the fear in time. He uttered the words too fast, and his voice cracked at the end. The first man wheeled on the spot, almost amused by the whole thing.

'Why?' the first guy said. 'What's the rush?'

'The husband.'

'They're not married.'

'You know what I mean. The boyfriend.'

'He's still at the gym.'

'You sure?'

The first man shrugged, and adjusted his grip on the 9mm in his hand. 'I almost hope he's not.'

And suddenly the second guy saw it all laid out before him. It almost seemed too obvious, in hindsight. He should have known there was room for error.

His co-worker had endless experience in the field, but sported nothing close to the reputation of this mystery man — the guy whose girlfriend they'd come to kill. The second guy saw envy and jealousy and bitterness in his co-worker, all rolled into one. The first man, despite his supposed "experience," wanted to confront the mystery man. Wanted to put a bullet in his head to prove a point. Hence the lack of surveillance.

The first guy *wanted* to meet the guy whose reputation had supposedly trumped his own.

Because of his own goddamn lack of humility.

The second guy said, 'I don't think you should be so confident about this.'

The first guy said, 'Supposedly this man is the stuff of legend. I want to see what he's made of.'

'If he's anywhere near us, he'll have heard the gunshot.'

'Good.'

The front door crashed off its hinges, ripped from its frame by a thunderous front kick.

Both men wheeled toward the sound, and the first guy

reacted accordingly. He raised his 9mm pistol and fired a couple of shots at the door as it clattered to the floor just inside the entrance. One round shredded the wood, and the other whisked out into the night.

Hitting nothing.

Because no-one was there.

They both froze in the shadows, wired to the eyeballs with adrenalin, and the second guy thought the world might end right then and there. He'd never been put on the back step like this. They both skewered their gaze on the doorway, searching for any sign of movement in the semi-darkness beyond.

Then a giant figure vaulted in through the open window beside them, impossibly fast.

Way faster than they had entered.

Neither of them spotted it until he was right there, only inches away from them in the lowlight, and by then it was too late.

The first guy tried to swing the 9mm pistol around in time but the newcomer seized him by the wrist and snapped his forearm with a stabbing elbow. The grotesque *crack* made the second guy hesitate for a moment, and he found himself unusually unprepared to react. He went for the 9mm pistol at his own waist, but by that point the newcomer had bundled the first guy up in a powerful bear hug, and then he hurled his foe like the guy was nothing more than an oversized bowling pin.

Inhuman strength.

Almost surreal in nature.

Two hundred pounds of the first guy hit the second guy in the chest and knocked him off-balance. He didn't go all the way down, but he lost his footing, and by the time he righted himself the newcomer was right there in his face.

Six foot three.

Well over two hundred pounds.

Short, thick brown hair.

A weathered, handsome face with a jaw like steel and eyes like ice.

Jason King head butted the second guy in the face, breaking the man's orbital bone with his own forehead.

The second guy collapsed back against the bungalow wall, in too much pain to think.

The first guy was unarmed and pale, his shooting arm mangled beyond repair.

King kicked him in the groin and threw him head-first into the same wall, where he slumped down alongside his colleague.

Through a haze of semi-consciousness, the second man felt fear like nothing he'd ever experienced before. It was a deep, guttural, primal sensation. He already couldn't see out of one eye. He couldn't feel the left half of his face. But the physical pain wasn't what bothered him. It was that King hadn't shot them on sight. He'd beaten them down like they were made of glass.

He'd kept them alive.

To decide their fate when he had time to deduce what had happened.

Through a mask of agony, the second man watched King approach the bed, labouring slowly across the dark room like a golem. He stood quiet for what seemed like hours, staring down at the body on the mattress. Pure emotion bristled in the air. The atmosphere crackled. The second guy opened his mouth to apologise, to say something — anything.

But what the hell was he going to say?

So he sat there, wallowing in pain as the left half of his

face swelled like a pumpkin, mute and forlorn. His colleague sat alongside him, in an equal amount of pain, feeling an equal amount of regret.

Finally, Jason King turned around to face them.

There was a look in his eyes that neither of them had thought physically possible.

They didn't know one man could possess so much rage.

King advanced toward them.

PART I

1

Budapest
Hungary
Present day...

'Do you understand who my husband is?' the woman hissed under her breath, her voice low. Trying to keep the conversation hushed.

But, seated next to her, Will Slater heard every word.

He was in a ruin bar, surrounded by artistic disrepair, silently savouring the aesthetic. The Budapest staple appealed to him. It was a battered, broken shell of a room. It had been converted from a rundown and vandalised office space, but most of the destruction dished out to the commercial premises had been left as is. Instead of cleaning up, the new owners had worked around it, adding bright colours and tables and chairs and a long wooden counter-top. It was gritty and unfiltered and suited him just fine.

He could appreciate anything that thrived in a state of ruin.

Atypically, he was as far from ruin as he'd been in quite some time.

After a harrowing stretch in Zimbabwe a few months earlier, he'd come away sporting a surprising lack of permanent injuries. His shoulder, chest, and sternum had healed promptly, no thanks to a generous dose of controversial stem cell therapy in a clinic he frequented on the outskirts of Tijuana.

It was illegal in mainland America, but Mexico provided guaranteed anonymity.

He was feeling fresh within ten days. Then he'd plunged into an exercise regime with a sickening level of dedication. He didn't know why. If he had to pinpoint a reason, he might ruminate that his life seemed to ebb and flow with every incident he got involved in.

And it seemed to move in a cycle.

There was a short burst of pain and war, followed by an extended period of downtime. He was learning to recognise the downtime for what it was and take advantage of it. He'd spent the past two months bettering himself in every way imaginable, even though there was little to improve upon in the first place.

And, somehow, he'd kept himself out of trouble along the way.

But then the woman next to him raised her voice in heavily accented English, and a dark premonition in the primal part of his brain told him the downtime was over. Her lithe figure was clad in an expensive black dress that ended halfway up her thighs. She wore knee-high boots and her straight black hair hung like a stage curtain over the back of her neck. He figured she was in her early forties. She was with a friend who looked awfully similar — tall, dark, sly — and they were embroiled in an argument with an unruly big guy on the other side of the line-up.

The new guy had a friend, too.

Two on two.

The women had been quiet and subdued until the conversation took a turn. The men were loud and drunk, as they had been for most of the last ten minutes. And then there was Slater, stewing silently on his own, as he always did.

He gulped down the last mouthful of the Old-Fashioned in his hand and gently placed the empty tumbler back on the bar's countertop. He looked at the bartender, who looked right back at him. Asking a question, and getting an answer from the level of detail in the guy's eyes.

Don't get involved, the bartender was silently telling him.

Slater swivelled on the stool and got involved.

The women were in a neat line, shoulder to shoulder along the bar, stomachs pressed to the countertop, facing directly forward. The age-old *leave-me-alone* pose. The men had started that way, opting to fire catcalls across the bar, but the guy furthest away had drifted over to get closer to them. Now they formed a rudimentary right-angle.

Slater leant away from the bar, so they could see him sitting there. All two hundred and ten pounds of him. He'd packed on muscle like nobody's business during this particular stretch of downtime. Usually sitting at one-ninety, he'd converted an extended calorie surplus into a near hundred pound increase in all his usual compound lifts. He rested a bulging forearm on his knee and stared directly at the two guys.

They were in their thirties, European, big, muscular, pumped full of testosterone. They must have come expecting a conquest, and it was getting late. Therefore they were getting desperate.

They needed some action.

Slater figured he'd give them some.

He didn't blink. He just kept looking at them until they noticed him. He had enough life experience to know how to antagonise. If they could hand out master's degrees in the practice, he would have received his ten years ago.

They noticed him.

They both stared at him, and then one of them looked away, anticipating that Slater would back down from his confrontational stance.

He didn't.

Then they both *really* stared at him.

The bigger guy said, 'What the fuck are you looking at?'

Like reading from a B-movie script.

Both women spun, and Slater made eye contact with them for the first time. They could have been twins. They both had black eyeliner piled on thick, which made their green eyes striking. They were tanned. But on top of all that, they looked dangerous. Maybe not to the common observer. But Slater could see a menacing spark in both their eyes.

And suddenly he thought he might have interpreted the bartender's look the wrong way.

It was always, *Don't get involved.*

But it might have been because of who the women were, not the men...

But now he *was* involved. And he'd enraged the two perverts. Which meant none of this was going to end politely.

Although he didn't exactly feel like wasting his energy in a barroom brawl.

So he changed the direction of the script. The following

conversation was supposed to hit all the prerequisite beats. Slater had seen it a thousand times before.

What the fuck are you looking at?

You.

Going to do something about it?

Maybe. Why don't you come over here and find out?

This is your last chance to leave. Beat it.

I'm staying right here.

Well, okay then...

It had a purpose in traditional bar fights. There had to be some kind of feeling-out process. You didn't see someone staring at you and instantly hit them in the face. There had to be that vital delay where you could size them up, read into their responses, try to discern how nervous they were, all the while injecting confidence into yourself in preparation for that first big swing.

But none of that happened.

Because as soon as the first guy said, 'What the fuck are you looking at?' Slater flew off the stool like he'd been electrocuted, and before either of them could blink he was in front of the guy with one hand wrapped around the back of his neck. Which didn't have to be taken as a dire physical threat at first. Men did it in bars all the time to establish dominance. Clasp a palm around the back of the neck and pull them in close.

But Slater didn't pull forward. He flexed his forearm and used tremendous grip strength to pull the guy's head down, and there was nothing the man could do to resist it. Then Slater hit him in the gut with a short uppercut, but he used the bulk of the guy's frame to mask the punch from the rest of the bar, so the altercation wasn't visible.

Then Slater stepped away, as fast as he'd darted into range, and he relaxed, diffusing the tension.

The guy he'd hit in the stomach threw up all over the bar's countertop, his insides spasming violently from the force behind the blow.

Then he slumped onto the nearest stool and continued to dry heave.

Embarrassed and going pale, his friend shook his head in resignation and hauled the guy away from the bar, muttering a half-hearted apology to the bartender. There was a brief moment of tension — he looked at Slater and considered seeking revenge.

But he'd been *right there*. He'd seen how hard Slater hit his friend. It probably hadn't even looked real.

Then the first guy threw up again, all over himself, and that sealed the decision.

The second guy opted not to risk any further embarrassment by lingering around in the contents of his friend's stomach. He looped his hands under the man's armpits and dragged him toward the exit.

The first guy retched again.

The second guy quickened his pace.

And then they were gone.

Slater sat back down on his stool and grimaced as he surveyed the puke littered across the countertop.

The bartender shot him a dark look and said, 'Thanks for that.'

Slater feigned ignorance. 'For what?'

'You didn't need to do that.'

'But I did.'

Then one of the women piped up, and in a scornful tone she said, 'You really didn't need to do that.'

Slater said, 'And yet, here I am.'

2

The dark-haired woman said, 'Who are you?'

Slater said, 'An accountant.'

'No you're not.'

'Then you can narrow it down yourself, can't you?'

'If you're the competition, you could get me in a lot of trouble for talking to you. That's why I'm asking.'

Slater said, 'What?'

She looked at him, then averted her gaze and said, 'Never mind. Said too much.'

'Who's your husband?'

She raised an eyebrow.

He said, 'You asked those guys if they understood who your husband was.'

'That still falls under the category of saying too much, I'm afraid.'

But her actions belied her words, because she sure as shit wasn't going anywhere. In fact, she was tilting herself toward Slater to make the conversation a little easier.

The opposite of the age-old *leave-me-alone* pose.

There was unrest all around them. The bartender

circled around the bar with a mountain of cloths and rags in one hand, and a mop in the other. The fetid stink of the vomit began floating across the space, driving patrons to the other ends of the room. Surprisingly, though, no-one had vacated the premises in a hurry. This was Budapest, and people had paid good money for their drinks. A light scuffle at one end of the room wasn't going to deter them.

But the bartender shot daggers at Slater as he set to work cleaning up the mess, so Slater deemed it prudent to move the conversation elsewhere.

He gestured to an unoccupied booth skewered into the corner of the far wall.

He lifted an eyebrow.

Wordless.

The women looked at each other, shrugged to themselves, and nodded in unison.

He slid off the stool and made an *after you* gesture. As they stepped away from the countertop, Slater passed a twenty-euro note to the bartender.

'Sorry about all that,' he mumbled.

'Watch yourself,' the bartender muttered back, flashing a pointed glance at the two black-clad women.

Slater said, 'I can take care of myself.'

He followed them toward the booth and sat down across from them. He hadn't a clue where the conversation might lead, but that was the nature of his life.

Venture boldly into the unknown and see what awaits.

'I'm not the competition,' he said. 'My name's Will Slater.'

'Is that supposed to mean something?' the first woman said.

The second woman had yet to say a word.

'It's just my name,' he said. 'I assume you've both got them too.'

The first woman said, 'Camilla.'

The second woman said, 'Dani.'

Slater looked at Dani and said, 'You speak.'

'Not often,' Dani said, but she managed the hint of a smile.

'I'm usually the one that does all the talking,' Camilla said. 'And I'm not about to break that trend, I'm afraid. Might I ask why you're sitting across from us right now?'

Dani mumbled, 'He's oblivious.'

'Evidently,' Camilla said.

Dani said in her trademark low tone, 'He's making a mistake.'

'Obviously,' Camilla said.

Slater shrugged. 'I make mistakes all the time. It hasn't caught up to me yet.'

Camilla's eyes sparkled, aflame with something eerily resembling desire. 'I like you.'

'Sounds like that could be a dangerous game to play,' Slater said. 'Based on what the two of you are hinting at. Who are you both?'

Camilla shrugged.

Dani stared.

Slater said, 'There *is* a mood, is there not?'

Camilla said, 'Of course there's a mood. Everything we do is deliberate. You should have figured that out by now.'

'I don't really know how to interpret it.'

Dani said, 'You're not supposed to. We're supposed to just give off a vibe.'

'Well, I can feel it.'

'What's it telling you?'

'That I should head as far away from you two as possible.'

'Then you're picking it up correctly.'

Slater said, 'But I think it's a test. To sort the men from the boys. You're putting the feelers out. You're trying to let me know — *hey, our husbands are involved in some shady shit* — without making it obvious. But you're still sitting here. And you're still looking at me. And I'm still looking at you. Do I look deterred?'

Dani said, 'Not at all.'

Camilla said, 'Keep talking.'

Slater said, 'Your husbands are the unscrupulous types, I imagine. And that's putting it nicely. The way you threw that information around when you got harassed just before... I think they're organised crime. That's how you two know each other. That's why you look like sisters. You're wives of powerful men that go for a certain type.'

'And what is that type?' Camilla said.

Slater said, 'Stunning.'

Silence.

Dani looked at her friend and mouthed, 'He's exotic, isn't he?'

Slater grinned his trademark grin and rested his chin on a tightened fist, his elbow skewered into the chipped surface of the table. Like a parody of Prince Charming.

He said, 'You're getting a real weird vibe now, aren't you? Because it seems like I couldn't give a shit about organised crime.'

Camilla said, 'You should.'

'But you don't want me to. You wanted someone like me to show up. Maybe just to shake things up. Stir the pot, so to speak. Someone who could give your husbands a run for their money on the danger scale. Am I checking the boxes?'

Dani said, 'We should leave.'

Camilla said, 'We should.'

But they stayed right where they were.

Slater said, 'How are your marriages?'

Camilla said, 'That's a topic we're not getting into tonight.'

'We don't need to get into it. I can tell exactly how your marriages are going. Because you're still sitting here. And you didn't turn and run when I put out the feelers.'

Dani said, 'Let's bring him to the hotel.'

Staring straight at Slater as she spoke.

Camilla said, 'He won't want that.'

'Why not?' Slater said.

'You will get yourself killed. If our husbands find out you will be worse than dead.'

Slater sat completely still, and he made sure to stare unblinking into each of their eyes in turn. He said, 'Do I look scared?'

They both said, 'No,' in unison.

Slater said, 'I'm not scared.'

'You should be.'

'But I'm not.'

'You enjoy this,' Camilla said. 'The danger. I can see it in your eyes. It's like you weren't alive when you were sitting at that bar with nothing to do. We saw you when we came in. You looked completely different to how you look now. You don't want to get away with this, do you? You want to screw us and lord it over our husbands. You don't want to slip away undetected.'

'I gave up on wanting any particular outcome a long time ago,' Slater said. 'I just take things the way they come. The question is — how badly do you want to avoid your husbands finding out?'

They looked him up and down, making no apologies for the blatant objectification. He didn't mind. He was doing the same to them.

Camilla said, 'Not bad enough to stop.'

Dani said, 'It's not our fault if you get yourself killed.'

Slater said, 'I've been told that a thousand times.'

'And what happened?'

'I'm still here.'

'You talk a good game,' Camilla said. 'There'd better be a payoff at the end of the tunnel. We wouldn't risk our reputation for anything less.'

'Let me show you,' Slater said.

Dani raised an eyebrow.

Slater said, 'You'd risk your reputation every day of the week for it.'

'That good?' Camilla said.

'So I've been told.'

'If you're exaggerating, we'll tell our husbands what you did.'

'Maybe I want your husbands to find out regardless.'

'That danger. You live for it, don't you?'

Slater said, 'More or less.'

'Has it been a while?'

'I've had a few weeks off.'

'A few weeks off from seducing the wives of criminals?'

'Trust me,' Slater said. 'I'm not rusty.'

'I believe it.'

'What do your husbands do?'

'A little of everything. They'd be on the Forbes list if their assets were in their own names.'

'Drugs?'

'Yes.'

'Guns?'

'Yes.'

'And everything else?'

'Yes.'

'I'd love to meet them.'

'That's not going to happen,' Camilla said. 'You're too dangerous for your own good. But you can still show us a good time.'

Dani turned to Camilla and said, 'I need him.'

'I need him too.'

Slater said, 'Let's go.'

He climbed out of the booth and led them out of the ruin bar with a hand placed on each of the smalls of their backs. On the way out he managed a final glance at the bartender, frozen in place in a freshly clean patch of linoleum flooring, jaw half-open in shock. The man couldn't believe what he was seeing.

Slater could tell what he was thinking.

Not only has this guy ignored my advice, it seems he's deliberately trying to do the opposite. He's got a death wish. He wants to die.

Slater winked to the man, waved farewell, and guided Camilla and Dani out into the night.

3

————

S later came to in a groggy stupor at nearly two in the morning, and as he peeled an eyelid open he focused on controlling the postcoital lethargy as best he could.

Satisfying them both had been tiring, but he'd proved his worth. It had taken a couple of hours, but he was nothing if not persistent. They lay on either side of him, fast asleep, worn out from the rigorous physical activity. The three of them were tangled in sheets, their naked chests rising and falling with each breath.

He rubbed his eyes and managed a half-smile.

It had been a pleasant evening.

But that wasn't the reason he'd seduced them.

Camilla had nailed it the first time.

'That danger. You live for it, don't you?'

He couldn't deny it. He'd sensed their husbands were bad men, and capitalised. He didn't ordinarily go for married women. Not his style. It didn't seem morally pure. An interesting dichotomy, considering most of his career had been spent putting bullets in heads and slashing throats.

But that was his life.

Extreme violence, coupled with a perverse sense of right and wrong.

That's the way it had always been.

And it would be that way until the day he died.

Which, judging by the comments Camilla and Dani had made earlier in the evening, might come sooner rather than later.

Camilla stirred next to him in the darkness. Slater propped himself up against the headboard and surveyed the room in the lowlight. He was on the top floor of a spacious townhouse in Budapest's fifth district, one of the city's most opulent and expensive areas. The ceiling sat far above their heads, masked from view by the frame of the four-poster bed they were lying in.

Camilla placed a hand on his chest and offered him a coy smile. There was none of the snark from before.

He'd proved himself, after all.

She said, 'Hey.'

He said, 'When do your husbands get home?'

'A long time from now,' she said. 'Or you'd have been kicked out already.'

'Maybe I want to hang around. Maybe I want to talk to them.'

'That'd be trespassing, then. If we wanted you out, and you refused.'

'That's a strange stance for someone involved in organised crime.'

'I'm not. My husband is.'

'You seem thrilled to be with him,' Slater said.

'Life isn't as simple as just walking away.'

'Yes, it is. When you break it all the way down, that's all it is. But you're used to this life. So you'll stay. And maybe you'll keep sleeping around until you get caught, just to liven things up. And see where it takes you.'

'You think we're using you?'

'If you want to call it that. I can't complain. I'm doing the same to you.'

Camilla raised an eyebrow, highlighting her beauty in the dark blue room. 'You are?'

'I don't like organised crime all that much.'

'I can tell.'

'I'd like to talk to your husbands. Maybe put them on a different path. I can be fairly persuasive.'

'You trying to save the world?'

'Piece by piece.'

'Well, it's too bad we're kicking you out now.'

Beside them, Dani stirred.

'What?' she mumbled.

'He was just leaving,' Camilla said.

Eyes half-closed, Dani frowned and pursed her lips. 'That's no fun.'

'Up for another round?' Slater muttered in her ear.

She giggled.

Camilla frowned and said, 'No, Will, you really need to leave.'

Slater shrugged, nonchalant. 'It's too late anyway.'

'What are you talking about?'

'You were both spent after we finished. You didn't notice that I didn't actually go to the bathroom. I took a quick trip down to that panel by the front door and flipped a few switches. Worked it out pretty fast. The silent alarm's been ringing for the better part of an hour now. I assume that doesn't go to the police.'

Camilla's face fell. 'What the fuck have you done?'

'We're about to find out, aren't we?'

She used the hand resting on his chest to slap him hard in the sternum. 'You moron.'

He smiled. 'That's not nice.'

'Fuck you.'

Then the reality of the situation hit her, and she scrambled out of the four-poster bed, snatching at parts of her outfit that had been tossed across the room at random. Her bra was resting in one corner, burrowed into the plush carpet, and her panties lay balled up a dozen feet away. The three of them had been ravenous when they'd first entered the room, and the aftermath spelled it out fairly succinctly.

Slater calmly slipped out from underneath the covers and slid on his underwear and the same pair of smart dress pants he'd worn to the ruin bar.

Then, downstairs, the sound of the front door flying open resonated through the empty townhouse.

Screw it, he thought. *I'll just have to do it bare chested.*

He figured that would be more humiliating for the new arrivals anyway.

He tiptoed across the room with bare feet, his toes sinking into the carpet. He reached the lavish double doors leading into the master bedroom and pressed his back against the wall nearby. The moonlight spilled in through the nearest window, accentuating the powerful physique he'd forged through hellfire over a decade of hardship. The barrel chest, the corded arms, the round deltoids, the veins like road maps along his forearms. He hovered there, watching Camilla and Dani intently, trying to figure out whether they would betray him or not.

He shouldn't have given them the benefit of the doubt.

As soon as Camilla recognised that Slater was lying in wait, she screamed.

Slater narrowed his eyes and gave her a withering look.

'That's not going to work,' he hissed.

Thumping footsteps sounded on the stairwell, racing up toward the master bedroom. Slater tensed up in anticipation.

At the last second, he muttered, 'Actually, that might have helped.'

The two men burst into the room with exaggerated bravado, Glock pistols in their hands, their chests puffed up like peacocks. They looked ridiculous. They came in out of position, narrowing to squeeze through the slim gap between the double doors. Both doors sat slightly ajar. It created a perfect runway for Slater to line up his offence.

The first guy came in with a near thirty pound weight advantage over Slater, all commercial fitness, like he'd dedicated half his waking existence to bench pressing a barbell. He had a beefy artificial body, but the equivalent of male breasts did nothing to prevent Slater's elbow from detonating off the side of his head and robbing him of his consciousness. As the guy collapsed forward Slater stripped the Glock off him and used it to pistol whip the second arrival in the nose. He smashed the butt of the gun on the bridge of the guy's nose with pinpoint accuracy.

Like cracking a whip.

Lash.

The second guy recoiled, horrified by the sudden explosion of nerve endings across his face, but he didn't go down.

With a near lifetime of experience in MMA, Slater changed levels by ducking low, and looped his arms around the man's lower thighs. He picked him up and dumped him on his head. All technique. He used what he saved on power to quicken his timing. So by the time the guy rolled forward with his head spinning, realising he'd probably just been concussed, Slater was already on top of him. He pinned him down and wrestled the second Glock away and threw both guns across the room.

Then he slapped the second man in the face.

Hard.

It sounded like a gunshot.

Camilla screamed again.

Slater said, 'Now that's *really* not going to work.'

Dani just sat there on the bed, half-amused.

Slater got the sense Dani was a fierce woman.

Camilla, on the other hand...

Camilla said, 'Lukas, I swear—'

Slater held up a hand above Lukas' head, threatening another vicious slap to her husband, and she went quiet.

Lukas bucked, trying to lever Slater off him.

Slater slapped him again.

This time, harder.

The man audibly whimpered and cowered into a ball.

Slater clambered to his feet, and all went still.

He had total control.

4

S later said, 'We've got a few things to discuss.'

But it wasn't going to end there. To these men, reputation was everything.

Lukas had experienced the full wrath of Slater's power — two open-handed slaps had puffed up his cheek and turned his jaw numb. One eye was already swelling shut.

He curled into a ball and offered no resistance.

The unnamed man, on the other hand, had just crawled out of temporary unconsciousness. He was brash and big-headed, and he didn't quite have a grip on how dangerous Slater was. And in a business like this, hesitation equaled death.

A man without a sinister reputation had nothing to live for.

He reared to his feet like a newborn giraffe and stumbled toward Slater with his fists raised.

Camilla flashed a horrified glance at Dani, as if silently saying, *Aren't you going to say something? That's* your *husband.*

Dani just kept the half-smile in place.

Slater moved his head forward a couple of inches, as if

going through the initial wind-up before a punch. He telegraphed it from across the room. He stuck his chin right out there and widened his eyes and tensed up his shoulders.

To his credit, the unnamed man crawled out of semi-consciousness just in time to react accordingly. He braced for impact, bringing his elbows up in a ludicrous defensive posture, as if Slater couldn't simply slip a jab straight through the guard and shatter his nose.

But instead Slater kicked the guy's legs out from underneath him.

The guy went completely sideways in the air and tumbled back to the carpet. He hit his skull against the floor and went right back to sleep.

Slater looked at Lukas, and raised an eyebrow.

The big Hungarian was in no state to protest.

Slater said, 'Okay. Where were we?'

In heavily accented English, Lukas said, 'You wanted to discuss a few things.'

Slater looked at Camilla and Dani, and pointed at Lukas. 'See that? Finally, someone reasonable...'

Camilla screwed up her face in disgust and said, 'Lukas, this man—'

'Burst into your room and assaulted you both?' Slater interrupted.

Camilla said, 'Yes.'

'That's the avenue you want to take?'

'Yes.'

'I don't like getting accused of rape.'

'It's not an accusation, it's the—'

Slater cut her off by turning to Lukas and saying, 'You've got a lot of enemies?'

Lukas didn't respond.

His tone deathly cold, Slater said, 'Answer. And make sure you tell the truth. Or I'll know.'

Lukas nodded.

Slater said, 'You take precautions to protect you and your family against these enemies?'

Lukas nodded again.

Slater said, 'You have CCTV in the house? In case of a dire emergency? In case something horrifying happens to you or your loved ones and you need to seek revenge?'

A third nod.

Slater said, 'You have CCTV in this room?'

A pause. Then a half-hearted shrug, followed swiftly by a fourth nod.

Camilla's jaw slackened and she paled. A hint of anger flushed hot in her eyes, followed swiftly by crippling guilt.

Slater said, 'There you go. Camilla, if you want to prove your accusations, tell your husband to check the tapes after we're done here.'

Lukas stared up at him.

Slater said, 'You're going to want to check the tapes. Just to make sure.'

Lukas scrunched up his face, half pained, half humiliated, and said, 'What do you want?'

'I want to know how you managed to afford this place.'

'I'm a businessman.'

'Crack? Heroin? What does best on the streets?'

Lukas sighed and bowed his head and said, 'Crack cocaine. It's all the rage in Budapest right now.'

'How do you import it?'

'Cargo planes.'

'How do you get away with that?'

'Pay the right people. Everyone takes bribes if you offer enough.'

'Are you the brains behind the operation?'

'No,' the man said, and Slater knew he was telling the truth.

Slater had first-hand experience with organised crime. Nearly a decade of it. He'd dived deep enough into the chain of command to understand that it effectively functioned like a normal business, besides the illegality. The only difference was the consequences.

If you break the rules in the normal world, you get fired.

If you break the rules in the criminal world, you get dead.

But it wasn't a dictatorship. Not even close. Competence came out on top, just as it did in the real world. And there was no megalomaniac sitting behind a desk controlling everything. It was an enormous operation with a million moving parts.

It was unlikely that Slater had stumbled upon the two men at the top of the food chain. The opulent surroundings didn't mean anything. You could do very well for yourself and still exist at a lower rung on the ladder.

Slater said, 'What do you two do?'

'We handle operations for the rural HQs. The airfields that are responsible for most of the incoming deliveries. There's a lot of behind-the-scenes work to be taken care of.'

'You work from there?'

'No. We work in an office, like regular people. We—'

Then all of a sudden he clammed up, as if the consequences of what he was saying had just hit him. Slater had seen this all before, too. Slater had a certain refined talent in interrogations. Both conversational, yet intimidating. He'd honed it to a tee over the years. Now he could extract information before any of his subjects realised what they were saying.

Now Lukas did, and he shut his mouth tight.

'You don't know where the airfields are, do you?' Slater said. 'You think I'm going to ask you to direct me there, but you don't have the actual locations. And you think I won't believe you. So you're keeping your mouth shut.'

Lukas stared at him, mouth agape. 'How the hell did you know that?'

'A wild guess. Don't worry — I understand. You're the equivalent of a system administrator, aren't you? You keep everything running, and all the lights turned on, but you don't need to know specific details for that. Like what's coming in, and in what quantities, and where. You just keep the programs up to date. Better for deniability if you don't know the details.'

Lukas nodded. 'We handle the business we're given, and we're paid well for it. We don't worry about anything else.'

Slater opened his mouth to ask another question, but shut it again promptly a second later.

He realised he already had everything he needed.

He had enough to work out this wasn't the fight for him.

5

S later said, 'You realise I could put you away for life if I got that on tape?'

Lukas looked up from his position lying on the carpet. Dejected. Defeated. 'Did you record that?'

'No. Not my style. I'm more of a vigilante.'

'What's your aim here?'

Slater put his hands on his hips.

He said, 'In truth, I don't know.'

'You're a weird guy.'

'I thought this would be more of a challenge.'

'Are you going to tell me to stop breaking the law? Is that what you're leading up to?'

Slater gave him a look. 'Would you listen if I did?'

'Of course not. And if you leave me alive, I'll make sure to hunt you down.'

'That's not the right thing to say in a situation like this.'

'I have a reputation to uphold.'

'And how's that working out for you right now?'

Lukas went quiet.

'What's your friend's name?' Slater said, pointing to the

half-conscious partner lying on his back with a dazed expression on his face.

Lukas said, 'Benicio.'

'Do you have the same job?'

'We're business partners.'

'If I felt like going down this avenue, where would you recommend I start?'

Lukas stared at him. 'Are you being serious?'

'Of course.'

'We're just one rung on the ladder. You'll be dead in a few days if you follow this trail.'

'I've heard that a lot lately. I'm still here.'

'You'd be tackling an entire crime family. You'd be tackling members of the government. Do you have backup?'

'Just me.'

'You're insane.'

'I thought you were two of the most feared men in Hungary.'

'We are.'

'Then I'm not so insane, am I?'

'What did we do to you? Family got caught in the crossfire? If it's that, it wasn't personal.'

Slater regarded him with the utmost contempt. 'It wasn't that. But I'm glad to hear it wouldn't have been personal.'

'I'm sorry for whatever we did to you.'

'You didn't do anything to me. I just thought I'd test the waters. I've been out of the game for a few months. I thought this might be the avenue to suck me back in.'

'I don't know what any of that means.'

'Count yourself lucky.'

'Why?'

'Because I'm deciding not to pursue it.'

'So what happens now?'

Slater went silent.

Choose your battles, he told himself.

He said, 'Now I leave.'

'Just like that?'

'Just like that.'

'What were you hoping to achieve?'

'I live a fairly unique life, Lukas,' Slater said. 'I don't know if you figured that out by now, but you should have.'

'So that's what this is?' Lukas said, his speech slightly slurred as it passed through his swollen jaw. 'You just get your rocks off by kicking the shit out of people?'

Slater turned to look at Camilla and Dani, and he said, 'Not quite true. I don't need to do that. I usually just get my rocks off the old-fashioned way.'

Then he picked up his shirt and fetched his shoes from the corner of the room, and gathered up both Glocks for precautionary purposes, and left all four of them sprawled across the master bedroom in a perpetual state of unrest.

Dejection swept through the atmosphere. There would be ramifications. Perhaps a fallout or two. A couple of quick divorces. Or not.

Slater wasn't about to hang around to see it play out.

Because he'd judged the situation very differently. He'd reacted on a whim, figuring he could sink into the underworld of organised crime resting under the surface of Budapest. But sometimes reality is a whole lot different to what you imagine.

And when he considered the logistics of waging war against a crime family, he envisioned a skirmish that could drag on for months, if not years.

He couldn't rearrange an entire country's black market. He didn't run a firm. He didn't have a small army of mercenaries working for him.

But he could help people personally.

At an individual level.

So he left, and sauntered down through the townhouse's three levels, and stepped out into a chilly Hungarian evening.

He took a deep breath, and detached himself from the madness of the last few hours, and promptly let it pass from his mind.

He picked a direction at random and set off walking, figuring he could bunker down in any luxury hotel he came across. He had the working capital for that kind of expenditure. He was deep in the fifth district, but after a few moments thought, the lure of the seventh district called to him. That was where most of the ruin bars lay, deep in abandoned buildings in the old Jewish quarter.

He needed a drink to delay the inevitable hangover and let the evening's lack of resolution fade from his mind. So he got his bearings and powered towards District VII.

Fifteen minutes into the walk, he figured out he was being followed.

I t had nothing to do with Camilla, or Dani, or Lukas, or Benicio.

He was certain.

Because the tail was far more adept at keeping to the shadows than a grunt employed by an organised crime family. If it was a typical Hungarian street thug following him, he would have spotted the guy in seconds. But this man was talented. Slater almost didn't pick up on him for most of the first five minutes. He caught whispers of movement in his peripheral vision, but chalked them up to stray animals, or the street lights reflecting off a car in a certain way. Only when he wheeled on the spot in a quiet residential street did he see a darkened figure dart into the shadows.

Slater froze.

The cold settled over him.

His breath steamed in front of his face.

He folded his arms over his chest, tucking his hands into his armpits. He waited, aware of the compact Glock 19 pressing into the small of his back. He could have the gun out in half a second. He could blast through anyone faster than they could get a beat on him. But he didn't pick up on any signs of hostility.

Intuition told him this wouldn't end in a firefight.

Which made him awfully curious about who was following.

He hovered there for another beat, all his muscles relaxed, maintaining nonchalance. Then he broke into a sprint, feet pounding the pavement. He made it to the lip of the alley in a few seconds.

He jammed his boots into the concrete and skidded to a stop, and wrenched the Glock from his waistband and aimed it into the shadows.

There was nothing there.

He stayed where he was, his breath coming out in clouds.

Indecision plagued him.

It wasn't organised crime. So what was going on? Who had an interest in him? How had they found him?

He went down the alleyway, holding the Glock by his side, at the ready. From the other end of the narrow passage — between two residential apartment complexes — he heard all the familiar sounds of a late-night entertainment district. He pulled up a rudimentary street map of Budapest in his head and figured he would be entering a familiar street he'd walked down a couple of days previously, packed with ruin bars and seedy strip joints, with a couple of expensive haunts thrown into the mix to liven up the choices offered to drunk passers-by.

He ran through the memory, replaying it over and over.

Nothing stood out as particularly threatening.

He doubted he would be walking into an ambush.

But he stayed prepared regardless.

Because this was his life.

A constant stream of indecision. No consistent routine, no familiar locations, no settling for comfort. He'd become used to it, in his own way. He thrived on the uncertainty inherent in constant travel.

He reached the end of the alley, and the shadows receded, replaced by dull lighting spilling out from a dozen nearby establishments.

Slater looked all around, scanning the street. Half the grimy ruin bars were closed at this hour. A handful were still open, drenched in glowing neon, populated by a diverse range of night owls in various states of drunkenness. He passed his gaze over them, searching for all the familiar signs of someone trying to put on an act. It wouldn't have taken much effort for the tail to leg it to the nearest bar, pick up a half-empty beer and pretend they'd been there the whole time.

But no-one had a thin sheen of sweat on their forehead, or nervous darting eyes, or a forced demeanour. Everyone seemed relaxed, at ease, seized by the alluring effects of alcohol. Couples laughed and danced, clusters of young men roared raucous laughter at each other, and older types sat back and watched the nighttime ebb and flow with a certain serene contentment. Those types had seen it all before. They were drawn to the ruckus of it all.

Slater wondered if he was simply being paranoid.

He studied the bars in a new light.

Searching for a place to continue finding the bottom of a bottle.

His night had been going well before the temporary detour with Camilla and Dani.

But he'd done what he set out to do.

Inject a little adrenalin.

Oil the internal mechanisms.

Kick the engine into gear.

What would it lead to? He didn't know.

He'd decide over a beer.

He set off, choosing a direction at random, making sure the compact Glock was once again tucked out of sight in the back of his waistband. He stepped out from the lee of the alleyway and found himself drenched in the yellow glow from the streetlights overhead. He merged into the foot traffic, and tried to let the war state of mind recede.

There was no-one following him. He was experiencing the remnants of his past, creeping up to plague him during his downtime.

It's foolish to always stay on guard, he told himself.

Then he walked past a ruin bar with an inner courtyard packed with flea market furniture, set up in a derelict old building. Neon light spilled out through the open entranceway, and Slater looked past a couple of bouncers to admire the interior.

In hindsight, he didn't know why he chose that place to stop.

But he would always remember it.

He swept the inner chamber, noting the decor had been arranged to convert the hollow shell of a building into a modern colosseum. Patrons sauntered across the open floor, entering conversations at random, swaying and moving to the rhythmic, pulsating thumping of bass.

His gaze caught on a particular table.

And a particular set of cold eyes.

For the first time in months, he made eye contact with a man he thought he'd never see again.

Sitting on his own. Cradling a drink. His posture ramrod straight. His face set like stone.

Slater had seen that look before.

He gulped back apprehension.

Looking like the hardened killer of old, Jason King lifted a palm and beckoned Slater inside the ruin bar.

7

L ike moving through a fever dream, Slater stepped inside the colosseum.

The cylindrical space had ruins on all sides, forming a harrowing perimeter around the bar's converted interior. Like the centre had been scooped out and drenched in hedonism.

Drinks flowed, music pulsed, and lights flashed on and off. It added to the surrealism. Slater stared hard at King as he moved across the space, wondering if he was making the greatest mistake of his life.

Because he almost didn't recognise the man he'd formed a brotherhood with over the last couple of years.

The Jason King he'd managed to corral to the Russian Far East had been a reluctant participant. King had resorted to his old ways to mow through an icebreaker packed with mercenaries, but he hadn't *wanted* to. The fight had left him, and it took an inhuman effort to bring it back.

Because it was nigh-on impossible to be a ruthless killer and keep your head screwed on straight.

You had to bounce back and forth between the two

worlds. Slater had built up a particular skill at that, but King had reached his wits' end long ago.

He was out of the game.

He'd returned for a brief spell, to prevent another world war, and then he'd disappeared back into self-imposed exile.

He'd told Slater to never try to contact him again, at risk of sending him plummeting into madness.

And right now, there was barely a shred of humanity left in King's eyes.

Slater pulled to a halt on the other side of the table, and stood there.

Unsure.

King beckoned to the seat across from him. 'Sit.'

Slater sat.

He couldn't remember the last time anyone had ordered him around so effortlessly.

They sat there in silence, two of the most feared warriors on the planet. Two solo operatives from a long-dissolved government division. They had a history that couldn't be summed up unless they sat there for hours, dissecting it, breaking it down. But there was no need for that. They'd both gone through it in the flesh.

They both knew what each other had been through.

Life flowed around them. Civilians laughed. The bass thumped. The lights wandered across the floor, catching their table at sporadic intervals. The rest of the time, the perimeter of the ruin bar was plunged in shadow.

It created a sinister effect. King sat draped in the darkness, but occasionally Slater saw him illuminated, and caught the lethal glint in the man's eyes.

Finally, Slater worked up the courage to speak. 'I thought you were out of the game.'

'I still might be,' King said.

Slater said nothing.

The music continued.

The bass thumped on and on.

Slater said, 'You're not the same. You're back.'

King said, 'You can tell?'

'What happened?'

'What do you think?'

Slater sat there, deep in a labyrinth of dark thoughts. A waiter drifted over, and Slater pointed to the half-empty pint glass sitting in front of King. A wordless command.

One of those.

He didn't respond until the man went away and returned a minute later with a full glass of the strong brew. He nodded his thanks, picked up the pint, and drank half the beer in a single gulp. Then he sat back, wiped his mouth, and let out a long sigh.

He said, 'Is she dead?'

King just nodded.

'Christ, King,' Slater said. 'I'm so sorry.'

'It was quick. That's some consolation, at least.'

'Why are you here?'

'Why do you think?'

'Did you track down who did it?'

'I found them right after. I wasn't far away. I just missed them.'

'I assume they're not around anymore.'

'You could say that.'

'How many?'

'Two.'

'Who sent them?'

'That's why I'm here.'

Slater paused. 'Maybe this was fate, then.'

King cocked his head. 'Why's that?'

'I was about to wrap myself up in a war with half the Budapest crime families. But I pulled myself away from it. That's something I rarely do. I just got the sense it wasn't the fight for me.'

'Lucky you ran into me, then.'

Slater paused to consider what had been said. King wasn't saying much. There was still the remnants of intense loss and pain and anger in his features. There were heavy bags under his eyes, and hard lines creased into his forehead. But apart from that he looked energised, revitalised, in phenomenal physical condition.

He was ready for a war.

Slater said, 'How'd you find me?'

'In Russia, you told me about stem cells. That night when I saved you from Ruslan and took care of you — before we stormed aboard the icebreaker. You were delirious. Semi-conscious. It was one of the worst concussions I'd seen. We talked about a lot that night, but I'd be surprised if you remember any of it. The brain is funny like that.'

Slater said, 'Most of the events around that time in Russia are a blur.'

'Does that worry you?'

'It's an isolated incident. If it spills over to the rest of my memories, I'll start getting concerned. But what good will that do, anyway? No use stressing over the inevitable. If it happens, it happens. I figure it's best to be blissfully oblivious to all of that anyway. I hope I don't realise what's happening to me until I'm a vegetable.'

King frowned, and scrunched up his face, and said, 'You really think that's the way it's going to go?'

'It wouldn't surprise me if it happened to either of us. We know very little about the brain. And we've abused ours.'

'At least we made hay while the sun shone.'

Slater nodded. 'That we did.'

'You didn't ask what you told me about stem cells.'

Slater shrugged. 'It makes sense. I would have told you about the clinic I found in Tijuana. I've used it repeatedly. I assume you saw the news of a one-man war in Zimbabwe. You read between the lines, and figured I'd need patching up not long after.'

'There was no guarantee.'

'Then count yourself lucky. Because I probably didn't need them. Zimbabwe didn't bang me up like I thought it would.'

'Then why'd you go to Tijuana?'

'Because it's a fountain of youth.'

'You ever wonder if there's side effects? As far as I can tell, none of it's scientifically proven.'

Slater paused for rumination, and sipped his beer with a wry smile. 'I don't think I'd have done ninety percent of the shit in my life if I was worried about side effects.'

King stared at his closest friend, and shrugged. 'Sometimes I worry about you.'

'You shouldn't. I'm doing fine.'

'You're redlining every area of your life. Don't you see that? Sooner or later you're going to break down.'

'You think?'

'From what I gather, you train like a fiend until your body's on the verge of collapsing. Then you're at peak capacity for a fight, so you throw yourself into some quest for justice. Then that leads to a host of injuries, so you pump yourself full of stem cells to streamline the recovery process and juice you up for the next go round.'

'That sums it up.'

'You ever think you're doing too much?'

'Are we really having this conversation?'

King shrugged again. 'You're right. I'm not one to judge.'

'When did this happen?' Slater said.

They were both hesitant to touch on the grim details, but they both knew it had to be done.

King bowed his head, composing himself. Then he said, 'Two months ago.'

'What have you been doing since?'

'Not a whole lot. I didn't think I'd ever find out what depression was like. I didn't think I was built that way. I'm sure you're the same. The amount of death we've seen. The amount we've caused...'

'But?'

'But I've never felt anything like this,' King said. 'And it worries me.'

'What exactly about it worries you?'

'The fact that I'm going to do something about it.'

'That's never worried you before.'

'If I'm back, then I'm back,' King said. 'And I'll never find anything like what I had with Klara. At least, not for a long time. I've been a shell of myself for two months. Keeping the same routine. Staying in shape. But just going through the motions. Relying on habit alone. If I decide to investigate what happened, and why, then I'm going down a one-way street.'

'You really think you can choose to walk away from this?'

King shook his head, rage in his eyes. 'No. That decision's already been made. I was just summing up the courage to translate it into action.'

'And now?'

'And now I'm here.'

'And what happens now?'

'Now I go back to the way things were. And I figured I'd ask for your help. Because you never changed.'

'Welcome back.'

'This isn't what I wanted.'

'It's not about what you want,' Slater said. 'It's about the way things *are*. And this is how it happened.'

King said, 'You ever lost someone close to you like that?'

Slater said, 'That's a complicated question with a complicated answer.'

'If you have, I need to hear it. I can't be alone with my thoughts anymore. It's driving me fucking insane.'

So Slater told him all about a young kid he'd fought tooth and nail to rescue from the depths of hell.

8

King listened to the tale with a pained expression on his face.

Slater figured most of it was a deliberate attempt to wrap himself up in the story. King had no doubt been dwelling on Klara's death for a couple of months now, and he needed something — anything — to change his neural pathways. He needed to plunge into someone else's problems. Just for a brief while. It was some sort of respite.

King said, 'You told me about Macau. I didn't know about the rest of it.'

Slater shrugged. 'How could you? It happened after Russia.'

'What happened to the Lynx program?'

'I don't know,' Slater said. 'But I met someone from it during my travels. She was raised in it. Her name was Ruby. They fashioned her into a killer.'

King said, 'They did that to us, too.'

'But we chose this life,' Slater said. 'She didn't.'

'Did she see your side?'

'Eventually. The last I saw of her, she was having a

forceful conversation with the man who started the program. In Northern Maine. Deep in the woods. I don't think it turned out well for him.'

'But you don't know for sure?'

'If I had to guess, the Lynx program is dead.'

'They might have tried it again. Re-engineered it. Adopted version 2.0.'

'If they have, I'll need to pay the mainland a visit soon. But not right now. I'm still number one on the covert world's shit list. That's why I went to Zimbabwe in the first place.'

'What did you do there?'

'Nothing pleasant.'

'But it worked out in the end.'

'That seems to happen a lot,' Slater said. 'Just the nature of our talents, I guess.'

'That's why I came,' King said. 'You're a good luck charm. You're the only ally I could think of.'

'Have you tried to follow the trail yourself?'

King nodded. 'I've hit a brick wall.'

'Is that why you're here?'

'I'm here because you're the only person besides Klara in my life.'

Slater stiffened. He drank greedily from his beer and his face turned to stone. He said, 'You were adamant about what you wanted in Russia. You chose a life of exile. You left me alone, which might have been what I wanted, but I always knew you'd be back. You tried to settle down when it wasn't in your DNA. At least I had the capacity to recognise that before I tried to start a family. I sent Shien away for her own safety. You didn't do that. Are you sure you made the right decision?'

King's mouth formed a hard line, and his voice turned

cold, and he said, 'Are you fucking insinuating that it's my fault she's dead?'

Slater cooled himself. He took a deep breath. 'No. I don't know what to think. Maybe I'm just as messed up in the head as you are, but I haven't accepted it until now. I think I'm just confused. I want to help you, but I don't know what I want to do with my own life. I'm at a crossroads.'

King paused. 'Is it because of something that happened in Zimbabwe?'

Slater said, 'I can't stop thinking about it.'

'About what?'

'What I'm not doing. Every second I rest, I feel like I'm letting people suffer and die. It's driving me insane, but I never stop to consider it. It's my personal life philosophy, right? Help people, all the time. Because if I don't, it's selfish. If I stop, and try to have a life for myself, I'm letting innocent people get tortured and maimed and raped in every country, all over the world. And I can't do it all, but I can attack it one step at a time. Which is why I supercharge my life — like you said. With stem cells and unbelievable workout routines and constant battles with anyone and everyone. Because the alternative scares me. But you were right, King. You can't do it forever. You burn out. It fries your neural pathways. It makes you lethargic, and depressed, and you don't know why the hell you started in the first place. Because I'm never going to fix everything, am I? So I'm remembering what I saw in Zimbabwe, and I'm thinking — that's what's happening everywhere. All the time. Why am I even trying to make a dent in it? So I go round and round in circles like that, and I never have the opportunity to voice my concerns to anyone, because if I'm choosing a life like this, then I'm choosing a life of solitude. And you're the only person who understands, but I thought you were gone forever. And now you're back. That's what I'm grappling with.'

He wound down, and ordered another beer from the waiter as the thirty-something man with a pencil moustache floated past once more. He sat back on his chair and put his hands behind his head and exhaled a deep, long breath.

King just watched him, silent, brooding.

Slater said, 'I'm sorry that I'm not focusing on what happened to Klara. It should be priority number one. But you said it yourself. I need to sort myself out before I help anyone else.'

'I can give you time,' King said. 'It doesn't have to be right now.'

Slater locked his steely gaze onto King and said, 'No. It does.'

'You said—'

'I just sorted myself out. By speaking it out loud. I never get the chance to do that. It's liberating. That's all I needed.'

'Slater...'

'Nothing would make me happier right now than finding who killed your girlfriend and tearing their head off,' Slater said. 'So let's do that.'

The waiter returned with a fresh pint, and Slater finished the entire beverage in a series of gulps. He put the empty glass down on the table and interlocked his fingers and raised an eyebrow at King. 'What now?'

King drummed his fingers on the table, and despite the circumstances the hint of a wry smile traced across his features. He said, 'You'll never change, will you?'

Slater said, 'Not for as long as I live. I think I've found the way to make the most of my short life. Should we get the fuck out of here?'

King said, 'Let's.'

The two warriors rose in unison. The ruin bar was emptying out as the clock kept ticking, entering the early hours of the morning. They set off toward the front door, and Slater passed the waiter halfway across the floor. He slipped the man a 10,000 Hungarian Forint banknote. The equivalent of roughly forty American dollars.

'I get change,' the waiter said over the racket of the music.

Slater shook his head.

The man gave a warm smile and melted away into the pulsating darkness.

King said, 'I assume there's plenty more where that came from.'

Slater looked at him. 'How much did I tell you in Russia?'

'Not all of it. But enough. Let's talk when we get out of here.'

Reunited once more, King and Slater made for the exit.

Like nothing had changed at all.

9

The night was cold, and the street was emptying out.

The pair set off in the direction of the fifth district, despite King's apprehension to return to the general vicinity of the townhouse.

'You sure you're not going to run into any more trouble with those two scum?' he said.

Slater had debriefed him on the situation with Lukas and Benicio on their way out.

Now Slater said, 'I'm sure.'

'You never know. Especially with those types.'

'I know,' Slater said. 'Trust me. I humiliated them by sleeping with their wives.'

King threw him a sideways glance. 'You do that sort of thing often?'

Slater shrugged. 'Not usually. I guess you could say I'm in a dark place at the moment.'

'I understand,' King said.

Slater shook his head. 'No, it's foolish. I shouldn't be

making that claim. I've got nothing between my ears compared to what you're going through. I couldn't imagine.'

'I've had two months to process it,' King said, but it was an empty, futile statement.

'Has it helped?'

'The time has almost made it worse,' King said.

The same dark rage crossed his features.

There were no tears, no emotion whatsoever. Just anger. The knowledge that King had the skills to do something about it, but had failed all the same. He probably blamed himself.

Slater put himself in King's shoes, and came away with a queasy picture of what he might be going through right now.

Slater assumed that the time for emotion had already come and passed. Besides, he'd never known Jason King as one to dwell on sorrow.

Just as he himself didn't.

But it had allowed them both to achieve longevity in a career choice that usually left its participants dead or broken within a few months, if not weeks. They'd thrived for years — close to a decade each — as solo operations for a clandestine black ops division of the U.S. government. Although it had shut down their capacity to treat other areas of their life like they were regular people. They'd seen death and torture every day when they were employed. They'd been taught — no, conditioned — to compartmentalise it and shut it away and pretend those uncomfortable feelings had never existed in the first place.

But a loved one?

Slater pulled up a mental image of Shien, the young girl he'd rescued from a casino in Macau and deemed himself responsible for protecting. He'd guided her onto a safe path twice — once after Macau, and again after he'd mistakenly handed her to a man with impure intentions the first time.

He imagined finding her body. He tried to consider how that would feel.

He went down a dark corridor in his mind, and it took him a few seconds to resurface. When he did, he found King staring at him. They were still striding down the desolate streets of Budapest, hands in their coat pockets, breath steaming in front of their faces.

But King was watching him.

The man said, 'What?'

Slater said, 'I was trying to put myself in your shoes.'

King got a bleak, soulless look in his eyes and said, 'Don't.'

'It'll get better.'

'She was everything to me.'

'I know. But you've got fifty years of your life left, at least. That's assuming we both die of natural causes.'

King half-smiled. 'It's ironic, isn't it?'

'What is?'

'All of it,' King said. 'The shape we're in. The dedication we need to get to the highest level. The way we're able to hone our bodies into whatever we want. It means that if we don't get ourselves killed in the interim, we'll probably live to be the oldest men on the planet.'

'I wouldn't go that far.'

'But that same level of dedication committed us to our career choice. So it should have got us killed right at the start.'

'But it didn't. And here we are.'

'Here we are.'

They kept moving. Down dark streets, completely at ease with the late-night stroll. For they were two of the most vicious, hardened killers on the continent, and any petty criminals looking to make a quick buck by relieving them of their possessions would find themselves in a world of trouble they knew very little about.

Slater almost hoped they got mugged.

Just for the entertainment.

King said, 'I know it'll get better. Eventually. But not right now. Right now I need to dwell on it. And right now I need to make it my life's purpose to find out who the hell did it, and why.'

'Did you ever consider that maybe I wouldn't want to help?'

King looked across. 'Never.'

Slater nodded. 'Then you got that right.'

'Thank you, brother.'

'What else was I going to do?'

'I thought maybe your own spark might have gone out. I thought you might be dealing with the same things I was. I thought there was a chance you'd have given up on this world for good. That you would want no part of it.'

'Even if that was the case,' Slater said, 'I would have brought myself back. Just like you did to help me in Russia. That's how this works between us. And that's the way it'll be until we get ourselves killed.'

'After Russia, I don't know what it will take to get us killed,' King said.

'Don't test your luck.'

'So what's the plan?' King said. 'I don't think I was expecting this all to go ahead so fast.'

Slater stared at him. 'What do you mean?'

'I thought you'd need some persuading. Even if I always knew you'd come around.'

'What a monumental waste of time that'd be. I'm ready. I'm not tied down to anyone or anything. So let's go.'

'I have a lead.'

Slater checked his watch. 'It's late as hell. Should we do this in the morning?'

King eyed him warily. 'You've had too much to drink, haven't you?'

'Story of my life,' Slater muttered.

'Let's find a place to crash.'

'Somewhere nice,' Slater said. 'I can cover it.'

'I do alright for myself.'

'Not like what I've got saved up.'

'What'd you do — rob a bank?'

'You could say that.'

King paused. 'Wait ... was this in Macau?'

'I got wrapped up in an altercation with the triad over there. I got their bank details. They weren't in need of the money anymore.'

'How much?'

'Four hundred million. But it rises and falls with the market. I check each morning.'

King simply stared. 'How's that feel?'

'No different to when I was worth ten,' Slater said. 'I have everything I need.'

'That's the way.'

They found a luxury five-star hotel with a lavish social club next to the lobby, consisting of broad armchairs and a massive fireplace and a bar staffed twenty-four-seven to accomodate any drink the patrons might crave. It looked like a private members' area, exclusively for use by hotel guests. Slater strode right up to the enormous entranceway with King in tow, and as soon as he had eyes on the social area he nodded his approval and went right in.

King said, 'Works for me.'

They stepped into the foyer.

10

B y now, Slater had the process systematically refined to perfection.

He checked in within five minutes, acquiring a pair of king-bed rooms right next to each other for a last-minute discount, considering there was only half the night left. He politely skirted around all the optional extras the concierge offered, and had a pair of matching keycards not long after that.

The man behind the desk had slick hair combed back straight, and clipped English, and a warm demeanour. He said, 'Is there anything else you require, sirs?'

Slater jerked a thumb at what effectively constituted the private members' club and said, 'Is that open to us?'

'Of course, sir,' the concierge said. 'First drink is complimentary, too. The bartender will help you with any specific requests. We have a fine selection, I must say.'

Slater nodded his thanks, and ushered King across the marble lobby, toward the secluded cluster of armchairs near the fireplace.

The concierge called, 'Sirs, would you like me to put your luggage up in your room?'

Slater looked at King, who looked back at Slater. They both shrugged to each other.

Slater turned to the concierge and said, 'No luggage.'

'I'm sorry?'

'It's a long story. We're simple folk.'

'Very well,' the man said, but he couldn't hide his confusion.

'We mean no harm,' Slater said. 'Trust me.'

He led King to the armchairs and dropped into one of them himself. The warmth of the fire washed over him, flickering in the dim lighting. King sat in the leather chair opposite. Despite their lack of luggage, they both carried themselves as if they were international businessmen. They wore expensive clothes, they both had expensive watches on their wrists, and their posture was ramrod straight.

They were well-built, and confident in themselves.

There was no one action that conveyed this — it all simply added up to make them look right at home.

As a result, the waiter was over in seconds.

'Greetings, gentlemen,' he said. 'I am the alchemist on duty tonight. What can I get for you?'

King said, 'I'm fine.'

Slater said, 'Your best whiskey.'

'Sir, I'm afraid that won't qualify as a complimentary— '

'No problem,' Slater said. 'Happy to pay.'

Perhaps if he was underdressed or less sure of himself the waiter might have listed the price, or made a gesture to indicate that Slater should reconsider dropping such an extravagant sum of money at four in the morning. Instead he nodded curtly and turned on his heel.

King rolled his eyes, and said, 'Yeah, what the hell,' and the waiter turned back.

King said, 'Get me one of those, too.'

'Certainly, sir.'

The man floated away.

Alone and capable of private conversation, King said, 'You're going to suck me right back into this world, aren't you?'

'What world?' Slater said, feigning ignorance.

'Moving from one place to the next like there's a fire behind us. Getting into trouble anywhere we can find it. Spending outrageously. Drinking plenty. There's a reason I got away from all this.'

Slater cut through the bullshit and said, 'King, I'm sorry about what happened to Klara. I didn't know her for long, but she seemed like an amazing girl. We're going to handle this situation, and then we can talk about the future. Sound good?'

King nodded.

Slater said, 'What's your lead? You mentioned you had something. I assume we're not blindly feeling in the dark.'

King reached into his coat pocket and took out a slim black smartphone. He twirled it in between his giant fingers for a few revolutions, then reached forward and placed it delicately on the table between them.

They both stared at it.

Slater opened his mouth to speak, but the alchemist returned that moment with two tumblers of glowing amber whiskey. They were some of the finest, most exquisite glasses Slater had ever seen.

He took his graciously and sipped at it.

It was warm and packed with flavour, and it burned all the way down his throat.

He settled back into the armchair, savouring the experience. Sometimes life passed him by, and he'd been learning to try to be grateful for more moments like this. Simple pleasantries in the palm of luxury, dotted through a life wrought with pain and death and suffering.

King sipped his own whiskey, and hummed with approval.

They put their tumblers down on the glass table and turned their attention back to the phone.

Slater said, 'You got it off one of the bodies?'

King nodded. 'They only had one between them.'

'What's on it?'

'I don't know.'

Slater stared down at the device. 'We can find out.'

'I don't think we can,' King said. 'Not on our own.'

'Why don't you know what's on it?' Slater said, taking care not to ridicule King for his short-sightedness.

But King read his mind. 'You think I found it password protected and gave up right then and there?'

'I don't know how good you are with technology,' Slater said. 'But I'll admit the thought crossed my mind.'

'It *is* password protected,' King said. 'But I'm not so stupid that I think that's the end of the line. I know there's a hundred ways around that. But I'm afraid that *is* actually where the line ends. Everyone I've taken it to comes up short. I've been told there's an arsenal of encryption that's stopping anyone from using a backdoor. The thing's a steel trap. The guys who killed Klara really didn't want anyone accessing the contents of the phone.'

Slater stared at the slim device and said, 'There's ways around that.'

'I'm telling you there isn't.'

'Then you haven't gone to the right people.'

'Who are the right people?'

'Tech wizards. But they're few and far between.'

'I thought you were one of them,' King said.

'Nowhere close,' Slater said. 'This is a different ball game I'm talking about. I know my way around a computer, but there's people who have dedicated more time to cracking encrypted technology than we have learning how to kill people.'

'Then how the hell are you surviving with four hundred million dollars of illegal funds to your name in today's society?'

'Because I'm very, very good at outsourcing. If there's any skill I have, it's being efficient. I know exactly what I can do, and I stick to that. Anything else — I pay the best people to set me up right. My money's untouchable. It's locked away so deep in Switzerland that you'd need the entire cyber crimes division of a few countries to come up with any evidence of it.'

'So you can use those guys to crack this phone?'

Slater shook his head. 'They're bankers. They won't talk to me unless it involves controlling staggering sums of money. And besides, they're the same as me in some respects. They're very, very good at one certain thing. Which is banking. If we want into that phone, we're going to need the kind of guru you'd usually see on a TV show.'

'Do they even exist?'

'Yes, but like I said, they're few and far between. If they're obscenely good, they're snatched up by Fortune 500 companies right out of college as developers or research scientists. Google and Apple and Netflix have a bunch of them, but they're institutionalised, law-abiding citizens, and I don't really feel like kidnapping anyone and forcing them to do what we say. We'd probably have to torture them.'

'Okay,' King said. 'That's out, then.'

'Option two for these whiz kids is the government. The same deal applies to tech wizards right out of college, but if Uncle Sam — or any other government — thinks they'd make a good fit, they'll approach discreetly. They'll offer a crazy pay packet and unlimited benefits and put them straight to work. But they'll make them sign a whole bunch of NDAs first, so we'll never find them. And even if we did, they'd be even less co-operative. They're even more institutionalised than the Fortune 500 company shills.'

King said nothing.

Slater said, 'Limited options, I know.'

'That's it? That's our only hope?'

'There's a third option.'

'And what might that be?'

Slater paused for rumination, and sipped his whiskey. Then he put his hands behind his head and said, 'King, I think there might be a reason you came into my life late tonight, and not a minute earlier.'

'And why's that?'

'I think it's fate. I think I was meant to run into a few certain individuals beforehand. Otherwise we'd be stuck in the mud here.'

King said nothing.

Slater said, 'The third option is organised crime.'

11

They spoke for another half hour, catching up on the less exotic details of their time apart, ignoring the waiter circling their table and offering the opportunity for more drinks.

The staggeringly expensive whiskey settled in Slater's stomach and a feeling of contentment washed over him. There was a way out of this mess. He could see it now, right in front of him, clear as day.

Before, he'd been treading water in uncertainty. He thought King had no leads, and would therefore be forced to wallow in his misery for the rest of his life — however long that entailed.

But now there was a phone, encrypted to the nines, and an avenue to crack that code.

But Slater didn't want to discuss details until the next morning. He was buzzed as hell, and he didn't want to admit it. He figured King could tell — they'd shared enough experiences to be able to read each other — but he didn't want the man thinking he had a drinking problem.

But you do, a small voice said.

He stuffed it back down where it belonged.

Locked it away in a drawer in his own mind and fought through the haze of alcohol.

He rose to his feet and gestured for King to wait one moment. Then he went over to the alchemist and offered a platinum-coloured credit card to cover the cost of the two tumblers of whiskey. The price had three zeroes next to the first number, and he almost fainted at the sight. But he reluctantly waved the transaction through and sauntered back to the fireside.

There was still a thin layer of alcohol in each of their glasses. Slater pointed to King's tumbler and said, 'Make sure you savour that.'

'How much was it?'

'Just enjoy it.'

They both drained the rest of the contents of their glasses, and left the social club behind. They took the elevator up thirty floors to their rooms, resting side by side in a lavish hallway.

Outside King's door, Slater offered a hand.

King shook it.

'Good to have you back, brother,' Slater said. 'I wish it was under different circumstances.'

'Me too, King said, a certain weariness behind his eyes.

Slater left him there, pondering his own misfortune.

He didn't want to tell King he was deep in the throes of an intoxicating buzz, and therefore not prepared in the slightest to tackle deep, weighty emotional issues. He focused on putting one foot in front of the other and used the keycard to let himself into a beautifully furnished, exquisitely put-together hotel room with a king bed and a stunning view over central Budapest.

Like something out of a spy movie, with the corners

drenched in shadow and the mystery and intrigue cranked up to maximum.

As drunk as he'd been in a long time, Slater stumbled to the bed and wrenched the covers back. The sheet was tucked tight into the base of the mattress. He worked it free, took his coat off, slipped into bed fully clothed, and found himself alone with his thoughts for those brief moments before he passed out.

He hated these moments.

He thought of the hopelessness he'd been dwelling on ever since he left Zimbabwe. He'd always stuck to the line of reasoning that he couldn't save everyone, and he'd parroted it to anyone he'd ever had to justify his stance on the world to. But there was something very different between spouting the same things he'd always said, and truly understanding them.

The reality was, he *couldn't* help everyone.

He would never be able to stop 99.99% of the suffering in the world.

In fact, less than that.

It was sobering. Depressing. It sometimes made him think everything he was doing was for nothing. And that was a dangerous line of reasoning. It was a scary path to go down.

Because he put his body and mind through hell for the sake of helping others, and that tested his willpower like nothing else. He justified it with the knowledge that he was helping people, but when he saw suffering on such a staggering scale — like in Zimbabwe — it sobered him to the bleak reality.

He closed his eyes and drifted into an uneasy, dreamless sleep.

He never dreamt.

Not anymore.

He'd suffered a brief bout of nightmares directly after retiring from active service, but now he just passed out, dead to the world.

Mostly due to the alcohol.

He wondered if it was normal to live like this. Then he figured he was scratching at the very edge of the spectrum, experience wise. He was living a life rich with emotion and sensation. It was unparalleled. It was pain and satisfaction in equal measure. Most people got up and went through the same routine, and sat behind a desk they hated at a job they hated, and came back home and dulled themselves with alcohol just the same as he did.

But at least he was living a life for the ages.

His last thought before he drifted off was whether it was a good omen that Jason King had walked back into his life...

...or the exact opposite.

12

He came awake at the crack of dawn as the booze wore off from the night before.

He hadn't closed the curtains, so the bleak grey light flooded into the room, inch by inch, as the darkness receded.

Instead of closing them and struggling through another few restless hours of sleep, he surrendered to consciousness and got out of bed. He crossed to the floor-to-ceiling windows and stood there, admiring the view. He stared out over residential apartment complexes and great basilicas, and Parliament House, and the Danube River flowing through all of it, cutting a path through the skyline. He lingered on the apartment complexes, with their quaint balconies and ornate railings. He spotted a couple of early risers hunched over small outdoor tables, sipping from steaming mugs of coffee.

Busy in their own worlds, with their own problems and their own relationships and their own goals and aspirations.

A whole world out there, ebbing and flowing as the city rose for the daily commute.

Sometimes Slater wanted part of it.

It would be dull and drab and monotonous, but hell, at least it would be *normal.*

Sometimes he yearned for that sensation. He always chided himself for caving into societal norms, but they were societal norms for a reason. They encouraged a sense of community. They brought people together in the same routines, the same leisure activities.

Like a billion fingers on the same pulse.

Slater was a world away from that reality. He couldn't compare his life to anyone, or anything. It didn't make the least bit of sense. As if he was coldly detached from the rest of the world.

But it was a dichotomy, because he could look at it the other way and realise no-one had the depth of emotional experiences he'd been through. They hadn't seen tyrants die, or saved innocent lives from the brink of death, or lifted people out of ruin.

He had.

And now he had someone in his life who'd been there before.

The only man who could relate to him.

The only man who understood what it was like to live like this.

He stripped out of his dress pants and cashmere sweater and stood poised in the centre of the room in his underwear. He studied his reflection in the mirror. Two hundred and ten pounds of rippling muscle. Nothing had changed.

But the trauma he put his muscle tissue through on a regular basis would be nothing if he didn't have flexibility, dexterity, and cardio.

So he took himself through his morning routine, honed

and refined over more than ten years of putting his body through hell.

Fifty minutes of vinyasa yoga, opening his hips. Oiling the joints, so to speak. Ensuring there were no kinks in the framework. Ensuring he didn't lift weights and get tighter and tighter until he could barely throw a kick or a punch without disrupting the fascia. He followed the yoga with a relentless string of burpees, leaping up and jumping down until his muscles screamed for relief.

Then he kept going.

He burnt himself out, sweating profusely, flushing the alcohol out of his system from the night before.

When he finished, he staggered to the bathroom and vomited. Not a typical part of the routine, but an unfortunate side effect of the amount of liquor he'd consumed.

Sometimes it happened.

Nothing he could do about it.

Yes, there is, he told himself.

But he ignored that voice.

As he'd become so extraordinarily adept at doing.

He took an ice cold shower, another discomfort he'd overcome early in his life. The benefits were profound. He couldn't pinpoint *exactly* how it had altered his life, but it was something about the willpower necessary to overcome water at its most chilling in a setting that was usually warm and comfortable. It set the course for the rest of the day. Get over the first hurdle, and you can tackle the next obstacle, and the next, and the next.

That's how all of life operated, as far as he could tell.

A strange philosophy, maybe, especially because it was something so simple, but he had taught himself long ago that often the only thing that separated a disciplined person from an undisciplined one was the tiny consistent habits they set for themselves each and every waking moment. Actions that seemed like nothing in the moment, but added up to everything over the course of his life. He'd put that theory to the test nearly fifteen years ago, and judging by the fact he'd cultivated more discipline than a thousand men put together, he figured he was doing okay.

He dried himself off, skin tingling from the chill, and dressed in the same clothes from the night before. He'd come to Budapest on a whim, as he assumed King had too, and he hadn't bothered to pack luggage. With four hundred million dollars to his name, a new wardrobe was the least of his concerns.

He had bigger fish to fry, most of them residing deep in his own mind.

What most people base their entire life around, he barely gave a second thought. Luggage was the least of his concerns.

Maybe that's it, he thought as he made his way out of the room and downstairs to the lobby.

Maybe when he mastered his mind, the rest of life's problems fell away, leaving him with only the most raw concerns.

Maybe that's why he got himself wrapped up in other people's problems.

Because he hadn't a single one of his own.

Somehow, some way, that gave him temporary peace.

Then he remembered why Jason King had walked back into his life, and all that peace fell away.

Nothing good would follow in the coming days.

He was sure of it.

He stepped out into the lobby and found King in the social club, still as a statue amidst a horde of early morning business meetings.

It seemed King had gone out and bought himself a fresh change of clothes earlier in the morning.

He wore a pair of slacks, and a long-sleeved shirt stretched tight over his fearsome physique, and the whole package was draped in an overcoat that looked like it cost somewhere in the mid-four figures. It was a new coat. Slater didn't know where King's old one was.

Slater walked up to him and said, 'Speaking of finances — you're not doing too bad yourself.'

'Living in Thailand is cheap,' King said. 'I had all I needed. My Black Force funds have been accumulating interest for the better part of a year now. I can afford to splash out.'

'If we get through this next chapter, I'll split my fortune with you.'

'You don't need to do that,' King said.

'You think I need the other half?'

'I've got all I need.'

'I've got all I need, too, and then I've got three hundred and ninety nine million dollars more.'

King managed a wry smile and said, 'At least use five. One is pushing it.'

'Let's call it two hundred even. I don't like our chances of getting through this, anyway. But when has that ever stopped us?'

'And why's that?'

Slater checked his watch — almost an impulse move by this point. He said, 'The day's barely started, and we're about to take on an organised crime syndicate.'

13

King said, 'Why don't we rendezvous in a few hours? You've barely slept.'

Slater sat down across from him and shook his head. 'I don't need that much sleep. Call me genetically blessed.'

King raised an eyebrow and said, 'I thought you told me you got more than eight hours a night usually.'

'Usually,' Slater said. 'Because it's vital for recovery. But I don't *need* it to function.'

There was a pause.

Slater said, 'Why are you down here, then?'

King said, 'I'm the same as you.'

'In sleep, or in life?'

King gave a subtle nod.

Slater sighed and said, 'I've got a feeling we've got a lot to discuss later.'

King stared at him. The lobby ebbed and flowed around them — men in suits and women in smart business attire strode past, late for various appointments, all wrapped up in their own individual bubbles. A few lingered in the social area, sipping steaming coffee from exquisite mugs and talking amongst themselves, or reading the newspapers alone, but no-one was in earshot.

Slater sat there, oblivious to it all, removed from the hustle and bustle of everyday life.

Finally King said, 'I think Klara was my one connection to the normal world.'

'See how you feel after we get the people responsible,' Slater said. 'It might change your perspective.'

'*If* we get the people responsible.'

Slater figured it wasn't the opportune time to go down that path, so he changed direction. 'What was life like in Thailand?'

'Good,' King said. 'Better than good. Better than I thought possible.'

'So why not give it a second chance?'

'Because she was the glue holding it all together.'

'It'll get better,' Slater said, mirroring what he'd said the night before. Except this time he was sober, so he meant it. 'With time. Trust me. It'll heal.'

'I don't think you're the best person to give advice in a situation like this.'

'Why's that?'

'Because you're just as fucked up as I am. It's like talking to a mirror.'

Slater laughed.

King laughed, too.

A waiter floated by, and Slater enquired about the breakfast options. He typically fasted in the mornings, but it had been quite some time since his last meal, and hunger reared its ugly head. The man explained there was a buffet on the other side of the ground floor, or for a small fee he could bring a designated selection of meals to their table so they could continue their talk in peace. The man seemed to sense the subject matter of their conversation was sensitive, and not for prying ears.

Slater nodded graciously.

The waiter said, 'What would you like?'

Slater looked at King, who looked back at Slater.

A knowing look.

Their brotherhood was forged in the fires of hell, after all.

They could almost read each other's minds.

'One of everything,' Slater said. 'Each.'

The waiter nodded. 'Certainly, sirs.'

He floated away, and in the meantime Slater and King made small talk the only way they knew how.

By diving straight into the deepest subject matter they could think of.

For, in Slater's humble opinion, there was no better way to live. He had long ago figured no-one really cares how the weather is, or if your favourite sports team is winning, or how office politics are faring. He figured it was all just noise to fill the gaping void people had in their lives. Perhaps that was the perspective of a sociopathic killer, but he didn't think so.

He had to admit he thought a little differently than most.

But so did King.

Slater said, 'What have you been doing these last two months?'

'Stewing over what happened. Blaming myself.'

'I know you. You're improving. At an exponential rate. I can see it. I've only known you were back in the game less than twenty-four hours, but it already seems like you're coping better with each passing moment.'

King said, 'I only pulled my head out of the sand when I figured I was mentally strong enough to handle it.'

'You're doing good, King,' Slater said.

More to reassure him than to tell the truth.

Because Slater could see in the man's eyes he'd never felt emotion like this.

King said, 'I'll feel better when I have the heads of the people who ordered the hit. Nothing else matters.'

The waiter brought back plates loaded with eggs, bacon, mushroom, spinach, crispy Viennese sausage, bread, and croissants. King and Slater devoured all the food at a lightning pace, much to the surprise of the waiter, who tiptoed back and forth across their line of sight with wider eyes each time he passed.

They were following the old rule, and they didn't care who judged them for it.

Eat when you can.

Satiated, they settled back into their chairs and bickered back and forth for twenty minutes as the food digested. There was no use powering toward the objective with enough calories settling in their stomachs to impede their movement. So they settled back into the same rhythm — it had taken time, but Slater found himself rapidly warming to King now.

The way it had always been.

He didn't know what it had been at first. Maybe hesitancy to dive into his old joking ways after hearing the brutal reality King had been dealing with for the last two months. Or because of Russia. They'd both felt a bond severed there, never to return.

But it had.

Almost immediately.

Proving they were one and the same after all.

Finally, King said, 'Okay. What needs to be done?'

'We're going to have to split up at the start,' Slater said. 'The way I see it, we need to do two things at exactly the same time. And each of them needs to happen fast. Or we'll miss our window of opportunity, and then we'll be relying on the first two options I told you about last night.'

'That wouldn't be ideal,' King said. 'What's the play?'

Slater laid it out, in all its detail.

14

———

Jason King stepped out of the hotel lobby with a renewed purpose he hadn't felt in months.

He pulled up a satellite map of Budapest on his smartphone and made straight for the eighth district, as per Slater's instructions.

Budapest, whilst scoring safe in most crime statistics, had noted a substantial increase in methamphetamine use due to the influx of the drug on the city's streets. Slater had his own business to settle, but the timelines had to align, so King kept himself to a strict schedule. Despite a lack of change in his circumstances, he felt different. He couldn't quite pinpoint it, but he thought he had a general idea.

He had a goal now.

Before, he'd been wandering across the globe, achieving nothing in particular, wallowing in self-pity. It had taken all his willpower just to stick to the same physical exercise regime of old, something that had previously come naturally to him. But now he was out of that hole, and although the emotional wounds wouldn't heal for some time, he had his head screwed on straight.

Or so it seemed.

He was in good enough mental shape to concentrate on the task at hand.

His instructions from Slater were simple.

Find a street-level dealer.

Follow the supply chain upward.

Use any means necessary.

That was it. Although it would be a little harder to put into practice than to discuss in theory. Thankfully, King didn't think he'd be stepping far out of his comfort zone to accomplish this particular task. He'd been doing this sort of thing for over a decade. Knocking a few heads together was part of his daily life by this point.

He'd had a couple of months off, though.

Maybe close to half a year, if he counted the time that had elapsed since Russia.

And that had been an isolated experience, a return from the dead before plunging straight back into retirement.

He hadn't been active in over a year.

Time to shake the ring rust off.

He figured it was better to overcompensate than under-estimate the competition. So he charged himself with adrenalin, the only way he knew how.

He visualised his life on the line.

He imagined a gun in his face.

He thought of the imaginary man standing across from him, trying to strip him of everything he had, trying to take his life away, to humiliate him and degrade him and leave his corpse in the street like a stray dog that had been shot out of mercy.

He balled up his fists, and tightened the muscles in his forearms, and strode into the eighth district like he had a death wish.

Then he cooled off slightly, recognising the disadvantage of charging into the fray like a wild bull. That was a mistake reserved for his youth. He'd been through several early solo operations using that strategy, but it didn't bode well for long-term health. It usually involved broken bones and torn muscles and a concussion or two for good measure.

That wasn't what he was going for this time.

But it was good to know he had the sensation in his back pocket. He could pull out the rage like a secret weapon, whenever he so desired. He slowed his pace, and levelled his breathing, and scoured the streets with a sweeping gaze.

It didn't take him long to find what he was looking for.

He powered down random streets and laneways and wider roads until he spotted a thin pale junkie lingering at an intersection.

The man was trying his best to blend into the hordes of passers-by. He seemed to be in his early thirties, but it was hard to tell. He had big bags under his eyes and wrinkly acne-ridden skin. He could have been eighteen. Meth had that effect on people. He was leaning against a concrete column that was propping up the portico of a big old building. The shadows spilled across him, giving off the intended effect. He was trying his best to look menacing. If cops wandered into the area, he'd scurry away, but to everyone else he was a person to avoid.

But he was attracting the right crowd.

King set up camp across the street, sitting down at an outdoor café in full view of the intersection. He ordered a coffee and put all his surveillance skills to use, only taking quick glances at the gangly junkie out of the corner of his eye every now and then. The rest of the time he spent on his phone, or observing the crowd around him. He was a businessman in an expensive overcoat with his concentration wrapped up in his smartphone, just like most of the men sitting on their own at cafés in Budapest.

The junkie changed positions, alternating between loitering against one of the columns or sitting on the steps leading up to the portico itself. There was no exterior signage, so King couldn't tell if it was a town hall, or a museum, or a government building.

He very much doubted it was the latter, for every now and then a hunched figure wandered up to the junkie and handed him a wad of cash.

The junkie returned the favour with a small plastic baggie that he passed across in a concealed palm.

The move was discreet, but King knew exactly what he was looking for. He only caught the occasional brief glimpse of the drugs themselves — anyone else looking might not have seen a thing — but it gave him all he needed.

He pulled out his phone and messaged Slater, tapping away at the screen.

Got one. Moving in.

Slater came back an instant later.

Okay. There's security on my end. I'll deal with them.

King replied.

Does the timing work?

Slater came back.

Not going in yet. Just dealing with security. That's all.

King replied.

I'll keep you posted.

As he was rising out of the chair, he drained his espresso and caught a final *ping* from his phone. He pulled it back out of his overcoat and checked the departing message from Slater.

Bring the old King back.

King typed two words.

He's back.

Then he paid the bill, shoved the phone into his pocket, and strode across the busy two-lane street towards the junkie.

15

Slater hovered in the lee of the alleyway across the street from Lukas and Benicio's townhouse.

In fact, he didn't know if it belonged to one or both of them. But both men had treated it as home the night before, storming through the bedroom doors in unison. Perhaps it was Benicio's place, considering he'd been the first man inside the bedroom. Or maybe that was just because he came through the front door first.

It didn't matter either way.

Camilla and Dani had taken him back there.

He doubted the girls were there now — the husbands were likely in damage control.

Hence the burly security standing guard on the steps of the front deck. They were staggered in a rough triangle, with two at the bottom of the narrow stairwell and one near the top. All of them were leaning on the metal balustrades.

Spending half the time scouring the street for any sign of a threat, and the other half checking themselves out in car window reflections, puffing their chests out and touching their hands reflexively to the Heckler & Koch pistols in leather holsters on their belts.

Openly carrying.

Lukas and Benicio must be damn confident they've paid off the right people.

It made sense, though. Hungary was relatively well-known for its corruption, and even if these boys were arrested by cops who weren't in the know, they'd be promptly let out of their holding cells at the local precinct after a quick and informative call from someone high up in government.

Slater kept to the shadows, employing the training of years past, aided by the dreary conditions overhead. The sky was overcast and a light drizzle began to fall, coating the street in a general air of misery. The occasional luxury vehicle drifted past, but the windows were all tinted to the maximum, and Slater couldn't make out any other details of note.

The three sentries stood there, shifting from foot to foot, ignoring the thin sheets of rain falling over them. It dripped off their coats and ran down their faces, but they stood there resolute, following their orders to a tee.

With organised crime, there was no alternative.

It was a ruthless amoral industry with no room for misinterpretation of orders.

You either did what your superiors said, or you got the hell out of Dodge.

Slater used a metal awning to shelter himself from the rain, letting it pour down in rivulets off the edge of the platform above him. From there it dripped to the grimy concrete and ran along the alley floor, coagulating with the dust and muck surrounding the big garbage dumpsters.

And there he waited, until his phone lit up with a message from King.

He fished it out of his pocket and went through the exchange, finally receiving a single phrase to sign off the conversation.

He's back.

In the darkness of the alley, surrounded by drizzle and shadow, Slater smiled.

He put the phone in his rear pants pocket and took off his knee-length coat. He folded up the expensive garment and placed it in a dry patch underneath the awning, resting it on a single step out the back of a restaurant. From deep inside the building, he could hear the unmistakable sound of food frying.

He rolled up the sleeves of his jumper, crossed to the dumpster nearby, and fished a full can of pasta sauce from the top of the garbage. It was well past its expiry date, and had been thrown out fully sealed. He tested its weight in an open palm, then considered his options.

It didn't take him long to decide.

He wasn't about to murder three men in cold blood just to send a message. He didn't know if any of them had been pressured into organised crime by their circumstances.

It sure wasn't an excuse, but he wasn't prepared to massacre them for it.

Besides, he needed them alive to contact their bosses.

So he left the Glock 17 in the rear of his waistband.

He kept low, masked by the shadows, and hurled the sealed tin like a fastball as soon as the three men were looking in the other direction. As soon as he'd let the can go, he stepped out from under the awning and sprinted out of the lip of the alleyway.

The can arced over their heads and smashed through

one of the townhouse's ground floor windows. The pane shattered with a noise like a gunshot, and all three men flinched. They wheeled instinctively toward the source of the noise, hands flying to their waistbands.

They scrutinised the scene, but couldn't immediately put two and two together. They'd just missed the sight of the can tumbling into the interior.

They couldn't understand how the window had exploded.

Then, almost as one, they thought, *Gun.*

They thought someone had shot the window out.

Maybe they'd even been aiming for the sentries themselves.

They wheeled back around in unison, tugging their Heckler & Koch pistols out of their holsters. But they hadn't prepared for a situation like this. They were fast, and they were big and muscular, and they looked mean, but they didn't have the uncanny reflexes of experienced combatants who had made their life revolve around getting a pistol out of its holster at lightning speed.

So they fumbled for a second or two.

And at that point Slater was on them.

He came out of the dreary morning gloom, coated in rain, and maintained the momentum of the sprint into a stabbing front kick. In the lowlight, it looked like a whip cracking. The sole of his hefty boot found the sternum of the first guy and shoved him off his feet like he'd been hit by a shockwave. He crumpled across the first few concrete steps with a disgusting *thump*, out of commission, but Slater didn't even see it, because by that point he'd used the same momentum to twist a half-revolution with his left elbow jutting straight out, cocked like a lever.

In the movies, spinning elbows are utilised because they look flashy on the big screen, but they're also utilised in real life mixed martial arts contests because they hit like a goddamn freight train. The momentum you can generate by twisting into a blow is monumental. Mixed martial artists don't rely on them, because it's awfully difficult to keep someone in place for a pinpoint accurate strike when they've been training for months to avoid that exact scenario.

But that wasn't the case here.

The second guy didn't even understand what was happening. He was deep in the throes of sensory overload, and he'd frozen like a deer in headlights, so Slater had all the time in the world to throw the elbow.

He didn't need all the time in the world.

He needed a half-second of hesitation.

It landed home, bone to skull, elbow to temple.

Lights out.

The third guy almost had his Heckler & Koch free, fumbling with the latch on the holster, but he'd be there any second. And he was at the top of the triangle, so Slater would have to cover the gap and then throw a punch with every intention of killing the guy. Given the circumstances, there wasn't enough time to...

Slater gave up.

He ripped the Glock 17 out of his waistband like he was moving in fast motion and had it pointed square between the guy's eyes before the man could even finish grappling with his own weapon.

Because Slater *had* made his life revolve around getting a pistol out at the speed of light.

Slater said, 'No, no, no, no, you stop right there.'

The guy froze with his hand on his weapon, eerily

similar to an old-school gunslinger who'd been beaten to the draw.

Which he had.

Slater said, 'Take that out of its holster with two fingers like pincers, please.'

The guy complied.

'No fast movements,' Slater said. 'I swear to God I'll shoot you dead right here.'

The guy complied.

The guy had never seen anyone move as fast as Slater.

He would do anything Slater said.

'Now throw it over the balustrade.'

The guy complied.

The gun clattered to the concrete a few feet below.

Slater lowered the gun, walked up the three steps, and feigned a punch.

The guy flinched.

But Slater didn't want to break his delicate fingers, so he waited for the guy to realise he'd been duped, then jerked forward at the waist.

The guy didn't flinch this time.

He didn't want to be humiliated twice in a row.

But this time, Slater wasn't faking it.

His forehead crashed into the guy's nose.

A colossal headbutt.

The man went down in a squirming heap, hands flying to his face.

Surrounded by three incapacitated goons, Slater calmly slipped his phone out of his back pocket and checked for an update from King.

16

K ing kept his hands in his pockets the entire way across the street. He weaved through traffic that had trickled to a standstill in the busy morning rush hour. He passed in front of a panel van and the frustrated driver leant on the horn.

King stopped dead in the middle of the road and wheeled around, staring the man in the eyes. He reared up to his full height, and let his broad shoulders bulge on either side of the giant overcoat.

The driver lowered his head, and lifted a hand in apology.

King continued onward.

He stepped up on the opposite footpath and beelined straight for the junkie. The man was sitting on the third step leading up to the portico, sheltered from the light rain by the stone ceiling overhead.

King stopped in front of him.

'Hey,' he said.

The junkie looked up, suspicion and anger in his eyes. 'What the fuck do you want?'

'You're coming with me.'

'What—?'

King kicked him in the chest, flattening him against the steps, smashing all the breath from his lungs. The junkie gasped and clawed at his shirt, but before he could ascertain exactly how injured he was, King bent down and used a sixty pound weight advantage to haul him off the stairs.

King threw the slight man over one shoulder, turned around, and walked off down the street.

A couple of passers-by stared.

King said, 'He's drunk. I'm taking him to the police station.'

They half-nodded, still suspicious.

Then they saw the man's behaviour — his eyes nearly boggling out of his head, his breathing laboured, his arms thrashing — and they turned their half-nods to full nods and went on their merry way.

King took the first right turn into a narrow laneway and dumped the guy down between a trash can and an empty van. He figured the van belonged to a cleaning company, and they'd currently be sweeping through one of the neighbouring office complexes.

He figured he had all the time in the world.

The junkie tried to scramble to his feet, and King shoved him back down into the damp gutter.

Then the skinny idiot tried to pull out a switchblade.

King lunged forward, seized hold of the guy's wrist, and smashed his arm into the trash can. There was a *crack* — either from the guy's arm or the metal caving in — and the whole trash can went over, spilling its contents across the alleyway floor. The switchblade came free and King kicked it away with reckless intensity, sending the knife skittering dozens of feet further inside the alleyway, where it was lost to the shadows.

The junkie reeled back, clutching his arm, and his entire demeanour shifted. He went from trying to escape to sporting a look of terrified complacency. He cowered against the wall, soaked in dirty water, and stared at King with pleading eyes.

King said, 'Don't play the victim.'

In accented English, the junkie said, 'I do not know what you want.'

'Answers.'

'What answer? I no have answer.'

'You have the answers I want.'

'What you want?'

'I need to know where you get your product.'

'What product?'

'Three seconds.'

'What?'

'I'm giving you three seconds to answer before I get mean.'

'You are mean.'

'You're selling meth to the general population. You're ruining lives. Don't get preachy with me. You don't get to play the victim.'

'I no play victim.'

'Where do you collect your product? Who gives it to you to sell? Give me an address.'

'I don't know.'

'One second.'

'Please...'

King squatted down and elbowed the junkie in the stomach, so hard that he threw up all over the alleyway floor.

King darted back to avoid contact with the projectile vomit, then dusted himself off and tried again.

He said, 'Where do you collect your product?'

The junkie said nothing.

King said, 'An address.'

'They kill me.'

'I kill you,' King said.

He pulled out the second Glock 17 Slater had collected off the organised crime thugs and pointed it square at the junkie's head.

King said, 'Same deal. Three seconds.'

'Please, man.'

'Give me the address, and then go buy a one-way train ticket to anywhere. Start fresh. Pull yourself together. Get clean and get a minimum wage job and save as much of it as you can. Work your way up from there. Take simple steps every day to improve your life. Read every day, exercise every day, and take your job seriously, no matter how trivial the work is. That's about the extent of my advice.'

The junkie said nothing.

'Or die, right here,' King said. 'Don't think I won't do it.'

The truth was, he wouldn't do it.

But the junkie didn't know that.

He blurted out an address.

King said, 'If that's wrong, I'll come back and find you. I know where you live. I'll finish you off. But it won't be a bullet. I'll use a knife.'

The junkie changed the address, giving a new one with an apologetic look on his face.

King said, 'Thank you.'

He put the Glock back in his waistband and entered the address into his smartphone's maps application.

Then he said, 'You got a phone?'

The junkie nodded.

'Let me see it.'

Hesitantly, the man pulled a slim iPhone out of his pocket. King snatched it up, dropped it to the alley floor between his feet, and stomped down on its screen with a weighty boot, demolishing it beyond any hope of repair.

He didn't need the junkie calling anyone before he reached his intended destination.

Then he strode off down the alleyway before the man even realised what was happening.

Leaving the guy alone, in a puddle of his own vomit, pale and nauseous and afraid.

But alive.

17

S later looked up and down the street for any sign of unintended witnesses, but he came up short. It was a series of residential cul-de-sacs, tucked away from the hustle and bustle of busy inner-city Budapest, like a private estate without the perimeter fence. There was no reason for civilian vehicles to be trawling up and down these streets. That's why the residences in this area were so expensive. They were afforded the luxury of peace and quiet.

It worked for him.

He kicked the first guy in the throat just as he started to recover, sending him straight back down the steps. The second man had started crawling out of unconsciousness, but he was in no state to listen to commands.

It didn't matter.

Two out of three was good enough for Slater.

He said, 'Listen up.'

Then he adjusted his tactics. He reached down and ripped the Heckler & Koch pistols from the first two guy's holsters and sent them tumbling over the balustrade after their buddy's gun.

The first guy had an unreasonable amount of fight in him, and started crawling back to his feet — even after the kick to the chest, followed swiftly by the kick to the throat. Slater sized him up. He was European, with caramel skin and black hair combed back and thick bushy eyebrows and eyes like crackling thunder.

There was a red mark on his throat and he seemed to be having trouble breathing, but he was persevering regardless.

Slater helped him to his feet, then smashed an elbow square into his forehead.

The guy's knees wobbled and he bent down in a squat and then tumbled head over heels down the first few steps. He clattered in an unconscious, messy heap at the bottom of the stairs. He'd wake up in half a minute, but he wouldn't be functional or cohesive for at least twenty.

Slater turned his attention to the third guy — the man he'd stripped of his weapon and shattered his nose.

Now he was the only conscious member of the party.

Slater said, 'Guess it's just us now.'

The guy nodded. Rivulets of blood ran out of both nostrils, and swept down his neck. The crimson had already soaked his shirt collar. He lay back against the concrete steps, utterly defeated. He offered both hands in the air, palms turned toward Slater. Showing he was unarmed, and wasn't going to offer any further resistance.

Slater didn't need the reassurance.

He already knew the guy meant no harm.

He said, 'You call Lukas and Benicio and tell them to get back here right this instant. Tell them there's someone here who wants to talk to them. And be quick about it.'

The guy paused, wincing in pain as the implications of

his broken nose started to set in. He screwed up his face and said, 'Wait, that's it?'

'That's it,' Slater said. 'Tell them to hurry, though. I'll be around.'

'W-what?'

Confusion. Utter confusion. These men operated in a world that had no room for error. If an unknown hostile got the jump on you, you were dead. He'd been ready to forfeit his own life, and he hadn't even considered any other possibility.

As if testing the waters, the third guy pointed to his two unconscious friends slumped at the bottom of the stairs and said, 'What about them?'

Slater regarded them for a moment. 'They'll wake up in a minute or so. They'll be confused. Help them through it.'

'You're not going to kill them?'

Slater said, 'No.'

'Why not?'

'I'm not going to kill any of you.'

'Why not?'

'It's Lukas and Benicio I want to speak with.'

'But they will tell us to help them when they get here,' the third guy said. 'And we don't want to do that.'

Slater almost widened his eyes, but made sure to keep his expression placid. It still shocked him all the same. This man had been beaten into such utter submission that he was aiding and abetting Slater in any way he could. He was offering suggestions, highlighting contingency plans, and doing anything possible to make sure he stayed alive.

What did you expect? Slater thought to himself. *This is organised crime. No-one has allegiance to anyone else.*

It's a dog eat dog world.

Slater said, 'Then don't be here when they arrive.'

'Where should we go?'

'I'm not your babysitter. Figure it out for yourself.'

'I don't want to help them,' the guy said. 'I don't want to make you angry.'

'I'm already angry.'

'I don't want to make you more angry. Neither do my buddies. They're just trying to earn a payslip. We all are.'

'You would have killed me just before.'

'I'm sorry.'

'Get out of here,' Slater said. 'But make sure you call them first. I need them here immediately. Then you can go.'

'They'll come looking for us.'

'Then you'd better move quick, hey?'

The guy simply nodded.

Slater turned on his heel and trotted down the steps. On the way past the two unconscious men he skirted around to the sidewalk near the left-hand side of the stairwell and collected the three Heckler & Koch pistols off the kerb. He gathered them up between his fingers and set off ambling back down the alleyway, following the trail from whence he came.

Leaving devastation in his wake.

18

The address fed to King by the junkie led him to a residential block of apartments near the north of the eighth district, only a few blocks away from the Hungarian National Museum.

The surrounding area was fairly upmarket, with wide paved roads and bright green London Plane trees arching their crowns toward the sky. Pedestrians were sparse, but the few that trickled around the area kept largely to themselves, chatting in their groups or admiring the scenery. King stood alone in front of the residential building, staring into its foyer, wondering if he'd made a mistake.

Wondering if the junkie had given him the wrong address, despite his warning.

There was only one way to find out.

He took the stairs two at a time and pulled the door handle, whereupon he ran into his first problem.

It didn't budge an inch.

Through the glass he spotted a resident heading for the entrance — a neatly dressed woman in her early twenties, with a small dog in tow on a leash. King stepped back and fumbled in the pockets of his overcoat, feigning irritation over not being able to locate his key.

The woman reached the entrance and thumbed a green EXIT button on the side of the wall.

The door sprang open, and she bustled past with her sausage dog trotting alongside.

King sighed with relief and caught the door as it swung outward.

She turned and offered him a warm smile, flashing brilliant white teeth.

He smiled back.

And then she was gone, and he slipped into the foyer with the most natural mannerisms he could muster. He knew he could turn his charm up to eleven if the situation demanded it.

The benefit of good genetics.

If he'd been stooped and squared away with a desperate, paranoid face, she might not have been so lax to let him in without visual confirmation of a key — especially not in this day and age. But he'd never had much trouble swaying people to help him out.

He should have entered the foyer with confidence, but the woman's warm smile reminded him of Klara.

So instead, he walked in angry.

He checked the apartment number on his smartphone — the number "705" rested in front of the rest of the address. He strode to the elevators, called one down, and punched the button for the seventh floor.

It whisked him upward.

Do it fast, a voice in his head told him.

The junkie might have found another phone by now. Unlikely, but pay phones still existed. This entire state of flow — from one address to the next to the next — required almost no room for hesitation. Slater had told him that earlier in the morning. Thankfully, that was the only way he knew how to operate.

He brought the adrenalin back, feeling it tickle the base of his spine and work its way up to his neck. He balled his fists again, and breathed deep, and considered the Glock 17 in the rear of his waistband.

He thought, *No.*

A surefire way to bring the impromptu operation to a screeching halt would be to fire a gun in an upmarket residential apartment complex. The police would be on the scene in minutes, and there'd be no guarantee he could get out of the building. Besides, he'd made it here in under ten minutes. He figured the junkie would sit around in his own misery for at least that long, wondering how he'd been struck by such misfortune.

The man would sit there in a state of analysis paralysis — going over all the possible outcomes. Would this mystery man really go to the apartment? Would he name-drop the junkie? Was his life now over?

King wanted him to sit there and stew. It meant he wouldn't run to the nearest pay phone and make the call.

So he was banking on that.

But he figured he could improvise if they knew he was coming, too.

He would just beat them to the draw, as he'd beaten anyone on the planet in a game of reflexes for ten years and counting.

The elevator deposited him on the seventh floor, in a corridor he'd seen a thousand times over in various upmarket establishments all over the world. He gave thanks for the plush carpet as it absorbed his footfalls, and he made it to the fifth apartment in the hallway in a few seconds.

Three digits had been stencilled into the dark wooden door.

705.

King backed up to the far wall, took a deep breath, and charged.

Locks were simple contraptions. Put two hundred and twenty pounds of raging muscle mass into the centre of a standard door with the charging speed of an angry bull, and bad things were bound to happen internally.

Either to King if the door didn't give, or to the lock if the force was too great.

And King had a hell of a lot of force to give.

It snapped, and the door shot inward at an uncanny speed.

King followed it into the apartment, and found himself in a small hallway, with a doorway at the end leading to an open-plan kitchen, dining room and living area all rolled into one.

He came in with all the momentum he'd built up, and if it had been an ordinary domestic scene he might have given the occupants a heart attack.

But it was far from an ordinary domestic scene.

In fact, his luck ran out almost instantly.

There was a fat bald guy right in front of him, in the entranceway, with a big .44 in his hand. He looked ready to use it. If he was, King didn't stand a chance — he put that together in the brief microcosm of time where the brain processes vital new information. There were six rounds in the cylinder, and one would go right through his skull and pulverise his brain if the guy had any kind of ordinary reaction speed.

But he wasn't ready to use it.

Not yet.

He was mid-stride, turning toward the doorway, and red in the face. Wheezing for breath, almost, even though there was barely room to move in this tiny flat.

Which meant they must have *just* got the call that King was on his way.

King envisioned the frantic burst of motion — running to a drawer, shoving clothes aside, rummaging around for the .44, pulling it out, hustling to the entranceway.

Another few seconds and the guy would have been in position.

So maybe luck was back on King's side after all.

He kept his pace and kicked the guy in the stomach, doubling him over and almost making him spew his break-fast over the wooden floorboards. King kept moving forward, and he snatched two handfuls of the guy's shirt and rammed him back into the far wall, knocking the back of his head against the plasterboard.

It hit with a *thud.*

The guy went wobbly.

Disoriented, but not unconscious.

But in a fight, they were one and the same.

They both rendered you useless.

King reached down and ripped the .44 out of his hands and smashed an elbow horizontally into the bridge of his nose, and he realised he'd put a little too much ferocity into it when the guy reeled back like he'd been hit by a baseball bat and bounced his head off the wall a third consecutive time, which seemed to be the straw that broke the camel's back, because after that he went down in an ungainly pile that King knew signified total unconsciousness.

It wasn't a practiced fall that protected his head from further damage.

His hands didn't fly to his face to absorb the shock.

Instead his legs turned to jelly and he collapsed straight down vertically and splayed across the floor with a grisly *bang.* His broken nose hit the floorboards next as he face-planted forward, and the pain woke him back up.

He started howling, curled up in the foetal position, as King advanced through to the next room with the .44 held at the ready.

King hesitated in the doorway.

Something wasn't right.

Then two new guys, crouching, poised in wait, fell on him with blunt weapons as soon as he stepped foot in the living area.

L ukas and Benicio ended up returning with the
cavalry.

   Slater figured there wasn't an urgent need for
tactical adjustment. He wasn't dealing with geniuses here.
Organised criminals had routines and patterns and systems
in place to manage their lifestyles, because most of their
time was spent ingratiating with ordinary society.

They couldn't descend into savagery in the same way
that a mercenary working in the jungles or at a remote
outpost could.

They had to go to dinners and attend social events and
bribe their way to seats at the right tables, so the actual
crime had to be reserved for whispers and occasional bursts
of violence, but that brought with it a certain reservedness
and apprehension to act like the mob thugs they were in
public view.

They weren't ready to flip the switch so easily.

Slater was.

So he stayed where he was, masked by the shadows in

the alley, crouching between two dumpsters and waiting for the three sentries he'd beaten down to get their shit together and sort themselves out.

It didn't take long.

They pulled themselves upright, the second and third guy helping the first to his feet. The first guy was the slowest to rise. Slater had dealt the most damage to him. He looked pale and shaky as he got his legs underneath him, and he gripped the balustrade with white knuckles. It seemed he was fighting the urge to vomit. He breathed in and out, in and out, in and out — like a human statue, frozen in time, except for his belly distending with each breath.

The third guy — the one with the broken nose — turned away from the other two and slid a phone out of his suit pants. He dialled, mumbled a few words, paused a beat, said something else a little more aggressively, and then hung up.

Then he turned back to his two colleagues and urged them to do exactly what Slater had recommended.

He urged them all to walk way.

The information had been passed along over the phone, and now they had to flee. *Hey boss, yeah it's me, no don't worry everything's fine — oh and by the way, we just got the shit kicked out of us and we're getting out of here before it gets any worse. Best of luck with the rest of your life.*

Slater saw the first two glance at each other with apprehension, and then the entire trio seemed to collectively shrug their shoulders as they arrived at the same conclusion. They had broken bones and concussions and pain up to their eyeballs. They were in no mood to hang around and test Slater's wrath. He'd warned them explicitly.

If they were still here when their bosses showed up, they'd just get hit again.

And harder.

None of them were willing to even entertain the possibility.

They all sauntered off with their heads bowed, wondering what the consequences would be. They would probably have to disappear. Lukas and Benicio would sniff them out if they stayed in Budapest. They'd walked off the job at the first sign of adversity. That wasn't something you did in a field like this.

But I'm a different kind of adversity, Slater thought to himself. *I'm demoralising.*

They were gone only fifteen minutes before Lukas and Benicio pulled up in a 4x4 Mercedes G-wagon, with three burly men in expensive tracksuits in tow. Lukas came out of the driver's seat, Benicio came out of the passenger's, and the trio of helpers piled out of the back, one by one. They were European and built like bodybuilders with jaws made of granite and identical buzzcuts.

Your cookie-cutter enforcers, like something out of a bad Mafia film.

The tracksuits indicated they were currently being used for intimidation purposes somewhere else in Budapest, but had been rounded up and carted to the scene just in case things had gone bad. There was nowhere in a tracksuit to store a gun without it being incredibly obvious, so they'd opted to hold the sleek Heckler & Koch 9mm VP9SKs in their hands, keeping them low and pressed to their side in case of civilian observers.

But there was still no-one around.

The five-man procession made for the steps out the front of the townhouse. Their eyes were wide and their gazes were searching for any sign of movement. It seemed they couldn't quite believe the initial three men had *actually* run off. The guys in tracksuits were in total disbelief, but Lukas and Benicio seemed a little more understanding.

And it made sense.

They were the only two who had previously met Slater.

They knew what he could do.

Slater stayed in the alleyway for a moment, weighing up when to make his approach, clutching his own VP9SK tight in his palm. They seemed to be the only weapons Lukas and Benicio's crew had. It made sense. Budapest was the kind of demographic where concealed carry was vital — the mob couldn't be openly walking the streets with firepower in their hands. They had to be subtle about it.

Slater tested the weight of the gun in his own hand and figured he could put it to good use.

Then he found his opportunity.

An elderly couple out for a stroll toddled across the mouth of the alleyway, just as he was about to emerge from behind the dumpsters. The five-man team on the other side of the street caught sight of the bystanders, and subtle panic rippled through them. The guys in tracksuits shifted their guns into their opposite hands, pressing them tight against their bulky thighs, masking them from view, and all five of them averted their eyes, as if pretending they weren't there.

Slater came out from behind the dumpsters when the old folks were three-quarters of the way across the alleyway's mouth.

He moved fast, and by the time they'd passed by, he was right there behind them. He darted out into the street, narrowly avoiding a collision with the pair, but he kept quiet. They barely noticed him on his way past.

Because that was what Lukas and Benicio and their goons had missed.

They'd just seen a couple of pedestrians and panicked.

But these geriatrics were pushing ninety, hunched over and supported by walkers, and by the time Slater had stepped out onto the asphalt they were already well out of earshot, slowly following the sidewalk as it curved around down the expensive avenue.

They were wrapped up in their own bubble.

And Slater could use it.

Because the five mob thugs were looking in any direction except the one that mattered. They'd instinctively averted their eyes from the elderly couple. They were focused on the road ahead, or the townhouse's front door, or the pavement between their feet.

Slater broke into as fast a sprint as he could manage without making a sound.

He flew across the road, screeching to a halt on the opposite sidewalk, and had his arm around Benicio's throat before any of them realised what was happening. He shoved the Glock into the side of the man's temple, and stared daggers into the other four.

Their guns didn't come up.

They stood there frozen, pumped full of disbelief.

Where the fuck did he come from? Slater could hear them all thinking.

Slater said, 'Guns down.'

He kept his voice low — the elderly couple weren't out of sight yet. But they were half blind and half deaf, so if they turned around to peer back down the street they would see six blurry shapes standing real close together halfway along the avenue.

Slater said, 'Guns down, now.'

The trio in tracksuits complied straight away. They had no intention of making a heroic gesture and getting their boss killed in the process. Too much risk. Too much potential for collateral damage. They let their VP9SKs clatter to the pavement, mirroring what Slater had done to the sentries just half an hour earlier.

Lukas was a little more difficult to persuade.

He started to bring his own Heckler & Koch up from where it rested in his palm, pointing at the ground.

Inch by inch, he raised it.

Slater gave him a stare that could melt steel and said, 'That's a really, really bad idea, Lukas.'

He shoved his own weapon so hard into Benicio's temple that the man cried out in anguish.

A shiver ran down Lukas' spine, and he dropped the gun.

Slater said, 'All of you inside.'

Lukas said, 'Why can't you just fucking leave us alone, man?'

Slater said, 'Something came up. After I left last night. Now I need your services.'

All six of them shuffled up the stairs. Lukas unlocked the front door, and they went through one by one. Slowly. No sudden movements.

Keeping his eyes on five highly dangerous, well trained men at once, Slater could feel the adrenalin pounding in his veins. When he shoved Benicio forward and scanned all five of them for potential second weapons, he figured he was safe. There was nowhere to hide more firepower. The tracksuits saw to that. And Lukas and Benicio would only have the one weapon each. They were glorified system administrators. Sure, they did mob work, but they weren't tough as nails. They didn't carry multiple weapons around like gangbangers. They sat at desks, and if they needed to, called in the muscle to help them out.

So Slater had stripped them all defenceless. Knocked them over like dominoes.

He lined them all up in the opulent hallway, and kicked the door shut behind him.

20

The problem with attacking Jason King with blunt instruments is the simple fact that it takes five or six well-placed blows to kill someone with a baseball bat or a two-by-four.

If you want to make sure you put Jason King down, you need to shoot him with a rifle from across the street.

Because anything close-range, anything in a claustrophobic space...

...that comes down to reaction speed.

And that was a specific skill that King had in spades.

No matter how long he'd been out of the game.

It was simply genetic, and it was why he'd pioneered a whole new division in the covert world of U.S. black operations.

A couple of street dealers was no problem at all.

The first guy came in from the left, and swung a steel bat at his head. King sidestepped it, but he didn't overreact. He could have thrown himself wildly off-balance — most people would. You see a steel object coming at your face, and you panic and hurtle out of the way, and stumble or even fall down, and leave yourself open for further attacks.

But King shot sideways, figured out exactly where he was out of range, and then stayed *right* there.

The bat whistled past, missing him by inches.

He kicked the guy wielding it square between the legs with enough force to rupture a testicle. He didn't know if it actually happened, but the man sure went down like it did, complete with the primal groan that came with taking a blow to the most sensitive region imaginable.

King pivoted and struck with the same leg, this time twisting sideways and opening his hips in a traditional close-range Muay Thai stance. He didn't know where the second hostile was exactly, but he had a general idea.

They'd taken up position on either side of the doorway.

King had disrupted the natural rhythm of things — obviously, the first guy swinging the bat was meant to connect. And he hadn't, so therefore there was a strange half-second of delay from the second attacker, because he had another bat in his hand but he'd deemed it useless to swing at the exact same time as his friend.

So King managed to connect with the kick before he had to deal with a second bat.

The second guy had his bat cocked back, ready to go, but he didn't follow through in time, and when King's shin bone caught him in the ribcage he flew off his feet like something out of a movie. But, really, it was grounded in reality, and it made sense given the circumstances.

King hit like a Mack truck, and the guy was lean and wiry, and he hadn't been bracing himself for an impact like that. He'd been focusing all his mental acuity on figuring out when to swing the bat, and he'd failed spectacularly at that anyway.

So he wasn't focused on keeping his balance.

He bounced off the wall and tumbled down to the cheap rug on the floor, clutching his stomach and retching violently.

King turned around and kicked the first guy in the chest, and he yelped.

Then he turned back and lined up another kick square to the chest of the second man, but he pulled back at the last second.

There was no point prolonging the suffering.

They were both down, and out for the count.

King crouched next to both of them, making sure he remained in the doorway, keeping the guy in the hallway in his peripheral vision.

He took a deep breath, and sent oxygen to his burning muscles.

It had been some time since he'd thrown full capacity strikes like that. He hadn't thrown anything with murderous intentions since he'd found Klara's body in Koh Tao.

He kept breathing, and the three thugs kept wincing and gasping for air and rolling around in horror on the floor. Their entire world had just been turned on its head. They were at the mercy of a vicious intruder.

There were few things on earth more horrifying than that.

King said, 'All three of you get up, real slow, and go sit on the sofa. I need information and I'm not leaving without it.'

They picked themselves up, still wincing, still traumatised, and stumbled over to a tattered old couch in the corner of the room. It had been wedged into place underneath a wide window with a tacky white sill and a plain glass frame. They dumped themselves down on it, and King held the .44 at the ready. For the first time, he could get a better sense of where he was, rather than only absorbing the necessary details as he fought for survival.

The living area was just big enough for three residents, with most of the floorspace occupied by a giant table positioned in the centre of the room. The surface was coarse wood, and it was packed with packaged bricks of hard yellow rocks. There were beakers and burners and jugs of water and bicarbonate soda strewn everywhere. And there were sachets of white powder all over the place, ready to be mixed and burned and left to set.

Cocaine to crack cocaine.

An age-old process.

King gave the contents a dark look, and then turned his attention to the three dealers.

'You three haven't been behaving very well,' he said.

He raised the .44 and pointed it at the head of the guy in the middle.

Six in the cylinders.

The guy squealed.

King said, 'I need to know where you pick up the drugs.'

The guy on the left sat up a little straighter. He squared his shoulders, and gave a slight smirk, which he quickly wiped away.

But King saw it.

King said, 'Did I say something funny?'

'There's no way we're giving you that information,' the man said, and he didn't have a trace of a European accent. He was a native English speaker. Australian, maybe. 'I thought you wanted something reasonable, like drugs or cash or guns.'

'I'm just climbing up the food chain,' King said. 'That's all. Where do you pick the crack up from?'

A pause, and then the man said, 'Another apartment.'

'Where?'

'In another district.'

'Give me the address right now or I'll blow your brains out.'

King held the .44 at the ready, and he put an expression on his face like he was going to use it at the slightest provocation. He added a certain derangement to his stare.

They seemed to believe him.

The guy in the middle softly elbowed the guy on the left in the ribcage. All their eyes were wide and unblinking. As if silently saying, *He's going to do it, man. Just tell him. I don't want to die here.*

The guy on the left sighed and bowed his head, suddenly realising he couldn't come up with anything believable on the spot, especially not with a gun aimed at his head, and finally he said, 'Okay, it's not an apartment. It's an airfield.'

'Where?'

'South. In the countryside. Middle of nowhere. Near Sárbogárd.'

'You got an exact location?'

The guy on the left raised his head with a quizzical look on his face and said, 'What do you think you're going to do?'

'Pay the airfield a visit.'

'And what to do you propose to do from there? You realise what this is, right? This is a production line. We're nobodies, man. We drive up to a gate that's fortified to the eyeballs, and a bunch of armed guards dump coke in the back of our truck, and then we drive off. We're not allowed into the airfield. That's where the drugs arrive, but we don't know how to get in. We're just grunts. There's nothing you can get from us.'

'Except the location.'

'It won't help you. It'll be like trying to storm a castle. I'm not kidding when I tell you it's fortified. How are you planning to get around that? You can't just drive a truck through the wall. It doesn't work like that.'

King said, 'Don't worry about that. All I need is the location. I've got a friend working on the rest.'

21

Slater later told them to stand shoulder to shoulder with their arms down and their palms facing forward. He told them if they made any sudden movements, he wouldn't hesitate to shoot them dead. There was no proof linking him to the townhouse. He could massacre them all, wipe the secret CCTV feeds, and then disappear into the wind like the ghost that he was.

They believed him.

They stood there in a row like toy soldiers, the colour drained from their faces. Even Lukas and Benicio had reached their wits' end. This mystery man was terrorising them, but it seems he didn't want to kill them. Did he just want to prolong their suffering?

Slater lined up the three men in tracksuits on the left, and in the silence of the empty townhouse he stepped up to the first in line.

He said, 'Please stay perfectly still.'

The guy complied.

Slater jerked forward and hit him with a trademark horizontal elbow, slashing it like a whip into the guy's forehead. The man's brain rattled, his legs gave out, and he collapsed. Slater had seen it a hundred times before.

He stepped up to the second guy.

He said, 'Please stay perfectly still.'

But he knew the man wouldn't.

He feigned an elbow, and the guy flinched hard.

Slater stared at him.

The silence dragged out.

Slater said, 'Either I give you a concussion, or I give you a bullet.'

The guy nodded, and sighed, and straightened up, and closed his eyes so he wouldn't see it coming.

Slater elbowed him, and it sounded like a starting gun going off at the races.

He repeated the process with the third man.

Lukas and Benicio stood there, mouths agape, staring at their only remaining guards wallowing in semi-consciousness on the floor of the entranceway.

Benicio shifted restlessly, as he was next in line.

Slater smiled and shook his head. 'Don't worry. That was just for them.'

'What the hell do you want?' Benicio said.

'One thing at a time,' Slater said. 'I can't keep tabs on all five of you at once, so I had to do that. Now the three of us are going to get something to tie them up. You got duct tape?'

'Yes.'

'Where?'

'Kitchen drawer.'

'Let's go.'

Slater followed Lukas and Benicio into the kitchen, keeping the Heckler & Koch aimed squarely at their backs, alternating between both of them every couple of seconds to make sure he didn't get complacent. Benicio strolled straight over to a drawer, and reached for the handle, but Slater stopped him with a sharp verbal command.

Benicio froze in place.

Slater crossed the kitchen and placed the barrel right in the small of Benicio's back. 'Now open it.'

Benicio gulped.

Slater said, 'If there's a gun in there that you were about to go for, I'm going to kill you right here. No second chances. You want to tell me in advance?'

'It's just duct tape,' the man hissed. 'That's it. I wouldn't risk it with someone like you.'

Slater nodded. They were getting the sense of what he could do. 'Good.'

Then Lukas lunged at him.

And it almost worked.

Lukas came at him at an angle, diagonally from behind, figuring he was just out of sight to try some final desperate dive for the gun. Slater had him *right* outside the edge of his peripheral vision, but it meant that when he twisted his head imperceptibly to the right he was able to see where Lukas *should* have been. And he wasn't there, so what followed was a violent pivot to the right, and at the same time he wrenched the gun inwards, bringing it closer to his body, putting some kind of awkward obstacle between Lukas and the gun.

Which was exactly the right decision to make, because Lukas slammed into him with enough force to send him skidding a few inches across the kitchen tiles. The man had his hands outstretched, his fingers splayed, searching for the Holy Grail — a grip on Slater's wrist. Then he'd be able to use all his strength to control the trajectory of any gunshot, which would leave Benicio free to punch Slater endlessly in the face until he dropped in a dazed and bloody heap to the kitchen floor.

But the lunge didn't work.

Slater composed himself and picked his next move wisely, getting a better sense of where Lukas had ended up after the desperate charge. He was flustered, unsure what to do next, contemplating whether to keep charging — and risk Slater shooting him dead — or surrender right there. It was only a half-second of hesitation, but Slater used it to make sure Benicio hadn't moved.

Benicio was effectively a prisoner by this point.

The man was standing by the kitchen drawers, his eyes wide.

Unmoving.

So Slater jerked forward and headbutted Lukas in the chin with his own forehead. He made sure to line up the strike so it had no chance of missing, and when it came down on the perfect target area there was a *crunch* and Lukas fell to the floor with a guttural moan.

His jaw might be broken.

Slater found it hard to care.

He came away unscathed, apart from a slight rattle to the head. But he'd taken a thousand of those over the course of his life, and here he was.

A forehead was considerably thicker and stronger than a jaw.

Slater levelled the VP9SK at Lukas' head and said, 'I should kill you right here. I don't need you.'

Everyone was a tough guy until the concept of instant death reared its head. Lukas went pale and started shaking, and Slater spotted beads of sweat forming on the man's brow. He imagined the guy's internal situation was no better

— a pounding heart, a churning stomach, lightheadedness, deep thrumming anxiety.

Slater said, 'You going to do anything remotely like that again?'

Lukas said, 'No.'

But it didn't come out right. It come out weak and stilted and his voice quivered. It had only been a single syllable, but he still hadn't pronounced it correctly.

Definitely some sort of serious injury to his jaw.

Again, Slater found it hard to feel a shred of empathy.

He turned back to Benicio and said, 'Get the duct tape.'

22

J ason King sat at the wheel of a beat-up old Peugeot
and floored it through the Hungarian countryside.

As he drove, he ruminated on how fast circumstances could change in the space of sixteen hours.
The night before, he'd sat in the ruin bar in relative misery,
figuring that Will Slater would want no part in whatever
barebones plan he'd concocted. It had all been a pipe dream
— he had a phone seemingly no-one could crack, and a
lingering sorrow over how quickly his life had been torn
apart, and a surprisingly resolute dead end, despite his past
ability to overcome almost any situation he found
himself in.

But he'd been out of the game for a couple of years, and
sometimes that was all it took.

The world was changing, and his kind were slowly being
phased out. All the reaction speed in the world ceased to
matter when you couldn't even find the hostiles you were
looking for. They buried themselves in a digital maze, under
a labyrinth of encryption, and the opportunity for a covert
solo operative to storm into a compound and run amok was

increasingly becoming rarer and rarer as time went on. Everything was done by tech prodigies paid handsomely by the government to sit behind their desks and burrow their way into the most tightly secured virtual locations.

You didn't need to actually pick up a gun if you could drain a terrorist's bank account, completely eliminate their funds and prospects, and then send a drone missile through their window for good measure.

But now there was hope.

Slater had encouraged a very hands-on approach to the problem at hand, and it had all gone swimmingly so far.

The three crack dealers were tied up in their apartment under enough duct tape to prevent them doing anything at all for the foreseeable future. King had taken their keys, gone down to the parking garage below the building, and commandeered the small Peugeot the three of them shared between them. He'd left the pieces of tape loose on their mouths, so eventually they could work their lips around and shift it free and scream for help, but by then he planned to be a ghost in the wind.

The timelines were aligning in all the right ways. Earlier that morning neither of them had expected this would work, but now it was, and it was all unfolding awfully quickly.

King accelerated faster, heading for a set of coordinates a couple of miles north of the town of Sárbogárd in Hungary's countryside. The journey would culminate at a very private, very secluded airstrip that for all intents and purposes did not exist. It was paid for by a shell corporation, and its tracks were covered up with the help of three or four prominent politicians who had enough influence and deep enough pockets to take a meaty bribe when required.

Therefore it wasn't *actually* an airfield receiving valuable cargo — instead it was an empty tract of public land resting between two giant privately-owned corn farms.

The three crack dealers had been *incredibly* hesitant to pass on that information.

King had persuaded them.

Somehow...

Half an hour on Route 63 and he was there, trundling down narrow roads, surrounded by endless undulating fields, tasting crisp countryside air through the open window. He rested a giant forearm on the sill and made sure to savour the present. For all he knew, he wouldn't get another moment like it...

He pulled up two miles from the airfield's supposed location in an empty overgrown lot, got out, and walked along the deserted gravel trail.

He knew the dealers hadn't been lying.

He'd promised them if they did, he'd come back well before they could get out of the duct tape and make life a living hell for them.

Considering the fact he'd already done so, he hadn't left much to their imagination.

They'd given him everything he'd asked for.

Without a moment's hesitation.

He crested a rise along the rural trail and surveyed a sweeping expanse of flat land fashioned into a couple of runways running parallel to each other, surrounded by a cluster of shoddy outbuildings, a warehouse, and a perimeter fence made of thick iron sheets. The whole thing looked unprofessional and thrown together with random parts — except for the runways themselves, which had all the bells and whistles that signified some serious coin had been dumped into their development. He saw shiny lights and smooth tarmac, and then noted he was standing atop the only slight incline in the surrounding terrain. Therefore, the contents of the airfield would be obscured from sight.

It was a private complex — not to be touched or interfered with in any way.

In fact, King saw a couple of signs slapped onto the perimeter wall that read — loosely translated from Hungarian — GOVERNMENT PROPERTY. KEEP OUT.

He scoffed.

These guys had connections.

He flattened himself to the earth, even though he would register as nothing more than a speck to anyone who had eyes on him. He was nowhere near any potential security cameras, and the trees and brush scattered all around him would provide perfect cover to wait.

He went prone, pulled out his phone, and dialled a number.

Slater answered. 'Yeah?'

'I'm in position.'

'Already? Where is it?'

'A couple of miles north of Sárbogárd.'

'Wish I knew my way around the Hungarian countryside. Doesn't ring a bell. You sure it's the place?'

'Oh yeah, I'm sure. Do you have what I need?'

'Working on it.'

'What's the hold-up?'

'This is more complicated than I thought. We're taking a trip to their office complex to get the information they need. Have you found an entry point yet?'

King scanned what little of the perimeter wall he could see from his vantage point. He took in the barbed wire and the curve of the iron. Entry would be literally impossible by trying to go over the top, and there would be cameras fixed on the top of the fence from every angle conceivable.

He breathed out and said, 'You know, if we did this my way, it never would have worked.'

Slater said, 'Aren't you glad we did it my way, then?'

'Thanks for all your help so far.'

'This is nothing. I've got a feeling there's a hell of a lot more coming.'

'Me too.'

'You didn't answer my question.'

King kept looking, and eventually he found a barely perceptible outline in the perimeter wall, like a small indent maybe five hundred feet from his position. He said, 'I think I found a side door.'

'Has it got an access code?'

King looked harder. He made out the shape of a small metallic box next to the outline. He said, 'I believe it does.'

'Perfect. That's all we need.'

'How long will you be?'

'As fast as I can.'

'And how long will *that* be?'

'I'm hoping less than an hour.'

'Okay. I'll wait.'

'Good luck.'

'I don't need it anymore. I've done my part. You need it.'

Slater said, 'I've never needed it before,' and hung up the phone.

King lowered the slim smartphone gently to the dirt in front of his face, and rested his chin on the earth.

He managed a half-smile.

He'd always liked Slater's confidence.

And, he realised, for the first time in two months he

hadn't dwelled on the image of Klara's body lying on the bed in Koh Tao.

For the first time in two months, he had momentum.

For the first time in two months, he felt alive.

S later sat in the middle of the rear seats of a metallic black BMW sedan as it whisked through the narrow Budapest laneways.

He had his gun trained on Benicio's head, who had both hands wrapped around the wheel, and white knuckles. That was all he needed. Lukas was in the passenger seat, but he was sporting a broken jaw, and it seemed he didn't have the mental fortitude to overcome the physical pain and make another lunge for the gun.

Besides, if he did, Slater would just pull the trigger and send a bullet through the back of Benicio's head, and then they'd all die anyway.

Slater had forced the pair to leave their seatbelts off.

He had his secured in place.

If they crashed, he'd be the only one not in for a world of hurt.

Benicio said, 'You're lucky there's no-one there on a weekend.'

Slater said, 'I'm always lucky.'

'Who was that on the phone?'

'None of your concern.'

'Let me guess,' Benicio said. 'He's already at the airfield. You mentioned an entry point. You're going to get us to get the codes for you, and then you're going to get him to open the door, and then he'll be inside.'

Slater shrugged. There was no harm in telling the truth. 'Pretty much.'

'But we don't know the location, which is why you split up,' Benicio continued, invigorated by the fresh lead. 'So he went round to a few street-level dealers, and went up the food chain and found out where the boys in the kitchen pick up their supply from, but he has no way in. So it's coming together like a two piece jigsaw.'

'You sound like you're happy to see us succeed,' Slater said.

Benicio shrugged. 'It makes sense now. I thought you were some lunatic. It's much more likely we'll get out of this alive if you've got more than two brain cells to rub together. But — hang on — why the hell do you need to get into the airfield? What are you planning to do?'

'None of your concern.'

'What harm will it do?' Benicio said. 'We're on your fucking side, man. We've got survival instinct.'

Slater said, 'It's nothing to do with you, or your careers, or your organisation. I ran into both of you by chance last night, and then something fresh came up with an old friend, and I figured I could exploit your resources to get what I need.'

'What do you need?'

'A tech wizard.'

Slater didn't much care whether Lukas or Benicio fed him lies when he told them what he needed. He fully expected to hear a spiel about how the airfield was a dead zone, devoid of valuable personnel who were integral to the organisation's survival.

But instead, Benicio just nodded and said, 'They've got a few people out there. You'll find them.'

Slater paused, taken aback. 'Thought you'd try to bluff me there.'

Benicio shrugged. 'I told you. Survival instinct. You're a different breed, man. I hope you find what you need and then carry on out of here. I don't want anything to do with you after this.'

'Good,' Slater said.

They pressed on north, into the fourth district, although Slater hadn't been keeping track of where they were. Even if they were leading him into an ambush, he figured he could shoot them both dead and escape out one of the back doors before they could properly approach the supposed blockade. Besides, he had no idea what they could have coordinated whilst held at gunpoint, and he believed Benicio's sudden change of allegiance.

The human brain was somehow predictable yet unpredictable at the same time.

Benicio had got it right when he'd voiced his concerns.

Survival instinct.

So when they pulled up outside a rundown three-storey office complex on the outskirts of Budapest, and Lukas silently gestured to the second floor with a knowing look, Slater suspected nothing awry.

'Let's go,' he said.

There was no-one else in the parking lot. For good measure, Slater tucked the VP9SK under his shirt, but kept it pointedly aimed in the direction of Lukas and Benicio. They both seemed to notice — they moved like robots across the cracked concrete lot, and if anyone had been peering out of their office windows they might have suspected something was awry.

But no-one did.

The mob had chosen an excellent location for their tech support — low on the totem pole, but compensated handsomely, given the townhouse they owned in Budapest's fifth district. Or one of them owned individually.

Slater had yet to discern exactly *whose* bed he'd slept in last night.

There was that dynamic at play, too, he realised. He'd slept with their wives. That was an emasculating concept in its own right. And here he was, ordering them around at gunpoint. No wonder they'd caved in so quickly.

Then he realised he'd probably gotten lucky by breaking Lukas' jaw and sapping all the fight out of the man in an instant. Benicio was much more compliant without the threat of significant injury.

They led him into an empty foyer and up an empty flight of stairs to a drab grey office with drab grey carpet and drab grey desks. The long low space was almost entirely devoid of furniture, save for the collection of desks adorned with all sorts of desktop PCs and monitors. Wires ran amok, and Benicio dumped himself down in a drab grey swivel chair and looked up expectantly at Slater.

'Okay,' he said, 'what do you need?'

He fired one of the computers to life and navigated around a desktop screen with at least a hundred icons on it. Then he took his hands off the keyboard and mouse with a sharp, sudden recoil.

He almost gasped, too.

Slater jerked involuntarily, and said, 'What?'

Still pale, Benicio said, 'I didn't want you to think I was alerting anyone by playing around with the computer.'

Slater stared at him.

And smiled.

'I've really got you wrapped around my thumb, haven't I?' he said.

Benicio gulped.

Lukas sat in the corner on another swivel chair, making sure to stay within Slater's peripheral vision. His eyes were wracked with pain. He offered no fight.

Slater said, 'You said you don't know the locations of the airfields. How does that even work?'

Benicio shrugged. 'Our employers extract that data from everything they send us. We just build systems. We're not told where they're needed. It helps split everything up so no one person knows everything. Doesn't seem to have stopped you, though.'

Slater said, 'How many airfields are there?'

'Only one that's live right now.'

'Live?'

'Taking cargo.'

'Where do you import it from?'

'Does it matter?'

Slater thought hard about that, then said, 'I guess not.'

'What do you need?'

'Gate codes for the perimeter around the live airfield.'

'There's only two.'

'You know which sides?'

'North and south.'

Slater slid his phone out of his pocket.

24

King took the call, and on the other end of the line Slater said, 'Are you on the north or south side of the airfield?'

'North,' King said. 'I came in from the north.'

'You sure?'

'Absolutely.'

There was a pause, and muffled voices from the other end, and then a few moments later Slater came back on. '845950.'

King said, 'Thank you very much. Same plan?'

'Same plan.'

Just then, an ancient Douglas DC-4 swooped in from the sky and touched down on the left-hand runway. It coasted down the last stretch and rumbled to a halt in front of one of the outbuildings. Workers materialised out of the blue like a swarm of ants, and began shovelling *something* out of the hold.

King couldn't make it out from this distance, and he hadn't had time to bring a pair of binoculars. But he knew exactly what it would be. Neat bricks of coke. They'd be converted to crack and sold for an obscene mark-up in tiny portions to the addicts on the streets, and the wheels would keep turning, endlessly on and on.

The international drug trade.

He had to compartmentalise. He wasn't here to fight all organised crime in the country. He was here to find out who had killed his girlfriend, and why, and it started with tapping into the phone in his pocket.

He took a moment to shake his head at the ridiculousness of the situation.

He and Slater had just dismantled the security around a top-secret airfield importing cocaine into Hungary, all to get access to a gang of tech prodigies who *might* be able to get access to the phone and see if there was anything of value on it. But, then again, it made sense upon further scrutiny. These planes coming in couldn't show up on any official radars, or the whole racket would come crumbling down, and there was enough money in coke to funnel millions to the right talents.

Just like the government did.

Just like the Fortune 500 companies did.

So Slater had been on the money, as usual.

But now was the pivotal moment.

He rose off the dirt and crouch-walked down the incline, vanishing from the line of sight of anyone inside the complex looking out. He checked for CCTV cameras aimed at this section of the airfield's perimeter, but the coast seemed clear. He was shoving and forcing his way through overgrown brush and weeds, and it seemed no-one had stepped foot on this ground for years.

Utterly deserted.

He skirted all the way up to the small indent in the perimeter wall, and lifted the phone to his ear again.

'Still there?' he muttered.

'Sure am,' Slater said.

'What was that code?'

Slater repeated it.

King punched it into the keypad, one digit at a time.

The single red bulb vanished, replaced by a green pinpoint of light beside it.

King reached out and tugged the handle.

The door gave a few inches, sliding out of its lock.

King breathed a sigh of relief, and said, 'I'm in.'

'Same plan?' Slater said.

'Same plan.'

'Be there soon. Text me the coordinates.'

King stood there, keeping the door exactly where it was, refusing to open it all the way, because he didn't know what the hell he was going to find on the other side — and he didn't want to go in alone. It seemed to contrast with how he'd lived the first ten years of his life — charging recklessly into anything in front of him. Always solo. Never relying on help. But he wasn't that man anymore. He was older, wiser...

...and he had a friend just as dangerous as he was.

A comrade.

A brother.

And Slater was coming.

So he held it a few inches away from its lock, his only lifeline to his only lead. Those few inches of space encapsulated all the hope inside him. Without it, he had nothing, and he might as well skulk off toward the horizon and fade into oblivion if the phone's contents resulted in a dead end. Klara had been the only thing holding his sanity together. He'd truly, truly loved her, and he couldn't remember feeling that way about anyone for as long as he'd been alive. Now he was a shell, with all the training and discipline in the world but none of the emotional connections.

If he could avenge her, then perhaps his future might stand a chance.

If not...

He didn't want to think about it.

It had taken every fibre of his being to wrench him out of the old life, and now he was back in it.

That did things to you.

Indescribable things.

He wasn't sure if he would ever be the same.

But at least he had Slater.

At least he had a brother.

25

To Lukas and Benicio's horror, Slater fished a couple of fresh rolls of duct tape out of his jeans. He'd pocketed them back at the townhouse, and now he smiled as he waved the gun in one hand and the tape in the other.

'You know what this means,' he said.

Begrudgingly, they pinned their arms to their sides and sat deathly still on their swivel chairs.

Slater took perverse pleasure out of binding them into their own personal cocoons — a technique he'd perfected over the years. Nothing quite rivalled the simplicity and the efficiency. For a few dollars at a hardware store, you could pin someone in place as effectively as handcuffing them with steel.

Slater made sure they were entirely enclosed in the poly-ethylene before he tossed the empty rolls across the room. Then he put a foot in each of their chair backs, and pushed them gently across the room. They rolled across the carpet, twirling as they moved, like makeshift merry-go-rounds.

Slater actually laughed.

'Just leave us alone, man,' Benicio said. 'I've had enough of this shit.'

'Sorry,' Slater said. 'I just like the image of leaving a trail of organised crime thugs across Budapest, all duct taped to the spot. Should be simple for the police to follow.'

Benicio's face fell. 'You'd do that to us?'

Slater shot daggers across the room. 'You might think we're all buddy-buddy here because you've been cosying up to me, but we're not. You both sit at a desk and handle administrative matters, but you're not oblivious to what you're doing. You keep the lights on and the codes secure for an organisation that flies in tons of coke and keeps the streets full of the stuff. You ruin lives from here, even though you might feel like you're detached from it. And then you use a portion of those profits that are distributed down to you to buy expensive townhouses and eat at good restaurants and buy your wives lavish jewellery.'

'Probably ex-wives now,' Benicio grumbled.

'But not because I slept with them,' Slater said with a wry smile. 'Because you'll be in jail.'

'Best of both worlds.'

'Enjoy your time in the hole,' Slater said.

He tucked the VP9SK into the back of his waistband and dialled 112 on his phone. He followed the necessary steps to get through to the police, and then fed a confused officer details surrounding a townhouse in the fifth district and what he would expect to find there. Three men — known mafia thugs — tied up with duct tape, wriggling around like fish on the sitting room carpet.

He hung up just as the officer started asking him for further information.

Lukas stared silently, and Benicio said, 'Why didn't you lead them here?'

Slater said, 'Because they might have experts with them, and I don't want them unravelling the puzzle too fast. The townhouse will lead to this office, and this office will lead to the airfield. But myself and my colleague still need time to get our work done at the airfield itself.'

'Your tech wizard?'

Slater nodded.

Benicio said, 'Good luck.'

Slater said, 'You don't have to pretend to like me anymore. Or wish me luck. You'll go to jail for this.'

'Or we won't,' Benicio said, and gave Slater a knowing look. 'If the right people find us. Our employers haven't survived for this long in this industry by ignoring the bribe systems. If we're processed correctly, it shouldn't be a problem.'

Slater thought long and hard about this, and about how deep the corruption might actually be entrenched, and then he shook his head and put the phone back in his pocket.

'Well,' he said. 'The pair of you had better hope for the best.'

Then, without fanfare, he turned and left them there in the middle of the giant office space, rotating ever so slowly on their swivel chairs, taped all the way from their waists to their shoulders. There would be no chance of destroying the evidence. Whoever came across them would find them sitting in front of their monitors, implicated in a wide range of crimes just for being in the vicinity of all this stuff.

But that was none of Slater's concern.

He'd got what he needed.

He took the stairs down two at a time and slipped into their BMW. He'd told them to leave the keys in the ignition for precisely this purpose.

At that moment his phone pinged with an incoming

message, and he skewered it onto the dashboard with the help of an adhesive patch on the back of his phone case. He brought up the coordinates King had sent through and gunned it out of Budapest, covering as much ground as he could manage before the emergency call went through and the web of crime in the luxurious shadows of the city began to unravel.

All to get access to a goddamn phone, he thought.

He emptied his mind of all the clutter on the long drive south. The GPS told him it would take just over an hour and a half to reach the airfield, and he wondered how long King could stay deathly still holding a door before his arms grew tired and he gave up.

Then, with a sly smile, Slater remembered who he was dealing with.

Jason King had never quit anything in his life.

He was an unforgiving man with an unforgiving past, just like Slater.

And therein lay the crux of it.

They were born and bred the same. Tried and tested fighters. Killers. Warriors. They were the solemn few that relished the opportunity to find that moment when your mind told you, *No more,* and then go right through it.

They'd been doing it for over a decade.

Between them they had more experience in ruthlessness than an entire platoon of SEALs, and they'd already demonstrated their ability to act cohesively after so long apart.

They'd done it in Russia, and now they'd do it here.

In a single morning they'd gained access to what might constitute the most private, most secured, most protected patch of land in all of Hungary.

Within which dwelled a couple of software engineering geniuses whisked into organised crime straight out of university, who kept the whole thing running smoothly and the cash flowing to the relevant parties.

And then Slater thought, *Why am I doing this?*

He could have died multiple times this morning. And it had barely fazed him. He'd pressed on without a moment's hesitation, when most people baulked at the thought of commuting an extra thirty minutes to work each morning. And why? To investigate the death of a friend's partner. A man he hadn't seen in months. A man he didn't owe a thing.

But that wasn't true after all.

Because Jason King and Will Slater owed each other everything, and they would prove it time and time again until their bodies broke down and they were forced to deal with the consequences of the life choices they'd made.

Until then, they'd keep on fighting.

He floored it past bright green fields that still managed to shimmer under the cloudy sky. The rain had receded, replaced by a drab monotony, but Slater savoured it. For some superstitious reason he didn't want the sun to be out. He wanted to be cloaked in shadow, infiltrating a place he had no business in, alongside a comrade who had only just resurfaced in his life.

He pulled up in the same dreary lot King had parked the Peugeot in, and he left the BMW right alongside the empty hatchback. He followed the same trail up the crest, and then down the decline, where he found King standing with a rigid, straight-backed posture alongside the side access door, keeping it prised open with just two fingers. The whole door hovered only a few inches away from the lock.

King had been cutting it close, but he'd clearly wanted to ensure anyone strolling past on the other side would suspect nothing awry.

Slater jogged down the last stretch of the slope, and came to a halt right alongside King.

Slater said, 'Any unexpected developments?'

Bored out of his mind, King eyeballed him and said, 'Does it look like it?'

They listened intently for a minute or two, and then King peered through the narrow crack in the doorway, getting his bearings, searching for problems on the other side. He found none. But he reached back and drew a .44 Magnum from his waistband all the same, and Slater followed suit with his own Heckler & Koch VP9SK.

'Let's go find our man,' King muttered.

They whisked the door open and stepped through into the airfield.

Like a well-oiled machine.

Each dangerous on their own, but together...

Together, they were something far greater.

26

T hey entered a zone that felt eerily similar to no-man's-land.

Just a sweeping patch of churned earth between the perimeter wall and a collection of outbuildings facing one of the runways.

It closed them off from the rest of the airfield, and they savoured the privacy. There was no-one in sight, but as they swept their gaze across a warehouse, an administrative building, and a small set of portable toilets, Slater got the sense this was a fluid operation, that could be dismantled and packed away and shipped off to an undisclosed location at any moment. They probably needed that in place, in case the bribe system collapsed on itself, or any number of things went wrong up the pipeline.

They moved in a tight formation, practically shoulder to shoulder at all times, and covered the gap of no-man's-land with quick strides. Slater aimed for the administrative building, figuring it was the best place to start. It lay directly ahead of them, composed of two portable modules with a walkway in the middle. The whole thing looked like it had been carted in on the back of an oversized truck. There were no windows facing the perimeter wall, and Slater counted his lucky stars.

They were ten steps from the walkway when, thirty feet to their left, a rusting metal door was thrust open out the back of the giant warehouse and a guy in a high-visibility vest wearing a plastic hard hat stepped through.

He had a cigarette in his mouth, and the lighter was halfway to his lips.

He froze when he saw them, but for the first time together, Slater and King utilised their reaction speed at precisely the same moment.

It was as if their brains were synced, and instead of wheeling their aim around to point the barrels of their weapons at the newcomer, instead they thrust the guns behind their backs in unison.

A pair of short, sharp actions, but it made all the difference in the world.

Instead of screaming for backup as he noticed two pistols coming toward his face, the guy simply paused for a beat. Lighter frozen halfway to his mouth.

King and Slater were big and powerfully built, but they didn't look like killers.

They were dressed expensively, and they carried themselves with a poise that screamed, *We belong here.*

And this guy didn't know how the whole operation worked. He was a cog in the machine, and who was he to question if a couple of higher-ups were back here, taking a break from an important meeting in one of the other buildings?

So he nodded to them, and they nodded back, and a second later the door swung shut behind him.

Following its natural trajectory.

Sealing him off from the inside of the warehouse.

And then the guy realised that none of those thoughts really held up to much scrutiny, but by then it was too late. As soon as the door clicked closed King and Slater brought their handguns out from behind their backs and had them both pointed at the guy's face before he could blink.

The worker was speechless.

Then he swore under his breath in Hungarian.

Slater said, 'Come here.'

'You don't want to do this,' the guy said, but he kept his tone low all the same.

He knew if he raised his voice, they might shoot him.

And Slater was entirely prepared to.

King said, 'Come here.'

Somehow his words held more weight.

The guy said, 'Okay. Don't kill me.'

His English was good.

He took a few steps forward.

Slater said, 'Don't make a goddamn sound.'

The guy said, 'Okay.'

He kept moving forward.

Step by step.

Foot by foot.

Then he entered the narrow laneway between the warehouse and the administrative building, and his eyes flitted sideways. Slater and King were close to the administrative building, and they didn't have a line of sight down that laneway.

They didn't know what was there.

Slater said, 'Keep walking.'

The guy kept looking down the laneway.

Then he opened his mouth to shout.

27

But Jason King had predicted the whole thing.

A pang of relief resonated through Slater as he watched the six-three, two hundred and twenty pound man lunge off the mark like an Olympic sprinter coming out of the starting blocks. He closed the gap in about two seconds of furious running, and the warehouse worker only managed to eek out a half-hearted '*Hey,*' by the time King's right fist met his jaw.

King had lunged into the punch with reckless abandon, a looping diving haymaker, and he connected without caring whether he shattered his knuckles in the process. It was why Slater so often relied on the elbow — because the bones in the fingers were delicate, and could break at the slightest provocation.

Mixed martial artists and boxers wore gloves for a reason.

It wasn't to protect the other fighter from head trauma.

It was to protect the hands.

But King hadn't the time or the range to lunge into the elbow, so he ended up throwing a punch so hard that it flattened the worker to the churned earth like he weighed twenty pounds.

His neck twisted to the right and he — *snap* — went unconscious and — *crash* — splayed into the dirt. Then King was standing over him and aiming his .44 rigidly down the laneway like it was attached to his hand.

Slater took off, and was alongside King in seconds, his own gun raised.

They found a pair of workers — one in an untucked shirt and tie, the other in the same high-visibility vest as the unconscious man on the ground between their feet.

An office worker, and a labourer.

One of them carted the coke off the planes, and the other sat at a desk and worked out where to send it.

Where there were shortages. Where there was high demand.

Slater said, 'Both of you come here right now and don't make a sound or we'll blow your brains all over this fucking alleyway.'

And it came out like that too — a long, uninterrupted string of words that poured out in a low tone. Much the same way they'd approached the situation with the original worker.

But now it was like dominoes, and Slater tightened up internally as he imagined all the ways this particular situation could go wrong. One of them could run off, and then they'd have to shoot them both, and that would resonate across the entire airfield unless another ancient DC-4 chose that moment to land and drown out the gunshots under the roar of its engines.

But that didn't happen, of course, because Slater and King weren't *that* lucky.

There wasn't another plane in sight.

The workers froze, slightly shellshocked by the savagery with which their colleague had been smashed into silence.

Maybe they considered another idea.

But then they caved.

They bowed their heads sheepishly and shuffled closer, covering ground fast, the laneway between them and the men holding them at gunpoint shrinking fast.

Slater's heart stopped pounding at a dangerous rate.

Everything might be alright after all.

King said, 'Come stand right here.'

They complied. Maybe they'd never had a gun pointed at them before. Just because you worked in organised crime, didn't mean you were an organised *criminal*. The packages they handled were illegal, but the entire operation was shrouded in supposed legitimacy. Politicians and officers of the law had been paid off left and right, and this particular airfield might never have run into adversity.

And that would make them complacent, and scared, and prone to being ordered around by a couple of intruders who knew *exactly* what the hell they were doing.

The guy in the shirt and suit pants walked up to King first.

King elbowed him in the face.

Which didn't knock him out.

To both Slater and King's surprise, the guy stumbled around like a newborn deer, his mouth open and his eyes wide, trying to keep his legs under him. King had hit him with a monumental shot, and Slater couldn't remember the last time he hadn't seen someone wilt under the sheer force of King's power.

But the guy was basically out on his feet.

He went through a wobbly pirouette, and when he came

back around to face forward again, King hit him even harder with the same elbow.

This time, he went down like someone had pulled his power cord out of the wall socket.

Before the other guy in the high-vis vest could react, Slater lunged forward and wrapped both hands around the back of the guy's neck in a traditional Muay Thai clinch. Still pinching the VP9SK between two of his fingers, he gave thanks for the compact undersized weapon as he locked his fingers together. Then he brought the guy's head down fast, and brought his own knee up even faster.

Bang.

Another unconscious casualty.

With three squirming bodies at their feet, they got straight to work.

King dragged two of them at once, using his inhuman strength to haul both labourers out of the laneway and behind the administrative building. Slater hefted the office worker over his shoulder and followed suit. Together they shoved the three men under the portable deck out the front of one of the modules, and left them there in the overgrown grass.

They wouldn't be cohesive for at least thirty minutes.

King had hit them *hard,* and Slater had followed suit.

He usually reserved that kind of ferocity for people he wanted to kill.

So they would wake up soon, but that wouldn't mean anything. They'd be confused and their minds would be dull, and they'd lie on their backs underneath the deck in the shadows, trying to piece together what the hell had happened. Then they'd sit up and vicious headaches would sprout to life, and they'd go straight back down into the dirt.

If they weren't severely concussed, it might be an hour before they managed to drag themselves upright and stumble to the nearest superior, to alert them about what was happening.

If they remembered what happened at all.

King looked fast at the administrative building, and Slater's heart skipped a beat.

He'd seen something.

Slater followed the man's gaze.

He saw a face flashing away from one of the windows in the right-hand module. Wide-eyed and pale. Mouth agape.

Someone had just seen them moving the unconscious workers.

Slater's heart skipped another beat.

'*Go,*' King hissed.

Slater leapt up the short flight of stairs and put his shoulder into the back door at the same time as he smashed a fist down on the handle. It twisted, and to his relief it sprung open.

Unlocked.

His shoulder-charge paid off and he tumbled into the narrow corridor in seconds. The walls were cheap and thin, and he could hear frantic movement in the adjoining room.

Slater sprinted flat out down the corridor and thundered a twisting side kick into the half-ajar door to that room, smashing it open as fast as he could. Without even thinking twice, he went straight into the room. Any delay would give the occupants time to phone for help, or arm themselves more than they already were. There was no nobility in hesitation.

There was only *forward.*

Slater barged into the long low room only a few seconds after they'd glimpsed the face in the window.

He expected to see multiple guns coming up to fire.

He raised his own VP9SK and prepared to go down in a blaze of glory.

28

B ut there were only three people in the room.

Two men, and a woman.

And they all looked scared to death.

Slater worked the barrel of his gun from left to right, his eyes wide, his veins pumped with adrenalin. One of the guys had a landline phone halfway to his face, and Slater raised both eyebrows and looked a question at him.

The man dropped the phone instantly.

It smashed back against its cradle and toppled off the desk.

Silence permeated the room.

Slater kept the gun in position, but he took a step back through the open doorway and peered down the corridor. He saw King on the open landing, gun raised, defensive posture initiated.

Ready for a war.

Slater mouthed, 'All good,' but he didn't vocalise it, because he had no idea who was in the adjacent room. King nodded and approached warily, his footsteps large and imposing on the cheap floorboards underfoot. He reached the doorway, and both he and Slater squeezed through into the room. Slater shut the door behind them, and they both sat down on the thin-framed chairs near the entrance. In unison, they rested the guns on their lower thighs, keeping a finger each on the side of the trigger guards.

Slater gestured for the three workers to sit.

They dumped themselves down in their swivel chairs with the colour draining from their faces. Slater figured they'd never been threatened before in their lives, and as he scrutinised them, he came away entirely convinced that these were the trio they'd been looking for all along.

He said, 'Do all three of you speak English?'

They nodded in unison, their mouths all hard lines.

Slater said, 'Because you're all geniuses, aren't you?'

Their faces were turning whiter and whiter. Slater could see the veins in their foreheads, the lumps in their throats. They were all in their late twenties with stooped postures and thin noodle-like arms.

They could have been from the same family.

Made in a lab somewhere, with similar properties.

The two guys had thin receding hair, and the woman's hair was frizzy and looked unhealthy.

But it was simply a byproduct of the environment.

They were cooped up in this dank office space with an absence of natural light and unending job stress. These were the tech prodigies, offered gross starting salaries to do private work for a private company, paid under the table whilst avoiding any tax implications with the help of government officials paid off with bribes. A perfect system, except for the expectations. They were designated to run a foolproof operation that had no margin for error — if they slipped up, and the wrong parties found out about the airfield, it would be their heads on the chopping block.

If the encryption they set up was bypassed, all of it would be right there for the taking.

All the flight logs, all the quantities of the imports — everything.

And now their jobs were about to get a whole lot more complicated.

But only for an hour or so.

Slater said, 'Okay. Ground rules established. We can all communicate with each other — that's good. Now who else works in this building?'

The woman sat up and said, 'There's a few guys in the other module, but we're the only people in this one.'

King said, 'You telling the truth?'

She said, 'Why the hell would I lie to you? Do you think I want to die?'

Slater exchanged a glance with King. They both tried not to smile.

She was smart.

Slater said, 'So we won't be disturbed for the foreseeable future?'

The man closest to the window gulped and mumbled something.

Slater said, 'What?'

The guy pointed a shaking finger at the dirty window pane. 'Did you kill those guys out there?'

King said, 'No.'

The man breathed a sigh of relief.

King said, 'But we will if we have to. And we'll kill the three of you too.'

Slater got up and strode over to the window. All three of the hackers flinched, but he kept the gun behind his back and peered out through the pane.

Assessing the scene.

He didn't like what he saw.

One of the warehouse workers was already upright — the guy King had hit twice to put down. He seemed to have a chin made of steel. Nothing could keep him down. He was wallowing in the shadows under the flight of stairs, surrounded by overgrown grass, but soon he would be on his feet and functioning mentally.

Slater said, 'King.'

King perked up.

Slater pointed out the window. 'Got a slight problem that needs dealing with.'

King nodded once. He'd intentionally drawn into himself. Reduced his communication to nods and single syllables. Playing the role of the enforcer. It made him seem more terrifying.

He rose off the small chair, listened intently for sounds of activity in the corridor outside, then threw the door open.

Slater heard his thudding footfalls on the other side of the wall.

He shook his gun at the tech team and said, 'All of you get up.'

They sprung off their chairs, completely obedient.

Slater said, 'Come over here.'

They joined him by the window.

In a shaky voice, one of the guys said, 'What's going on?'

'I want you front and centre for the big show.'

'The big show?' the woman said.

Slater looked at her, then looked back out the window.

King threw the back door of the module open a moment later, and hustled out onto the deck. He flew across the landing and down the steps, all two hundred and twenty pounds of him moving like a gymnast, and he caught the barely conscious worker by the corner of his high-visibility vest. The guy spun round, reacting to the touch, but he was operating at far less than normal brain capacity, so it took him vital seconds to register who stood in front of him.

Then his face fell.

King hit him with a blocky forearm, thrusting it horizontally into his face, sending him straight back to the shadow realm. He collapsed back underneath the deck, and for good measure King kicked his legs out of sight. When the body was firmly tucked away in the overgrown grass, he looked up to the window and nodded a confirmation to Slater.

He won't be getting back up for a while, his look said.

Both an operational necessity and a measured performance, in equal parts.

The tech team was suitably horrified. Slater told them to sit back down, and they wandered back to their chairs on shaky legs. When they planted themselves down, each of them appeared to be grappling with their own version of an existential crisis. Would they have taken this highly illegal, very risky job if they knew it would ultimately lead to this?

This hadn't been in the job description.

They'd been told they would never fall into harm's way, no doubt.

King re-entered the room, and gently closed the door behind him.

He stared at the three workers.

Slater said, 'Are you going to help us?'

All three of them blurted, 'Yes,' at the exact same time.

29

S later said, 'Good. Just making sure.'

King said, 'Here are the ground rules.'

Three sets of eyes darted in his direction in unison. Slater hadn't done anything to demonstrate his abilities yet, so for now King was the most terrifying person in the room, and they reacted accordingly. They hung onto his every word like the mere idea of them not paying attention could get them killed.

King said, 'We're not going to kill you if you do exactly what we say. And we mean follow every word. Nod so you understand what I'm telling you.'

Three nods.

'You've all been recruited straight out of university?'

Three nods.

'Are you all Hungarian?'

The two guys nodded. The woman shook her head.

She said, 'I am German.'

King said, 'Okay.'

Then he looked at Slater.

Over to you.

Slater said, 'Do you know your way around military-grade encryption?'

Three nods.

King said, 'Why should we believe you?'

The woman said, 'We have to know our way around it. This operation needs to be conducted without anyone on the outside realising. That takes a lot of work. More than we can realistically achieve. But the three of us work well together, so we get it done. We've been asking them to hire more people for a long time.'

'What are your qualifications?' Slater said.

'We all have Masters' in software engineering, and we all graduated magna cum laude from separate universities,' one of the men said. 'And we all displayed certain ... traits that put us on the radar of this place.'

Slater raised an eyebrow.

The woman looked sheepishly at the ground and said, 'Are you cops?'

King pointed a finger out the window. 'Would cops do that?'

'Depends which cops.'

'We're not cops,' Slater said. 'So you can tell us.'

'We were all implicated in financial crimes before this organisation approached us.'

Now King raised an eyebrow. 'Implicated?'

The woman shrugged. 'University is expensive. And most security systems aren't anything impressive. Not to people like us.'

King nodded, seemingly satisfied, and rose off the chair. All three of them flinched. He crossed the room, step by step, and approached the end of their desk. He took the slim black smartphone out of his pocket and placed it delicately on the table. He tapped the screen with a single finger.

'I need you to get into this phone,' he said. 'However you can. And as fast as you can. You're going to need to put all those skills you've been acquiring to the test, because if you don't get it done we're going to kill you. And we might not just shoot you either. We might beat you down like we did to those guys outside. Because you got yourself into this mess through your own mistakes, and now you're going to face the consequences for it. If you don't get into this phone you're going to wish we were police. Have I made myself clear?'

Three nods.

Three pale faces.

Even Slater bristled at the spiel. He knew full well that neither of them were prepared to kill a trio of scared, talented kids fresh out of university, but King almost had the acting chops to convince Slater, too.

Slater tapped the barrel of his VP9SK against the desk and said, 'He's not kidding. And I'll be the one to do it.'

One of the guys gulped.

'Okay,' King said. He put his .44 down on the table and clapped his hands together. 'Get to work.'

Slater circled around behind the three swivel chairs, so he had a view of the monitors splayed out across the desk. He kept his gun in his right hand, and made sure all three of them could see it.

'I'm not going to tell you to slow down your workflow for me,' he said, keeping his voice low. 'I get that you'll need to do things fast. It wouldn't feel natural to walk me through it. But I don't need to keep an eye on what you're doing. Because the simple fact is — if you even think about tripping some kind of panic button, I'm right here. The second someone charges through that door in response to your alert, I'll shoot all three of you through the backs of your heads. It won't even be a contest. Security might get the jump on us after that, but that won't matter to you. We'll have killed you long before it turns into a proper firefight. You won't be around to wonder whether we got away or not. So don't try it.'

They all nodded.

'Okay,' Slater said. 'Permission granted to proceed.'

They huddled around the phone and plugged it into one of the CPUs. Instantly, the woman pulled up a specialised software program and said, 'Yeah, it's encrypted. We'll need to do an offline attack.'

'Like I said, you don't need to walk me through it,' Slater said. 'Just get it done.'

They got to work, and Slater stepped back in awe at the speed with which they flashed through tabs. They pulled up information on what seemed to be a dozen different ways to breach an Android phone and absorbed enormous amounts of data in minutes, speed-reading their way through a collective bible of instructions.

Then they broke down what would and wouldn't work, and started running different potential options in a rapid explosion of code.

They typed at inhuman speed, fingers flashing across the keyboards, but there was none of the Hollywood glitz and glamour.

They were just obscenely good at their jobs, and Slater knew if they'd decided to contact their superiors for help through one of the open tabs, he would have no way to tell.

King sat in the corner, seemingly counting the minutes ticking by, and Slater was so enraptured by the speed of the tech team that he didn't notice his colleague stand up and slip out of the office.

He did, however, notice King return a few moments later with both the semi-conscious warehouse workers draped over each of his shoulders.

30

The tech team went pale, and Slater hissed, 'What are you doing?'

King dumped them down in the corner of the room and waved his gun in their faces. 'Stay fucking quiet if you want to live.'

The pair nodded uneasily, and sat with their arms around their knees and their heads bowed.

Again, Slater said, 'What are you doing?'

The tech team visibly slowed down. Slate tapped his own gun against the backs of their chairs.

'Don't look at them,' he instructed. 'Keep doing what you're doing.'

Then he turned back to King, and for a third time said, 'What are you doing?'

King pointed at the workers. 'They're waking up. We needed to bring them in here. What else would we do with them?'

'Knock them out again.'

'You want me to turn them into vegetables? Because

that's how that happens. They can't take another hit each. We need to watch over them.'

Slater almost sighed outwardly, but he kept it in.

Yeah, great, King, he thought. *This really adds to our aura. Getting concerned over our victims taking one too many knocks to the head.*

Instead, he said, 'Okay. Go get the other guy.'

But King was already halfway across the room, and a moment later he threw the door open and disappeared back out into the corridor.

Then Slater heard multiple footsteps at once, and a sudden pause, as if two separate parties were sizing things up, and that preceded a surprised, *'oomph,'* and a moment after that King returned hauling another office worker by his shirt collar. A man Slater had never seen before. The guy was bleeding from the mouth and nose, and King dumped him down next to the warehouse workers with a disgruntled expression plastered across his own face.

King looked up at Slater, and muttered, 'New arrival. Stepped into the corridor as I was on the way out.'

Slater regarded the scene all around them, and shook his head in disbelief.

This was quickly getting out of control.

Soon they'd be babysitting half the employees at the airfield in a semi-conscious state.

Slater said, 'Make sure that doesn't happen again.'

King raised two bruised hands and said, 'How the hell am I supposed to control that?'

'We can't track seven people at once.'

One of the tech guys said, 'I'll watch them.'

'Yeah, right.'

The guy said, 'Think about this for a second. All three of us wanted out of this job as soon as we realised exactly what it entailed, but they kept us doing what we're doing by showing us how we'd go down just as hard if we burst the bubble. So we're implicated in this whole thing, and you two clearly have nothing to do with this operation. This phone isn't related. You just needed our services, right? So why shouldn't we help you?'

Slater said, 'That's a noble speech. But I still don't trust you. Keep doing what you're doing.'

The three of them turned back to the desktops.

King vanished again, and came back half a minute later dragging the final office worker in tow. He practically threw the man across the room as he re-entered, frustrated by the mounting complications and the increasing likelihood of detection.

Slater felt the same.

They exchanged a weary glance as they surveyed the four airfield workers in varying states of disrepair, and the three tech workers hunched furiously over their monitors. It was a lot to juggle at once.

But they could do it.

The tech team seemed compliant, at least.

So they took up positions on each side of the room — King stood over the four workers and kept his .44 aimed at each of them, daring them to make any sudden movements. At the same time Slater maintained his position behind the desks, even though it was growing more and more useless with each passing moment. The three tech workers were deep inside their own bubble, speaking their own language, ignoring all outsiders. He very much doubted they were going to rat the intruders out. He'd believed the man who had spoken about their lack of allegiance, even though he hadn't shown it at the time.

Finally, after nearly twenty minutes of silence — interrupted only by the clacking of keys and the clicking of a computer mouse — the woman spun around in her chair to face Slater.

He flinched involuntarily. He was aware of the four workers in the corner slowly coming to their senses. Their increasing lucidity was worrisome. King was staying vigilant, but he only needed to slip up for a second, and four bodies would pile on him. All the reflexes in the world wouldn't be able to save him if he was stripped of his weapon and overwhelmed by sheer numbers. And if Slater had to intervene, it would leave the tech team unattended, giving them room to make a break for it. He wasn't sure if he'd swayed all three of them over to his side yet.

So, getting more and more tense with each passing second, he said, 'What?'

She said, 'We've got a text message sent to the phone sixty-four days ago. Does that add up?'

King bristled. 'That's two days before it happened.'

She furrowed her brow, confused. Slater didn't elaborate. She didn't need to know about that. He just said, 'What does it say?'

'It just reads, "Go ahead."'

King swore, and Slater scrunched up his features. 'Got a location?'

'Yes, actually,' she said. 'It was sent from a set of coordinates that seem to lead to farmland near Tapanui.'

'Tapanui?'

'It's a small town on the South Island of New Zealand. Middle of nowhere.'

Slater sighed.

King didn't say a word.

He stared across the room vacantly, looking into space, his gaze focused on nothing.

He said, 'I don't like this at all.'

Slater said, 'Guess we're flying halfway across the world.'

'Could be a ruse. Just to get us out of the picture for ... something.'

The woman shook her head vehemently. 'No.'

Slater raised an eyebrow.

She said, 'It's genuine. I'd bet my life savings on it. They tried so hard to mask all the sensitive data. It's a miracle we got text logs out of the phone. They definitely didn't want anyone seeing this. It was a nightmare to crack. Even when we got into the phone itself, the location the texts were sent from was scrambled. We had to decrypt that, too.'

'How'd you do it?'

'You got all day?' she said.

'What else is on it?' he said, moving on.

'Almost nothing,' she said. 'That's the truth. It was a burner phone, in case you didn't put it together. Supposed to be untraceable. Supposed to mask everything. I'm telling you — no-one other than the three of us together could have got through that encryption. Whoever's doing it is damn good.'

Slater said, 'Then they won't expect us to show up on their doorstep.'

The woman said, 'Who are they?'

'We don't know.'

'What did they do?'

Slater glanced imperceptibly at King, who shivered as something cold ran down his spine.

Slater knew what it was.

Dark, black rage.

Unfortunately, the pair of warehouse workers deemed it a suitable time to mount a resistance.

They leapt to their feet in unison and charged at King,

thinking they were taking advantage of some kind of lapse in attention.

Slater winced.

They fell on him, and one of the office workers decided he was lucid enough to pile on too, but what they hadn't predicted was something out of their worst nightmares rising up to retaliate.

Jason King lurched around to face them with pure anger in his eyes.

B ad timing, was all Slater could think.

Don't attack the man when he's mourning the loss of his life partner, you fools.

The warehouse workers were strong and short and built like tanks, almost wider than they were tall. Their forearms rippled with muscle, resting over thick calloused fingers, their physiques hardened by manual labour. In a civilian confrontation, they might have intimidated the competition nine times out of ten. But this was a world away from the civilian sphere, and King whipped around with lightning speed to meet their oncoming bullrush.

He raised the .44 over his head and pistol-whipped the first worker, somehow slashing his way between the guy's outstretched hands, splitting the guard and sending him careening off-balance in response to his broken nose.

King didn't stop there.

He was angry as hell, furious at the turn his life had taken, and Slater could see it in the man's eyes. He could almost see the gears turning in King's head.

These guys have been supplying the country with crack for years.

Imagine the untold devastation they've caused.

The addicts' families won't mind if I take out my rage on them.

King lashed out with a vicious leg kick, tearing cartilage in the first guy's knee, sending him half-falling, half-bowing toward the carpeted floor. King encouraged him down by grabbing the back of his neck and wrenching downward, helping him along his journey. He slammed the guy face-first into the carpet and then sprung upward, leaving the broken man in a pool of his own blood. The second guy hesitated, shocked by the sudden violence, but he'd already shown his hand and King wasn't about to deliver any mercy.

He kneed the guy in the mid-section as soon as he realised his adversary had left his stomach exposed.

Bone crunched against muscle, and bone won.

Slater heard the impact of the knee and visualised the worker's insides seizing up, cramping and screaming for relief. The guy bent over with all the breath smashed out of him and King followed up with the same knee directly to the unprotected face. The worker shot back, and King thundered a kick into his chest, bouncing him off the wall like he weighed ten pounds.

The office worker piled in, seemingly unfazed by his two colleagues' demise.

Slater figured he was either dumb or brave.

Probably both.

King clenched his teeth and threw another looping overhand haymaker of a punch, this time out of sheer irritation instead of desperation. He wanted to throw something with mean intentions, and he wanted it to hurt.

It hurt, alright.

Four knuckles landed against a jaw and broke the bone.

The office worker moaned and collapsed.

King shook his hand and winced, testing to see whether he'd broken any of his fingers, but he seemingly came away without significant injury.

He straightened himself up and flashed a glance at the tech workers, surrounded by three men all seriously injured, and a fourth so intimidated he might have wet his pants.

'Sorry,' King said. 'This isn't a great time in my life.'

'We can tell,' the woman said.

Suddenly eager to get the hell out of here before King made things worse, Slater slid his own phone out of his pocket and said, 'Those coordinates, please.'

The woman read them off the screen.

To make sure she wasn't bluffing, Slater leant in and cross-checked them with his own notes, but it all added up. She had a maps application open in the desktop background, and he could see the same latitude and longitude entered in. As she'd told him, it narrowed in on a tract of land a few miles east of the tiny New Zealand town of Tapanui. The map feed was from a satellite, and Slater could see staggering peaks of mountains dotted with snow all around the bright green fields.

He glanced from the monitor to King. 'Ever been to New Zealand?'

'No,' King said. 'But there's a first time for everything.'

Slater put his own phone back in his pocket and straightened up. He surveyed the damage. There were three men lying flat on the carpet in the corner of the office, bleeding everywhere and moaning to themselves. The fourth was sitting in the same position, with his knees tucked up to his chest and his gaze fixed on the ground, as if he could wish his way out of his predicament. The tech workers seemed slightly more subdued, resigned to whatever fate Slater and King had in store.

Slater turned to them and, wishing he could rewind the last minute of their lives so they weren't intimidated by King's ferocity, said, 'Here's the deal.'

They listened in.

Slater said, 'You've got no reason to trust us, but you nailed it the first time. We have nothing to do with this airfield, or this operation. It's too big for us to take care of, and quite frankly it's none of our concern. You three can carry on doing what you're doing and keep your same jobs, and we couldn't care less. We needed information on that phone, and we needed it fast. This was the only way. If you hold that against us, then that's alright. But we'd prefer if you were as vague as possible about what happened here for as long as possible. We need a head start and it sounds like whoever runs this operation has connections everywhere. We'd prefer not to get shut out of the airports before we can get out of the country, because we need to get to New Zealand. So ask yourselves if it'll affect you in any way if you're sparse on the details for twenty-four hours. Once we're gone, call this in, but you don't know what happened to these guys. You only saw a glimpse of us. We never spoke to you. None of this will ever come back to haunt you.'

They shrugged and nodded in turn, but there wasn't the slightest guarantee they'd stick to their word.

He'd used all the persuasion he could manage.

Now he bored his gaze into them.

Deep into their souls.

He tried to show them, with just a look — *I'm not a bad guy.*

One by one, they seemed to genuinely believe him.

He nodded silently to each of them.

He mouthed, 'I'm sorry.'

Then he pointed King toward the door and gestured that it was time to leave.

They stepped outside simultaneously, and Slater gently shut the door behind him. Before he pulled it closed in its entirety, he gave the tech team one final, pleading look.

He wasn't going to kill them to protect himself.

He had to hope like hell they would follow his advice.

They stared back at him, but there was very little fear in their expressions.

He shut the door, and followed King out of the module. They crossed silently to the perimeter door and re-entered the same code Lukas and Benicio had provided them with, this time from the other side. The green light buzzed and they slipped out of the airfield.

On the other side, King let out a hearty sigh.

Slater did the same.

It felt like they'd beat down half the damn complex.

Slater's bones were weary. He had the beginnings of a throbbing headache. But he tuned all of it out, because there was work to do. He had to admit he'd expected a hell of a lot more information off that phone.

They had almost nothing to work with.

But they had a location.

New Zealand, he thought. *Never been there.*

And he was due for a vacation.

32

As they clambered up the incline and made for the small rural lot nearly two miles north, they both let the silence drag out. It was something subtle between them. They didn't need to pour out their conflicting emotions about what they'd found. They just dealt with it on their own, going deep into their own heads.

Processing the recent developments the only way a couple of solo black-ops killers knew how.

King said, 'A goddamn burner phone.'

'We've got a location.'

'Yeah, but it's not enough.'

'It's more than enough. Look what we had to work with today. If we stayed on this path, we could have shut down an operation that would have made international news.'

King hesitated at that, mulling over it. 'Maybe we should have…'

Slater said, 'I wish I could hold a mirror up to your face right now.'

'Why?'

'Because you're a mess, King. Your head's not right. You almost killed those three guys back there—'

'They deserved it.'

'I could see you running that through your head. Weighing up whether you could live with yourself if you beat them all to death. But that's not what we came here to do. We're not sociopathic. We needed information, and we got it, and you might have crippled all those guys you beat down. If they pulled a gun on you, then fair game. But you only did it because you were angry.'

Alone on the deserted trail, King turned to look at Slater as the country wind lashed their faces. 'Do you understand what I'm going through right now?'

'Yes,' Slater said. 'I haven't told you much about what I've been through recently, but I've experienced something similar. I had someone I considered a daughter. I had to give her away because of my own lifestyle. Because of the way I'm wired. Because of what I do day to day. And that made me angrier than I ever thought it could. So I went to Zimbabwe to try and get away from it all, to grapple with the fact that I'll never have anything resembling a family because I can't go two days without getting into some kind of chaos. And I was slowly coming to terms with it, and then everything went to hell in Zimbabwe, too. Because that's my life. And it's yours, too. You tried to avoid it for so long, but the bottom line is that neither of us are going to be able to avoid it in future.'

King said, 'Then what's the point?'

'You know what the point is. You know what we can do. You know what we're capable of. It's what I was trying to accept this whole time, when you were on a tropical island trying to live a peaceful existence. It was never going to work, King. But at least you got the chance to give it a shot.'

'Don't act like you're superior.'

'I'm smart enough to know where my lane is, and to stay in it.'

The fist came at his face so fast that for a moment he thought he was hallucinating. He'd never dealt with a combatant like Jason King in his life, and the blinding speed nearly deceived him. If he'd hesitated a half-second longer, it would have crashed against his jaw and knocked him unconscious.

But, under the surface, it seemed King had been holding something back. It was imperceptible, barely noticeable, but Slater sure picked up on it.

His own speed rivalled King's, and he knew the man had second-guessed himself as soon as he'd thrown the punch. He'd thrown it with anger and animosity and frustration, all rising up like an unstoppable ball in his chest, and as soon as Slater had insinuated it was King's fault, he had unleashed it with all his rage.

But Slater was fast as hell, and he knew King hadn't dealt with anything like that in a long time either.

He recalled an encounter at an airport in Corsica a couple of years ago. Back when they'd first met.

He'd beat King then, and he'd do it again now.

Because he was quick, and relentless, and he considered himself a little more unhinged than his counterpart. King had morals and a rigorous code. Slater was a cooped-up bull, and it didn't take much to set him off.

A fist flying at his face from someone he thought he trusted was enough to do it.

He flipped a switch and jerked out of the way, and the fist missed him by inches. King had overcompensated with it, throwing caution to the wind as he channelled all his anger, and Slater took advantage of the speed difference. He was behind King in a half-second, and wrapped around his back like a boa constrictor in another half-second.

He bucked with his hips and wrenched downward and used every morsel of his jiu-jitsu ability to lever all his weight across King's upper back. King weighed more, so he kept his feet under him, but Slater reached down and seized hold of King's left wrist and jerked it down, sending him stumbling to the left wearing a two hundred pound backpack, and that was enough to tip the equilibrium and seize control.

To a bystander, it would have seemed incomprehensible. Two of the fastest, most dangerous men on the planet locked in a vicious battle of leverage, both aware that with a third-degree black belt in both their possessions, it would be a matter of who got to the ground in an advantageous position to tip the scales in their favour.

King went down into an awkward half-squat, fighting with all his might to stay on his feet, but it was a test of technique, and Slater had come in with bulletproof composure. King was getting his awareness back, but he'd been furious at the start, and as that flowed out it translated into a loss of momentum.

As soon as he was down in the half-squat, Slater sunk the hooks in, wrapping both his legs around King's mid-section, securing the metaphorical backpack. King's hands flew to his face, knowing full well that a choke attempt was coming, but Slater knew he'd do that. So he jerked again at the hips, jolting King in place, and he lost his balance and fell forwards without the use of his arms to stabilise his stance.

He ploughed into the dust, and on the empty gravel trail they fought and squirmed and battled for every inch of control.

But the fight was done.

Slater had every advantage.

And there was an unspoken agreement in the air not to resort to blows. Jiu-jitsu was just enough of a test of competition as a straight-up fight, without the accompanying brain damage that came from men of their calibre smashing fists against skulls.

Because they both knew they could kill each other in a heartbeat.

Slater flattened King out on his stomach, his legs still looped around the man's abdomen. He tried to squeeze with his legs and crush the breath out of his opponent, but King had abdominals that felt like steel. Slater ignored it, concentrating on what he could control. He forced King's face into the dirt by pressing down on the back of his skull with a calloused palm, and used the momentary discomfort to loop his other hand around King's throat.

But he was slightly out of position.

He crushed the head down harder, and King fought against it with animalistic strength.

Slater adjusted his hips, sliding a few inches down to get better leverage.

King bucked hard, threatening to throw him off.

Slater held tight, and nearly broke a nail off on the ground as he clenched his teeth and forced his arm through the gap.

Nearly there...

Just a few...

More...

Inches...

There.

He felt the crook of his elbow touch the soft flesh of King's throat, despite the man's efforts to crush his chin into his chest and prevent any attempt at a rear naked choke.

And then he knew he had it, so he stopped forcing King's head down and used his other hand to wrench the choke in tight, the muscles in his arms screaming and straining and crushing tight against King's windpipe, and as he held it he channelled his own anger at what his life had become over the last few years, feeding off the chaos and uncertainty, wondering if he would ever live a stable, comfortable life, and then he realised that wasn't what he wanted and instead he would be happy to do this forever, fighting and struggling for every inch of space and finding out what he could truly become when he wasn't tethered down by personal and emotional burdens.

All that played out in the space of a couple of seconds, and King rolled him over so now Slater's back was on the ground, but the choke sunk in tighter and tighter, and King's face turned red as Slater cut off the carotid artery and any moment he would pass out...

But he tapped.

He reached up and patted Slater's forearm, twice, and surrendered.

Slater let go and skirted over on his butt, moving a foot to the left, and he rolled into a seated position and caught his breath.

King sat there, too, silently working for breath, his throat already red and aggravated and swollen.

Then he said, 'I'm sorry.'

And it echoed down the trail.

33

They sat there for a couple of minutes, not talking, because that was how they operated.

Instinct.

Bred into them over time.

They'd spent their whole careers out in the field, alone, compartmentalising their own emotions and grappling with their life choices, bogged down in muck and sweat and blood and dust, outnumbered almost every time.

And here they were, fighting each other.

King piped up eventually. He said, 'I was angry.'

Slater said, 'I know.'

'Would have gone differently if I'd been calculated.'

'Keep telling yourself that.'

'Is this going to happen again?'

Slater said, 'You tell me.'

'I'm surprised it doesn't happen more often. This is a mad world. I don't know how we stay sane.'

'We don't.'

King just nodded.

Then he picked himself up and dusted himself off, and

offered Slater a hand. Slater took it, and clambered to his feet, and they set off back down the trail like nothing had happened at all. The sky turned steadily more overcast with each passing minute, shrouding them in grey, adding to the uncertainty they both felt churning in their stomachs.

They walked on and on.

Eventually Slater said, 'I really don't want that to happen again.'

King said, 'I know.'

'I fucking mean it. I see a punch coming like that again and next time I might not let go when you tap.'

'I understand.'

'If you're going to do it again, make it count. Because there won't be a third time.'

'I'm telling you — that was it. I'm not myself.'

'I can tell.'

'But that shouldn't mean I should place you at risk.'

'Exactly.'

'You could turn and walk away whenever you want.'

'You're goddamn right I could.'

'In fact, you probably should. I've asked for your help, and put you at risk, and I just tried to attack you. You owe me nothing. I have a location, and really ... I've got all I need, don't I?'

Slater raised an eyebrow and looked at King quizzically.

King turned, palms spread, face open. 'I mean, you did what I asked. You helped me out. You got into the phone. There wasn't much on it, but that's all I asked you to do. This isn't your fight and I don't expect you to help me. I'll go in alone. It's probably better that way — given how our careers unfolded.'

Slater said nothing. He let their footsteps echo ahead, and behind, and he kept his gaze wired down at his feet.

Finally King said, 'Slater.'

Slater looked up. 'What?'

'I can't do this anymore. This silence. I need an answer.'

'You said it's better if you go in alone.'

'Isn't that what we spent a decade each doing? Learning to thrive on our own? Shouldn't it go that way? And besides, don't you want to fight your own fight? Why fight mine?'

Slater said, 'You don't remember why Black Force was founded in the first place, do you?'

King said, 'You kidding?'

'No. I'm not.'

'That shit was my life. I poured my heart and soul into it. I remember every goddamn moment.'

'You were pulled out of Delta because you didn't mesh with your unit, and neither did I in the Navy. And you know why that was? Because we were simply better. That's the cold hard truth of it. We reacted faster, we went our own way, and we felt like our team bogged us down in combat. Even though we were operating with the best of the best — it wasn't enough. Black Force's founding principle was that those outliers work better alone, because there are no contradicting orders and nothing to hold us back. We can go at our own pace. We can go deep into our own inhuman minds. We can do extraordinary things. And we did. We did them over and over again until we were the stuff of legend.'

King said, 'Where are you going with this?'

Slater let the silence drag out, and they trudged on a little further, and then he said, 'They never thought of putting us together.'

King said, 'Maybe they tried it with the others.'

Slater said, 'I don't think they did.'

'Why not?'

'Because if they ever put the two of us together in the

field, I don't think they ever would have gone back to the way things were.'

'That's a stretch.'

'Look what we just did. We didn't butt heads until after we got what we needed. Until then we were operating in the red zone, but we were doing it effortlessly. We ticked off our separate objectives and then came together to get what we needed. Who else could have done that? Certainly not either of us on our own. It took a whole plethora of moving parts, but it felt streamlined in the process.'

King let that sink in. They reached the secluded dirt lot, and both of them silently selected the BMW as the vehicle of choice to get them to the airport.

It was quicker than the Peugeot, and in this business speed was everything.

Slater got behind the wheel, and King sank into the passenger seat.

Slater fired up the engine.

King said, 'Maybe everything happens for a reason.'

Slater said nothing.

King said, 'Maybe I was never supposed to settle down.'

Slater turned out of the lot and got back on Route 63 and gunned it in the direction of the closest airport, which the GPS told him rested on the outskirts of Budapest.

King said, 'Let's see how we do in New Zealand.'

Slater said, 'I agree. You read my mind.'

'And then we can figure out where to go from there.'

'If we make it through this.'

'They won't know we're coming. They won't think we cracked the phone.'

'But we did it. And we did it easily.'

'So we'll do this easily.'

'Because we're two of the toughest bastards that ever lived.'

Slater smiled.

'That's why I didn't answer your question,' he said. 'Of course this is my fight. Every goddamn fight is my fight. Especially if it's yours. Because I don't think we're ever going to meet a warrior like each other. No-one's wired like us, which is why they isolated us in the military. But now we're out, and we're free, and we're unburdened. Where do you think that could lead?'

'We'll find out,' King said.

He offered a hand across the centre console, and Slater reached over and shook it.

'New Zealand sounds like a nice place for a vacation,' King said.

'You read my mind.'

'Let's raze hell.'

'Always.'

They redlined it toward the unknown.

As they'd been doing all their lives.

But this time, they did it without a haphazard plan. They did it unified. Not thrown together by fate or happenstance, but deliberately coming together as a team.

Slater felt it in the air.

He wondered where it would lead.

But the possibilities were endless.

Jason King was back, and the future was bright.

PART II

34

As they'd suspected, it turned out to be a mammoth of a journey.

Halfway to Budapest International Airport, King sat up straight in his seat, as if suddenly struck by a sinister premonition.

Slater said, 'What?'

King said, 'Didn't you tell me things had gone south with Uncle Sam recently?'

Slater nodded. 'I'm not in their good books, to say the least.'

'Are they actively looking for you?'

'I think so. Maybe not as intensely as they were when I went AWOL back in Russia. They've got their own problems to worry about. When the Lynx program dissolved, it made the news. It was a PR disaster. But they mitigated most of the damage, and came away relatively unscathed by downplaying what was going on in the North Maine Woods. And then the media cycle kept churning, and everyone forgot about it real fast. So I think they were more concerned about recovering their image in the headlines than actively hunting me.'

'But I assume you're on every flight list in the world.'

'Is that what you're worried about?'

'I don't want to trip at the first hurdle by not thinking things through.'

'How do you think I got into Hungary?'

'There's a dozen ways to do that illegitimately.'

'And there's a dozen ways to do it legitimately.'

'You've got a fake passport?'

'Did I mention how much I was worth?'

'Right. That didn't cross my mind.'

'Four hundred million dollars buys you any kind of access you want. And I'm creative.'

'Right,' King said.

They left the car five miles away from the departure terminal, parking it well away from the airport in a narrow side street, surrounded by industrial developments and the stink of smoke and steel. They got out and slammed the doors and left it unlocked. If petty thieves chanced across it, then all the better. If not, when the inevitable investigation began into what the hell had happened around the airfield, the necessary parties would take their time linking it to Budapest International Airport.

They'd scour the immediate search area, and find nothing amiss in the industrial zone, and then finally make their way to the conclusion that the two occupants had fled the country.

As long as he and King were on the ground in New Zealand by the time that happened, it didn't matter in the slightest.

'What's your status with our government?' Slater said as

they strode through empty industrial laneways in the darkening afternoon.

A stormy grey sky infiltrated above, lengthening the
shadows and adding to their unrest. They had nothing but a
location near Tapanui, one of the most isolated and scenic
locations on the planet. They had no idea what was in store
for them.

All King needed was revenge.

Now he said, 'Nothing's changed.'

Slater said, 'Well, technically, everything's changed.'

'Not since you told me I was cleared. No-one came looking. No-one came knocking. The government didn't care
about me anymore, and I was free. I was happy. I had no
burdens. I was...'

He trailed off, glancing up at the sky, fighting back a
wave of guilt. Slater could see the expression on his face, his
eyes wracked with pain.

King said, 'Everything was good, man. Real good. Better
than I deserved — that's for sure.'

'It was quick,' Slater said, but he kept his voice low.
'When it happened, it was quick. She wouldn't have known
what was coming.'

'The bullet went through her forehead from close
range,' King said. 'She would have seen it coming. Trust me.'

'Only for a moment. If I had to choose how to die, that'd
be it. Quick. Painless. Nothing to it. I know you feel the
same. We've talked about it.'

King said, 'It's not that. She died because of me. That's
the problem. I don't know what she did to deserve it. Is it
because of what I've done?'

'It's not because of anything,' Slater said, and suddenly
all his ruminations about life bubbled to the surface. 'It's
just because shit happens. That's the truth. Life goes that

way sometimes. We've all got to suck it up and deal with it. Do you really think anything we do is going to make a dent in the suffering going on in the world? We could spend our whole lives fighting this shit and we wouldn't change a thing. That's the truth, too. Nothing means anything, but at least we can do our best in the moment. Understand?'

King didn't respond for a beat, and briefly the hairs on the back of Slater's neck bristled as he anticipated another violent outburst.

He made a mental note to not test King philosophically at such a sensitive time.

But the punch never came.

Instead, King smirked. 'Thought I was going to hit you?'

'Maybe the part where I said your girlfriend dying doesn't mean anything might have been taking it too far,' Slater said.

King shrugged. 'And yet, the point stands. Life's going to go on. What am I supposed to do? It happened. I was a wreck for two months. I'm still a wreck, but now I can cover it up. So do I sit in solitude and let it break me, or do something about finding out why it happened? Do something about finding the people responsible...'

'Exactly,' Slater said.

They let their thoughts play out as they made for the airport. They powered down a sidewalk adjacent to an endless stream of gridlocked traffic flowing toward the departure and arrival terminals.

Inside the terminal, they approached one of the counters warily, expecting an army of secret policemen to descend on them at any moment.

Which was realistic.

They didn't know what sort of connections the airfield operation had.

How high up the totem pole it ran...

Slater took a deep breath, and asked how fast they could get to Christchurch on the South Island of New Zealand.

The thin man in uniform behind the desk looked at him like he'd asked to go to Mars.

35

S later said, 'I understand it's going to take some work. But that's where we need to go.'

The guy set them up with an initial flight to Dubai, then a four hour layover before a connecting flight to Sydney. From there, they could take a short flight across the ocean to Christchurch. Altogether, the journey would take nearly twenty-eight hours.

Slater said, 'That's fine.'

King also didn't look fazed in the slightest.

Something about getting shot, stabbed, and beaten half to death for a living made monotonous travel a non-issue.

And Slater knew they both felt the same.

They had the same mindset.

They were very nearly the same person.

They paid for first class, got their tickets, and shocked the worker a second time when they revealed an absence of luggage.

Their clothes were dotted with dirt and had the faint smell of stress from the sweat they'd exerted whilst beating half the airfield to a pulp, so they moved straight through the check-in process and bought two fresh new sets of cold weather gear from a luxury outlet in duty free.

Slater changed into chinos, a smart dress shirt and a cashmere sweater — altogether totalling nearly a thousand U.S. dollars — and left his old clothes in the change room for the next lucky soul to stumble across.

They were good as new — they just needed a wash.

He passed through each checkpoint without issue, and breathed a sigh of relief when he met up with King on the other side of customs.

But he needn't have worried.

As soon as he'd been excommunicated from the secret world for the second time, Slater had got to work behind-the-scenes, making use of the time it had taken to heal up his injuries. He'd put all his resources to work, and come away with nearly a dozen ready-to-use passports, as well as an additional layer of secrecy over the top of his Swiss bank accounts. This was the new world, where geography no longer mattered and the best experts on the planet were available via a phone call.

He was a ghost.

And King didn't need to be.

So they made their way to the boarding lounge and sat in meditative silence as they waited for their plane to arrive at the gate.

Slater could feel the after-effects of the punches and knees and kicks he'd thrown over the course of the day. It was only mid-afternoon, and he'd barely taken a single strike in return, but sometimes throwing a punch hurt just as much as receiving one.

Not in the moment, per se, but in the uncomfortable hours afterwards when your bones and muscles ached from the exertion.

He maintained a respectable posture, but everything hurt.

A first-class seat would give him ample opportunity to recover.

He could tell King was feeling the same way.

When the boarding announcement floated over the speakers, they peeled themselves slowly off their chairs, both of them masking limps. King had his arms hanging straight down by his sides, and he kept them that way as they sauntered to the front of the queue.

They nodded and smiled to the staff, who checked their tickets and ushered them down the long dreary tunnel to the plane.

As they strode out in front of the rest of the passengers, Slater said, 'Banged up?'

King just grimaced.

'Ring rust,' Slater said. 'Happens to us all.'

King glanced across. 'You don't look one hundred percent yourself.'

'I'm not. You're never in good shape after throwing strikes with that sort of force. But the repetition gets you used to it.'

King nodded. 'Damn right. It doesn't get easier. You just get stronger.'

'You'll be back to your old conditioning before long.'

King managed a half-smile.

Slater said, 'What?'

'You don't need to pump me up with reassurances,' King said. 'I did this solo for more than a decade. I can take care of myself.'

'Sometimes I forget who I'm dealing with.'

They made their way aboard and stretched out in first-class seats across the aisle from each other.

Slater put himself in a familiar deep meditative trance, and he could feel King's eyes on him, curious yet silent.

Eventually, after the rest of the passengers had settled into their seats and the plane was in the air, Slater cracked an eyelid open.

King still watched.

Slater said, 'What?'

'Just seeing when you'd snap out of it.'

'I need to eat,' Slater said. 'That's why I stopped. But I'll be doing this for the rest of the flight.'

'How long have you been meditating for?'

'Years. You can't deal with the chaos of our lives without balancing it with silence.'

'Interesting.'

'Give it a try.'

'How do you do it?'

'Close your eyes and focus on the breath. Over and over and over again. Inhale, then exhale. When you feel your mind drifting, bring it back to the breath.'

'That's it?'

'It's not as simple as it sounds.'

'I don't know how easily I'll be able to distract my mind. It hasn't shut up in two months.'

'Then you need to meditate more than I do. Work at it with the same intensity you work at anything else. Soon you'll start reaping the benefits.'

'Is that all you do?'

Slater paused, then shrugged. Most of his mindset he'd forged on his own, without vocalising it. But he had to recognise that he had a comrade with him, and it wasn't guaranteed to be that way forever. In this game, either of them could die at a moment's notice.

He figured he might as well share everything with King.

There wasn't anyone on the planet he trusted more.

He said, 'I've been playing around with visualising myself healing. It seems to have an effect.'

Instead of ridiculing him, King sat up straighter. 'Like a placebo?'

Slater shrugged. 'That's how I first heard about it. Because what the hell *is* a placebo, really? What can our brains do? I know what mine can do, because I went from a homeless teenager with no family to an elite operative in an exclusive black ops division of the government. And I had to change my mental pathways to do that, because hard work wasn't something I knew about in my youth. I was an aimless kid who made something of himself, so I'm just carrying that concept of transformation as far as I can, I guess.'

'I get it,' King said. 'Sometimes I feel like ninety-nine percent of the shit in my life is mental.'

'And you learned that the hard way, just like I did. Through going into hell. Through operations in the field. We're capable of a lot more than we thought, because if we weren't we would have died on our very first assignment.'

King said, 'How do you visualise it?'

'I picture myself healing, from head to toe, over and over again. If there's anything this motherfucker of a life has taught me, it's the power of repetition. I just do it relentlessly — ten, twenty, thirty times. I concentrate on every spot I can feel pain ... and I mean really, really concentrate on it. You can only build up that sort of mental focus by mastering meditation first. I find the silence, and then I fill my head with the pain I'm feeling, and I visualise it dissipating. By the time I get off this flight I'll feel like a new man.'

'Interesting,' King said again.

The flight attendant arrived to tend to their needs, and

both of them ordered one of everything on the menu. She hesitated, unsure if they were joking, and opened her mouth with reservation on her face — no doubt to list the cost of the extra meals.

Slater handed a credit card over before she could even start her sentence.

She took it and returned fifteen minutes later with a metal trolley, stacked with steaming plates of their own food.

Slater wolfed down quality pasta and chicken tagine and beef and kingfish and a few generous side servings of salad, then settled into a reclined position to resume his meditation. Beside him, he sensed King doing the same.

And with his eyes closed, he smiled.

He relished the open-minded individuals — the men and women who were willing to try anything for that edge in self-improvement. By no means did he consider himself a guru, but he couldn't deny his track record, and although the spouts of alcohol and drug addiction along the way showed up as black marks on an otherwise pristine career, for the most part he'd continuously fashioned himself into a better individual with each passing year.

Because that was the essence of his life. To get better at *everything,* so he could help anyone.

He'd been following it since he first began his ascent through the military structure, and he still maintained those principles to this day.

It took someone like Jason King to show up to allow him to vocalise them.

To bring them forth from his subconscious.

He focused on his sore muscles and joints and bones and dissected the pain, piece by piece, step by step. Thankfully this had been his life for as long as he could remember.

He wasn't used to existence with the absence of pain. He'd taught himself to savour it, for better or worse.

Rocketing toward New Zealand with four hundred million dollars to his name, and an endless list of innocent victims he'd pulled out of their own personal version of hell, Will Slater figured it had all ended up for the better.

36

The layover at Dubai International Airport passed in a blur, then Sydney followed swiftly afterward.

When they touched down in Christchurch, it certainly hadn't felt like twenty-eight hours had passed. Slater arose from a groggy stupor — he'd napped intermittently over the journey, but most of it had been spent deep in his own mind. He knew that was the fastest and most efficient way to get anything done. Go deep into your own head, figure out what's wrong, and then chip away at it. When the wheels touched down on New Zealand tarmac, Slater's eyes came open and he breathed in deep.

King stirred too.

They'd barely spoken since leaving Budapest. Both understood the value of utilising downtime, and neither were the type to waste it on pointless conversation. When they spoke, they kept it short and sharp, and then they went back to dissecting the pain in their own bodies and figuring out ways around it.

Now, Slater glanced across the aisle and gave a thumbs-up gesture.

His eyes asked a question.

King answered with a thumbs-up of his own.

And Slater looked into his eyes and saw something new there.

Right then and there, he realised a new Jason King had awoken on the flight over.

Whatever King had done over the course of a full day in a deep meditative trance had fundamentally altered him. Slater didn't know if the effects would be permanent or not, but he could see them now. There was none of the rage or the unrest, or the discontent he'd seen in Budapest.

There he'd met a King with his life in turmoil, his emotions conflicted and his mental health a mess.

And then Slater realised what had happened.

He said, 'You never half-ass anything, do you?'

King said, 'What do you mean?'

The man's eyes sparkled with intense energy.

Slater said, 'Whatever the hell you did, you look like the Terminator now.'

King said, 'I'm ready.'

'Ready for what?'

'I broke myself down over the last twenty-four hours. I compartmentalised what I needed to, and I worked through the rest of it. I used exactly what you told me. But I didn't just use it for physical pain. I sorted myself out. I went deep inside my own head and I organised the clutter. That's the best way I can describe it. I can't tell you how I feel now. It's...'

'Astonishing?'

King stared at him with vigour swirling behind his eyes. 'I know one thing, at least.'

'And what's that?'

'Whoever the hell is on that farm near Tapanui is in for a world of hurt.'

'They already were.'

King rolled his wrists, cracked his neck, and worked his jaw open and closed. Then he said, 'I feel brand new.'

'Likewise.'

'How did you teach yourself to do that?'

'I had demons you didn't,' Slater said. 'When I was in Black Force. You could bear all the burdens and take them in stride, and I couldn't. I turned to drugs. I turned to drinking. I fucked myself up just as hard as I was training. I went way off the rails in both directions. Pushing myself into sickening workouts, and then drinking my problems away. I was a mess when I got out. I had to sort myself out, or I wouldn't have made it. I had to learn to quiet my mind, and when I did that I discovered there was a whole lot of other shit resting in there that I hadn't tackled yet. And when I tackled it, I found out what I could do with my own mind. And I knew you'd experience the same thing. Because you're just as hard-charging as I am.'

King said, 'This is incredible.'

'Let's make it count. Let's find who killed Klara, and get it done, and then we can close that chapter.'

'There's no way they'll be expecting us, right?' Then King paused, before finishing with, 'Although, does it make a difference?'

'You're confident, and that's a good thing. But it would work wonders if they didn't know we were coming.'

'I can't see how they would.'

'Who do you think it is? What enemies have you made?'

King just stared at him. Then he raised an eyebrow, as if to say, *Really?*

Slater understood.

As in, *What enemies haven't I made?*

Slater said, 'Any of them stand out in particular?'

King shivered, then said, 'You think it might have anything to do with Russia?'

Slater shook his head. 'We closed that chapter. Besides, they wouldn't go for your girlfriend. They'd go for you.'

King didn't say anything for a long moment.

Then the plane finished taxiing along the runway, and the seatbelt light flickered off. They held that thought as they sliced their way to the front of the queue — thanks to the added benefit of not having to fumble with their carry-on luggage — and powered off the plane as soon as the doors opened. Separated from the rest of the passengers once more, they resumed.

King visibly fought off another shiver and said, 'You made it sound like they were toying with me.'

Slater shrugged and said, 'I'm trying to look at it without any bias. If they were going for you, they wouldn't have made themselves known. They were able to get to Klara without either of you realising, which means they were good enough to conduct adequate surveillance. So they would have kept doing that if their plan was to kill you. I don't think they were after you specifically.'

'But ... what the hell would they want with Klara? She's never done anything to anyone. She was with us in Dubai, all that time ago, but she was a bystander. No-one could have tracked her to Koh Tao. I was the weak link. It's like they were using me to get to her. But I can't, for the life of me, figure out why. I think that's what makes me so angry. All of this is such a mystery...'

'Calm,' Slater instructed. 'Don't lose what you spent the whole flight working toward. Don't get angry again. There's nothing to gain from it.'

King clenched a fist, and released it, and then he was calm.

Slater shook his head in disbelief.

It seemed King was heading fast toward mastering his emotions, just as he'd mastered nearly everything else in his life.

King said, 'It's all a mystery, but you can be damn sure I'm getting answers before it's over.'

Slater said, 'We'll find them. Don't worry.'

They made their way through customs without any fanfare, and headed straight for the nearest car rental service. King filled in the details under his name, just in case there was a chink in the armour of Slater's false identity, and after everything was verified and a hefty deposit was laid down they got their hands on a plain four-door Toyota sedan.

They climbed in, slammed the doors, started the engine, and peeled out of the lot.

Out of Christchurch International Airport.

Out of comfort.

Onto the open road.

Toward chaos.

37

The South Island of New Zealand was stunning.

There was no other way to put it.

Jason King and Will Slater, two of the baddest men on the planet, stared wide-eyed and slack-jawed out the windscreen as the landscape revealed itself in all its glory. They were out of Christchurch in less than an hour, and when they cleared the perimeter of the city the farms sprawled out on either side, flat and green and stretching for miles in every direction.

But past that they saw stunning snow-capped mountain ranges draped in mist, like something out of a fantasy film. The morning dew hung in the air, and the atmosphere crackled with a sense of wonderment Slater had never experienced.

He likened it to driving through a prehistoric landscape — all the natural wonders preserved by time, brimming with the potential of adventure.

It certainly added to the unease that, deep in this ominous wilderness, rested someone who had actively targeted Jason King.

Someone who had found him on Koh Tao, and decided to *toy* with him, instead of attempting to take him out.

That sent a shiver down Slater's spine more than the vastness of the landscape did.

King upped the pace, plowing toward their destination. Slater had entered the co-ordinates into his phone and zeroed in on the location. Christchurch to Tapanui was a six hour drive, and as soon as they'd cleared the congestion and traffic surrounding the airport they were free to coast up to a considerate speed.

King drove, pushing the Toyota to its limits in his haste to lay hands on whoever had harmed Klara, but Slater urged him to slow down.

'We need to think about this tactically,' he said. 'What's your plan? Stroll right up to the front door with empty hands and hope for the best?'

'They don't know we're coming,' King said. 'Whoever they are. That's all the tactical advantage I need.'

'Your head's clear, but you're still not thinking straight.'

King took a hand off the wheel and raised it, palm up, as if saying, *What the hell do you expect?*

Slater said, 'What?'

King said, 'This is New Zealand. You see anywhere we can get guns around here?'

'I'm not saying we need to load up with an arsenal,' Slater said. 'It'd be useful, but it's not exactly practical in these parts. There's probably only a handful of guns on this entire island.'

'We should have bought space on a cargo plane,' King muttered. 'Then we could have brought our own.'

'That's the price we paid for speed,' Slater said. 'There would have been valuable time spent negotiating, and finding a place, and even then you know the risks that come with that side of the world. There's nothing to stop us getting locked in a container, and shipped off to slavery.'

'I think we could fight our way out of that.'

'You can't fight your way out of a metal box. No matter how talented you are.'

'Okay. So we sacrificed that for speed. Which is why I'm putting the pedal to the floor now. That's all we've got, Slater. We can sneak up on them before they have the chance to get the hell out of here, which is becoming increasingly likely with each passing second. Did you see the level of encryption they had on that phone? Maybe we triggered a failsafe by breaking into it. That's a fairly simple mechanism, and there's every chance it went undetected by that tech team. Hell, we were holding them hostage. Maybe they knew they'd tripped something, but they weren't willing to piss us off by telling us. Maybe we're walking into a trap.'

'Then we should turn around.'

'No — we should approach faster. The less time they have to prepare, the better. And there's no way in hell I'm turning away from this.'

They continued down State Highway 1, en route to Dunedin. That would take them all the way to a small town called Milton, whereupon they would turn right and head toward the colossal mountain range.

Tapanui and the surrounding farmlands rested in the lee of the breathtaking mountains spearing toward the sky. Slater turned his attention to the scenery, awed by the mountains hovering in the distance.

The fog intensified as they headed further south, and eventually Slater dwelled so deep in his own head that new revelations began to dawn on him.

'King,' he said under his breath. 'Why am I here?'

King said, 'Because I need your help.'

'Then you should listen to my advice. We need to slow down. We're in unfamiliar terrain that looks like something out of Jurassic Park. We're heading to an unspecified area near Tapanui. Could be a farm, or it could be a goddamn fortress for all we know. We've got nothing. Speed isn't always the answer. We survived through Black Force utilising its advantage, but we're older now, and I'd like to think we're wiser.'

King said, 'Listen...'

Slater slammed his hand against the centre console. 'No — you listen. You tracked me down in Budapest, and you tailed me to make sure I got to that bar, and you confronted me. That's a lot of effort to put into finding someone just to ignore their advice. You wanted my help, but I'm not just a body to use and discard.'

'That's not what you are.'

'We need to—'

'Wait.'

'What?'

'What you just said before.'

'Which part?'

'I never tailed you.'

'What?'

'You said I tailed you to make sure you got to that bar. I never did shit. I sat in that ruin bar drinking, wondering when to approach you, and then you walked straight past. And then you saw me.'

Slater paused.

And thought hard.

And came to a sinister conclusion.

He said, 'Then who the hell was following me? Who was that sentry?'

King said nothing.

The silence drew out, and they both stared out the windows, watching the impossible landscape flash by. Both deep in thought. Both thinking through endless possibilities.

Finally, King said, 'What exactly did you see?'

'Nothing. Just someone tailing me. I was sure it was you.'

'So someone had eyes on you.'

'On us, potentially.'

King didn't respond. Then he said, 'I can't get my mind off what you said. *Toying.*'

Slater said, 'What if they wanted us to crack that phone?'

'They couldn't have. You said it yourself. It was next to impossible to find someone who could do it. It took all our resources.'

'We've been doing next to impossible things for our entire careers,' Slater said.

A pit of anxiety started to form in his stomach.

His blood ran cold, and beads of sweat broke out across his forehead.

Slater said, 'What if they knew they had to make it next to impossible? Because that's the only way we'd believe it. That would get us here. On this goddamn desolate island. Right where they wanted us.'

King said, 'It's unlikely.'

Slater said, 'But ... what if?'

Then they passed a crossroads, where the State Highway intersected with a rural gravel trail, and a jet black vehicle roared out of the mist and crumpled their flimsy sedan like it weighed nothing, spinning them across the asphalt with the shriek of metal and the explosion of airbags in their ears.

38

S later held on for dear life.

The impact lashed him against his seatbelt and the airbag burst forth from the dashboard, pummelling him. Out of the corner of his eye, through blurred vision, he saw King hit with his own airbag.

It billowed into the man's face, erupting from the steering wheel.

The mountains and the farmland and the mist outside turned to an impossible blur, and the chassis all around them groaned and protested the collision.

Then they were off the road, bouncing and jolting over uneven terrain. A geyser of displaced mud poured in through the open driver's window, showering them in debris, and Slater found himself temporarily blinded as he fought the airbag away. He reached down and held onto the seat, as if that would help, as the G-forces worked their way over him.

His muscles screamed in protest.

His eyeballs felt like they were about to bulge out of their sockets.

Then they came to a standstill. It was abrupt, and jolting, and the Toyota *slammed* into place at the bottom of the
shallow ditch.

They'd come to rest only a dozen or so feet from the side
of the highway, but it felt like they'd travelled a mile during
the uncontrollable skid.

Slater *slammed* back against his seat at the same time,
and as he caught his breath he reached down and stabbed
the seatbelt release with a pointed finger. It came free and
he punched the rapidly deflating airbag away, still in the
process of getting his bearings.

When he looked over at the driver's seat, he found
it empty.

King was already out of the car.

Turned out that King had reacted with impossible
speed, untethering himself from the seatbelt and the closed
driver's door in the vital seconds when the car had been
slowing down.

Now he was out of the wrecked vehicle and halfway up
the side of the muddy ditch, making a beeline for the road.

Slater gawked when he realised how slow he'd been in
comparison.

He shook himself free from the seat and thrust his own
door open. It jammed in the mud, but there was enough
room for him to spill out.

He fell into the churned earth and scrambled to his feet,
rounding the hood a moment later.

By that point, King had made it to the top of the ditch.

And he'd timed it to perfection.

The truck that had rammed them was only a few feet
from the lip of the ditch, trundling to a halt at an almost
leisurely pace after brutalising the smaller sedan.

It had rumbled across the highway and come to rest

above the Toyota's muddy grave, the aftershock of the impact still reverberating through its steel chassis. It was a big brute of an armoured vehicle with a giant bull bar and dark tinted windows.

But the line of sight was hindered by the slope of the ditch. To see the aftermath of ramming the Toyota, the occupants would have to climb out.

The hood of the truck was too big to allow a view of the ditch from within, unless they pulled up horizontally, which they hadn't.

So the driver and passenger were halfway out of the vehicle. Big bulky men with hard faces, carrying fearsome weaponry. Slater spotted the glint of automatic rifles and knew he didn't stand a chance where he stood.

But King was *right there.*

And then King was on them, barrelling into view as he sprinted out from the cover of the ditch. He rose up out of the chilly gloom and made a mad dash for the passenger door.

It was only a few feet away, and he was there before the passenger could react.

The big man with the rifle only caught a glimpse of *something* right nearby before King thundered a boot into the door, knocking it back into the guy with incredible force, and as fate would have it the top of the door caught the guy in the throat and crushed him momentarily against the chassis, startling him enough to freeze up.

Only for a second.

That was how it always happened.

And that was all King ever needed.

Slater watched King heave the door aside and crush an elbow into the same point of the guy's throat, and as always Slater marvelled at both the speed and the accuracy. The guy's neck was already numb and swelling from the metal door catching him in the soft tissue, and now the elbow put him down for the count. He folded at the waist and splayed back into the passenger seat he'd just burst up out of.

And then the real magic happened.

King had control of the guy's rifle — a shiny new M4 carbine — as soon as the guy went down, and he had effective use of it a second after that. He had a finger in the trigger guard and his frame was already compensating to aim *through* the vehicle.

He shot the passenger twice in the chest as the guy crumpled into the seat, then aimed past him to the driver, who was still trying to work out what the hell was going on.

Because Slater had seen every move play out almost in slow motion, but in reality it had been *bang-crunch-blam-blam.*

The kick to the door, the elbow to the throat, the seizing of the weapon, and the two shots through the passenger's chest.

The driver was still reeling, because he'd spotted Slater in front of the Toyota, so he couldn't work out which threat to deal with — him or the immediate problem around the passenger side — and he only had milliseconds to make the choice.

He didn't make the right one.

He aimed at Slater, figuring he'd take out the stationary target first.

Slater closed his eyes.

The situation was out of his control.

There was a gunshot.

39

W hen Slater opened his eyes again, the driver was lying beside his vehicle with half his face missing.

King swept the carbine ruthlessly over the rear seats, searching for any backup, but there was none.

Just the two men.

King backed out of the car, carbine held at the ready, breath steaming in the cold air.

Slater clambered up the embankment and joined King on the asphalt.

He looked at the empty armoured vehicle and said, 'Guess we've got a new ride.'

'There's more than that on the way,' King said. 'Look.'

Slater followed his gaze, spotting the faint glow of headlights down the overcast misty highway.

Coming from the north.

Blazing toward them.

An arsenal of vehicles, just as big and fearsome as the one they stood beside, probably packed with armed combatants juiced up on Dexedrine and ready for war.

Right on their heels.

Slater said, 'Shit.'

'How many? Can you see?'

'Looks like five. Six. Maybe seven … Christ.'

King looked down at his own carbine, then watched Slater collect the second M4 off the dead driver.

They both studied their own weapons, followed by the open terrain around them, stretching on for miles endlessly, desolate and sweeping all the way up to the mountains in the very distance.

Like something out of Jurassic Park.

Just as Slater had described.

Standing like twin beacons on the empty highway, Slater said, 'We make damn good targets out here.'

'We can get behind the truck,' King said. 'Use it as cover.'

'They'll just drive around us. There's seven goddamn vehicles. They can surround us, or just drive into the fields if they find that too dangerous.'

'You sure there's that many?'

King squinted, trying to ascertain for himself.

His eyesight evidently wasn't as good as Slater's.

Then he said, 'Shit, you're right.'

Slater said, 'Make the call.'

'We run.'

'Good call, soldier.'

They piled into the armoured vehicle. Slater hauled the dead passenger out onto the asphalt and clambered in — King skirted around the enormous bull bar and slotted into the driver's seat.

Slater took one look at the interior and figured the truck was a Mercedes G-wagon with aftermarket Brabus modifications to tune its performance. King confirmed it when he stepped on the accelerator and the truck responded with a deep, thrumming, throaty *roar.*

The truck had been outfitted with armour plating on top of the original Brabus modifications. It must have cost somewhere in the vicinity of three hundred thousand dollars.

And there were seven more on the way.

Whoever the hell they were dealing with had a metric shit-ton of money.

Slater vocalised this.

King said, 'I think we already knew that.'

He twisted the sleek black wheel and pulled away from the two corpses they'd left on the side of the road. Slater wondered how long it would take for police to get involved, and whether they'd even survive until then.

His heart pounded in his ears as he checked the passenger side mirror.

The fleet of seven trucks roared forward, only a few hundred feet behind them.

A muzzle flash flared from one of the windows — someone leaning out with a carbine rifle — and a moment later the round whizzed by the open passenger window, sending displaced air washing over Slater's face.

He recoiled from the window and gripped his own carbine with sweaty palms.

'They're good shots,' he said. Then he gulped back anxiety. 'You can't push this thing faster?'

'Pedal's on the floor,' King snarled. 'It's a big beast. Takes a while to accelerate.'

Then it picked up steam, and Slater held onto the windowsill with white knuckles as the 4.0L Biturbo V8 used all of its seven hundred horsepower and the big Brabus surged forward with ferocity.

King kept the pedal on the floor and suddenly they were

at top speed, barreling down the desolate State Highway, heading further and further south.

But the fleet behind them was gaining.

And gaining fast.

More shots flew past, and one impacted the rear of the wagon. King flinched involuntarily, ducking low, and Slater followed suit. But the tinted windows were bulletproof, and soon enough they sat back up and corrected their course.

Then the worst case scenario unfolded at horrific speed.

They crested a rise in the highway, and when they plunged into the decline, the scene before them revealed itself.

There were two civilian vehicles in sight, both heading in the opposite direction — toward Christchurch — but one of them was in the process of overtaking. It was a small blue hatchback — a Volkswagen GTI — and its driver had made to dart past a rusting old pick-up truck with alarming speed.

It was side-by-side with the truck, opting to overtake it at that *exact* second, and King and Slater were rocketing toward it in their Brabus.

The steel bull bar attached to the front of the truck would obliterate the Volkswagen.

The GTI driver saw the oncoming Brabus at the last second, and in his panic he accelerated instead of braking, trying to complete the overtake manoeuvre before impact.

King braked.

He had to.

If he didn't, he would pulverise a civilian.

He hadn't factored that into his day.

Slater said, 'No,' but it came out muted, and he took it back almost immediately.

It was the lesser of two terrible options, and the Volkswagen made it into the correct lane with mere inches to spare.

The two vehicles blew past each other, so close they could almost feel the wash of wind against each other's chassis'.

But then the Brabus slowed after braking, and the fleet of seven oncoming trucks crested the rise only a few seconds later.

Slater twisted in his seat to survey the damage, and winced as one of the bull bars on the rightmost truck simply crushed the Volkswagen to a pulp, pulverising the driver and spinning the hatchback like a child's plaything off the highway. It landed on its roof in the ditch by the roadside.

Inevitably fatal.

Then the pick-up truck it had been attempting to over-take followed suit, driven by an old farmer with slow reflexes and not a shred of time to get out of the way.

The Brabus caught it with a glancing blow, unwilling to slow down or veer off into the ditch, and the pick-up truck shredded to pieces as its rusty old parts crumbled and blew apart from the impact.

It spun away too, its driver flung from the vehicle.

Two casualties, just like that.

Slater clenched his teeth and said, 'Fuck.'

It was all he could think to say.

The fleet approached.

'Faster,' Slater muttered.

'Trying,' King snarled back.

Then the first of the pursuing vehicles caught up to them and all hell broke loose.

40

T he oncoming fleet had expertise in the realm of aggressive takedowns.

The first vehicle to catch up to them was an identical black Brabus with tinted windows and a vicious bull bar attached to the front, but the guy behind the wheel was much more adept at tackling the weight of the truck than King was.

So he came in at an angle, expertly weaving toward them, and at the last second he twisted the wheel tight and the enemy vehicle steamed toward them from the side.

'King,' Slater yelled.

Too late.

King braked at the last second, attempting to outmanoeuvre the oncoming truck, but it proved futile. He only served to worsen the blow. Slater didn't blame him — this was a brutal and barbaric realm to learn how to handle such a massive vehicle, and Slater knew he wouldn't have fared any better.

But understanding why it had happened didn't change the consequences.

The enemy vehicle caught them in the driver's side door, coming in from the right, crushing against the armour plating. Steel met steel and sparks flew, and King recoiled away from the window.

He had the bulletproof glass pane raised, so when three rounds impacted the glass right near his head and splintered into a trio of spider-webs, he came away with his head intact.

Slater gripped his carbine and vaulted out of his seat, leaping through the narrow gap above the centre console into the rear seats. He sprawled out across the leather, almost tumbling into the footwell from the inertia as the Brabus screeched and careened across the highway.

He found the electronic button that controlled the right-hand window and pushed it halfway down. He shoved the M4's barrel through the narrow crack and let off a volley at the enemy vehicle, the big beast still grinding and pressing into their side.

The passenger in that vehicle was leaning out the window, almost half his body extended into empty space, a carbine of his own in his hand.

Slater saw the determination in his dark eyes, and spotted the sharp jawline and hair shaved to the scalp.

Ex-military.

Guns for hire.

Slater worked his aim to the left, and squeezed the trigger again from his makeshift bunker, and caught the passenger in the forehead.

He didn't actually see the bullet strike home — there was too much happening.

Too many variables.

King fought for control of the truck, and the metal on the right side of the chassis groaned, and the enemy vehicle continued its attempts to force them off the road. But amidst all that the passenger's head snapped back like someone had tugged it on an invisible wire, and a spout of crimson blew out the back of his skull, and then his body overextended and tumbled out the open window. It disappeared under the truck, squashed like a rag doll, and wound up somewhere on the other side to be run over again by the fleet of charging vehicles.

Then the rear window on the enemy vehicle buzzed down and a volley of shots came right at Slater. He recoiled away from the window frame, but a couple of rounds made their way through.

One buzzed over his head, so close he could feel his own death *right there,* and the other struck his carbine rifle, still halfway out the window.

From there, it ricocheted into the roof, and then down past Slater's shoulder.

He didn't actually conceptualise any of this — he just felt lead sizzling through the air all around him, and he collapsed into as small a target area as he could manage.

'Shit!' he roared.

'You hit?' King roared back.

'No, no, I'm good. How are we doing?'

King didn't respond — he just swore at the top of his lungs.

Slater scrambled to get a view through the windshield, staring between the two front seats.

He swore too.

King was skirting a precipitous line between the edge of the highway and another sizeable ditch resting at the bottom of a muddy embankment. The Brabus' left hand wheels were spinning against mud, and the right hand wheels were gripping the asphalt, naturally turning them away from the side of the ditch.

But King was fighting against that, because it left them open to the vehicle alongside them. If they got rammed again, they'd be going straight into the ditch.

King was threading the needle.

Slater felt his brain going into overdrive. They were doing nearly ninety miles an hour, the ground all around them flashing by at impossible speed. One slight overcorrection to either side could send them spinning end over end into the ditch. Without seatbelts on, they'd be smashed and crushed and squashed to a pulp.

Slater said, 'Ram them.'

'What?!'

'Ram them. Fuck it. Just do it. I can get to them. We don't have any other options.'

'What the hell are you talking about?'

'King,' Slater yelled. 'Just *do it.*'

King clenched the wheel and swore under his breath.

Then he did it.

He jerked the wheel to the right and the Brabus went back in the direction of the enemy vehicle, and the driver of that vehicle seemed to sense the opportunity to capitalise, and Slater could almost see him snarling with glee.

The driver of the other Brabus came back at them with reckless abandon, so they'd collide at diagonal angles, side to side, and one of them would be sent spinning off toward destruction, given the velocity they were both travelling at.

And King knew he'd lose.

He wasn't experienced enough with lining up the trajectory. The other driver came in at a better angle, and he would crunch into King's hood and send the Brabus plummeting off the road.

But Slater, crouched in the back, was the wild card.

King came in reckless too, and Slater sized up the gap and the primal part of his brain made the calculation and said, *Yes.*

So he went, without even thinking of the risk.

He dashed forward a moment before impact and threw the rear driver's door open and hurled himself out onto the step running along the exterior of the Brabus.

The wind lashed him *hard,* turning his hands and face numb, and the mountains in the background loomed into the heavens.

Through the open passenger's window of the other truck — still stained with blood from the headshot Slater had landed — he saw the driver go wide-eyed.

The driver realised what he was about to do.

And the man had to keep both hands on his own wheel, because he was in the process of ramming King.

The two hoods collided, and King's Brabus bounced away from the impact zone like it had been slapped by a giant. It zigzagged across the highway, sliding out with its massive bull bar hanging in a state of disrepair. It plummeted over the embankment and turned end over end before crumpling into a twisted mass of metal, resting on its roof with its fat tyres spinning, clogged with mud.

But Slater wasn't there.

He'd leapt across the narrow gap, threading a needle of his own, and piled in through the open passenger window. There were two men in the rear seats of the enemy vehicle — and the driver, of course — but neither of them could reach over and wind up the window pane in time. Slater went in head-first, tantalisingly aware of the ground speeding past him underneath. If he missed and tumbled out, he'd skin himself alive on the asphalt.

But he didn't.

He landed on his neck on the soft leather, and it broke his fall. It still hurt like hell, but adrenaline quashed the pain, and with no serious nerve damage he was free to control himself as his legs followed suit, toppling in over his neck and lashing the driver in the face.

The guy swerved, irritated yet unhurt, but it didn't matter.

Slater was inside.

41

H e lurched around, shoving his feet into the passenger footwell so he could lever himself upright.

The driver swung a closed fist sideways, taking one hand off the wheel to try to smash the side of his hand into Slater's unprotected face.

Slater jerked backwards, and it hit him in the chest. It cracked against his sternum and he wheezed for breath.

Holy shit, he thought.

The guy had fists like bricks.

The driver pulled back and tried another sideways hammer fist, but this time Slater was ready for it. He jerked *away* from the seat, bouncing off the dashboard, hoping he didn't set the airbag off.

The driver stamped on the brakes, suddenly aware that he had his precious cargo in the vehicle and there was no need to speed.

At the same time, one of the guys in the rear seats made a lunge for Slater in the cramped interior, trying to dive over the centre console and tie him up.

Unfortunate timing, Slater thought as the guy sailed head-first into the dashboard, encouraged by the momentum of the Brabus decelerating *hard.*

Slater helped him along with a vicious close-range elbow to his temple, and the unconscious body collapsed across the centre console. It restricted the driver from throwing another fist, and Slater lunged across and head butted the guy in the side of the skull.

The driver recoiled against his own door, rattled by the impact, close to unconsciousness.

Slater helped him along, too.

He threw a fist with maximum intensity, literally leading with it across the cabin. If he missed, he'd break all his fingers on the door behind the driver.

But he didn't miss.

He struck the guy in the side of the head, right where his own forehead had slammed home.

The man collapsed against the driver's door, and Slater reached over and tugged the handle, and the guy spilled out onto the road at sixty miles an hour.

Slater didn't want to see the grisly aftermath.

He grabbed the unconscious guy who'd lunged from the rear seats and threw him out of the car after his comrade.

Then, in one fluid sequence of movements, he leapt up onto the centre console with one leg in a crouch and jack-knifed the other close to his body, then he aimed into the back seats and let loose with a stabbing front kick, and he hit the last guy square in the jaw with the sole of his boot. The guy was slack-jawed as it was, frozen in place as he tried to comprehend the rapidly unfolding crisis, and the kick broke his jaw and sent him crumpling into the footwell in a literal world of pain.

Slater slotted into the empty driver's seat, slammed the door closed and grabbed the wheel.

Just in time.

The Brabus was heading fast for the opposite side of the highway, veering into the oncoming lane. Thankfully there was no civilian traffic this far south of Christchurch, so he hadn't pulverised any vehicles coming the other way.

He swerved back into his own lane, and pushed the accelerator all the way down, and when the guy in the back with the broken jaw sat up with his hands against his face, Slater whipped around and elbowed him hard in the nose, breaking that bone too in quick succession.

The guy collapsed against the seats, overwhelmed by the pain and receding into unconsciousness.

Slater glanced to his left, searching for King's vehicle alongside him.

It wasn't there.

His stomach fell.

He gripped the wheel and scanned the side and rear mirrors, and he saw the bulky shape of a black vehicle nearly half a mile back, resting on its roof in the shallow roadside ditch.

He swore.

He slowed down.

He wasn't leaving without King.

No matter what.

The brakes kicked in and the Brabus began to slow, and the asphalt flashing past underneath lost its motion blur as Slater receded to a more traditional speed. He could survey the landscape now, but nothing had changed. They were still deep in the endless plains of farmland, and an approaching road sign told him he was bearing down on the town of Orari. Soon the state highway would branch to the left and sweep along the coastline, no doubt paving the way for more stunning views. To the right, he spotted the same sinister mountain range — capped with snow, draped in cloud, faded by the mist in the air.

It was a cold, wet, miserable day on the South Island, and Slater's sinking stomach reflected the weather.

When the Brabus reached an appropriate speed, Slater turned around in the driver's seat.

'You're probably in too much pain to comprehend this, but if you want to live you need to get out of the car right now. I won't tell you again.'

Sporting a broken jaw and a broken nose, the crippled mercenary nodded once.

Without considering the consequences for a moment, he opened the rear door and tumbled out of the cabin. Slater was still travelling at thirty miles an hour, and the guy didn't land correctly. Slater saw him tumble head over heels in the side mirror. But clearly the terror he held toward Will Slater overpowered any of his natural survival instincts, and he'd willingly leapt free at the first command.

Slater reached back and tugged the door closed, then sat in the empty Brabus and sighed.

There was another M4 carbine in the passenger footwell, loaded and ready for use. When Slater had shot the passenger the man had tumbled out of the open window clutching his own rifle, but this was clearly a spare.

He reached over, picked it up, and held it in one hand.

He checked his rear view mirror.

Four of the massive vehicles approached him. Two had peeled off to subdue King, and they were out of sight.

Actually, Slater thought he could make out their faint outlines, but it was pointless. He had four armoured wagons bearing down on his position, and if he took off now they would probably double back and make sure King was dealt with.

Even though King was likely already dead.

When King's Brabus had veered off the road, it hadn't looked survivable.

But without him, Slater was here pointlessly.

Alone on a misty island, with no friends or family left in the world.

And that wasn't somewhere he wanted to exist.

He had to give King some sort of chance if he was alive, and that involved doubling back. At least he could separate the two groups long enough for King to have hope.

What hope?

He just flipped his truck, and he hadn't been wearing a seatbelt.

It was futile, but Slater had nothing without King.

So he twisted the wheel and turned around on the highway, facing the oncoming fleet.

He readied the carbine in his right hand, and gripped the wheel with his left.

He took a deep breath.

The mountains and the mist and the chill bore down on him — crushing, oppressive, sapping the hope out of the air.

He had nothing.

Which meant he had nothing to lose.

He stamped on the accelerator.

42

King's eyes came open.

He was bleeding. From the forehead, from the shoulder, and from a deep cut along the top of his right wrist. Any deeper and it might have nicked an artery.

And he was upside down.

Suspended from a seatbelt he'd thrust into place at the last second.

He'd spotted the embankment coming up to greet him and wrenched it across his body and felt the *click* just as the front end of the Brabus rocketed off into nothingness, and then pitched and groaned and fell and smashed into the earth and spun the car over vertically, where it came crashing down in the ditch in an explosion of mud. Metal had screamed and he'd squeezed his eyes shut and the force of the seatbelt wrenching against his collar bone had sapped all his energy.

An obscene impact.

He thought he'd snapped his collarbone clean in two.

And that would be that, because even if he managed to

peel himself out of the wreck, he'd have no ability to use his right arm, and he couldn't survive surrounded by trained militants armed with automatic weapons without the use of his good hand.

But when his eyes came open and he got past the sight of all the blood and tested his limbs, he found himself almost entirely unhurt.

And he didn't chalk it up to chance.

He'd put his body through the ringer on Koh Tao. Retirement hadn't lasted long, but that hadn't meant he'd become civilised. He relished the animalistic part of his brain, and he'd vowed to never let it go. He'd taken all the energy he normally channelled into life-or-death black operations and put all of it into the gym. Into training and pushing himself with weights and obscene cardio workouts, and sparring in the Muay Thai gym every day, and generally hardening and callousing his mind and body until it ran like it was made of pliable steel.

Which allowed him to take a bump that might have shattered bones in a soft-bodied civilian.

The same way Muay Thai practitioners kicked trees over and over and over again until their shins hardened and became near indestructible.

He wasn't superhuman, but he was as close as you could get to a perfect physical specimen.

He didn't dwell on this — he just gave thanks for it. He reached up and unbuckled his seatbelt and dropped into a small pool of his own blood. He landed on shattered glass fragments and grimaced as he squirmed and writhed and worked his way out of the truck.

And then he pulled the M4 carbine out after him.

He stood up in a half-crouch, his ears ringing and his head pounding, but already the presence of all the blood had disappeared from his mind. It didn't matter. You could lose three or four pints before things got disastrous. Instead his senses were wired, having descended totally and completely into operational mode. Clutching the carbine in front of him, he vowed to make it through this coming fight by whatever means necessary. He'd been beaten and cut and bruised, but none of that mattered. None of the men chasing him had caused a significant injury.

The first Brabus appeared at the top of the embankment, but it didn't pause there. It seemed its occupants had been taught a valuable lesson by their late predecessors. They'd driven past the corpses of those who had hesitated at the side of the highway before King ambushed them.

Now this vehicle dipped onto the muddy embankment, its fat tyres chewing up the earth, and it made a beeline for the bottom of the ditch where King's vehicle lay on its roof.

King squatted down behind the crumpled Brabus.

He tensed up.

He breathed.

Calm.

Focus.

Reaction speed.

You know what you can do.

So do it.

On the other side of the wreck, the enemy vehicle pulled to a halt.

The engine growled throatily as the enemy Brabus idled.

Doors opened.

Now.

King came up into view and trained the carbine on the first man to get out of the car and shot him through the head. He put two bullets into the guy to make sure he was dead, and the blood and brain matter spraying across the door confirmed it. That man had come from the passenger seat, so when the driver materialised a half-second later he quickly realised his error and tried to duck back behind the safety of the bulletproof windows.

King shot him in the face before he could react.

The third guy tumbled out of the back in a desperate attempt to close the gap, probably figuring he had a better chance of succeeding if he bull rushed King's position rather than cowering and exchanging gunfire in a tactical shootout.

But that was the worst strategy imaginable against someone with King's reaction speed.

He zeroed in on his target and put a three-round burst into the guy's chest before the man made it three steps away from the car.

The enemy Brabus sat there, its engine still rumbling, its occupants slaughtered.

King breathed out, settled his racing heart rate, and watched for the other vehicle. He'd seen four of the trucks blazing down the highway after Slater when he'd climbed out of the cabin, so there could only be one left on his tail.

You can do this.

A soft breeze blew against his back. He threw a glance over his shoulder — both to assess the new landscape and search for potential ambushes — but he saw nothing except a grid of manicured fields, separated by thin wire fences, some packed with cattle and horses. And further beyond that, he saw the mouth of a forest — enormous coniferous trees standing at least a hundred feet high, visible from a mile away. The woods had been chopped back to make space for additional farmland.

King filed the terrain away for future use.

Then he turned back to scrutinise the top of the embankment, and he saw it.

Not a truck.

Five men, walking shoulder to shoulder. Four of them armed with carbines. One clutching some sort of electronic device. Slightly larger than a phone. A customised device. Purpose unknown.

King ducked below the line of sight as a hail of withering gunfire assaulted the overturned Brabus in front of him.

43

S later quickly realised his options were scarce.

The terrain was too flat. It was the same problem he and King had faced when they decided to run, but now the hopelessness had amplified without King's presence. He was alone, facing twenty times the level of fire-power he possessed on his own — and ordinarily he would have overcome the odds, but this time he had nothing to work with. He was surrounded by fields, and he thrived in claustrophobic conditions. He relished tight corners and dark spaces and shadows — it enhanced the need to react faster than the opposition, something he excelled mightily at.

There was no chance of that on the open highway, with farmland the only terrain in sight.

Actually...

He saw the faint outline of a forest far in the distance, back the way he'd come from, but he had no chance of reaching it. He'd have to find a way through the rapidly approaching blockade of vehicles. King stood a better chance of making it there, but Slater doubted King was still alive.

Then what the hell are you doing?

He quickened his pace, speeding toward the line of armoured trucks, wracked with doubt and guilt.

Why are you fighting for a man you know is dead?

Because it was Jason King, and if there was anyone who could find a way to survive the impossible, it was him...

And even if there was a one percent chance King was alive, Slater would go to war for him.

So he put more pressure on the accelerator. At this speed, they were due to collide in seconds. He didn't budge. He put his seatbelt on, lay the carbine across his lap, and tightened his grip on the wheel.

There was no strategy here.

There was just brazenness, and recklessness, and the capacity to put his heart in his throat and attempt the impossible.

Because he had one distinct advantage.

None of the approaching combatants were as crazy as he was.

None of them had walked the fine line between life and death as often as he had.

He could steel himself in the face of certain loss, but they couldn't.

Which meant he'd win a game of chicken every goddamn time, because he just didn't *care.*

And the two oncoming trucks in the middle recognised this at the same time.

If there was an impact, it would kill all of them.

Their drivers jerked the wheel simultaneously in opposite directions, grating up against the sides of the trucks along the perimeter, creating a narrow gap through the middle.

Slater gunned for it.

It wasn't wide enough.

The sides of his hood detonated against the two side mirrors of the vehicles on either side of him, smashing them off in twin showers of debris.

Then the side of his Brabus grated against the others at nearly eighty miles an hour. A split second later he was through and barrelling down an empty road.

The four trucks had passed him by.

He stamped on the brakes and waited a few seconds, then twisted the wheel to the left and screeched around in a tight arc and switched straight back to the accelerator.

He surged after the group.

He didn't know what exactly he would achieve.

He was still vastly outnumbered, and wielding only a single carbine with no spare magazines in sight. He couldn't hope to take down four carloads worth of combatants with a single clip.

But he could try.

Heading for King's position was futile without taking care of the larger group first.

He pushed the Brabus faster, and the engine screamed and roared in response.

He picked up the M4 carbine again — more for reassurance than anything else. He wasn't about to hang out the window at ninety miles an hour, but he figured if he gained some ground he could run one or two of the trucks off the road and pick his shots selectively.

He gripped the stock with a sweaty palm.

He felt a brilliant surge of hope, as if the situation might be salvageable after all.

Then the engine died.

It didn't choke and splutter and wheeze and finally give out with a pathetic last gasp. Instead it just died in an instant, going entirely silent. The stretch of highway he was tackling rested at a slight incline, so the Brabus started to slow immediately.

Slater cursed, and put both hands on the wheel, rattled by the sudden quiet inside the cabin.

The four trucks ahead sensed his retreat, and they slowed and turned around on the highway like hungry stalking predators.

'Shit!' Slater roared. He punched the dashboard, bruising his knuckles on the leather, suddenly seized by helplessness.

He tightened his grip on the carbine.

It was his last hope.

Sitting in a rapidly slowing box, he reached for the door handle. He figured he could lever himself out onto the step and aim over the top of the door, using its bullet-proof window and armour plating as a makeshift bunker. He had no control of the Brabus now, so it was his last port of call.

He took a deep breath, and saw a couple of the trucks coming right at him, and threw caution to the wind and heaved the door outward.

It didn't budge.

He rocked back in his seat, overwhelmed by that same feeling of helplessness. It threatened to choke his insides, constrict his breathing, send his heart rate sky high. He looked around the luxurious cabin and saw nothing but a steel trap.

The passenger window was still down.

He lunged out of the driver's seat but the seatbelt caught

him, so he reached down to unclasp it, and the second he worked it free the window came up, sealing him in.

Fighting the urge to panic, he angled the carbine into the back seats and shot the rear passenger window, making sure to fire at a diagonal in case the bullet deflected.

It bounced harmlessly off and embedded itself in the roof.

Bulletproof.

Just as he suspected.

Then he turned and braced himself as the four trucks surrounded him like a pack of vultures circling helpless prey.

He gripped his carbine in the silence, and the only sound he could hear was the *thrum-thrum-thrum* of his heart against his chest wall.

'Well,' he whispered to himself. 'If this is it...'

Sweat dotted his brow. He watched as the four enemy vehicles reversed alongside his truck, waiting for it to slow completely. He could see them leering openly out the windows. They weren't protecting themselves, even though they could see the outline of the carbine in his hands through the tinted glass.

They knew he wasn't able to fire at them.

Someone in their crew had used a kill switch.

Embedded in every car, and...

Fzz.

He heard the soft electronic stutter emanate from within the M4 carbine. He almost jumped out of his skin, figuring if a small explosive charge had been rigged in the gun he would be helpless to escape.

But nothing else happened.

Then Slater figured out what was going on.

Another kill switch.

He aimed the carbine at the dashboard and pumped the trigger, and sure enough...

...nothing happened.

'Oh, Christ,' he whispered. 'What have you got yourself into?'

As if instructing him through an elaborate theatre production, the driver's door unlocked with a muted *click*.

Slater tossed the useless carbine aside, wrenched the door handle, pushed the door outward, and stepped out onto the blacktop as soon as the Brabus slowed to a crawl.

More than twelve men piled out of the four vehicles collectively, and all of them had assault rifles.

They trained them on him like professionals.

He stood awkwardly in the middle of nowhere as the Brabus rolled away, driverless and dead.

He put his hands over his head.

He swore under his breath.

His heart hammered away, incessantly, endlessly.

Then a man stepped out of the fourth car and raised his open palms wide, like unravelling a master conclusion to the same theatre production. There was a broad smile on his face, and a cunning intelligence in his eyes. Slater didn't think he'd ever seen anyone look so *sharp*. He had a presence unrivalled in his crew — he was similarly physically imposing, but there was a cold calculation in his slate blue eyes that Slater knew meant unparalleled smarts.

And he exuded an energy the others didn't — a feverish excitement to be right here in this moment, surrounded by life-threatening tension and vehicular carnage and the eternal thrill of the hunt.

He said, 'Will Slater. It's a pleasure.'

He had an unruly mop of dark black hair swept back off his forehead, and a five o'clock shadow resting over a rigid jawline, and a physique like something off a magazine cover. He had the appearance of a man who'd taken advantage of every opportunity in life — gruelling workout routines, optimal nutrition, endless self-discipline.

He looked like Slater.

He looked like King.

He had that same energy.

Slater said, 'Have we met?'

The man said, 'Now we have.'

'Who are you?'

'My name is Ali Hawk.'

'Okay.'

'I'm glad you could join me out here, Will.'

'You wanted us here, didn't you? The both of us?'

Hawk turned to look at the closest mercenary to him, and said, 'Told you he's smart.'

'Not smart enough,' Slater said.

Hawk shrugged. 'Can't win them all, can you?'

Slater said nothing.

The man grinned devilishly and said, 'But I can.'

'What happens now?'

'I let you fight me hand to hand and give you a chance to escape.'

Slater stood there with his hands by his side and felt a twinge of hope.

He readied his reflexes.

Then Hawk said, 'Just kidding.'

And he detached a handheld taser from his utility belt and fired the prongs into Slater's thigh.

Slater's world went mad.

44

King withstood the barrage of gunfire by crushing himself into the muddy earth and praying a stray shot didn't ricochet through the open Brabus windows, come out the other side and rupture his internal organs.

But that didn't happen.

The metal storm softened for a moment, allowing him a brief respite. His ears rang and throbbed, and a headache was forcing itself to the forefront of his consciousness despite the rush of adrenalin. He knew that didn't bode well for the future — *if* he survived the coming moments.

But, despite everything stacked against him, he liked his odds.

He raised his head above eye level, only pausing there for a half-second, refusing to allow the mercenaries any time to lock their aim on. He assessed where the opposition were, how they were spread out, how easily he could hit them.

He caught a split-second glance of the guy on the right

staring at the electronic device, working it with both hands, tapping away at its touch screen.

When he ducked back down, his carbine died.

That was the only way he could describe it. He registered a slight vibration from within the rifle. He didn't pick it up on the edge of his hearing — his eardrums were temporarily deafened. Instead he felt a palpable *shift* in the carbine's mechanics, and with a sinking feeling in his stomach he test-fired a round into the ground from behind his concealed position.

Nothing happened.

The gunfire from atop the embankment ceased.

King bowed his head and weighed his options.

None of them were good.

'Come out now!' a voice with an Australian accent roared. 'We'll play nice.'

'No you won't,' King said.

He could barely hear himself talk. The unsuppressed gunfire had rivalled an airhorn going off in both his ears at once.

'You don't understand, then,' the same voice said. 'He wants you alive.'

'Who?'

'This isn't a fucking debate,' the guy said. 'Come out now, mate. Don't try anything stupid.'

They knew about your reflexes, King thought. *Otherwise they wouldn't have risked unloading half their magazines at you.*

They were laying down suppressive fire so the guy with the phone could flip the kill switch on your gun. But they wouldn't have tried that with anyone else, or it might have killed them. You were too fast.

They knew about him.

Who he was.

What he'd done.

Of course they did. They were the ones who'd gone after his girlfriend in Thailand.

All to get to him.

He pieced together a plan. He visualised each movement, putting it together into an entire sequence. He imagined their instructions coming down the pipeline. Very specific instructions, not to be ignored. Not to be disobeyed.

Shouldn't have told me you need me alive, he thought.

Then he stepped out from behind cover.

With his hands up.

And he put as much dejection on his face as he could muster.

The guy up on the embankment doing all the talking smiled.

'Good lad,' he called down.

'You want me up there?' King said.

'No, stay right there. We'll come to you.'

'What's the point?' King grumbled, and put his head down and set off walking toward the slope.

'Hey!' the guy called, but King didn't *seem* to be a threat. So he hesitated a beat.

King said, 'Be right there.'

'No, I said—'

'Oh, what?' King said.

Moving forward the whole time.

Then he made it alongside the idle Brabus — the vehicle whose occupants he'd gunned down effortlessly, before the man with the kill switch arrived on the scene.

The driver's door was open.

It was right there.

The guy doing all the talking worked out what he was doing.

'Shoot him in the fucking leg,' he snarled.

Too late.

No-one was willing to. Not for a couple of seconds at least, and King knew full well how fast he could take advantage of a few seconds' hesitation. They had to line up their aim and get it exactly right, knowing in the back of their minds they'd probably be killed for accidentally murdering a valuable target. So they were preoccupied with getting their aim right, which wasn't easy with the wind whipping at their backs and the cold seeping into their bones and their hands shaking from the adrenalin.

King and Slater had been lured here, so these men had known for weeks, possibly months in advance that they'd be coming.

That was a lot of time to get in their own heads.

They would have heard rumours. *These are the pair of warriors. The best of the best. You'd all better be on your A-games.*

And now they didn't want to choke, which made them more likely to choke in the first place.

So King leapt into the driver's seat and shifted the gearstick from "Park" to "Drive" and stamped the accelerator and the big Brabus roared in response. A couple of gunshots blared then, and a bullet ricocheted off the open driver's door, sparking off the bulletproof window pane.

Then a voice said, *'No!'* sharply, and King knew they couldn't risk killing him.

He slammed the door closed and the tyres spinning in the mud finally found traction and he floored it up the other side of the ditch, which was shorter and far easier to traverse.

A couple of bullets pinged uselessly off the back of the Brabus, but they were shots fired out of pure frustration alone. King made it to the edge of the farmland and demolished the thin wire perimeter fence, making sure to hit it in the middle so it caved without resistance.

The armoured truck flattened the barricade and handled the flat ground with ease. It picked up speed, moving incessantly forward, and without any obstacles in the vicinity King could keep a close eye on his rear view mirror. He saw the five men lined up on the other side of the ditch, growing rapidly smaller, locked in indecision. They knew where he was heading.

A beeline for the woods.

It was mid-afternoon, and the sun would start to set a couple of hours from now.

They'd be searching for him in the dark, in unfamiliar terrain, with the threat of an ambush looming.

King had only made it five hundred feet from the state highway when the group decided to retreat.

They shrank away from the embankment, and he let out the breath that had caught in his throat.

For now, he was safe.

But then he checked his side mirror, and noticed a new field of view had opened up with his retreat into farmland, giving him a look at most of the state highway for a mile in either direction.

He saw a silhouette that looked eerily like Slater, way down the road, surrounded by armed mercenaries.

Another kill switch, he thought.

But it didn't work out so well for him.

He stifled the urge to turn around and barrel toward Slater, knowing it would get him killed. He was wrapped up in something far greater than himself. He still couldn't grasp the lengths their enemy had gone to just to get them here.

Their foe was intelligent beyond comprehension, and the best move now was *not* a brazen attack.

That had worked wonders for King in the past, but he got the eerie sense he'd never faced anything quite like this.

Weaponless, defenceless, stripped of everything he had to work with, he had no option but to retreat to the woods and wait until the enemy force dispersed.

He bowed his head to the wheel and maintained his trajectory.

His stomach turned over and over.

45

W hen the pain receded to a manageable level, Slater came to in the back of one of the trucks. It was moving.

Racing off south down State Highway 1, away from the remnants of vehicular warfare.

The Brabus' rear seats had been stripped out, leaving an enclosed area the size of a panel van's hold. He was strapped to a metal bed, handcuffed at both wrists, with coarse leather straps around his ankles. He didn't bother squirming or struggling or screaming for help — actions so prevalent in modern day movies.

He recognised his helplessness immediately. He didn't waste any energy.

He just accepted it.

He sat back, dealt with the aches and pains in his body, and waited for someone to speak.

Ali Hawk sat on a steel bench built into the side of the space.

He watched Slater intently.

'You caused me a lot of trouble,' the man said. 'This was supposed to go smoothly.'

Slater didn't respond.

He scrutinised the man across from him.

Hawk appeared to be in his mid-thirties, but he might have been far older. He had the aura of someone who took impeccable care of himself. Someone who had every facet of life sorted out, from his physicality to his mentality. What still stood out the most to Slater was the man's eyes. They were cunning and wise and they pierced right through him. So he kept his mouth shut. He felt like anything he said would be futile — Hawk would dissect it, deconstruct it, break it down, and after only a few minutes of conversation the man would know exactly what made Will Slater tick.

Slater didn't want to allow him the privilege.

Hawk smiled as the silence played out, and eventually said, 'You're going to have to speak eventually.'

'I'm in pain.'

'That's never held you back before.'

Slater raised an eyebrow.

Hawk almost looked irritated. He said, 'What? That really surprised you?'

'Frankly, all of this is surprising me.'

And he was telling the truth. On top of that, it was terrifying him. Everything from the bed, to the shackles, to the handcuffs — it all seemed like it had been customised to fit Slater *perfectly*. Like they knew exactly how this would unfold, right from the start. Hawk had been planning this for weeks — maybe months.

Hawk said, 'If it blows your mind that I was able to get access to blacked-out government files, then you're in for a world of terror when you find out what comes next.'

Slater said, 'What do you know about me, exactly?'

'About you and Jason King? Everything.'

'Up until retirement, I assume.'

'I admit, it's hard to find out what the hell went on after you two went off the radar. It's a shame that Black Force had such a messy dissolution, especially after all that potential. All that achievement. But in the end, it doesn't matter what happened afterwards. The two of you are still alive, and I've had time to browse your track records, and that's all I needed to know.'

Slater said, 'I'm not dead yet. I'm guessing that means something.'

'Of course it means something.'

'I assume it doesn't bode well for me.'

Hawk shrugged. 'That depends which way you look at it. After I'm done with the pair of you, you won't have much of anything left upstairs. You'll be mine.'

Slater didn't say anything.

He thought long and hard about what that might mean, and a bolt of ice ran down his spine. It started at the top of his neck and worked its way down his back, and he masked a shiver as he lay against the metal.

Slater said, 'Where are we going?'

But Hawk wasn't concentrating. He was staring down at his phone, an expression of distaste on his face. But a moment later it vanished, replaced by the same cold calculation Slater had grown used to.

Hawk thumbed something on the touch screen and pressed the phone to his ear and said, 'Yes?'

There was a muffled reply from the tiny speaker. Slater couldn't hear it.

Hawk said, 'The woods?'

Another muffled reply, shorter, only one syllable.

It sounded like, *Yes.*

Hawk swore, and rapid decisions flashed in his eyes.

When he spoke, it was measured and patient.

He said, 'Okay. Pull everyone back for now. I've read their files and I know exactly what these two will do for each other, so we don't need to go on the offensive. Jason will come to us. He won't leave my new friend here behind. So get in touch with Teams C and D back at base and bring them out here. Set them up at regular intervals along the highway and give them everything we've got in our arsenal. It's the only way Jason will get to our complex unless he decides to trek through the backroads, and that'll take him too long. He won't be willing to risk it. He'll come south eventually and we can bag him there. Got all that?'

The same muffled reply. Once again, it sounded a lot like, *Yes.*

'Good,' Hawk said. 'Give me an exact body count from Teams A and B.'

Another muffled reply. Inaudible.

But Hawk winced.

'Okay,' he said. 'When you're finished setting up the roadblocks along the highway I want the feelers put out for new recruits. Contract work. Maybe a couple of months at the most. We won't need them after that. I've got all I need right here in this truck.'

Then he hung up, and once again Slater felt the same icy shiver work its way down his spine.

Slater said, 'What is this? What are you running here?'

'You'll see,' Hawk said. 'Trust me, you'll see.'

Then he stared at Slater like he was a prized treasure, and some sort of dark passion flashed in his eyes, and he said, 'I can't believe I've finally met you in the flesh. I've been looking for a pair like you for so long. We're going to do fucking *unbelievable* things together.'

Then he turned his attention to the road ahead.

Slater could almost *see* him dreaming of the future.

Slater settled back into the metal bed, and felt his pulse thrumming in his neck.

He wondered where King was.

46

B unkered down under a rapidly darkening sky, Jason King put a full hour's thought into his next move.

It was all the time he gave himself. He told himself if he couldn't reach a conclusion in that time, he would pick the first available option and go for it.

Because time wasn't on his side, and as the night approached he bottled up his unease and focused on what he could control.

He'd seen them take Slater. At the very edge of his vision, nearly two hours ago, he'd made it to the tree line and watched the silhouette on the road struck with something — maybe a bullet, maybe a taser — and drop without resistance to the asphalt.

Then he'd been manhandled into the back of a truck, legs still kicking, and King knew the man was alive.

The truck had sped off, and King pulled his own Brabus to a halt between two massive conifers with his stomach sinking by the second.

Now he lay submerged under large ferns, draped over him in sheets, his stomach pressed to the cool dirt. He was a hundred feet inside the tree line, in a particularly overgrown patch of forest, and the sounds of wildlife came alive all around him as the evening chill set in.

Crickets and cicadas shrilled and chirped, and with each passing moment he sensed his time running out.

Whoever was behind this was ten steps ahead.

That was the ultimate conclusion he reached, after twenty minutes of going around in circles in his own head.

He didn't think there was anyone coming, but he had to make sure. It would pay dividends for the five men who'd shot at him to double back and approach the woods from some unseen angle, and he didn't want to be caught in the open, unarmed and exposed. So if they stalked through the forest around him, he'd get up and slaughter each and every one of them. But he doubted that was going to happen.

Then he got to work, processing and thinking.

Someone had wanted them in New Zealand. Their base of operations was established here, so they figured they'd lure King and Slater to the South Island with a labyrinth paper trail. King's mind lurched at the level of detail in the plan — they'd known King and Slater were competent enough to go out and get what they needed to decrypt the phone, even though very few people on the planet could do so. And they'd known, somehow, that they would *actually* do it instead of baulking at the mammoth effort it would require.

So their enemy knew all about who they were, and what they were capable of.

Which meant he'd seen what they'd done in Black Force.

Which meant he had some kind of connection to the organisation, or the files themselves.

Or he was just competent enough to get to them.

So the enemy could predict that King would come for Slater.

Therefore they'd focus all their attention on State Highway 1, but that wasn't the only way to Tapanui.

King pulled his phone out of his pocket and lowered the brightness so the glare was invisible in the twilight. Then he set to work using the maps application. He figured he could double back to Christchurch, then go north up State Highway 73, through Arthur's Pass, which would drop him off on the west coast of the island. From there he could make his way all the way down the west coast, passing Fox Glacier and a handful of other natural wonders, and use State Highway 6 to travel back across the mainland and approach Tapanui from the north.

Altogether, it would take nearly twelve hours of continuous driving.

But he'd slept for hours on the plane, anticipating an endurance feat precisely like the one laid out before him.

As the sky grew dark his resolve stiffened, so he gave himself ten more minutes to listen out for any signs of approaching combatants.

But the woods were dead and quiet and dark, and finally he made up his mind and rose up like Bigfoot coming out of the forest. He saw a weak beacon of light deep in the farmlands before him — a low ranch-style dwelling with a cluster of outbuildings around them.

A farmer and his family.

The deck light glowing weak and muted in the middle of nowhere.

King put the phone back in his pocket, and set off at a jog across the empty fields.

'Hang in there,' he whispered, hoping the wind carried his voice all the way to Slater. 'I'm coming.'

47

They drove on and on.

As the sky darkened Hawk fished a Tupperware container out from under the bench and detached a metal fork clipped onto its side.

Slater momentarily thought he was about to be subjected to some sort of medieval torture, but Hawk snapped the lid off the tub and gorged on a collection of smoked salmon, avocado, goat's cheese and braised beef.

Slater watched him with fascination.

Halfway through the meal, Hawk looked up. 'What?'

'You're not what I pictured an evil mastermind to be.'

Hawk smiled through a mouthful of nutrition and said, 'Well, that's because society's idea of an evil mastermind is moronic. I'm just a guy with enough brain cells to see the way the world's heading and adapt accordingly.'

'What do you want with me, exactly?'

Hawk finished the meal, checked his watch, and shrugged. 'What the hell — right? It's another few hours' drive. Are you up for a chat?'

Slater said, 'You've got me chained to a bed in the back

of a truck. What else would I be up for?'

Hawk waved the fork in Slater's face and said, 'Point taken. What do you want to know? Ask away.'

'Did you want King and I because of our reaction speed?'

'Yes.'

'And our track record?'

'Yes.'

'And our ability to dish out violence?'

'Yes.'

'Anything else?'

'No. I'm changing the rest of it.'

'What?'

'Your files speak for themselves,' Hawk said. 'You're both morally pure, if you want to call it that. You're basically prehistoric mentally. You can't get over the fact that the world is quickly going to shit, so you wrap yourselves up in your own individual brands of vigilante justice. You go from one task to the next thinking you're making a difference, when really you're not making a dent in global suffering. A thousand clones of you couldn't. And you fail to look at anything from the big picture. The world's population is getting out of control with each passing year, so really the handful of innocent people you save are only making things worse, if you really want to break it down like that.

'You see, the world's not going to shit because of suffering. In fact, we're getting less and less of it than any time in history. But that poses its own problems, because everyone's going to keep breeding like rabbits until the population peaks, and then everything's going to hell. If you've got two brain cells to rub together you know it, but if you don't recognise it you're just living in denial.'

Slater scoffed.

Hawk said, 'Did I say something funny?'

'So you're just another crackpot with a plan for an endgame. What is it — a nuke? A virus?'

Hawk leered, then bent over and tapped Slater's forehead with a manicured finger. 'You watch too many movies, kid. There's too many fantasies swirling around up there.'

'That's not what this is?'

'Not even close.'

'So what are you doing here?'

Hawk spread his arms wide, to encompass the whole fleet of armoured vehicles racing through the darkness. 'I'm fascinated by efficiency. I want to build myself an empire. I want to see how far one man can take that concept. How much can one man do in a single lifetime? Because apart from that, what the fuck are we even doing here? What are we living for? Simple pleasures? No, I'm past that. I want to keep expanding until I can just go *anywhere* and do *anything.* And that starts with the pair of you. Because you two might be the most vicious bastards I've ever heard of.'

'You're talking like you're going to use us.'

'I am.'

'Not much chance of that happening.'

Hawk raised an eyebrow. 'Oh?'

'You said it yourself. We're "morally pure." We wouldn't help you.'

Hawk edged closer to Slater, until his face was only half a foot away. 'You're not going to have a choice in the matter.'

'What?'

'I want to actualise something new. I want to create something that hasn't been done before. It started with supplements like nootropics. Brain enhancers. The archaic versions are just starting to hit the markets today. But behind closed doors, research into physical control of the brain has been going on for decades. A personal hero of mine pioneered the movement. José Manuel Rodriguez Delgado. Have you heard of him?'

With physical fear compressing his chest, Slater said, 'No.'

He looked down at the shackles around his hands and feet.

Now he tried to budge, but it didn't do any good.

The ramifications of his imprisonment set in, and for a moment he thought he might have a heart attack. He actually wished for it to happen, because it might free him from whatever the hell Ali Hawk had in mind.

But there was no escape from this fear.

Hawk said, 'He did most of his work in the fifties, sixties, and seventies. He used electrical stimulation to control the brains of animals. He built a stimoceiver — it was a device that connected to a receiver so he could monitor the EEG waves in a subject's brain and control them through electrical impulses. This is real shit, Slater. He could stimulate the motor cortex and get *actual physical reactions.* The fucking madman stopped a bull in its tracks on a ranch in Spain nearly fifty years ago. Can you believe that? Fifty years ago. I read this, and I figured — what the hell could I do with this in today's day and age?'

Slater sat in horrified silence.

Hawk said, 'I'm not much of a fan of ethics. And, it turns out, neither are the pioneers of different fields. So I hired the best of the best, and I brought them out here. I let them do their work without restriction. Without all the menial bullshit that goes along with verified studies. It's a free market out here, baby. I let them *thrive.*'

Slater stayed silent.

Hawk said, 'I bet there's a million thoughts going

through your head right now.'

Slater said nothing.

Hawk said, 'This is the new world, kid. This is *real life*. Can you believe it? I'm going to put a goddamn piece of technology the size of a pea in your head, and it's going to give me access to all of you. *All of you*. All those juicy genetics. All that reaction speed. You can't program that. But you can find the toughest men on the planet, and you can reel them in with bait, and you can *transform them*. And when I get your friend — and I will — I'll do the same to him. You'll be the muscle. My muscle. I can get rid of all these useless fucks around me. I can have the two of you all to myself. Imagine the places I could go. The things I could do. You two are unstoppable. You're like the Terminator on steroids, and so is your friend. Jason King and Will Slater — my personal bodyguards. You won't be able to stop me. I'll kill that part of you and keep the rest. You'll do what I say. Every day. All the time.'

Hawk inched forward even further.

'You'll be mine,' the man said.

A sickly smile spread across his face.

Slater physically recoiled from Ali Hawk. The man had a look in his eyes the likes of which Slater had never seen before. Hawk was off the deep end, wrapped in his own head, succumbing to his own genius...

...but he wasn't bullshitting.

Slater could tell.

Ali Hawk meant every single word he was saying.

This wasn't the rambling delusions of a psycho.

This was the new wave of terrorist.

This was a technological wizard without a shred of morality.

This was the new world.

48

King stepped up onto the rickety porch.

He took a deep breath, winced, and then did exactly what he needed to do.

Anything else would hinder Slater's survival, and he couldn't risk it.

He figured no-one would answer the door at this time of evening, and he also knew about the lack of firearms in New Zealand.

He wasn't likely to get shot breaking and entering.

So he took a deep breath, tested the weight of the flimsy wooden back door to the ranch, and smashed his shoulder into the wood.

It rattled, and nearly gave.

But the foundations were strong.

It stayed in place.

King put everything into the next charge, and the lock snapped like it was made of plastic. He forced it inwards, splintering the wood around his hand — where it gripped the handle — and charged into an entranceway. He followed the weak light, turned left into a small living room, and came face to face with a horrified family. A Maori husband with a weather-lined face and calloused hands, a white woman wearing a nightgown, and a small boy — no older than six — looking up with wide, terrified eyes.

Sometimes, King hated what he had to become.

He expanded his back so he spread out in the doorway, displaying all two hundred and twenty pounds. He stood up to his fullest high, and he put a look of black rage on his face.

He said, 'I don't want to hurt you. I need your car.'

They looked at him like he was a demon risen from hell.

The father started to get out of his chair.

King could see him clenching his fists.

Probably thinking, *Protect the kid at all costs.*

King roared, '*Don't!*'

The boy broke into tears.

The father rocked back on his haunches, rattled by the explosiveness. And there was something in King's voice, some added weight. Something palpable in the air. This was not a man to trifle with. This was not a man to take a chance against.

King lowered his voice and said, 'Just the keys. That's all I need. Don't be a hero. Just give me what I need and I won't hurt any of you.'

He wasn't going to touch them, but they didn't need to know that.

Eventually the father nodded, and King saw micro-expressions on his face that confirmed his obedience. The man stood up, and held his palms out on either side.

Trying to signal that he meant no harm.

'Just don't touch the kid, man,' the guy said.

I would never, King thought.

'The keys,' King snarled.

The guy bowed his head and sighed, and crossed to a chest of drawers on the other side of the living room. King kept a wary eye on him, watching for any sign of deception, but he found none. The man retrieved a key fob from the topmost drawer and tossed it across the room.

'Just bought it, man,' he said. 'Brand new. It's my livelihood. Ain't much money to go around out here, so we take pride in it.'

King listened, then pocketed the key. It was a Volkswagen, judging by the emblem on the key fob.

He said, 'Do you know your bank details off by heart?'

The man stood in rigid silence, as if he didn't know whether King was playing a practical joke on him or not.

'What?' he said.

'Your bank details,' King repeated. 'Do you know them off by heart?'

'Yeah,' the guy said. 'We don't have much, though. There's nothing to take.'

'How much did you pay for the car?'

'Thirty five thousand dollars.'

'Give me your details.'

The man gave King his Bank-State-Branch number, followed by his account number. He uttered the digits as if reading them off a page.

King memorised them, then pulled his own phone out and spent a few minutes organising an electronic funds transfer from the bank he'd been using in Switzerland for the better part of the last two years.

He said, 'Listen, and listen closely. I just sent you fifty thousand dollars. Consider the extra fifteen thousand interest. For the shock I've inflicted on the three of you. As soon as I leave here, you can go to the police, and I'm sure they'd find me on one of the highways within a couple of hours and have me arrested. But there's no guarantee they'd get me on the first try, and if that happens I'll come back here hunting for all three of your heads. Or you can chalk the entire thing up to a strange dream and go buy the same version of the car you worked hard for, and then you can use the rest of the cash as an emergency fund for tough times. Two choices. If you choose option two, you will never hear from me again. It's your call to make. Best of luck.'

Then he turned on his heel and left the room.

No-one followed him.

The family were frozen in place, stunned by what had unfolded, probably wondering if they were going to wake up in their beds a moment later and laugh off the crazy nightmare they'd mutually shared.

King made straight for the garage, and when he clambered behind the wheel of the Volkswagen Tiguan, he had a sneaking suspicion both the mother and father would see the light. All they had to do was open the banking application on their phone. They'd see the funds sitting there. That would make them pause, and ruminate on the options King had given them.

After all, he'd forced himself into their house so effortlessly.

Maybe he was telling the truth when he said he would come back for them.

Maybe he truly *did* have the capacity to avoid the police for long enough to make them pay for it.

They could pick up a new Tiguan from the same dealership, and no-one would know the difference.

King accelerated out through the open garage door and plunged into dark farmland.

He set the GPS on his phone to take him on a round-about loop of the South Island, and steeled himself for the long night ahead.

Something told him he had no idea what he was truly in for.

49

At ten in the evening the fleet of armoured trucks pulled into a rural ranch-style compound near Tapanui.

Slater soaked in the details out the rear window. The nature of his imprisonment prevented him from turning around to see what they were approaching, but he watched the long gravel track with a keen eye as it trailed all the way from the perimeter fence to the centre.

Everything he could see appeared unassuming.

He figured that was Hawk's intention.

As the Brabus handled the terrain, Slater turned to the man and said, 'Bet you're not happy about how much carnage we caused back there. Wouldn't want the aftermath to intrude on your privacy.'

Hawk waved a hand dismissively, shaking off Slater's attempts to rattle him. 'That's what I pay clean-up crews for. I've got them on standby for messy situations like this. By now the wreckages will be cleared and any trace of civilian casualties will be eliminated. I'm hearing reports that two innocent people were killed. How does that make you feel?'

'We didn't do it. Your men did.'

'But you caused it. If you went to me submissively like you should have, that wouldn't have happened. I wonder how you justify that to yourself. You see, being morally pure is horse shit. It's convenient for you. It's convenient for the world to pretend they're doing good, when deep down everyone is a piece of shit just like me. I'm just honest about it. I tell the truth.'

'I—'

Hawk held up a hand in derision, cutting Slater off. 'Is this the part where you somehow try to convince yourself that you and King are more important than those civilians that died?'

'No. I'd never do that.'

'You would have said something along those lines, in a roundabout way. I know how you tick.'

'Do you?'

Hawk paused for thought as the convoy reached its destination and the four trucks spread out in a fanning semi-circle across a wide dirt lot.

The driver killed the engine, and everything descended into silence.

The interior light went out, and the only illumination came from the weak porch light outside filtering in through the windshield. Slater couldn't see the house itself — he was still bolted to the bed.

The driver and passenger quietly exited the car over his shoulder.

He didn't see them either.

He was left alone with Hawk in the gloom.

The dull lighting exacerbated the shadows.

Hawk didn't budge.

He said, 'I think it's time you and I had a little chat.'

'About what?' Slater said.

'I feel obligated to give you the courtesy of knowing what's going to happen to you before we go too far down the rabbit hole. I respect efficiency, and you and Jason King are two of the most efficient people I've ever seen. You've mastered almost every aspect of your lives. So I owe you a great debt. I'll answer any questions you might have. King won't be so lucky. He irritated me when he got away, so I'll keep him in the dark until he's a vegetable on an operating table. And what I do with both of you after that will be beyond your comprehension anyway. So now's the time to ask.'

Slater said, 'Who are you, exactly? Do you have a grudge against us?'

Hawk almost looked frustrated at Slater's ineptitude. 'Haven't we already covered this?'

'How did you find out about Black Force, then? If you really have no connection to either of us...'

'By doing my research.'

He said this as if it was the most obvious concept in human history, and Slater recoiled from the conversation.

Hawk said, 'What?'

'Just do whatever you're going to do to me. I don't want to go round in circles with you. Get it over and done with.'

'You're uncomfortable, aren't you?'

'Wouldn't you be?'

'But I don't think it's because you're chained to a bed. I think you've cheated death so many times that barely fazes you anymore. I think it's the fact that you know you're not going to win this one.'

'Is that so?'

'You seem defeated already. Isn't Jason King out there somewhere? Isn't he going to come to your rescue?'

'I'd hope so.'

'You don't seem confident.'

'Should I be?'

'Usually you are. I've read your files, after all. I know everything that happened between the two of you when you were employed. You were each other's knight in shining armour. You saved him from certain death in Russia. I know all about what happened in that abandoned mine. Black Force wrote up a report on it before they dissolved. Now you're expecting him to do the same to you.'

Slater stared across the space.

'What?' Hawk said. 'Not feeling talkative?'

Slater kept his mouth shut.

Hawk said, 'You know I'm better than him. You know I'm better than both of you. I mean, think about it. You two are a nightmare for someone like me. I didn't want to have to subdue you halfway across the world and then deal with the gargantuan task of getting you both to New Zealand without incident. Both of you are too dangerous for that. So all it ended up taking was a bullet in the head of King's girlfriend, and a bit of high-level encryption on a phone I planted on the guy I sent to do it. And then you were here, like clockwork. I wrote that goddamn code myself. That's who you're dealing with.'

Slater stared blankly into space.

Hawk smirked and said, 'And you still know nothing about me.'

'You're some kind of genius who figured the two most efficient solo operatives in U.S. government history were a perfect place to start with your experiments.'

Hawk pointed a finger in Slater's face. 'Almost there.'

'Good luck with that.'

'You sound confident. You sound smug. You shouldn't be feeling anything like that.'

'You're going to put a chip in my head — is that what you said?'

'That's the simplified version.'

'I'm keen to see how well that works. Because I don't know if you should have targeted the two men on the planet with the amount of willpower we have. I don't know how well this is going to work out for you...'

Hawk nearly laughed, but cut himself off.

Then the man said, 'I shouldn't scoff at you for not knowing anything. That's wrong of me. I should be helping you understand.'

'What don't I know?'

'You don't know that it doesn't matter how much willpower you have. I'm going to fry certain parts of your brain, and you're never going to be the same. The old Slater isn't going to exist anymore. You'll have all that reaction speed, all those priceless reflexes, but the rest of you will be pliable. I'll shape you into what I want. Your capacity to resist doesn't even come into the equation. You're a computer up there — it's all hardwired in — so I can change parts of you.'

Slater squirmed.

Hawk said, 'And what you *really* don't understand is that you're not an experiment. I've been able to do it for some time now.'

The rear doors of the Brabus opened, and faceless silhouettes reached into the back to manhandle Slater's bed out into the cool night.

On the way out, Hawk reached over and gripped the back of Slater's neck.

Hawk pulled him in close.

He said, 'Jose Delgado removed a bull's aggressive instincts fifty years ago. Imagine what I'm able to do today. I can't wait to show you around.'

Then Ali Hawk gave the metal bed a gentle shove from behind and it slid from the truck into the waiting hands of his hired thugs.

50

T he first leg of the road trip passed without incident.

King stayed true to his original plan and took State Highway 73 across the mainland. He made a beeline for Arthur's Pass, and as he headed further away from the coastline, the terrain loomed up out of the dark. He stared in awe out the windscreen at the gargantuan mountains on either side of the highway.

They dwarfed him, and an eerie feeling of inconsequentiality settled over him.

Amidst this landscape, his efforts felt futile. He didn't think he was going to achieve anything in the first place, given how effortlessly he'd been lured here by an unknown enemy.

But this only added to it — this unease, this quiet, dark desperation.

The snow-capped mountains spread for miles in every direction, like rock golems in the night.

Silently judging him.

Silently criticising him for even attempting to rescue Slater.

A couple of hours later, King breezed past a cop car parked on the side of the highway. Plenty of time had passed since he'd stolen the Tiguan, and he could feel eyes in the back of his head as he imagined the cop running the plates, waiting for approval. If the sirens lit up, he knew he'd have a tough time outmanoeuvring the vehicle in a big SUV on a desolate highway at night.

There was one road to take, and nowhere to hide.

But nothing happened.

The family at the farm had made the right choice for all of them.

King continued through Arthur's Pass. He left the radio off, and he gripped the wheel with both hands, and he inadvertently got himself bogged down in endless thoughts about how the next day might go, and how well he would operate on no sleep.

But that wouldn't be a problem.

Back during the foundations of his career, he'd come out of a Navy SEAL Hell Week unscathed.

This was nothing in comparison.

He plunged out of the mountain range and made it all the way to the west coast an hour later. From there he branched left at Kumara Junction and headed south at as fast a pace as he could manage. To his left lay the same impossible scenery, and to his right lay a dark and rippling sea. The Tasman Sea swept away into the black horizon, endless in its vastness.

As the clock ticked closer to midnight, a light rain began to fall.

And then a car fell in line behind him.

He must have dropped his awareness for only a few

moments, because it all happened fast. One moment he was alone in the dead of night, and the next there were headlights right behind him.

Ordinarily nothing to stress over, but the speed at which they'd materialised rattled him.

Either the vehicle had approached fast with its headlights off and then flicked them on as it bore down on him, or King's concentration had lapsed so severely that he hadn't seen the car approaching at all until it was far too late.

Both possibilities were cause for concern.

Either the vehicle was hostile, or he was experiencing lapses in time.

A common side effect of blunt force trauma.

If he was concussed from the vehicular warfare, and he hadn't realised yet, it wouldn't bode well for his chances.

He slowed along the coastal highway, and pulled onto the first available service road, and then continued to slow until he was moving at a crawl through the night. He came to a wide gravel lot functioning as a pit stop for long road trips, devoid of life at this hour.

Totally desolate...

The car followed him in.

He couldn't make out anything in the darkness aside from the twin headlights, but they unnerved him. He slowed all the way down until he came to a halt in the middle of the service lot, and he flicked his own headlights off.

A long shadow stretched out in front of the Tiguan, accentuated by the glare behind him.

He sat still, and hunched down low, and waited for the inevitable to happen.

He already knew nothing good would come of this. It wasn't an innocent traveller asking for help or looking for directions. They wouldn't have trusted him if he'd turned into a service road. And it wasn't a cop. There were no lights. No sirens. Just silence, and the soft thrumming of both their engines in the night.

The driver's door opened.

King watched it in the rear view mirror.

All he could see was a dark silhouette in front of the headlights as the driver circled round the door and gently pushed it closed.

It was a man, and he was enormous.

And he had something in his hand.

In both hands, actually...

One object was a flashlight. The other was small and dark.

About the size of a gun.

King reached for the handle, then thought better of it.

He waited.

His pulse rose.

His breath steamed the windshield.

He sunk down lower in his seat.

The silhouette approached.

When the guy made it to the right-hand side of his car, King knew he would approach the driver's door. The flashlight came on, impossibly bright in the darkness, and the small, dark object came up to head height.

The driver, getting ready to approach the door.

To shine his light in.

To identify the occupant of the Tiguan.

To carry on if it wasn't who he was looking for, but if it was...

King threw the car in reverse and crushed the pedal to the floor and wrenched the wheel to the left. The Tiguan's tyres spun on the gravel, and then caught.

When they found traction the three movements

combined into a single vicious sweep, consisting of the hood swinging to the right in a near hundred and eighty degree turn.

The silhouette didn't have time to get out of the way.

Instead he tried to fire a shot through the driver's door, but the panic surrounding the sudden explosion of movement rattled his aim.

He fired over the hood, missing the car completely.

Then the Tiguan caught him at the waist.

It crumpled him, and King felt the vibration through the chassis. He didn't concentrate on the results — he just saw the silhouette vanish as it bounced off the car, and then he knew he had to move.

He had no gun, and he only had seconds to work with.

So he threw himself out of the moving vehicle and landed in the gravel only a few feet from the silhouette. The guy was dark-skinned, nearly six foot six, wearing dark khakis and a dark shirt. Powerfully built. Like an oversized version of Slater. He had a hard cruel face, currently creased in pain, and he had both hands on his ribcage.

The Tiguan skidded away across the gravel, driverless, and it coasted to a stop twenty feet away.

The man's gun was somewhere on the ground.

King figured the impact against the car had broken several of his ribs, or torn muscle around his stomach. Whatever sort of injury it was, it had to be debilitating. The guy wasn't concentrating on King in the slightest. He took a knee, his eyes squeezed shut and his mouth twisted into a grotesque contortion of agony.

King found the gun lying in the gravel only a few feet away.

He walked over and picked it up.

It was a Glock 26 with tritium night sights.

King said, 'Has this one got a kill switch too?'

The man didn't respond. He went down from one knee to two. He doubled over further.

He still hadn't looked King in the eye.

He was crippled.

King said, 'Pull yourself together. Then we're going to have a talk about who sent you.'

51

The handcuffs on Slater's wrists and the straps around his ankles bit tight.

Hawk's goons had slotted the bed onto a small flat trolley, and now they were wheeling it through a staggering entranceway with an expensive carpeted rug underfoot. The ceiling stretched out dozens of feet over his head, and a stairway at the other end of the hall ascended to a second level overlooking the ground floor.

Hawk strode in front, hands behind his back, admiring his own residence.

'Like it?' he said.

Slater said nothing.

Hawk spun around and slapped him across the face.

He hit hard, with an open palm, and the *crack* echoed off all the walls.

It resonated through the empty house.

Slater lay there with one side of his face on fire. He could barely see out of his right eye. But he didn't let a shred of his discomfort pass over his features. He refused to react.

He stared up at the ceiling, and tried his best to look bemused.

Hawk let his hand fall to his side. He nodded to the four guards wheeling the metal bed, and they stopped it in its tracks.

Hawk loomed over the bed.

He said, 'I shouldn't have done that. You forget that I know everything about you. I know you relish pain. You wouldn't have done the things you did throughout your career if you didn't embrace pain every day of your life. So hitting you isn't going to do much, is it?'

Slater said, 'You're on the right track. Shame you can't control your urges. Not as superhuman as you thought, are you?'

Hawk's eyes turned to stone. His expression slackened. He stared down at Slater for ten seconds, then twenty, then thirty.

Then he turned around and kept walking.

He said, 'We're going downstairs.'

'Why not stay up here?'

'What I've got in store for you is downstairs.'

'How do you get away with all this?' Slater said.

'All what?'

'You're living in a house like this. What is it — ten bedrooms? Ten bathrooms? Ten car garage? I saw a few buildings around this place, too. Guest quarters. All of that is very public. The authorities haven't come asking where you got your money from?'

Hawk barely registered the enquiry.

Slater saw the corner of his mouth tilt upward.

He was amused.

Hawk said, 'We haven't covered who I am, or where I came from, have we?'

'Evidently not.'

'I made my money legitimately. I don't hide. It's only recently that I've taken an interest in expanding into uncharted territory. That's all I need to hide. I'll keep you downstairs until I'm done with you, and then when I'm finished there'll be nothing suspicious. I can parade you around in public and no-one will know the difference. That's how intricate the human brain is. That's how rapidly technology is advancing. The brain is controllable. It's binary. Like a computer.'

'And you can do that on your own?'

'Of course not. It's time for you to meet the team.'

The four thugs wheeled him into a service elevator — an enormous metal box underneath the stairwell. The trolley under the bed got caught on the metal grooves on the floor, so the four men lifted the bed right off the trolley and dumped it down in the middle of the metal room. Hawk followed them in, slid the safety screen across, and hit a button on the side panel.

The elevator creaked and groaned and began to descend.

Slater finally got a good look at the four men around him.

Two white guys, an Asian man, and an African man.

If he was to break free, they were his competition.

He didn't like his chances.

They seemed *different* to the mercenaries he and King had fought earlier that day. They were a different breed, a different class of athlete. A different level of warrior. He could see it in their mannerisms — they were confident, and that was half the battle right there.

Staring up at them, Slater got the sense the men who'd

been dispatched to run him and King off the road were cannon fodder compared to Hawk's private security.

These men were all tall, all broad-shouldered, and all patient. There was no unrest as the elevator moved slowly downward. They had calmness of mind in spades, and all four of them stared straight ahead through the safety screen at the twisted concrete of the elevator shaft.

Awaiting commands.

Slater hadn't seen combatants with their demeanour since his Black Force days.

They looked like Ali Hawk.

They looked on top of the world.

The elevator thundered home at the bottom of the shaft. It was an old contraption, at odds with the opulence and luxury overhead. Hawk slid the safety screen open, and the four guards dumped Slater's bed back on the trolley and wheeled it out of the elevator.

They rolled into a dark concrete tunnel eerily similar to a mine shaft. Wooden supports rose up on either side, forming a latticework across the roof. At regular intervals harsh white light shone from doorways branching off. The light spilling out of the adjacent rooms was the only illumination.

Shadows spread out, long and fearsome.

If Slater's predicament didn't scare him enough, the aesthetic of the basement made sure to pull the fear out of him.

But he put on a brave face.

Because what the hell else was there to do but be resilient in the face of your darkest fears?

'Love what you've done with the place,' Slater said.

'Look closely enough and you'll see it's all artificially constructed,' Hawk said. 'I just liked the idea of an underground lair. I don't know about it. Thought I'd play around. Nothing else to do until I got my hands on the both of you.'

'You don't have King yet.'

'But I will.'

Indeed, as Slater scrutinised the tunnel he noticed it was a mine shaft by resemblance alone. The supports were purely aesthetic — not structurally integral in the slightest — and parts of the rock seemed carted in, as if integrated during post-production of a feature film. Like a sick wonderland.

Like a kid's playground.

Slater said, 'Who were you before all this?'

His voice rang off the walls, and echoed down the tunnel, and Ali Hawk turned around to face Slater with the same bemused look.

'You're still searching for some elaborate conspiracy, aren't you?'

Slater shrugged. 'It'd make things easier to digest.'

Hawk gestured to one of the first holes in the wall. Halogen light flickered as it emitted from the doorway.

'This way,' he said. 'I'll tell you all about exactly who I am.'

The four silent bodyguards pushed the trolley toward the light.

52

King quickly realised that if not for his last-second attempt to use the Tiguan as a battering ram, he would have come out the other side of the fight a battered, broken man.

The guy kneeling across from him in the dirt lot was well in excess of two hundred and fifty pounds, and all of it was muscle. He'd suffered a vicious blow from the hood of King's vehicle, and it had either ruptured internal organs or broken bones, but if not for that he might have crushed King with a single punch, or backed up a few steps and shot him through the face when he tried to get out of the car.

And there was also the fact that he'd chanced across King, merely by sweeping the state highways for anyone travelling alone.

How many more of them are there?

King knew he couldn't get lucky forever.

He aimed the Glock at the man's head as he knelt in the gravel and said, 'Feel like talking yet?'

The guy tried to get up — some sort of vain attempt to preserve his dignity — but a wave of pain washed over his face and he rocked back like a baby, going all the way down. He kicked his legs up in the air, then let them fall to the ground. He lay on his back, staring at the stars, clutching his stomach with both hands.

He was hurt bad.

If not for his hardened physique, the impact against the Tiguan might have killed him.

King walked slowly over and sat down on the gravel, six feet away from the big man.

He had no reservations about a surprise attack.

You couldn't fake that sort of agony unless you were an Oscar-level actor, and this guy wasn't. He'd broken out in sweat. Perspiration poured off his forehead and dripped to the ground beneath him. There were large pit stains on his shirt. He was gnashing his teeth together, riding out the pain.

King pointed the Glock at the man's head and waited for the initial wave to subside.

When the pain receded, the man stayed on his back. He looked up at the stars, panting for breath. Finally he rolled his gaze over to King, and he swore under his breath.

'You should just shoot me,' the guy said.

'Why's that?'

'I've got nothing to tell you.'

'I think you do.'

'Whatever you're going to threaten to do to me, the man I work for will make it ten times worse.'

'Do you know anything about my friend?'

'Who?'

'I had someone with me. He was taken by your organisation — whoever you are and whatever you do. Do you know anything about what happened to him?'

'He's still alive if that's what you're wondering. Other than that, I don't know a thing.'

'You sure about that?'

'Very.'

'That man was a close friend. Almost like a brother to me.'

'Look, man,' the guy spat, and blood ran out from both corners of his mouth.

Internal bleeding, King thought. *I don't have long.*

'Look,' the guy repeated, composing himself. 'I'll give you that. They've got your friend, but he's not going to be the same friend when you find him. Even if he's still alive.'

'He can handle torture. We've both been trained for that.'

The guy just smiled, exposing bloody teeth. 'Not torture.'

'What, then?'

'I told you to shoot me.'

'And I'm still saying no. You're going to give me answers.'

'I ain't telling you shit. Whatever you can do, my boss will do worse. I told you that.'

'But your boss isn't here, is he?' King said, getting to his feet. 'I'm the only one here. So right now, I'm the only one you need to worry about.'

King stepped forward and kicked the man in the ribs.

He screamed, and spat blood high into the air. The cloud rained down on him. He rolled over into the foetal position and clutched his abdomen.

It was already destroyed from the car hitting him.

Now it was ten times worse.

King squatted down and said, 'I could keep this up for hours before anyone finds you. You want to play that game?'

The guy audibly whimpered. Then he said, 'Your

friend's not going to be the same because my boss is going to change his brain.'

King didn't respond. He maintained the squat, and tapped the gun against his thigh.

Then he figured what the man had said was too ludicrous to invent on the spot.

He said, 'What?'

But something tickled the back of his neck. A premonition. A deep, dark primeval feeling. From the deep, dark primeval part of his brain.

An ancient instinct of sorts.

Something told him, *You're in a world you know nothing about.*

The guy said, 'Change his brain, man. Like he did to me.'

King tensed up.

The wind howled off the ocean and swept up the coast, buffeting the empty lot.

The sounds of nature rose up, drowning out the man's laboured breathing.

King said, 'What did he do to you?'

'He changed me, man. He made me better. More disciplined. More logical. I wasn't shit before he found me. He's my saviour.'

'What were you? Ex-military?'

'Just a grunt. A private. EV2.'

'U.S. military?'

'You couldn't tell from my accent?'

'Just making sure. Where are you from?'

'Tennessee.'

'When did you enlist?'

'Three years ago.'

'What happened?'

'I got dishonourably discharged. Wasn't doing things

properly. I had no self-discipline so I was trying to coast through the P.T., and they noticed. Started putting me to the test and I responded by throwing all the insults back in their faces. They kicked me out real fast. But Hawk saw potential in me. I'm smart, man, but I couldn't get the discipline to do things right. He went inside my head and he fixed me right up, man. Now I'm free.'

King said, 'Hawk?'

'Ali Hawk. He's my saviour.'

'He's a brain surgeon?'

'No. But he knows the right people.'

'What's he going to do to my friend?'

'He'll change him, man. For the better.'

'My friend doesn't need changing. He's got enough discipline for a hundred men.'

'It's not just discipline,' the guy said with a manic glint in his eye. 'It's … *anything.* Maybe your friend is a rare breed of soldier.'

'You have no idea.'

'Then maybe Ali Hawk wants him all for himself.'

'And me?'

'Are you the partner?'

'Of sorts.'

'Then he wants you alive. I was told to hand-deliver you.'

'How did you figure you'd do that?'

'At gunpoint.'

King muttered, 'You obviously haven't met me, then.'

'What?'

King said, 'Tell me exactly how I can get to Ali Hawk or I'll kick you in the ribs again.'

The man opened his mouth to respond.

A jolt seized him, starting in his head.

He jerked back against the gravel.

Blood ran from the corners of his eyes.

It spilled out his mouth.

It streamed out his nostrils.

He jerked once more in his death throes and lay still.

King watched him in horror, and quickly realised he was now alone in the darkness.

He nudged the body once with his toe, just to check.

No response.

Treading water in an unfamiliar realm, he trudged back to the car with an impending sense of doom lingering over him.

53

————

Ali Hawk turned away from a trio of sleek black desktop monitors and said, 'Sorry. Had to clear up a slight problem.'

He'd just minimised three separate windows displaying a collection of charts and graphs. Slater thought he saw a heart rate monitor somewhere in there.

Hawk had turned away from their conversation as an alert rang out on the main computer in the room. He'd worked like a fiend at the keyboard and mouse, moving so fast across both that the tech team from the Hungarian airfield seemed comparatively amateur.

He'd assessed some unseen, unknown situation, came to a conclusion, and acted fast.

He'd initiated a final series of commands, entered a couple of passwords, and then shut it all down.

'All done,' he said now. 'Where were we?'

Slater stared at the triple monitors behind him, each displaying a minimalistic desktop wallpaper.

He had the uneasy feeling something incredibly sinister had just happened.

He said, 'What was that?'

Hawk said, 'Nothing you need to worry about. I'm doing exactly what I said I was going to do, and that's all you need to know.'

Slater's stomach constricted into a knot.

'Did that have something to do with King?' he said.

Hawk managed a slight smile. 'Perhaps. It seems I know where your friend is now.'

'What did you just do?'

'Had an alert from one of my men show up on the screen. I took care of him. King won't be able to get anything out of him, so we're in the clear. And now I know exactly where he is. He's on the west coast. Smart move, but it won't take long to flush him out now.'

He looked at one of the four bodyguards standing behind Slater. 'Send Teams C and D to the west coast. Intercept him at Fox Glacier. Go all out. I want this done. Rustin and Blake — you go and lead. Fisher and Rodgers, stay. Got it?'

Four nods.

Two of the bodyguards peeled off — the dark-skinned man and the Asian man. They disappeared out the door without any palpable shift of emotion at the new orders. Taking their instructions like true professionals.

The two white guys stayed.

Fisher and Rodgers.

Slater filed the names away, and watched Hawk closely.

Slater was still tied to the metal bed, now seated in an upright position. Hawk had thumbed a remote ten minutes earlier, and the bed had folded in half with a mechanical whir. The handcuffs stayed on his wrists, and the shackles stayed around his ankles. But the top half of the bed tilted upward like a hospital gurney, so Slater could see the contents of the room without having to crane his neck.

It was a modern office, styled with architectural flair, complete with a triple-monitor setup on an enormous metal desk and a bank of CPUs — central processing units — wrapped up in sleek modern containers, arranged in rows on a series of shelves on the opposite wall.

Everything was state of the art.

Nothing was out of place.

Slater gazed around and felt the same unfamiliar shiver seize hold of him. It wasn't the technological wizardry he was laying eyes on that troubled him. It was that Hawk seemed ten steps ahead in every moment.

Slater figured there would be no Hail Mary rescue this time.

He figured this time, whatever the hell Ali Hawk wanted to do to him, it would be done.

Slater said, 'What do you mean you took care of your man? You told him to retreat?'

Hawk smiled like a patient carer and said, 'No, you idiot. That's impractical.'

Slater didn't respond.

Hawk said, 'I told you what I'm going to do to you. Work out for yourself what I did to my employee.'

Slater stayed silent.

Hawk said, 'He's not around anymore, if that's what you're wondering. He was hurt, according to his vitals. King was probably interrogating him. So I finished him off.'

'Remotely?'

'Yes.'

Slater said nothing. His stomach sank further and further. He bowed his head and tried to stifle the beginnings of a panic attack.

Hawk smiled again and said, 'I told you this was the new world.'

'What did you do?'

Hawk waved the question off. 'No need for specifics. Use your imagination.'

Then he dismissed Fisher and Rodgers with a wave of his hand, and they bled out of the room.

It was just Slater and Hawk, alone, surrounded by the cold incessant hum of the underground maze.

Hawk pulled up a chair and sat down in front of the metal bed. He crossed his arms over his chest.

He said, 'Now, what were we talking about before I was so rudely interrupted?'

'Who you are.'

Hawk nodded, suddenly serious, and said, 'I have no connection to you, if that's what you were wondering. I wasn't bluffing earlier. And maybe that's the scariest part of it all for you.'

'And why would that be?'

'Because I'm the new breed. There could be a hundred like me across the world, but I doubt it.'

'And what are you, exactly?'

'I'm smart, I'm efficient, and I'm switched on. I was raised correctly, by well-meaning parents. I was taught self-discipline at an early age. I took advantage of a passion for learning. And that's me in a nutshell. There's nothing extraordinary about me. Anyone can do what I've done if they had reasonable smarts.'

'I doubt that.'

'I made my money legitimately. I bought and sold companies I saw value in. I almost never got it wrong. I focused on biotech for a while, then moved into corporate lending when I amassed a rainy day fund far in excess of what I needed. And then I nailed that too. I gave out nearly a billion in venture capital, and got back ten over five years. You don't see that reported in the news if you do it through shell corporations. I'm the best kind of billionaire.'

'The unknown one?'

'Exactly. It lets me move out here and work on my passion projects. It lets me take a step back in private so I can go to the next level.'

Slater said, 'I need to know one thing.'

'What?'

'Am I the first person you're testing this on?'

Hawk smiled the same way, as if he were babysitting a toddler. 'You think I'd risk the first test on a specimen like yourself?'

Slater said nothing.

'You're out of luck. I've already perfected this. There's no more delays. There's no more time for you to escape. I've put the right team together, and now I'm going to reap the benefits.'

'Does your team know exactly what you're doing here?'

Hawk raised an eyebrow. 'Of course.'

'So they're just as morally bankrupt as you are?'

'They're interested in progress,' Hawk said. 'Not peer-reviewed research papers. I find it fascinating how easily I can entice people out to the middle of nowhere with a blank cheque and a promise to avoid all restrictions.'

'Then I doubt you have the best.'

'You and Jason King are anomalies in a morally bank-rupt world,' Hawk said. 'You're stubborn, and you're dumb, and you'll never achieve anything of significance without taking away the blinkers.'

'We'll have to agree to disagree about that.'

'The smart ones are like me,' Hawk said. 'The smart ones recognise the importance of what I'm doing here.'

'And what are you doing here, *exactly?*' Slater said. 'I've heard some vague threats, but nothing concrete. Nothing exact.'

'Then let me show you,' Hawk said. 'Let me give you a first-hand demonstration.'

He ushered in his team.

54

King drove for ten miles in a state of shock.

It wasn't that the man had died in front of him. He'd lost count of the number of people he'd seen killed. Death was as much a part of his life as eating, sleeping and breathing were.

It wasn't that.

It was that King couldn't understand how the guy *dropped dead.*

That didn't happen without external stimuli.

He'd seen people succumb to internal injuries before. It was a long, gruelling ordeal — painful to watch, yet a thousand times more painful to experience. It took a long time — if mercy was on their side, only minutes, but often up to an hour. During that time they existed in some sort of delirious fugue state, barely conscious, holding onto life as best they could. Often King had dealt with treating injuries like that far from civilisation, where medical aid was hard to come by.

The man who'd ambushed him hadn't succumbed to internal injuries.

He'd just died.

One second he was here, and the next he was gone.

And he'd *jolted,* like it had started in his brain, like there was something independent in there, deciding when and where to flip the switch and send him to the great beyond.

King gripped the wheel with both hands and drove through the night, heading fast for Fox Glacier.

Outside, the temperature dropped, and he passed the first major glacier near the highway — Franz Josef.

A sign signalled its presence, and he peered out into the gloom.

His eyes went wide.

He spotted the pale outline of the glacier in the soft moonlight, branching away to his right. It was tucked between two looming mountains, like an ethereal fissure in the earth. He stared for a while, and then concentrated on the road.

The windows fogged up from his own body heat, and he blasted the Tiguan's air-conditioning and directed the air through the front vents, up at the windshield. A hole cleared on the glass, just wide enough to see through. He hunched forward and concentrated on the only thing he could control.

Forward progress.

And then a fresh set of headlights lit up the highway behind him.

He felt his pulse rate spike — felt it pound in his neck, the veins throbbing. He quickened his pace, and rounded a bend in the highway, and a sign loomed up out of the gloom.

FOX GLACIER - 5KM AHEAD

He knew from a rudimentary online search that Fox

Glacier was the name of the town. The actual glacier itself rested off the highway, a looming eight-mile jagged gash of white in the foreboding landscape, much like the Franz Josef Glacier he'd just passed.

He buzzed down the window a crack — to test the conditions — and cold alpine air howled in, chilling him to the bone.

He rolled it back up and grimaced.

The car behind him stayed right on his tail.

You're paranoid, he told himself. *Everyone can't be out to get you.*

Or could they?

The next challenge presented itself immediately.

Commotion materialised up ahead — many headlights, frozen in time, illuminating a large dark object across the highway.

A fallen tree.

A *colossal* fallen tree.

It had cut off the entire two lanes, slipping down an icy embankment and coming to rest with a final, dying sigh. Its dark brown trunk, twisted and knotted, blocked any access on either side of the road. King saw flashing emergency lights through his foggy windshield, and as he grew closer and put pressure on the brake pedal, he noticed the line of cars stretching back on his side of the highway, resting like individual beacons in the gloom.

There were at least fifteen of them — it was late, but there were always people with places to be.

King coasted to a dead halt in the line, and slammed a palm against the wheel in frustration.

The steering wheel rattled, and silence enclosed the cabin.

The windows fogged, and fogged, and fogged.

There was no way out. No alternate route, aside from turning around and heading back for miles and miles the way he had come. And no matter how long it took to clear the tree off the highway, retreat was not an option. He'd end up on the same path Ali Hawk expected him to approach from, racing down the east coast and praying he didn't get caught in the trap the unseen, unknown enemy had laid out.

Whoever the hell Ali Hawk is.

He had a name, and little else.

That harrowing fact sunk in as the car behind him pulled up close, adding to the queue.

King instinctively shrank down in his seat, fearing the bullet that would come smashing through the rear window and obliterate the back of his neck.

He was vulnerable here.

Yet still, there was the possibility he was simply deeply paranoid.

He held the Glock he'd stolen at the ready, eyes darting this way and that.

Cars joined the line, piling in minute by minute as the traffic banked up.

Like an endless row of fireflies, surrounded by cold darkness.

Then one of the cars right up the back pulled into the oncoming lane.

King saw the headlights in his side mirror, approaching at a methodical pace. He stiffened.

Horns blared in the night, cursing the queue jumper.

King thought he knew why the car had dipped into the oncoming lane.

He held his Glock tighter.

He readied himself for war.

The car pulled up alongside his Tiguan.

It stopped.

King rolled his window down, and started to bring the gun up into the line of sight, accepting the consequences of shooting a hostile dead in front of a crowd of dozens of witnesses.

Then he froze, with the Glock only inches from the windowsill.

The passenger window of the queue jumping car was down, and an elderly couple were scrutinising the stoic expression on King's face with some level of concern.

The man called across the divide, 'Excuse me, sir.'

His heart thrashing in his chest, King said, 'Yes?'

'Do you have any idea how much longer this will take? We're desperate to get to a motel. My wife needs her medication. She can't be sleep deprived. It's not good for us.'

King said, 'I'm not sure, sorry.'

His throat was dry.

His mouth was dry.

His lips were dry.

The old man in the driver's seat nodded, and smiled politely, and threw the car into reverse.

It set off back the way it had come.

Hoping to slot into the same position in line.

King rolled his window up, and sat in the claustrophobic box, and controlled his breathing.

He almost wished for a fight. He wished for the sudden fury, and the scramble for the upper hand, and the gunshots and screams.

He was a junkyard dog in a fight.

He wanted to bite down on the metaphorical mouthpiece and get to work.

He couldn't handle the tension. He knew they were coming for him — but where, and when?

And then his prayers were answered.

The headlights *right* behind him flared in the darkness, suddenly beaming.

They were close.

Far, far too close.

The SUV rear-ended him and thrust the Tiguan into the car in front.

Jamming his vehicle in place.

Jason King tightened his grip on the Glock, bit down on the metaphorical mouthpiece, and went to war.

55

T he team came in, silent and morose.

They didn't introduce themselves.

There were four of them.

Three men, and a woman.

They entered quietly, crossed to the opposite wall, and stood shoulder to shoulder. They were dressed simply in tracksuit pants and loose-fitting sweaters — Slater figured Ali Hawk favoured getting results over implementing a strict dress code. It matched the man's penchant for efficiency. He didn't care about how people looked.

He wanted progress.

One of Hawk's guards stepped into the room next. Slater watched it all unfold like some sort of sick silent film. The guard nodded a polite greeting to his boss, and stood at attention just inside the doorway. He crossed his hands behind his back and waited for further instruction. It was clear he'd been told to enter after the team of scientists, but hadn't been informed of anything else.

He was short — maybe five eight — and stocky. He had coarse weather-beaten skin and a grey five o'clock shadow and rough fat fingers. He was an outdoorsman, used to toiling away beneath an open sky — no matter the weather. He seemed loyal enough to his boss.

The woman in the team of four unclipped a small electronic device about the size of a smartphone from her utility belt. She checked the screen — glowing softly in the dim lighting — and nodded once to Ali Hawk.

Hawk turned around, looked Slater deep in the eyes, and said, 'Watch this.'

His voice came out louder than before, and the tone had changed. It was still patient and methodical, but now it dripped with authority.

Slater got the sense something awfully sinister was about to happen.

Hawk said, 'Ray, please show our prisoner your scar.'

The guard named Ray looked at Hawk for a beat, mulling over the strange request. Then he shrugged, and nodded, and turned a hundred and eighty degrees on the spot to face the opposite wall. He reached over his shoulder and lifted his hair up at the back of his neck, revealing a jagged purple scar perhaps six inches in length, running all the way down to the collar of his shirt.

He dropped his hair back into place, turned around, and nodded again.

'Ray was one of our first test subjects,' Hawk said. 'He volunteered. We've substantially cleaned up the insertion process since then. No more scars like that. But would you say it's been worth it, Ray?'

'Absolutely, boss,' the man said.

He had a thick, rough Australian accent, and Slater got the impression he was ex-military.

Slater knew the type — just from the man's micro-expressions.

He'd seen them a thousand times before.

The eagerness to impress, the ramrod straight posture, the capacity to take any order from the man paying the bills. And on top of all of that, the ease at which he blended into a macabre setting like this.

A disillusioned ex-soldier wondering why he put himself through hell for a measly paycheque when individuals like Ali Hawk were perfectly happy to pay for his services post-retirement.

Sure, he had to look the other way every now and then to preserve his morality.

But what did that matter in the grand scheme of things?

Hawk said, 'Ray, come over here.'

The guard approached tentatively, aware of Slater tied to the bed in the corner. A trickle of unease crossed his face, but only for a moment. He didn't like the weird pacing of the conversation, or the apparent performance he was putting on for their prisoner.

But the need to please his boss trumped everything else, so he crossed the room and pulled to a halt right in front of Hawk.

They were nose to nose, or they would have been if Hawk hadn't stood a considerable amount taller. Almost six inches, Slater figured.

Hawk reached around to the small of his back and pulled a Glock 19 from a holster.

He pressed it into Ray's palm.

He closed Ray's fingers around the sleek black metal.

He said, 'Ray, go stand over there.'

Ray looked down at the Glock in his hand.

Slater could taste the tension in the air.

Ray nodded.

His default setting, it seemed.

He crossed to the other side of the room, putting a dozen feet of distance between himself and the rest of the occupants. Slater saw him place his back against the far wall. He stood at attention, and raised an eyebrow in question.

The guard said, 'What are we doing here, boss?'

Hawk said, 'I just want to show my prisoner something.'

'What do you want me to do?'

Silence.

'What's with the gun, boss?'

Silence.

'You want me to shoot that guy on the bed?'

Silence.

Slater stayed perfectly still.

He could hear his own heartbeat.

Hawk turned to the team of four.

The woman glanced down at the device in her hand.

She studied a reading.

She looked up, and gave a final nod of approval.

Whatever was about to happen, it was primed and ready to go.

Hawk said, 'Ray, I want you to shoot yourself in the head.'

'What?'

'Under the chin. Just aim the barrel toward the ceiling and pull the trigger.'

If not for the deathly stillness in the air, Slater wouldn't have noticed the woman reach out and thumb something on the screen of her device.

But he did notice.

And a moment later Ray jerked imperceptibly — just a tiny, subconscious twitch in the limbs — and then he smiled and nodded and put the Glock under his chin and took a deep breath and pulled the trigger and a geyser of blood exploded out the top of his head and his lifeless corpse crumpled to the floor.

The gunshot blared *loud* in the confined space.

Deafening.

Slater couldn't cover his ears with his hands — they were shackled to the bed.

Instead he winced and closed his eyes for a moment to deal with the headache pulsing through his temple, and when he opened them again Ali Hawk was standing bedside.

Hawk said, 'You see? It's not about how much willpower you have. I can make anyone do whatever I tell them.'

Slater sat in stunned silence.

'Physical control of the mind,' Hawk whispered, astonished at his own achievements.

Then he ordered in a fresh crew to remove the body and mop up the blood.

56

King unbuckled his seatbelt and leapt over the centre console, landing in a heap in the rear seats. He moved fast — surprisingly agile considering his size and weight — and when he came down in a pile of flailing limbs across the rear seats, only a couple of seconds had passed since he'd been rear-ended.

A dark silhouette materialised on the driver's side of the car.

It threw the driver's door open and unloaded half a clip of fully automatic rifle fire into the empty seat.

The polyester shredded, and the unsuppressed gunfire resonated down the highway.

Screams rose up from the line of civilian vehicles, but King didn't hear them.

He lined up his aim with the Glock, and shot the silhouette in the face from the backseat.

The bulky figure jerked back and tumbled to the freezing asphalt outside.

King came straight back over the same centre console, and scrambled out of the driver's door. He caught the next guy en route to intercept him, but the newcomer wasn't in the right headspace. He'd just seen his co-worker's brains fly out the back of his head, and it made him screech to a halt, disrupting the flow of the attack on the Tiguan.

King made to bring the Glock up and shoot him in the face, but then the impossible happened.

He lost his grip.

The icy conditions froze his hands, and in his haste to capitalise he overcompensated and lost control of the pistol. It flew out of his hands, and he made a wild snatch for it and missed.

No matter.

Before it even hit the ground, King thundered a boot into the guy's rifle, knocking it aside and breaking the finger resting in the trigger guard. Before the man could open his mouth to scream, King grabbed his head like a bowling ball — one palm flat on each side, crushing his ears — and used the leverage to throw him to the ground. King had massive hands, and it didn't take much effort. The guy went down head over heels, tumbling and turning, and when he finally righted himself and sat up into a crouch, King snatched his Glock off the asphalt and put a round through the man's face.

Screams rose from the line of vehicles, this time louder.

This time, King noticed them.

He searched frantically for any more hostiles, but the road was empty save for the horrifying sound of traumatised onlookers. He became keenly aware of his isolation — standing in the oncoming lane between two dead men, illuminated by the headlights stretching down the highway.

Blood coated the road.

His chest rose and fell with each heaving breath.

He looked at the empty SUV that had almost been the

death of him. It rested nose-first against the back of the Tiguan, wedging it in place.

No good.

He couldn't keep using the Volkswagen.

It would take time to back the SUV out, then get back in his own car and navigate out of the line.

And then what?

It was precious time he didn't have.

In the eyes of the law, he'd just committed a double homicide.

A couple of brave individuals got out of their cars. They were both men, and they were both older, and perhaps they thought they'd try to perform a citizen's arrest.

It wouldn't work.

King steeled himself and prepared to dodge a couple of geriatrics en route to his next destination.

But where?

He was on foot.

Surrounded by wilderness.

Nowhere to go, and no help to rely on.

And then fate or happenstance made the decision for him.

Three cars peeled out of the line into the oncoming lane, at regular intervals down the queue. Stretching away from the blockage, they accelerated toward the crime scene.

There were no flashing lights.

No sirens.

And they were coming on *fast.*

Not cops.

King turned and took off sprinting for the fallen tree across the lane.

Toward lights.

Toward sirens.

Toward police that were just now starting to realise what had happened a hundred feet up the highway.

They'd heard the gunshots, and now the culprit was sprinting right for them.

Caught between a rock and a hard place, King ran for the only option he had.

57

'Democracy and office politics and unending meetings,' Ali Hawk said. 'It's all bullshit. It's a waste of time, and there's nothing I despise more than wasting time. Thankfully the four of them saw the light. The four of them were on the same page as me. They didn't take much convincing. I showed them what I'd built out here. I promised them as much leniency as I could. They signed on the dotted line.'

Slater said, 'Who are they?'

The four-person team in sweatpants and sweaters had filed out moments after killing Ray. Slater had scrutinised the looks on their faces as they left. He didn't pick up a hint of guilt. Not a shred of empathy.

Now it was just him and Hawk, alone in the room again.

There was a faded crimson patch on the shiny floor behind them.

Hawk said, 'They're the best.'

'At what?'

'Neuroscience. What you and King were to Black Force, they are to the secrets of the brain.'

'It didn't raise any red flags when they left tenured positions to come out here?'

'Sometimes I wonder if anything I'm saying rubs off on you,' Hawk said.

'Oh, it does — trust me.'

'Then you'd understand I leave nothing to chance. Three of them are officially dead, and the other is officially retired.'

'How'd you manage to pull that off? Convinced three of them to leave everyone they ever loved and cared about?'

'When you get to this level of the game,' Hawk said, 'you don't get wrapped up in sentimental bullshit. The four of them were the best neuroscientists in the world, spread across the globe, and it took painstaking research to find the right crew. But I did it, and when I made the offer they pounced on it. Think about it. They were already working obscene hours. They never saw their families anyway. And then I gave them the opportunity of a lifetime — to advance human consciousness. To make the next leap in human evolution. They all knew it would take a gargantuan commitment to go through with it, and when I gave them the choice, none of them turned it down. Three of them left their old lives behind in an instant, and the fourth had no family or friends so we didn't need to fake his death. They're ghosts out here, and we're slaving away to do things that no-one on this planet has the balls to do anymore.'

'So you'll never be investigated out here,' Slater said, his stomach sinking. 'Because nobody knows you exist, and there's no red flags being raised because nobody knows that four of the top neuroscientists in the world are here, together, in a work environment that would usually put them on a watchlist.'

'I cover all my bases,' Hawk said. 'You'd know that by

now. But you don't listen, because you don't want to comprehend the gravity of what's about to happen to you. You're wrapped up in an insulated bubble that's very, very close to bursting. I can't wait to see how deep down the rabbit hole you go when you finally lose it.'

'I'll be okay,' Slater said.

'I don't think you will be.'

'Do you have King yet?'

'I'm not sure.'

'You'd best follow that up.'

Hawk picked up a ballpoint pen from a metal tray alongside the bed and began to click it incessantly. He stared down at it, and Slater saw his pupils darting left and right, as if breaking down an infinite number of possibilities in his own head. Then he put the pen back down and turned back to Slater.

'It doesn't matter whether we get King or not.'

'I thought you said that was vital.'

'We've got you,' Hawk said. 'And I think he'll run.'

'He won't run.'

'Are you sure?'

'More sure than you are.'

Hawk said, 'I wouldn't count on loyalty in a world like this. In the new world.'

'Doesn't matter what world it is. He won't run.'

'And if we set you against him?' Hawk said. 'Will he run then? Or will he kill you?'

Slater lifted his hands imperceptibly upward, and the raw skin on his wrists bit into the handcuffs. He dropped them back down, and claustrophobia swelled in his chest.

Entrapment.

The feeling of approaching, impending doom.

He said, 'I still don't believe you.'

Hawk laughed. Loud and shrill in the quiet of the underground lair.

Hawk said, 'What else do I need to show you?'

Slater shrugged.

Inwardly, he squirmed and writhed and fought for control.

Inwardly, he lost his last morsel of hope.

Even if King was coming, he wasn't Ali Hawk.

No-one was Ali Hawk.

Slater said, 'What's the hold-up?'

Hawk stared at him. Stared right into his eyes. Pierced through to his soul.

And found nothing in his expression that resembled fear.

Hawk said, 'You're a fascinating specimen. It'll almost be a shame to change you.'

'Then don't do it.'

Hawk shook his head. 'Hell, it was worth a shot, wasn't it?'

Slater said, 'You might have a change of heart. You never know.'

Hawk said, 'Never.'

'Don't worry. I can tell.'

'You really aren't scared, are you?'

Yes, Slater wanted to say.

Oh, yes.

I'm terrified.

I'm fucking terrified.

Instead he said, 'I've got out of worse situations than this.'

Hawk smirked. 'I dare you to get out of this one.'

'King is coming.'

'And if he's not?'

'Then I'm fucked.'

'You've got all night to consider how fucked you are,' Hawk said. 'It's a twelve hour procedure tomorrow, and I don't want any of my team slipping with the scalpel in their hand. You're too valuable for that. So rest up. Dream about all the ways you might be rescued. And then, hour by hour, lose hope.'

I've already lost hope, Slater thought.

But vocalising that would be admitting his own death.

So instead he said, 'You should do it now if you knew any better.'

'Maybe if I was someone else, I would,' Hawk said. 'But I don't cave to fear. Sleep tight.'

'You too.'

Hawk made for the door, and then stopped halfway across the room. He slowly turned one hundred and eighty degrees, so he was facing Slater.

He looked at him for a full minute. Maybe two or three.

Then he said, 'Sooner or later it's going to hit you. I don't know when. I wish I was here to see it, but I have to sleep too. Can't stay up all night watching my passion project. When it *does* hit you, I want you to feel every part of it.'

'When what hits me?'

'The knowledge that you're never going to get out of here. I'm going to rearrange the tiny, intricate segments of your brain and make something that does *exactly* what I say. I'm going to use you as my right-hand man. If we get King, then I'll use him, too. If not, I don't think it will matter. I know I'm going to do great things with you. Unbelievable things. I get goosebumps thinking how far I could go. I can't wait to put you to the test.'

'I'll still be there,' Slater said. 'Locked inside my head somewhere. I'll get out.'

Hawk smiled. 'You won't exist anymore. You won't have consciousness. There'll be something else there. A clean slate. No memory. Just a blank personality that I can shape into whatever I want.'

Slater didn't know how to respond to that.

So he just sat there, dejected, wrists aching as the hand-cuffs bit deep.

'Sleep well,' Hawk said.

And he turned out the lights.

58

K ing could sense the trio of vehicles on his heels.
He didn't know what make they were, or model, or the number of occupants. He could be up against fifteen men for all he knew. Five per car.

It wasn't a significant stretch of the imagination.

But he didn't have time to check.

He ran faster, and faster, and faster, and the light behind him grew brighter. But no-one shot him in the back of the head, and for a moment he grew cocky.

He figured, *They need me alive.*

That guy told *me they need me alive.*

They won't shoot me.

But he wasn't thinking straight. He didn't realise the orders had changed — even though, minutes earlier, a silhouette had unloaded half a clip of fully automatic rounds into the driver's seat of the Tiguan.

Then a round went whizzing past his head, so close he could almost *feel* the bullet, and then he thought, *Now they just want me dead.*

So he picked up the pace and bolted for the fallen tree.

He made it and threw himself over — hands on the coarse bark, pulling, tugging, wrenching his big frame over the tree — and he came down on the other side in as ungainly a fashion as possible. He landed hard on his feet, but the momentum carried him into an ugly tumble-roll across the road on the other side.

Then there were hands on him, snatching at his shirt, trying to drag him down to a prone position.

King cleared his head, and realised it was a cop grappling with him.

Thank God for New Zealand police, he thought.

Even though there was practically a gang war unfolding in front of him, the policeman had decided to try and wrestle the nearest culprit to the ground instead of pulling out his firearm and shooting him dead.

Which he full well could have done as soon as King came over the tree trunk.

But instead he froze up, maybe hesitant to kill his first resisting arrestee in the line of duty, and resorted to the non-violent option.

Unfortunately, King didn't have time to reason with an officer of the law.

As the policeman wrapped his arms around King's chest and tried to drag him to the ground, King pivoted into an uppercut, which he placed in the centre of the man's sternum. He hit flesh and the shock carried through into bone, and the officer gasped and crumpled and loosened his grip all in the same movement.

King kicked him in the sternum to add insult to injury and sent him reeling back across the asphalt, and then he sprinted for the cop's waiting vehicle.

It was a plain sedan, pulled over beside the fallen tree, its driver door open.

King darted into the driver's seat and pulled the door shut just as a low vibration echoed through the tree trunk.

'What the fuck...?' he muttered.

Then he realised that, instead of slowing down, his pursuers had opted to ram the tree trunk head-on to minimise the time they needed to spend slowing down. A pair of silhouettes materialised on top of the trunk, like gargoyles in the gloom, rifles in their hands. They'd leapt onto the hood of their vehicle and scaled the tree in record time.

King threw the car into reverse and smashed the accelerator and twisted the wheel as hard as he could to the left.

The sedan spun, and for a moment the flashing lights on top disoriented his pursuers.

He could sense them looking from the downed policeman, to the sedan now in motion.

He could sense them putting two and two together.

The cop's not in his car.

So who's in his car?

They opened fire on the sedan.

The rear window shattered and King ducked low, fighting for control of the wheel. When he lifted his head, a pair of policemen were sprinting at him from the front. They'd both leapt out of a neighbouring vehicle, and the flashing lights alternating red and blue lit them up in the otherwise gloomy night.

King saw one of them going for his gun.

He swerved again, into the oncoming lane, and narrowly avoided a collision with the backed up line of civilian vehicles on this side of the tree trunk. The cop car fishtailed and he came back into the correct lane, narrowly avoiding the pair of policemen with the trunk of his vehicle.

If he'd connected, he might have paralysed them both for life, and that wasn't his preferred outcome.

But he missed them, and carried on, and there was a moment of hair-raising tension as another volley of rounds from the silhouettes atop the trunk riddled the back of his car. He felt the *thud-thud-thud* as the chassis absorbed some of the bullets, and he couldn't see a thing in front of him, and his vision blurred and his pulse pounded and his head spun...

And then suddenly it all fell away.

Just like that.

One second — uncontrollable chaos.

The next — a welcome breath of calm.

He kept his foot on the pedal and suddenly he was out of range of the silhouettes. The cops had no chance of catching him on foot, and their own sedan was parked awkwardly — they'd been using it as a barrier for the civilian traffic. He was flying past an endless row of stationary civilian vehicles facing the other direction. He blitzed past them and took the sedan up to its limit, until the headlights fell away and were replaced by absolute darkness.

He coughed, and braced himself against the icy wind howling in through the shattered rear window, and tightened his grip on the wheel, and let the adrenalin subside.

Chaos.

Utter chaos.

Somehow he'd come out of it unscathed.

As always seemed to be the case.

He knew what it was. The reaction speed. The uncanny reflexes. To an innocent bystander, his actions in the heat of combat would seem like a blur. Frenetic movement after frenetic movement. Blood, death, bodies, violence. And then calm.

To an innocent bystander, it all unfolded in seconds.

To King, that sort of chaos felt like years.

Because he processed information at an obscene rate.

He recalled what the man in the gravel lot had said before he died.

He went inside my head and fixed me right up, man.

King shivered.

Maybe that was what Hawk wanted.

His reaction speed. His hardwired genetic predisposition. If Hawk could change the rest of him, he could take advantage of both King and Slater's reflexes and use them for his own benefit. He could make human slaves. That was worth luring them both to New Zealand. That was worth trying to take them alive, despite their unofficial status as two of the world's most dangerous combatants.

That was worth the risk.

Dreading the consequences of failure, he floored it toward Fox Glacier. Gunshots flared in the rear mirror — but they weren't directed at him.

King knew the worst had unfolded.

The police were dead.

He concentrated on the rear view mirror, and he thought he could make out the sight of faceless silhouettes slipping into empty cop cars.

Tyres spun.

Engines roared.

The pursuit continued.

59

S later didn't sleep well.

He stayed wide awake, dwelling on how fast things had gone south. Finally alone with his thoughts, he alternated between beating himself up over his carelessness and worrying over his fate.

He'd always thrown caution to the wind in combat situations precisely because of his nonchalance toward death. He'd never talked to anyone about it, but he figured King felt the same. He figured, if he had to die, best it be quick. Best he be in the heat of the fight, waging war against his enemies, and catch a stray bullet square through the temple. He wouldn't even be able to comprehend the fact that he'd died. There would be no delay, no sick feeling in the pit of his stomach as he stressed over the potential outcomes.

Just *bang-snap-gone.*

This, instead, was torture. This was the realm of the unknown — and there's nothing more terrifying than the unknown.

Slater sat on his metal bed and felt the pain in his wrists

and the stiffness in his ankles. He hadn't even thought about the fact that if he got out of his restraints, he'd be mostly useless for the better part of ten minutes. He hadn't moved in hours, and it would get progressively worse with time. His joints would ache as he got stiffer and stiffer, his muscles locking tighter and tighter. Then, even if through some miracle he peeled himself out of the handcuffs and the shackles, he'd have to stretch out and get blood flowing back into his limbs if he had any hope of winning a fight.

So he sat, and stewed, and as the darkness closed around him his mental health steadily declined.

It began in his chest. He experienced a sensation he wasn't familiar with. His heart felt fit to burst out of his chest, and for a moment he thought he might have a heart attack and succumb to massive organ failure before Ali Hawk got his hands on his brain. But the initial panic subsided, replaced by a consistent tightness in his chest.

He controlled his breathing, and felt sweat appear at the sides of his forehead, and fought for control.

This wasn't his specialty.

He was a hard charger. He went directly toward the fight, and he stayed there until either he or his enemies wilted. So did Jason King. It was how they'd both been doing it for a decade, and neither were about to change. He didn't play the psychological game. But now he was deep in his own head, wondering exactly what Hawk would do to him.

Wondering whether he'd still be able to conceptualise reality after Hawk physically destroyed parts of his brain.

Wondering if he'd just be an automaton, coasting through a meaningless existence.

Doing whatever the hell his master told him to.

This is sick. This is fucking sick.

Get me out of here.

Just get me out of these—

He pulled both wrists up instinctively, jerking them toward the ceiling. They caught on the handcuffs and the metal bit into raw skin. He yelled into the darkness, letting out all the discomfort in his chest, and it whisked out through the open doorway and echoed down the tunnel.

All went silent.

He sat still, heaving for breath, crippled by anxiety. Something about physically changing his own mind sent a terror through him he couldn't describe. It was unparalleled. It was mental torture. It was—

A voice floated out of the darkness. It said, 'Not taking it well?'

Slater thought he could make out a figure leaning in through the doorway, scrutinising him in the lowlight.

He said, 'Am I supposed to be?'

A light came on in the corner of the room. Dull. Muted. Barely providing any illumination at all.

But it gave enough.

It was one of the scientists.

The woman.

She sauntered into the room, backlit by the weak light, her features indiscernible.

She looked like something out of a horror film, with her hair down and her face masked by shadow.

But Slater remembered her from the live demonstration with Ray.

He recalled her features.

Late thirties. Sharp colourful eyes. Smooth skin. Hair pulled back tight. A severe expression. But something there apart from cruelty. Something else. An actual personality. Not an automaton.

Could there be a chance? he thought.

He opened his mouth to speak, and he could almost see her smile gleefully in the lowlight.

He cut off what he was about to say, and instead said, 'What?'

She said, 'You were about to try and convince me to cut you loose.'

'I—'

'Did you miss the part where Hawk told you I'm a neuro-scientist?'

Slater simply shrugged — as best he could in the restraints.

She said, 'I'd bet I know what you're going to say before you say it.'

'And what am I thinking right now?' Slater said.

'You're scared, but at the same time you're reserving some hope, because you don't really know what you got yourself into. It all probably feels like a bad dream. You're wondering when you're going to wake up, but that's starting to slowly decline as this keeps playing out. So now you're probably thinking — are they crazy, or are they right? Can they actually do it? And then you'll start going down all sorts of dark mental pathways as soon as I leave this room. Because surgery is tomorrow, and then you get to find out whether we're all full of shit or not.'

'I guess I'll never know,' Slater said. 'You might kill me on the operating table if you're incompetent.'

'We're not incompetent.'

'I figured.'

'You're starting to believe all this, aren't you?'

'I don't find myself with many other options.'

'How does it feel?'

Slater stared at her. 'You're the neuroscientist. You tell me.'

'I'm asking you.'

'Shouldn't you know?'

'I can physically control parts of the mind, sure. But the brain is still a mystery to even the most qualified of us. It's staggeringly complicated. So emotions always interest me. I want to know how all this really makes you *feel*. Can you tell me?'

'Fuck off,' Slater said.

She stood there, silent, observing him. Which almost made it worse. He wanted her to lash out, to lose control, to do *anything* besides stand and watch.

She said, 'This is overwhelming to you, isn't it?'

'I said, fuck off.'

'But why are you saying that? I'm your last hope, aren't I? Shouldn't you somehow try to convince me that I'm crazy?'

'You want the truth?' Slater said.

'Obviously.'

'You're not crazy. I'm a soldier, but I'm not stupid. I can see that this is the natural progression of things. As we get more and more advanced, this was bound to happen. Sucks that I'm the guinea pig, but I guess considering how insane my life was before this, I had it coming.'

'You were only chosen because of your physical gifts,' she said. 'It's nothing personal.'

'What's your name?'

She smirked, and a flicker of emotion crossed her face. 'That would make it personal.'

'I'm Will.'

'I know.'

'Give me something. Please. I'm going insane here, and

the thing that scares me the most is that you're not insane. Because that would be easy, wouldn't it? To attribute all of this to some lunatic. But you and the others and Ali Hawk — you're not insane. Which makes it a little easier to accept, I guess.'

'You're rambling,' she said.

'Tell me your name.'

'Why is it so important to you?'

'Might be the last chance I have to ask for something with my own mind. When you change it, it won't be me.'

'You'll still be in there.'

'Not the same.'

'You're right. Technically.'

'So?'

She looked at him. 'I admire it. I'm Renae.'

'Where are you from?'

'That's all you get.'

'Do you care about what happens to me?'

She looked at him with a strange fascination. Then she said, 'No. Not really.'

'Why not?'

She paused for a long time, as if trying to put a concept into words — something that she'd always thought, but never vocalised.

Slater waited.

Then she said, 'To you, you're everything. When your life ends, the whole world ends. That's the same with everyone, isn't it? Individually, I mean. But to me, it doesn't matter. When your life ends, mine goes on. Which makes you a test subject. So I guess I look at you as an opportunity to advance civilisation. If we nail it with you, you become totally compliant. You do whatever we say. And on top of that, you're one of the most dangerous and feared men on the planet. So we can use you for whatever we need.'

'Is that really advancing civilisation?'

'It's the next step in decoding the mind.'

'So that's where we differ, then,' Slater said. 'I'm not ruthless enough to look at things from the top down.'

'I am.'

'I can see that.'

Then he chuckled. Only for a moment. But Renae noticed.

She said, 'What?'

'Nothing,' he said. 'I just had this same conversation with an old acquaintance. His name was Russell Williams. He looked at the world very similarly to you.'

'And what did that involve?'

'Looking at things from the top down. Looking at the big picture.'

'And you don't agree?'

'I'm not a philosopher. I fight.'

'So primitive,' she said, and floated back to the doorway. 'And that's why you're strapped to that bed. That's why we're free. That's why our way is right.'

'I don't care about who's right,' Slater said. 'I just want out of here.'

'Shame.'

'You still haven't caught my friend.'

She said, 'I don't think that matters. He's got enough problems of his own. He'll be dead in minutes.'

'And how do you know that?'

'Because, as far as I can tell from the radio chatter, there's all sorts of hell going on around Fox Glacier. He won't last long.'

And then she was gone, leaving him alone with his thoughts.

He sunk deep into them, and didn't notice the slightest tremor in the earth beneath him a few moments later.

A foreshock.

If he had noticed, he might have expected what followed.

60

With the lights still flashing atop the sedan, King twisted through staggering mountains.

He wiped sweat off his brow, keeping a close eye on the rear view mirror.

He fought back the sensation of treading water in an ocean trying to suck him endlessly down.

There were three cop cars on his tail.

Each commandeered by unknown forces.

Just ghastly silhouettes in the night.

He knew nothing. He didn't know if Slater was alive. He didn't know if there was any point in continuing.

He imagined fighting his way through an endless army and finally collapsing at the front door of his destination, only to find Will Slater's body hanging from the rafters.

He figured that would probably break him for good.

But he tuned those thoughts out and pushed the sedan to its mechanical limits. He barrelled into the lee of Fox Glacier only five minutes after traversing the roadblock. He was covering ground at a lightning pace, and he didn't quite know why. In the back of his mind, he understood that sooner or later he would have to face the hostiles on his heels.

But there was something symbolic about it — if he stopped to fight, he didn't know if he would have the capacity to get back on his feet.

Not if they sent ten, twenty, thirty men to delay him.

For all he knew, that was their only objective.

Maybe they knew they likely wouldn't kill him, but they were doing anything to slow him down.

Slater needs me.

So he didn't address the pursuing vehicles. He tried to put more distance between them, overtaking civilian traffic at a hundred miles an hour.

The scenery out the windows — foreboding and dark — flashed past.

Then he entered the outskirts of Fox Glacier, and all went mad.

He slowed as he noticed buildings rise up on either side of the highway, piercing the gloom. There were a couple of porch lights glowing softly, and the road constricted as it passed through the small alpine town.

King brought the sedan down to sixty miles an hour, favouring control over speed. The last thing he wanted was to accidentally obliterate a civilian crossing the road late at night. He searched the dashboard for any kind of additional controls, and found the switch to turn the police lights off.

The red and blue died out, and the night wrapped around the car.

Still travelling fast, he passed a couple of motels, a cafe, a dormant petrol station, a general store, and a lodge. He glanced over the tops of the buildings and saw the glacier itself on the right, stretching away in a long pale dagger underneath the night sky. The moonlight gave just enough illumination to see the massive natural wonder.

When he brought his eyes back to the road, they sprung the ambush.

Three sets of headlights flared bright in his rear view mirror, and King noticed the hijacked police cars rising up out of the blackness. Their flashing lights were off, but their headlights burned. King quickened his pace instinctively, keen to flee the town's limits and minimise the potential for civilians to be caught in the crossfire.

As soon as he sped up, the waiting vehicles roared out of a side street onto the main road.

There were three, four, *five* of them.

King could barely count.

It was chaos.

They sped into view, passing underneath a sign from the street they came from. King thought he made out the words COOK FLAT ROAD before the vehicles were on him.

They weren't the armoured Brabus tanks from earlier that day. Hawk must not have been able to bring them over from the east coast in time.

They were a mixture of ordinary civilian vehicles, but the armed gunmen in the back seats were far from ordinary.

They opened fire on his sedan, and in that moment King knew for sure.

They don't care if they take me alive anymore.

They just want me out of the equation.

Which means they've got Slater exactly where they want him.

And that lit a fire underneath him.

Because if Slater was dead, Hawk would stop at nothing to secure King. The plot to lure them both to New Zealand had been staggeringly complex, made up of a number of moving parts that had no guarantee of paying off. Ali Hawk had risked everything to do it. But it seemed he'd determined it wasn't worth the trouble of trying to take Jason King alive. And that meant Slater was unharmed, still alive, and there was potential for King to do something about it.

So, in that moment, the cloud of indecision lifted. All this time he'd been considering whether it was worth it to stay in the fight. And the clarity came to him in a sudden rush of understanding — like a calculator producing an answer at an incredible speed.

Slater is out there somewhere.

He needs you.

King ducked low and memorised the *exact* position of each of the speeding vehicles spreading out across the road in front of him. When his head dropped below the line of sight, a cluster of bullets smashed the windshield and hit the polyester seat behind him with meaty *thwacks.* King ignored all of it — he'd been shot at before.

This was just another day.

He used all the instinct he could muster and aimed the steering wheel at where he figured the leftmost car would end up in exactly three seconds.

Then he crushed the accelerator into the footwell and counted.

One.

Two.

Three.

He steeled himself against the seatbelt.

Nothing.

Half a second passed, and he figured, *Fuck. I've overshot it.*

He started to raise his head up, to make sure he didn't plummet off the road.

Then he T-boned the enemy vehicle.

He hit it in the rear door, and it seemed his aim held up. He heard the sound of twisting metal, followed by a terrible, guttural scream. It was barely audible above the rest of the racket, and the shock of the impact ruined his perception right afterward.

But he heard it all the same, as imperceptible as it was.

It was the rear gunner, crushed either to death or paralysis as the hood of King's sedan smashed into the rear door.

King then heard screeching tyres, and a laboured shout of panic as the brutality of the car crash faded away.

He lifted his head back up, and took in his surroundings.

The enemy vehicle screeched and twisted and flew off the road a moment later.

It fell a couple of feet to a gravel ditch, but that was enough to disrupt the balance. Its right-hand wheels lifted up, and momentum did the rest. It tumbled end over end and crashed down on its roof. King thought he saw the driver and passenger spill out the shattered windshield, their bodies and faces bloodied, but he might have imagined it. He was past the crash site in another half-second, and that was when he felt the surge.

The surge?

He'd never put a label on it, but he knew what it was.

It was the first victory notched on his belt. In the heat of a war zone, surrounded by enough chaos to make any lesser warrior wilt, he was *wired.* Primed. Ready for anything. It didn't matter that he was still in maximum danger, surrounded by vehicular carnage as the ambush party swerved and skidded in the darkness, aiming to cut him off, aiming to riddle him with bullets, aiming to tear him limb from limb. Aiming to shred him to a pulp.

None of that mattered.

What mattered was the first victory, and he took it in stride as he saw the first enemy vehicle incapacitated alongside him.

1-0, he thought.

How's the rest of this going to go?

It was a ludicrous thought to have. Especially considering there were four vehicles left, all containing armed killers, all with the tactical advantage over him. They knew the terrain. They had faster cars. They could box him in, entrap him, remove any chance of escape. They could aim assault rifles at him from four separate directions.

Who cares? he thought.

And he gritted his teeth as manic focus descended over him.

He twisted the wheel, ripped the handbrake, fishtailed wildly across the two-lane road, and aimed for the nearest car.

They expect me to run.

No-one would ever know, but in that moment a small smile crept across King's face, and he figured if he'd gone insane it was best to come out a psychotic winner than a psychotic loser.

He thought he saw a horrified face through the windshield of the oncoming car, but he might have been imagining that too.

He hit it head on, slamming against his seatbelt, stopping both cars in their tracks.

Then, before the aftershock of the collision had even worn off, he leapt out of the groaning vehicle and sprinted the few feet toward the enemy.

The rear gunner of this car was reeling — perhaps a couple of ribs were broken. He'd been hanging out the open rear window with a carbine rifle in his hand when the impact occurred. The sudden deceleration had thrust his mid-section into the window frame at an incredible speed.

He was half in and half out of the car, barely hanging onto his weapon.

King was on him in a heartbeat, and he wrenched the M4 carbine out of his hands.

A brand new rifle.

It shone in the moonlight.

Hawk spared no expense.

King used the carbine to kill three of Hawk's thugs in the idle sedan — two in the front and the incapacitated guy in the back.

Three quick headshots.

Then he turned to the other three cars making sharp turns on the desolate mountain road and said under his breath, 'Let's go.'

61

Somehow, Slater slept.

Except it wasn't really sleep, because he couldn't quite comprehend where reality started and the dreams ended. He dreamt of automatons and faceless robots. He dreamt of a changing world. A dark world. A world where the limits of what was possible turned fuzzy. And then he woke up, and realised he was in the same world. He tossed and turned and the bloodstained metal of the handcuffs bit into his raw wrists. He sucked up the pain, and fought down the panic, and sat still.

His hip flexors ached from being locked in position overnight.

A pounding started behind his temples, perhaps from the accumulation of stress.

He closed his eyes and breathed, and figured that was all he could do until they came for him.

It happened in the early hours of the morning.

Renae stepped back into the room either minutes or hours or days later. Slater had no way of knowing. There was no natural light down here, and there were no clocks on the walls. He couldn't keep track of his own wakefulness, so he figured it was best to ask.

But from her puffy face and slightly damp hair and relaxed demeanour, he figured she'd managed a good night's sleep before she came for him — so it was probably morning.

He hadn't had a good night's sleep by any stretch of the imagination.

She had a plate in her hand, and a fork in the other. Slater spotted the same food groups he'd seen Ali Hawk gorging on in the Brabus the previous afternoon. Smoked salmon. Avocado. Goat's cheese. Braised beef. And a heaped pile of spinach, freshly sautéed.

'You got a chef here?' Slater said.

Renae said, 'Of course. Hawk has everything here.'

'Is that for you or for me?'

'For you.'

'I'm not hungry.'

'You haven't eaten since yesterday afternoon,' Renae said. 'You're definitely hungry.'

'Then consider this a hunger strike.'

'You're going to eat this,' she said. 'Whether you want to or not.'

'How do I know it won't kill me?'

She narrowed her eyes, as if wondering whether he was truly that stupid.

She put the fork down and picked up a Glock pistol from one of the free-standing metal trays.

She pointed it at his head.

'This will kill you,' she said.

'But you won't. I'm the man of the hour this morning. I'm the human guinea pig. You wouldn't dare kill me before the big moment. I take it I'm not going under for at least six or seven hours if you're trying to feed me. Otherwise I'd be fasting.'

She said, 'Surgery is at midday.'

'And the time now is...?'

'Four in the morning.'

'So eight hours until I become an automaton.'

'Unless I kill you first.'

'You won't. Why are we even entertaining the possibility?'

'Hawk and I have a ... special kind of working relationship. I'm sure he'd understand almost anything I do.'

'So you're sleeping with him. Good for you. He's an attractive fellow. Doesn't change the fact that you're not going to touch me without his permission.'

She set the plate down on the tray, freeing up her other hand, and walked all the way up to the foot of the bed. She stood there, cold and silent, watching Slater. Daring him to speak.

He did.

He said, 'Are you going to stand there all day?'

'No,' she said, and shot him through the top of his foot.

At first he didn't understand what had happened. There was a delay as his brain saw the blood erupt from his sock, and then the limb went numb.

He thought, *Am I dreaming?*

He wasn't.

The pain quickly followed.

Out of some sadistic competitive instinct, he refused to react. Inside his head, his brain was a cesspool of white hot fire. His nerve endings screamed for mercy and his leg twitched uncontrollably against its shackle, but some deep primal stoicism kept his gaze unflinching.

He stared Renae right in the eyes, and he said, 'Is that all you've got?'

And he broke her.

Not on the surface.

In real time, she simply put the gun down, furrowed her brow, and left the room.

But Slater had been analysing micro-expressions for over a decade, and he saw everything. He saw the twitch in her eyes as she paired what she was seeing with the rumours that had probably been spread about Slater and King throughout Hawk's private army.

He could almost see her thinking, *Is this fucking guy human?*

Is he really the Terminator like they say he is?

And then the twitch in her eyelids gave way to very real, very perceptible anxiety. He could *feel* her heart rate increasing and her chest tightening and her throat constricting as she wondered if *she* was the one dreaming. She'd just blasted a 9mm round through the delicate bones in his foot and he'd stared at her with a bored expression on his face.

And then she realised that if she stayed there, those anxiety symptoms would compound and come out to bear, no matter how hard she tried to stifle them. She needed to be alone, *right now,* to calm down. Which was a foolish position to put herself in in the first place, which only made it worse in her own head.

That was why she turned around and left the room.

Slater's foot poured blood onto the cold metal.

When she disappeared from sight, his face contorted into a mask of pain.

He closed his eyes and crushed both rows of teeth

together and flared his nostrils and took long, ragged, deep breaths.

Because he was human.

Very human.

But what she didn't know wouldn't hurt her.

He sat there, eyes closed, bleeding all over himself, for what seemed an eternity. Then he heard commotion all around him, and the next thing he knew there was pressure on his foot. He opened his eyes and winced at the same time, and saw a man and a woman resembling nurses cleaning up his foot, ripping his sock off, assessing the wound, stopping the bleeding.

Renae, or Hawk, had sent them in.

Because what Slater said was accurate.

He was the man of the hour.

And the hour was quickly approaching.

They needed him alive for the procedure, whether Renae wanted to admit it or not.

Hurting all over, Slater imagined Jason King barrelling toward Tapanui and whispered under his breath, 'Please hurry up.'

He didn't know how much more of this nightmare he could take.

62

K ing almost immediately realised his temporary bravado wouldn't win him the rest of the fight.

The three cars skidding in semi-circles and recalibrating their aim were loaded with hostiles. The two sedans he'd already removed from the equation had three occupants apiece, but the three vehicles still alive and kicking were bigger.

Two of them were SUVs, and one was a long Mercedes sedan. The SUVs were Toyota Klugers, but the bodies had been jacked up on modified suspension, and the tyres were fat and built for off-road use.

King figured the windows were armour-plated. They had the same tint as the Brabus' from the previous day.

So King made up his mind in a heartbeat.

He hauled the dead driver out of the second sedan and dove in himself.

The three enemy vehicles completed their turns and roared towards him.

King slammed the door shut and cut off the mountain wind lashing his frame. The engine seemed to still work, so he reversed away from the crash site as fast as he dared. The hood removed itself from the empty police car opposite, and both cars shrieked in protest. When King was free, he navigated around the police sedan with one hand on the wheel. He used the other to drop the carbine across the lap of the dead passenger.

The skirmish was unfolding at lightning speed.

He completed his short detour around the wreckage and weighed his options. Ahead he saw the state highway stretching past Fox Glacier — Slater lay somewhere ahead, almost beckoning him into the darkness.

But the road was long and flat and there was no cover in sight.

Then King glanced at the entrance to Cook Flat Road.

It spiralled into the mountains, heading in the general direction of Fox Glacier.

There were no streetlights that way. King stared into the gloom and winced. Neither option appealed to him, and the fleet lying in wait to ambush him had come from Cook Flat Road.

It was familiar territory to them.

But nevertheless, it would provide a hell of a lot more cover than the open highway.

King cursed his luck and slammed a palm against the wheel.

Then he twisted it to the left.

He rocketed up the dark rural trail, flashing past a pair of broad log buildings. Then civilisation fell away as the town receded into the emptiness behind him. He quickened his pace, feeling the suspension rattle and shake as the sedan fought to handle the uneven terrain.

And suddenly there was nothing to his right.

He glanced out the driver's window — more to get his

bearings than anything else — and his heart thudded a hefty *boom* against his chest wall when he saw a darker black than the rest of his surroundings.

There was a precipitous drop right there, but his headlights did nothing to illuminate the gorge. He figured it was a valley of some kind, perhaps not as vicious of a fall as he first thought, but in these conditions it would be fatal all the same.

He reached across and tugged his seatbelt across his chest, and that was when the first hostile vehicle caught up to him.

It was one of the Toyota Klugers — big and blocky and built to handle the potholed road. King's sedan struggled and coughed and wheezed in comparison. As soon as clicked the seatbelt into its buckle, a bull bar came out of the night behind him.

It hit the back of his sedan, tearing metal and destroying the trunk beyond repair.

King fought with the wheel as all four tyres lost traction on the loose trail.

The sedan skidded diagonally to the left.

King had no time to react.

The first hit from an enemy truck, and he was going over.

He fished for the buckle, undid his seatbelt, threw the door open, and leapt out of the car.

Time stopped.

Only for a moment.

He savoured the silence. It wasn't *true* silence, but in comparison to vehicular warfare it was bliss. He fell and heard icy wind howling all around him and the distant grumble of tyres on gravel and the distant screech of metal on metal, but it was all so far away. He couldn't see a thing. It was pitch black out here, and the endless stars overhead did nothing to illuminate the rural road.

Then the ground rushed up to meet him.

He heard and felt it before he saw it. There was an ominous *woosh* as he dipped closer to the gravel, and in that moment he figured he'd only been airborne for less than a second, but the brain goes haywire in the heat of battle. Time becomes inconceivable, and the fall dragged out another few moments in his mind — when in reality no time at all had passed — and then the ground was right there and he hit it.

He'd been trained to absorb an impact.

He'd spent his whole life doing it successfully.

This time, despite the circumstances, was no different.

As soon as he felt the horrid *slap* of the soles of his feet against the ground he buckled at the knees and bent at the waist, preventing any joints from contorting the wrong way. Then he threw himself forward and tumbled headfirst, twisting a full revolution in the air. He came down across his upper back and went head over heels again, then again.

He rolled a grand total of three times, absorbing a litany of superficial injuries.

Bruises and cuts and bumps and scrapes all over.

But no broken bones. No shattered limbs.

The vital components of his physique remained intact.

He came to rest in a seated position only a few feet from the lip of the drop, and a moment later a wave of air washed over him. It took him a second to realise it was his own car barrelling past, followed swiftly by the enemy Kluger. They'd come within inches of smashing him to a pulp, almost ruining his mad leap.

But he didn't tumble to his death in an enclosed metal box.

The next moment his empty sedan plummeted over the edge.

King realised the gradient was shallow enough for him to come to a halt even if he'd gone headfirst off the side of the road — it was actually a giant hillside sloping down to a shallow valley.

But a full-sized vehicle wasn't so lucky.

The sedan went over, and pitched and groaned and spiralled down to a broken grave.

And the Kluger followed.

To his credit, the driver tried in vain to correct his fish-tail. But ramming King's sedan with the bull bar had thrown him harder off-course than he ever could have anticipated, and by the time he realised he was going over it was too late. The passengers also tried desperately to escape the moving vehicle.

King saw the rear door facing him fly open.

He jolted in shock, and waited for an armed hostile to spill out of the car before it went over. Then they would be alone atop the hillside. The pair of them sitting there in shock. One armed, one not. The mercenary would line up his aim, and then...

Bang-bang-bang.

Triple shot to the chest.

Jason King, slaughtered in the lee of a glacier, late at night on the South Island of New Zealand.

But none of that happened, because none of the men in the rear seats made it out of the Kluger before its front tyres went off the trail and the rest of the chassis followed.

The guy closest to the open door tried his best to escape the death trap.

He got one leg out of the car.

Then the doorway tilted up toward the sky, and he toppled back into the vehicle.

It disappeared from sight, replaced by the cacophony of a large SUV tearing itself apart as it tumbled down a hillside.

King tentatively clambered to his feet, and looked all around.

He was alone in the dark.

Far below, both pairs of headlights died out, smashed to pieces by the multiple impacts.

And the last light whispered out.

Two cars left, King thought.

He stood unarmed and ready with the glacier looming behind him.

And he shivered in anticipation as he heard the rumbling of engines approaching.

63

———

Slater's misplaced bravado caught up to him as the pain intensified.

He'd been shot multiple times in the past, broken countless bones, torn muscles — faced practically every injury under the sun. He thought he'd be prepared to deal with the waves of pain and nausea associated with a bullet through the top of his foot, but it tested the limits of his threshold.

The silent nurses sanitised the wound and bound it up tight. They gave him a shot of a painkiller to numb the agony, but it did nothing immediately.

Then they vanished from the room, leaving him alone to wallow in his own misery.

By now, the hopelessness was setting in. Even if King made it to the compound, there was no guarantee he would get down here. All it would take was one locked door to defeat his plan in its entirety. Ali Hawk would shamelessly kill all his guards to prevent King from getting in, and he could do that remotely. Perhaps in another scenario, King would use one of the guards to open password-protected doors and force his way in, but that wouldn't happen here.

Hawk was too smart.

Too switched on.

Too good.

They'd lost the moment they stepped off the plane.

Now he let all the pain wash over him. He closed his eyes and tuned out his surroundings. The metal room, the metal bed, the metal surgical trolleys, the cold hard surfaces, the harsh fluorescent lights, the surgical instruments arranged neatly across tabletops, the dizzying array of technological firepower on display on shelves.

It all indicated the workspace of a man who knew *exactly* what he was doing. Nothing was in this room that didn't belong.

Except Slater himself.

He didn't belong here.

But soon he wouldn't be Will Slater.

Soon he'd be a slave.

When he opened his eyes, Ali Hawk was right there in front of him.

Slater blinked, wondering if he was imagining things.

Hawk said, 'You're not dreaming.'

Slater mumbled, 'Didn't hear you come in.'

'I heard you didn't want to eat your food.'

'Your girlfriend isn't very nice.'

'She's not my girlfriend.'

'She seems to think so.'

'She knows exactly what she is.'

'Then I assume you've killed her for her disobedience,' Slater said, nodding at his bandaged foot.

Hawk pulled up a stool and dragged it in close. He sat down and said, 'It doesn't work like that.'

'And how does it work?'

'She's the best of my four specialists. She calls her own shots. I'm the CEO, in every respect, and I know how to delegate. I know how to assign control to certain individuals. She can do whatever she wants to you. Because she's the brains behind the operation.'

'I thought that was you.'

'I'm good at the big picture. She's good at neuroscience. Which do you think is more important today?'

Slater changed topics and said, 'Why the hell are you feeding me this stuff anyway?'

'Because it's good for you.'

'This is insane.'

'Is it? You're a physical specimen. I need you for your genetic makeup. You can't code that sort of reaction speed — at least, not yet. And I need you and your friend right now. I've got grand aspirations, and I'm an impatient man. So I need you in the best condition possible. No point leaving you malnourished out of spite. I'm more level-headed than that.'

'But you're not operating until later today,' Slater said. 'Otherwise I'd be fasting.'

Hawk regarded him warily. 'Very good.'

'Just common sense.'

'Common sense often falls away in times of intense panic.'

'You see me panicking?'

Slater might have been expecting Hawk to come back with an instantaneous response, but he quickly realised that wouldn't be the case.

Ali Hawk stood solemn and quiet, staring Slater in the eyes.

At no rush to get anywhere, or do anything.

More than happy to wait it out.

The tension in the atmosphere ran thick.

And Slater started to sweat.

It was the combination of the humidity below ground, the pain in his foot bolting up his leg, and the sheer unease at Hawk's calm, placid demeanour.

Slater wasn't used to this. He wasn't a master of psychological warfare. He was tough, no doubt, but there was more to intimidation than being tough.

His restraints cut deep into his wrists, and sat tight around his ankles, and he squirmed with a sudden sense of uncontrollable claustrophobia.

And Ali Hawk smiled.

'There you go,' Hawk said. 'Feel it building in your chest. Feel like your heart's about to *pop*. That's the stress I want from you. That's all I've ever wanted.'

Slater squirmed and blinked hard as a bead of sweat ran through his eyebrow and stung his eye.

But he couldn't reach up to wipe it away.

He just had to sit there as the lab experiment he was, completely at the mercy of a man he couldn't decipher, no matter how hard he tried.

Calm down, he told himself.

Calm.

Down.

It was Hawk's unending patience. The man was in no hurry. He had all the time in the world to prolong the anguish, to stretch Slater to the limits of his panic before the anaesthesia went into his arm and he woke up a very different person to the man who went under.

Slater stared at Hawk, hating the silence, hating the metal room, hating everything about his predicament.

And then something changed.

He wasn't sure what it was at first.

A slight wrinkle in Hawk's facade.

The man visibly stiffened.

As if he sensed something Slater didn't.

And then Slater started paying attention to the world around him.

He noticed it too.

The faintest rumble in the ground, intensifying with each passing second, getting more and more noticeable until it consumed the whole world and Slater wondered how the hell he hadn't noticed it in the first place. If he wasn't tied to a bed he might have panicked, but he was in such a dark headspace that he appreciated any volatility.

And he relished the look on Hawk's face — the disbelief, the irritation, but above all the fear.

Because everyone got scared.

It just took the right trigger.

And it was all the worse when you were supposed to have planned for all contingencies. You were supposed to have solidified your home to protect against New Zealand's rampant earthquakes. It seemed Hawk hadn't even done that much. Slater could tell by the look on the man's face. He was scared — but even worse than that, he was frustrated.

Not at the earthquake.

At himself.

So Slater smiled, almost laughing as the walls shook and jumped and bounced all around him, and the metal trolleys slid across the room. Their wheels went haywire, racing in all directions at once, and a couple of them pitched and spilled surgical instruments across the floor. Then the shelves went, one by one, rattling out of their supports and tumbling to the floor. Computer casings smashed and hardware fell to shreds, and Slater almost couldn't believe his luck.

Could it be?

Is this fate?

And then it continued worsening with each moment.

And the smile on his face dissipated.

His own fear reared its ugly head.

He thought, *Oh, fuck. This is bad. This is really, really bad.*

Hawk was clearly feeling the same.

This wasn't a typical tremor. This was a full-blown catastrophe, one of the ugly natural disasters that spewed out of the earth every few years on an island like this. All the hope in the room vanished — first Hawk understanding that there would be little for him to salvage, and then Slater realising that even if his captor's plans were thwarted he was still trapped down here in a death chamber.

The walls shook harder and harder until Slater figured he would die from the vibration alone.

His bones rattled. His vision blurred. The ceiling let out a long, low moan. It was dull and terrifying and demented all at once. Slater felt himself tense up all over, expecting the roof to come down on his head at any moment.

He took a desperate look at Ali Hawk, as if silently saying, *Time to let me out?*

Hawk stared back with his own perplexed expression.

Slater recognised it.

It was utter disbelief.

Faint echoes of outcries came through the open doorway, emanating from the corridor outside. Slater figured it was a couple of the neuroscientists screaming at the top of their lungs, but amidst the uproar of the earthquake he could barely hear it.

He tugged desperately at his restraints, even though his

wrists and ankles were raw. He didn't feel the pain. He didn't feel anything except the burning desire to be free, to be *out,* to be in control for the first time in this whole goddamn carnival ride.

And then, somehow, it got even worse.

There were deep rumblings from everywhere at once, in the walls and floor and ceiling, and then a colossal—

Boom.

Dust and debris blew in through the open doorway, and Slater squeezed his eyes shut. The fine cloud washed over him fast, whipping his face with sharp fragments, and he figured it might have blinded him if he'd kept his eyes open. He tasted blood between his lips, and when he opened his eyes again he found something out of a nightmare.

The air was thick, and the shadows stretched out, elongated by the lowlight. The harsh fluorescent lights overhead flickered on and off, on and off, on a loop.

Then the power went out.

Slater's world plunged into darkness.

He sat still on the metal bed and figured it couldn't get worse. He figured this was what hell felt like. Unable to see, unable to breathe, hurting everywhere, with his surroundings vibrating horrifically.

He closed his eyes and counted to ten.

Slow.

Very, very slow.

He breathed in, and out, and he counted to ten again.

When he opened his eyes for the second time, the lights were back on.

A backup generator had kicked in.

And he was in the middle of a wasteland.

64

K ing thought he felt the earth shift underneath him.

But he chalked it up to an active imagination and focused on the two vehicles barrelling toward him.

He was bunkered down in the gloom. He'd only had seconds to act, but he figured he'd made the best use of the resources he had access to.

They were slim, but he figured they were enough.

Headlights flared.

Two powerful vehicles came roaring past him, and then he heard the inevitable screech of brakes as they saw the small white object King had left in the middle of the road. They came to a halt, one by one, and armed men spilled out into the night.

And Jason King lay in wait.

He counted three silhouettes coming out of the first truck, and two coming out of the second.

Five on one.

He could do it.

He knew he could.

He had the element of surprise, and that was a rare occurrence.

One of the silhouettes bent down to pick up the object.

It was a shoe.

A white sneaker.

Its laces undone.

It had been wrenched off a foot and had tumbled out the open rear door before the Kluger spilled off the trail.

King had put it right where he knew they would see it.

One of the trucks had driven straight over it before they'd slowed down. Now one of the silhouettes picked it up and trundled over to the side of the road, peering down into the gloom. But he saw nothing. Both pairs of headlights had been smashed out in their respective descents.

'How the fuck did that get there?' one man swore.

His accent was American.

Imported muscle, King thought.

To their credit, they did a decent job of securing the perimeter. As one man scrutinised the shoe, the other four fanned out in a tight semi-circle around the two stationary trucks. But they weren't *truly* paying attention. They were concentrating on the shoe, and the absence of anything else. They kept throwing curious glances over their shoulders. Their assault rifles were trained on the surrounding darkness, but they didn't seem to actually believe that something would come out of it.

That something would come for them.

So King surged out of the brush the moment the closest guy took his eyes off the land in front of him. He closed the gap in three easy strides and kept his resting heart rate low as he drilled a right hook through the guy's nose.

Like a brick cracking an egg.

The guy reeled back out of both surprise and pain,

and King ripped the carbine out of his hands and shot the guy on the right three times — in the stomach, chest and head.

That man fell too, dead on impact, and King leapfrogged his twitching corpse and put two rounds through the head of the third guy.

The third man's head jerked back and King ducked low and caught him around the mid-section, pirouetting on the spot to accommodate the inevitable assault from the fourth man.

But it didn't come.

Exactly what King had expected.

It was dark, and chaotic, and loud. The gunshots were unsuppressed, and the massive violence was harrowing up close. The fourth guy had his gun in his hand, but he still wasn't sure exactly what was happening, and as his comrades crumpled and dropped all around him he found it hard to focus on any one thing. Adrenalin surged through his skull, and he lined up his aim on what he thought was the hostile.

But then King was propping up a dead body in front of him...

And the fourth guy couldn't confirm whether his friend was dead or not...

Is he a human shield? King could hear the guy thinking.

So the man hesitated.

He didn't shoot.

He didn't want to gun his colleague down in cold blood.

Noble, King thought.

Then he shot the fourth man once through the eye socket.

He dropped the body he was holding, and put both hands back on the rifle — another state-of-the-art carbine

— and had it aimed on the guy holding the shoe in an instant.

But there was no need to rush.

The fifth guy wasn't armed.

He was a big Asian guy. Maybe six three, maybe two hundred and twenty pounds. A mirror image of King. He stood clutching the sneaker in one hand, and the other arm hung loose by his side. There were no weapons on his belt. He surveyed the bodies, and bowed his head in shame.

King said, 'Want to get out of this alive?'

The guy looked up.

But he didn't respond.

King said, 'Do you talk?'

'I talk. But you've got nothing to offer me.'

'That's what the last guy said. And he talked.'

'I doubt that.'

King kept his mouth shut. He thought of the guy in the gravel lot earlier that evening. Opening his mouth to speak, then *jolting,* then nothing.

Dead.

Just like that.

The man holding the shoe said, 'You know what's going to happen, right?'

King said nothing.

The man said, 'You've seen it before.'

King tightened his grip on the carbine.

'It's inevitable, man,' the guy said. 'That's how he keeps us here. He doesn't even pay us.'

'You're slaves?'

'Basically.'

'I can help you.'

The guy smiled a sad smile and shook his head. 'No. You can't.'

And King knew he was right.

'Get it over and done with,' the guy said. 'Better this than the alternative.'

'What's the alternative?'

'You know.'

King said nothing.

'You know what's in my head.'

'I've seen it happen,' King said. 'I don't know what it is.'

'It's the future.'

'Is it irreversible?'

'It's in my head. You can't get it out. If he knows I'm talking to you, he'll flip the switch.'

'We can try to fix this.'

'*No,*' the guy hissed. 'He'll see the heart rate monitors die out, one by one. Those four bodies around you will show up on his computers. And then he'll flip the switch and make sure I don't get taken alive. Just to be safe. He likes to play it safe.'

King said, 'I'm sorry.'

'No hard feelings. This is the world we live in.'

'What's your name?'

'Blake. I—'

King shot him in the head.

Mid-sentence.

He figured that was the best way to do it.

The guy would have never seen it coming. He never would know what had hit him. The man's lifeless body tumbled off the trail and King heard the steady *thump-thump-thump* as the corpse bounced and rolled down the hillside.

And then he was alone again on the trail.

It was somehow colder. He couldn't help but feel like his whole world had changed in the last few days. Technology was shifting the ground underneath his feet. There would be no more primitive enemies. If he stayed in this mad game, he'd only be dealing with the best of the best. People who knew things he couldn't dream of comprehending.

Chips in heads.

Physical control of the mind.

It nauseated him.

Sickened him to the pit of his stomach.

With the wind whipping against him, he tossed the carbine into one of the empty trucks — another Kluger — and climbed into the driver's seat.

He shifted the gearstick into "drive" and executed a three-point turn on the dark road.

Then he gunned it straight back down to the town of Fox Glacier.

Slater still needed him, despite his pessimism.

And as he drove, he thought he felt another slight tremor in the ground underneath him.

Once again, he chalked it up to either his imagination or the uneven terrain.

He wasn't ready.

65

Above everything else, Slater had a nightmarish feeling of *confusion.*

He couldn't exactly put together what had happened. He was isolated down here, cut off from the outside world, at the mercy of whoever had survived the earthquake.

But had it been an earthquake, or had it been something else? Something worse?

No way to know for sure until he *got out of these fucking shackles.*

For all he knew, the world had come to an end. It wouldn't surprise him. It would fit the theme of the last few days. The helplessness, the understanding that life was shifting, that society was moving toward something incredibly dark.

Why would it surprise him if the apocalypse had arrived?

But as the dust settled, he calmed.

He wasn't dead. The room was ruined, and the air was thick with silt, but apart from that he was unharmed. The bed he sat on had avoided the bulk of the damage. The metal sheeting on the walls and floor and ceiling was twisted and warped, and the contents of the room were strewn everywhere, and most of the hardware was destroyed. Outside in the hallway Slater could see debris and rock and support beams cast around like children's playthings.

But he was alive.

Then Ali Hawk rose from the debris.

The man picked himself up slowly, assessing for injuries, and wiped a few thick locks of hair off his forehead. Dirt caked his face and a thin bead of blood trickled its way down the side of his head. He wiped that away, too. When his finger came off his skin, he peered down at it with a certain detached bemusement.

'Blood,' he said.

'Yeah,' Slater said.

Hawk jolted, as if he hadn't known Slater was there. He stared at his prisoner, then braced himself against one of the overturned trolleys as a series of aftershocks rippled through the basement.

A man in a white lab coat stumbled into the room with blood covering his face, and it took Slater a moment to realise it was one of the neuroscientists.

'Ali,' the man said.

Hawk jolted again.

Like no-one had ever used his first name.

The neuroscientist's voice was shaking.

Hawk said, 'What? What is it?'

'Renae. She's fucking ... oh, Christ.'

Hawk grimaced. 'You sure?'

'I saw it.'

'Where?'

'Just outside. George is in bad shape, too. But he'll live. Quinn is fine. But Renae ... oh, man, I'm sorry...'

'What did it?'

'The ceiling fell in. She was under it. I saw it happen. I'm sorry.'

Hawk ran a hand through his hair, and fought desperately for calm.

Then he said, 'Okay.'

The neuroscientist said, 'What do we do?'

'Proceed as planned.'

'What?'

Hawk narrowed his eyes. 'What's changed?'

'Ali, Renae is—'

'Yes, you told me. What do you expect me to do? Break down in tears?'

'I—'

'I'll ask you again — what's changed?'

Slater couldn't believe it. Perhaps because the shock was still fresh in his mind. He couldn't imagine Hawk doing anything other than collapsing in on himself. But then he weighed everything the man had told him up to this point, and it started to make a lot more sense.

He truly is psychotic, Slater thought. *He's obsessed with efficiency, alright.*

No wasted time.

No stalling.

That was the crux of it.

The neuroscientist wiped blood off his forehead and said, 'There's more.'

Hawk said, 'What?'

The man threw a glance at Slater. 'Should he be here?'

'He's chained to a bed. You think he's going anywhere? It

doesn't matter what he overhears. He'll be mine in a few hours.'

'Ali, we can't do the surgery. We can't even get out of here.'

Hawk paused. 'The elevator's damaged?'

'It's crippled. And the emergency stairwell is buried under what's left of your house. The door won't budge. It's a nightmare. Have you even seen outside this room? Come, let me show you...'

Hawk said, 'It doesn't matter.'

'What are you talking about?!'

'So what — we can't get out of here? That's fine. We've got men above ground.'

'The ones you sent after King — what happened to them?'

'Rustin and Blake will have taken care of him.'

'You sure?'

Hawk let the silence drag out. 'What — you having second thoughts?'

'I think we might be underestimating him.'

'So what? Let's say Rustin and Blake fail. Fisher and Rodgers are upstairs. They were in the house when the earthquake happened. They'll rally whatever resources we have left and work on getting us out of here. They're the four best mercenaries on the planet.'

'No they're not,' Slater said.

Hawk looked over. 'Shut your mouth unless I tell you to open it.'

'They're B level,' Slater said. 'And you know it. You might have screened them based on their track records, but there's only so much you control. They're not Jason King.'

Hawk ignored him, and turned back to the neuro-scientist.

'Get in contact with Fisher and Rodgers. See how bad the damage is upstairs, and tell them to get to work getting us out of here without drawing too much attention. For obvious reasons.'

'That'll be fine,' the neuroscientist said. 'There'll be an excavation company willing to take a bribe. But then what?'

'What do you mean?'

'This damage,' the man said, waving a hand around the space. He wiped more blood off his forehead. 'This is bad, Ali.'

'Doesn't change a thing. We—'

Another tremor cut him off, violent and sudden. Slater jolted against his restraints out of fright, and both men lunged for a handhold. Hawk braced himself against one of the trolleys, and the neuroscientist clutched the door frame with white knuckles.

More debris rained down in the corridor outside.

Hawk snarled.

When it subsided, Hawk stumbled through the mess and seized the neuroscientist by the shoulder.

And there was a manic smile on his face.

He said, 'Don't you get it?'

'What?'

'This is a blessing in disguise.'

'Ali, Renae is dead...'

'But the elevator's fucked. And you know what that means?'

The neuroscientist shook his head, at a loss for words. He stayed clutching the door frame.

Hawk said, 'I've got a feeling King beat all our guys at Fox Glacier.'

The neuroscientist stayed quiet.

Slater stayed quiet.

Hawk said, 'I've got a feeling King's on the way here right now.'

The neuroscientist stayed quiet.

Slater stayed quiet.

Hawk said, 'But he can't get in. And he has to deal with Fisher and Rodgers. And even if he does get through them, which I seriously doubt, he'll be trapped up there in the wreckage of the house. There's no way down. We're insulated.'

The neuroscientist stayed quiet.

Slater stayed quiet.

Hawk said, 'We'll proceed with the surgery. He didn't end up eating what we wanted to feed him, so we don't have to wait for the fasting window to expire. How quickly can you prepare everything?'

The neuroscientist stood still with his mouth flapping open and closed. He couldn't put it together. He couldn't figure it out.

What Hawk wanted was blasphemous.

The man said, 'Ali, George is hurt.'

'How bad?'

'Pretty bad.'

'That doesn't sound catastrophic.'

The neuroscientist leaned out through the open doorway and called, 'How's he doing?'

A voice came back saying, 'He's resting. He'll be okay. Christ, man, Renae got crushed...'

Hawk said, 'You hear that? He's resting. He'll be okay.'

'This is sick.'

'This is life,' Hawk said.

'I won't do it.'

The atmosphere got cold.

Very, very cold.

Hawk said, 'What?'

'This is madness. One of our own is dead, someone the three of us cared about, even if you didn't. George nearly had his arm severed by a piece of falling debris. He's lucky to walk away with a functioning limb. But we're all shaken up. We can't do delicate brain surgery. Not in these conditions. Look around you, man. Look at what's happened. You're in denial.'

Hawk looked around.

Slowly.

Then his gaze came back to the neuroscientist. 'I see dust, and some broken computers. Since when has that deterred you?'

'Ali, think about this.'

'I have. You're going to perform this surgery or I'm going to kill all three of you.'

'And how are you going to do that without your bodyguards down here?'

Slater stiffened.

Not a good idea, he thought.

If Ali Hawk relied on his hired muscle to do his dirty work, it was purely because of his delegation skills. Slater could tell the man was a physical specimen. Whatever he put his mind to, he achieved. He would be more than capable of holding his own in a brawl, and the neuroscientist hadn't realised it yet.

Then Hawk stepped forward and hit him in the gut.

He came in low and lazy, as if he wasn't going to put any effort at all into the punch, but at the last second he cracked his fist like a whip and hit the neuroscientist so hard the man vomited all over the floor. Hawk pushed him gently through the doorway so he stumbled on all fours out of the room like a disobedient pet, and Hawk followed.

At the last second, he turned around and said, 'I'll be right back.'

Slater swallowed hard.

And then he was alone again.

He imperceptibly moved his right wrist — his raw skin burned and ached, and he needed to shift it in place to give himself some shred of comfort.

When he moved it, the handcuff sprang open.

66

King had barely made it past the outskirts of Fox Glacier when a quiet, ominous *click* sounded from the passenger seat.

He looked across the centre console, and instantly he knew the M4 carbine was now useless.

Whoever Ali Hawk was, he had intelligence beyond anything King had ever seen. He had his mercenaries and his arsenal on lockdown. No-one was taking advantage of his resources. For good measure, King reached over and squeezed the trigger, making sure to point the barrel toward the footwell in case the gun actually went off. But he was greeted by a resigned silence, just as he knew he would be.

In frustration, he buzzed down the passenger window and hurled the gun out into the abyss.

Then he drove with both hands on the wheel and his head reeling with intrusive thoughts. All his common sense was telling him to turn around. Slater was as good as lost, but he could still create some kind of life for himself without needlessly sacrificing it for a stubborn set of morals.

But then again, there was a chance Slater wasn't lost.

Not yet.

And Will Slater would do the same for him.

So he kept the Kluger moving forward — despite the fact he was driving an enemy vehicle and would be identified easily; despite the fact he wasn't armed; despite the fact he was getting tired; despite the fact he hurt all over; despite the fact that Hawk probably had another hundred men stationed at his compound.

King ignored all of that and re-entered the coordinates into his phone. Then he followed the GPS, and simply hoped for the best.

He could strategise when he got there. Until then, there were too many extenuating circumstances. He hadn't an idea what he'd be walking into, and there was no use pondering the possibilities until he had concrete evidence in front of him.

And then he came to the outskirts of the destruction zone.

At first he couldn't believe his eyes. The Kluger rumbled down the state highway without incident for hours, but as it approached the general vicinity of Tapanui, a nightmarish scene unfolded across the landscape. King crested a rise in the highway as he branched away from the coast, and what he saw sent a tremor of unease down his spine.

There were sirens, and lights, and general panic.

Everywhere.

He saw farms lit up with flashing red and blue, and then he kept driving and came across the first of the giant jagged cracks in the highway. The asphalt had split in two, leaving a gaping maw in the road. He slowed, and tried to navigate around the crack, but it covered too much of the surface area of the highway to avoid.

The rear tyres grumbled and bounced and jolted over

the gap, and then it became clear to King exactly what was going on.

An earthquake.

Staggering in scale.

He'd felt the faint rumblings on Cook Flat Road, high in the mountains around Fox Glacier. He couldn't imagine the significance of the damage closer to the epicentre. He tightened his grip on the wheel as he passed the first of the farms affected by the quake. The tremors themselves must have subsided some time ago, but they'd smashed everything above ground to pieces before they'd dissipated. King saw a long farmhouse with its roof caved in, surrounded by emergency personnel, lit up by the ghostly spectre of emergency lights.

He continued onward.

It no longer felt like he was moving toward an objective. The landscape had become surreal — churned earth, twisted fences, the occasional visible farmhouse broken and mangled and discarded. He drove around cracks and gaps in the highway, and wondered what he should be thinking. Should he be grateful that the quake had struck so intensely and severely that it was nearly impossible for Slater to have survived? Was a quick natural death better than prolonged torture at the hands of Ali Hawk? What had become of Hawk? Had he prepared for all contingencies, or had he perished too?

In that case, why are you still driving?

The thought hammered home, and King's fingers twitched on the wheel. He almost turned it. He almost touched the brake. Looking back, he figured he might have never returned if he'd allowed even a moment's doubt to creep into his mind. Looking back, he knew that was the pivotal moment.

All hope was lost.

But he managed a final glance at the GPS, and he saw Hawk's compound only ten miles away. He could make it there in fifteen minutes — he'd have to pass through Tapanui first, but then the coordinates were right there on the map, burrowed in the foothills of the land around the town.

He thought, *Why not?*

You've come this far.

He kept driving.

Dawn broke, and the sun forced its way up over the horizon, almost reluctantly. King knew it would be a harrowing sunrise. It would reveal the staggering destruction the earthquake had caused.

Under the drapes of night, the damage had been tucked away. Hidden from prying eyes.

Now everything was exposed.

Laid bare for all to see.

A few minutes later he entered Tapanui's limits, and he saw exactly what kind of havoc a major earthquake wreaked on a small town.

67

S later forced his heart rate back down, and flexed his free hand.

He couldn't believe it.

He was staring at a ring of raw skin around his wrist, bleeding and oozing, in awful shape.

But he could see it.

It wasn't cuffed anymore.

He watched the handcuff dangle uselessly to one side, and he noticed a tiny piece of metal tumble off the side of the armrest and fall to the floor. The earthquake had shaken it loose, and Slater started wondering what else might fall in his favour.

Then something intoxicating hit him.

Hope.

It came back.

And the steely resolve of years past settled back over him.

He'd almost given up. He couldn't articulate how close he'd been to permanent demoralisation. Ali Hawk and his psychological warfare had almost broken him. It was ridiculous that something as simple as a free limb could restore him back to the monster he used to be, but in that moment he knew it had happened.

Grunts and moans of pain emanated from the corridor outside, but Slater barely heard them.

'Tell me what you're going to do,' a voice that he identified as Hawk hissed.

'The surgery,' the man gasped. 'I'll do the surgery.'

'Good.'

Slater could hear the desperation in Hawk's tone — it had lost its monotony, lost its control. He was reeling now.

Slater savoured that, too.

Then he heard footsteps.

With one finger he gently lifted the cuff back over his wrist. It sat there against his raw skin, the ends hovering half an inch apart.

Will he notice?

Slater could only hope to find out.

But Ali Hawk didn't step into the room.

The other two neuroscientists did.

George — the injured one — and a yet unnamed man in his early thirties with prematurely greying hair and cold eyes.

George had his arm pressed tight to his chest, and there was fear in his eyes. He was European, with thick black hair in a mop over his forehead and blue eyes that Slater figured were usually alive with passion. Now they were riddled with anxiety. This wasn't part of the plan. They were supposed to be allowed to conduct their research without all this madness unfolding around them.

The unnamed man wasn't scared. He had the same monotonous expression on his face as Hawk. They were cut from the same cloth. The earthquake, and the death of a close friend and colleague, were mere inconveniences.

What mattered was scientific advancement, and the unnamed man stared at Slater like he was a piece of meat.

George regarded him with confusion.

Torn between two choices.

Slater figured his best hope was trying to usher George toward doubt.

Slater said, 'What are you two doing in here?'

The unnamed man said, 'We've been told to clean this place up for surgery.'

'How do you feel about that?'

Slater made sure to stare at George as he spoke.

George said, 'I've told him it might not work. My arm, and—'

The unnamed man cuffed him around the ear, and George visibly grimaced.

'Don't talk to him,' the unnamed man said. 'Ali wouldn't want you talking to him.'

'Fuck what Ali thinks,' Slater said. 'You two can't make your own decisions? Or does Hawk have both your balls in a vice?'

The unnamed man laughed and said, 'It's almost cute that you think this will work.'

But George had a hazy, unfocused look in his eyes.

The man was deep in his own head.

And the unnamed man didn't like it.

He turned to look at his colleague. 'George. Do I need to go get Ali to beat some sense into you?'

George let his gaze drift lazily over to his co-worker, and said, 'What's the point of him beating me? He can just...'

As he said it, he tapped the back of his neck.

And Slater understood.

Hawk's chipped all of them.

Christ, what a nightmare.

George said, 'Actually, Quinn, aren't you the only one without a chip?'

Quinn said, 'Don't need it. Wouldn't even think about being disobedient.'

'That's awfully convenient down here.'

'Down here?'

Slater said, 'It means we're all trapped down here for a long time. There's no getting out without some serious excavation. Leaves a lot of room for allegiance switches.'

Quinn strode up to him and slapped him across the face.

Slater laughed back. 'Didn't Hawk tell you anything about me? Keep hitting me — I don't care.'

'You're some super soldier. Doesn't matter. You'll be our super soldier by midday.'

As he spoke, Slater scrutinised him. He had no weapons on him whatsoever, which meant if Slater revealed he had a hand free he'd quickly come up against the other three restraints.

No, he needed someone with a gun to walk right up to him and threaten to pull the trigger.

Then he could disarm them with one hand, and use the gun to control the other occupants of the room. Because he sure as hell wasn't getting out of another handcuff and two leather straps any other way.

Then Quinn got a funny look in his eye. He said, 'I'll be right back.'

Then he turned on his heel and strode over to George. He snatched the neuroscientist by his injured arm and dragged the man out of the room, ignoring his feeble protests and gasps of pain.

Slater rocked back in the bed, confused by the sudden change in the atmosphere.

Quinn's last words had given him an uneasy sense of déjà vu, but he shrugged it off.

He thought he heard the words, 'Disobedience will not cut it,' softly spoken from the corridor outside.

'I'm sorry,' George yelped. 'I made a mistake.'

'What's this?' a new voice said.

Slater recognised it.

Ali Hawk.

Quinn said, 'He's acting up. Don't worry about it.'

'Why shouldn't I be worried?'

'Because I told you not to be. That's not good enough?'

Then silence unfolded, and Slater thought of it as the tensest silence in human history. He could feel it in his bones. Either Ali Hawk was about to kill someone, or all would return to normal very shortly.

Slater had no idea which it would be.

He couldn't see a thing. His foot ached with pain, he was sweating in the stifling underground heat, and the air was still thick with dust particles.

Then Hawk said, 'Fine.'

And he stepped into the room to deal with Slater.

68

King saw desolation, and ruin, and despair.

Several buildings had collapsed, the foundations torn apart by the viciousness of the quake. There were civilians out in the street in various states of distress. Some were placid, shocked into quiet, and some were sobbing.

There were a handful of people visibly injured on the sidewalks — some with bloody faces, some pressing arms to their chests that had clearly been damaged by blunt falling objects. The roads were a mess, with cars swerving this way and that, paying no attention to the road rules.

King took it slow through Tapanui, overwhelmed by what he saw.

When he noticed an elderly woman with a grandmotherly look standing at a crossroads looking somewhat calm, he pulled up next to her and rolled the window down.

She finished instructing a pair of teenage boys on where to head for relief efforts, and noticed King looking at her.

'Yes?' she said.

'Can I help?'

'Of course. There's still people trapped in buildings. We need all the help we can get.'

'I'll be back in half an hour.'

'Where are you going?'

'Need to check on a friend in the area. But it won't take long. I don't think there's much hope for him. I'll be back to help as fast as I can.'

'Not much hope?' she said, with a look on her face he couldn't figure out.

Then he realised what it was.

It was her sudden understanding that her perspective had changed — an hour ago, she might have been horrified to hear that there was little hope of a stranger's friend being alive, and now she was realising it was the least of her concerns.

She didn't know if half the town was alive after such devastation.

So she shrugged, and gave him a glassy-eyed look, and said, 'Best of luck.'

'I'll be back,' King promised.

'We'll need you,' she said, and then she strode off down the street to take care of the first pressing concern that rose up to greet her.

He continued onward, and his stomach sank as he left the town's limits behind. Now there was nothing between him and his destination but the open road. Although ... there was some morsel of hope resting below the surface of his consciousness, floating around in there, accompanied by strange emotions. He didn't know whether he wanted to find Slater alive or dead.

He'd consistently come across people with foreign objects in their heads, and that was Ali Hawk's own staff.

What might the man do to his prisoner if he was

messing around with the minds of his own men?

That same feeling returned.

The thought that he was out of his depth.

He was in a world he knew very little about.

He pressed forward, dreading the arrival, dreading the fight — he wasn't used to a sensation like that. He'd spent his entire career barrelling toward every objective, terrified to slow down at risk of getting stagnant and losing his hardened edge. But now it seemed he wanted nothing to do with this particular fight, despite the fact that his dear friend's life might be hanging in the balance.

Unlikely, he thought.

But possible.

The GPS beeped.

You have arrived.

He slowed down, and he saw the white brick fence running around the perimeter of a vast property on the left.

The front wall was set a few dozen feet back from the highway, and a pale gravel trail led down to the start of the driveway.

From his vantage point, stopped in the middle of the highway, surrounded by nothing but churned farmland and damaged asphalt, King peered over the property wall and saw ruin.

A colossal mansion rested in the middle of gorgeous green fields.

It was a shell of its former self.

The foundations had cracked, spilling the roof into the house itself, crushing most of the top floors and dumping the entire churned pile through the ground floor's ceiling. From King's perspective it looked like a makeshift arena, as if the centre of the ruined mansion had been fashioned into a miniature colosseum.

There was a sizeable excavator picking uselessly at the rubble around the walls of the building. A driver in a high-visibility vest sat behind the wheel. Even from this distance, King recognised a civilian when he saw one.

Probably carted in to clear a path to...

To what?

There was valuable cargo in the wreckage of the house.

Or underground...

King felt a pang of hope.

Then he scouted the rest of the perimeter, because there had to be somebody above ground who called the excavator in. And they must have promised to pay him a small fortune to ensure he prioritised them over the rest of the surrounding area, even though everything in sight was just as badly affected as Hawk's compound.

King found them sitting on the cracked porch in front of the mansion. They had their knees tucked up to their chests, and they were resting their forearms on their knees.

Although they were specks in comparison to the landscape King could see, he made out their dejection.

But why?

They'd survived getting buried under a mountain of brick.

Then King noticed their hands.

Empty.

Bare.

No weapons in sight.

And it hit him.

They hadn't been armed when the quake had struck. They'd been above ground, but perhaps in their mad scramble to get out they'd left their guns on a table, or a chair, and focused entirely on preserving their own lives as the building threatened to come down on top of them. Now they were stranded outside the house without a weapon in sight, unnerved by the fact that King hadn't been caught yet, expecting him to show up and shoot them dead at any moment.

They didn't want to hide, because if their boss caught wind of that they'd be summarily executed as soon as he was pulled free from the rubble.

But at the same time it struck them as odd to sit there and sacrifice themselves the moment King showed up.

What they didn't know was that King wasn't armed either.

The situation revealed itself in all its uniqueness, and King couldn't help but chuckle.

The hairs on the back of his neck bristled.

He revved the engine, and waited for the two men to notice him at the mouth of the trail.

They looked up, and spotted his vehicle resting idly on the highway.

Neither of them reacted.

No panicked reaching for hidden weapons.

Just a look of resignation.

Which dragged on, and on, and on.

And then they seemed to realise he was stalling too.

Something clicked in the air — a mutual realisation. No-one was coming in with guns blazing. Neither of them were in a hurry to rush toward each other and finish the foe off. Because they were all weaponless, and waiting for the other party to show their hand.

But none of them had a hand to show.

The two men stood up and walked out to the middle of the circular parking lot in front of the mansion.

King turned into the property and accelerated toward them.

69

Hawk was mad.

Really, really mad.

He barged toward Slater and pulled to a halt in front of the bed. He put his hands on his hips and bore his sharp gaze downward. Slater didn't flinch.

Hawk said, 'You're still trying to win, aren't you?'

'No harm in trying,' Slater said.

'You really think you're going to convince one of my staff to switch allegiances? You really think that's going to fucking happen?'

'Judging by how angry you are, I'd say he almost did.'

Hawk snarled and yelled, 'Bring him in.'

Quinn materialised in the doorway, dragging George behind him. George had blood matted to his scalp. He looked broken. His eyes went everywhere except to Ali Hawk. He stared at the floor, then the walls, then Slater for a brief spell.

Slater saw defeat in his eyes.

Hawk said, 'George. Care to tell us if you're going to get disobedient again?'

'I didn't do anything,' the man whimpered.

Quinn slapped him in the ear.

George whimpered and cowered away.

Quinn said, 'Yes you did.'

Slater said, 'It's not too late.'

Hawk came at him with reckless abandon. Perhaps the ramifications of the earthquake were sinking home, but the illusion of calm disappeared. The rage came out in all its intensity, and Slater saw something incredibly strange in the man's eyes. Something he hadn't seen before.

A loss of control.

And when Hawk spoke, he sure didn't sound like the same Ali Hawk.

He had a completely different accent...

He said, 'Listen here, you scum. Get this through your thick fuckin' skull. You need to fuckin'—'

'Hawk!' Quinn barked.

Hawk ignored the neuroscientist. Slater was shocked by the change in demeanour, and it was only when he looked past Hawk's raging silhouette that he saw Quinn standing there with deep concern plastered across his face. At first Slater chalked it up to Quinn's boss acting erratically, but as Slater continued to watch Quinn, he saw something like frustration setting in.

Then Hawk made a lunge, and Slater stopped thinking about anything other than survival.

Hawk snatched a scalpel off the floor, resting next to one of the overturned trolleys. He came at Slater's throat with it, his teeth bared and saliva dripping from both corners of his mouth. The rage had taken him entirely. Slater had no choice but to reveal his cards.

Reveal his last desperate effort to come out the other side alive.

He wrenched his right hand out of the loose cuff and caught Hawk's knife hand in an iron grip.

Hawk froze, flabbergasted by the sudden movement.

Slater jerked Hawk forward by the knife hand and threw a colossal headbutt. The thick bone in his forehead smashed against Hawk's nose, breaking it clean. Blood sprayed and Slater kept a vice-like grip on the man's wrist, making sure the knife went nowhere.

Now the tricky part.

A single error would lead to his death. This was a game of inches, unfolding at lightning speed. But he had no other choice, so as Hawk writhed and moaned and concentrated on his broken nose Slater leant forward and opened his mouth and closed his teeth around the scalpel's handle. He crushed his fingers into Hawk's wrist, making sure the man didn't jerk reflexively and cut Slater's mouth wide open.

Then Slater wrenched the knife free from Hawk's grip using his teeth.

It came out of Hawk's palm without incident.

Slater burst into motion. He let go of Hawk's wrist for a half-second, and he recognised it as the most vulnerable moment of his life. If Hawk found the strength to pull away and managed to dart out of Slater's reach, he would be left defenceless, still chained to the bed.

It would leave him with a knife in his mouth and little else.

But Hawk didn't utilise the half-second. His nose was badly broken, and he was still reeling from the pain. And Slater's mind was moving in overdrive — barely any time had elapsed at all.

Those genetic reflexes Hawk wanted his hands on were now useful after all.

Slater grabbed the back of Hawk's shirt and pulled him

down, throwing him off-balance. He stumbled and dipped into a crouch, and Slater reached out and wrapped his arm around the man's throat.

Hawk choked and spluttered, and Slater wrenched him in tight and held him there.

There we go. You're not going anywhere.

Gently, moving carefully with the scalpel between his teeth, he pressed the tip of the blade into the soft nape of Hawk's throat.

Slater tightened his forearm, and heard the man wheeze for breath as his thorax constricted. He sensed blood rushing to Hawk's face, turning it crimson red, making veins protrude from his forehead. Then Slater squeezed harder. He let the breath sputter and wheeze out of Hawk's mouth, and just as he was about to slip into unconsciousness Slater slackened his grip a little.

But he kept his forearm pressed tight like a boa constrictor, and he kept the knife handle between his teeth. He tickled the scalpel under Hawk's chin.

'Want to save your boss?' he screamed, and saliva dripped from the corners of his mouth as he fought to keep the knife in his mouth. 'Get me out of these cuffs, right now.'

George went pale and for a moment Slater thought the man might pass out. Then George backed away — to the corner of the room. He sat down and put his head in his hands and moaned.

It was a moan of despair. Of utter horror.

And it didn't gel with the situation at hand.

Slater got a dark, dark feeling in the pit of his stomach that George knew some terrible truth. Some truth that would make him look like a fool when it came to light.

But he didn't have any more time to consider that, because Ali Hawk struggled against his grip, and Slater was forced to squeeze his forearm even tighter. That put Hawk into pure survival mode, and he kicked and thrashed his legs like he was dying. Which he was, if Slater kept his grip this tight.

But he eased off again, and muttered through clenched teeth, 'Stop fucking moving or I'll slit your throat right now.'

Hawk went still momentarily.

Then the man lifted his eyes to Quinn and said, 'Ali.'

He said his own name.

Slater paused, confused.

He figured it was just the ramblings of a man on death's door.

A man whose life hung in the balance of Will Slater's teeth.

Slater said, 'Get me the hell out of these cuffs, Quinn. You told me you respect your boss. I'll kill him right here. Then all your dreams are gone. He told me how he convinced you to come out here. To advance neuroscience. To take it to unseen heights. You can't do that if he's not bankrolling you. Think of yourself. Think of your future.'

Quinn stood still as a statue, contemplating, thinking it over.

Then he said, 'Cut his throat.'

Hawk moaned.

Slater said, 'What?'

Quinn said, 'Do it.'

Slater said, 'I'm serious here. I'll do it.'

'I know you will. So do it.'

Hawk said, 'Please.'

And Slater froze in place. He'd never heard Hawk sound like that before. It was like his voice had shifted completely. Like a new person was speaking through his body, using it as a vessel.

Then Quinn lunged at Slater.

In hindsight, Slater should have known it was calculated. He should have known Quinn never intended to actually follow through with the gesture — only to startle. But hindsight achieves nothing in the moment, and in the moment Slater thought an attempt was being made on his life.

So he twitched involuntarily, jerking forward himself to intercept what he thought would be a raging Quinn.

Then Quinn pulled back.

The neuroscientist screeched to a halt and a sickly smile spread over his features.

It had been a fake charge.

Slater felt warm blood on his neck.

He looked sideways.

The blade had plunged into Ali Hawk's artery.

The man was bleeding from the mouth, bleeding from the neck, bleeding from everywhere. Out of shock, Slater released him. Hawk slid to the floor and twitched on his back, staring up at the bright lights, his eyes nearly bugging out of his head. Then the bleeding got worse. Slater stared down at him, both horrified and resigned to his fate. Ali Hawk was his final lifeline.

There would be no mercy now.

Quinn would probably murder him in a blind rage just for having the gall to follow through with the move.

Then Slater lifted his eyes to Quinn, and realised that was exactly what the neuroscientist had been wanting to happen.

Quinn had a smug, satisfied grin on his face.

He crossed his hands behind his back and said, 'Well, that's that. Did you enjoy the show?'

Slater didn't respond immediately.

He let the silence drag out.

Quinn raised an eyebrow, and said, 'You don't understand?'

'What is this?'

Quinn strode over to Hawk's corpse and dug one foot under the man's shoulder. Then he rolled the body onto its front.

Slater stared down at Hawk's backside.

'What is this?' he said again.

Slowly, Quinn bent down and swept Ali Hawk's long hair off the back of his neck, exposing the skin.

There was a scar there.

Quinn lifted his eyes to meet Slater's shocked gaze.

Slater said, 'Oh, shit.'

Quinn said, 'There we go. Now you understand.'

'You're...?'

Quinn nodded and smiled. 'Think about it. I have physical control of the mind. You think I'd risk all of that potential on you or King pulling out some Hail Mary plan to save your own lives? You two are goddamn invincible. Seems like you cheat death every day of the week. I wasn't about to put myself in the crossfire, even though I thought I had all my bases covered. So I got to work on a few new updates and put it in the head of one of my men.'

'One of your men?' Slater said, still barely able to comprehend it. He pointed down to Ali Hawk's body. 'Who *is* that?'

'Just a grunt who looked the part. His name's Quinn. He's ex-Special Forces. I realised that most of what we think is vain. He was a fairly simple man, but he had that aura of charisma about him. He could charm anyone, and he had unending confidence. So I put the chip in his head under the guise that it would help him get smarter, better and faster. Instead I cranked the control up to eleven and fed him all my philosophies. Like the most advanced form of hypnosis on earth. We subjected him to this for weeks on end until he walked and talked like a supervillain. And you bought it hook, line and sinker.'

Slater sat in silence, stunned, unable to form a cohesive sentence.

Ten moves ahead.

The real Ali Hawk said, 'You watch too many movies, Will. You don't understand the world you're in. You think because you got one handcuff loose you stood a chance?'

Slater slumped back against the metal.

He said, 'What happens now?'

'Now we go through with the surgery.'

'You're actually a neuroscientist?'

The real Hawk laughed. 'Far from it. Everything the decoy told you was true. It just came out of his mouth instead of mine.'

Ten moves ahead.

The thought wouldn't leave Slater's mind.

He dropped his head, defeated.

70

King sauntered up to the pair, and the trio stood facing each other in the lee of the ruined mansion.

No guns.

No knives.

No weapons of any kind.

A combination of Hawk's ruthless planning, and the devastation of the earthquake.

It meant they could walk right up to each other without risk of a surprise gunshot. This would be a fight to the death with their bare hands. And there was something primal about it.

King had always preferred a weaponless fight. There was less room for luck. It came down to skill, and timing, and technique, and strength, and willpower. If you were lacking in any of those categories, the tide would shift against you and you would cave to the momentum swing. It tested your limits in a way that was unrivalled.

It was pure.

If there was anything still pure in the mad world he lived in.

King said, 'Guessing you're the muscle.'

'That's us,' the guy on the left said.

He was short, but built like an angry bull. He had thick slabs of muscle hanging off his frame — a barrel chest, rounded shoulders, thick fingers, veins on his biceps, massive traps, and tree trunk legs. King put him at five eight, but they both probably weighed the same. His face was red and there were veins in his neck.

He wouldn't last long if it came down to a tactical fight, but King doubted it would be anything like that.

King said, 'How'd the pair of you end up out here?'

The guy on the right said, 'Not a whole lot of career options after leaving the Army.'

He had an American accent and he was a whole lot bigger than his counterpart. He was lanky, sporting long limbs corded with muscle, but at his core he looked impossibly strong. King didn't quite know how he pinpointed it — he could just tell. The guy was built to inflict bodily harm. A genetic trait.

Same as King, only with sharp elbows and sharp knees and a wiry build, like a praying mantis designed to draw blood with a single strike. He had the cool predatory look of a seasoned combatant.

The shorter guy wasn't as relaxed. He was trying to be, but he couldn't mask the adrenalin coursing through him, so he shifted back and forth in the dirt.

'U.S.?' King said.

'Yeah,' the tall guy said.

'Maybe we were in the same unit for a spell.'

'Maybe.'

'Maybe we could have been friends.'

'Doubt it.'

'Why don't you walk away?'

'Can't.'

'Why not?'

'Our boss is down there.'

'You can't be sure he survived the earthquake.'

'He's alive. He called us.'

'Oh.'

'Yeah.'

'You know anything about my friend?'

'This isn't the time for conversation.'

'What is it the time for?'

'You know.'

An uneasy silence elapsed.

'I'd rather not kill you,' King said.

'Part of the job. You've got the right to try, and we've got the right to protect our man.'

'Do you know who your boss is? What he does?'

'Not all of it.'

'Is that deliberate?'

'Best not to know.'

'Why are you out here?'

'We told you. Money.'

'There's a lot of places to make money.'

'Not like this.'

'So what's it going to be?'

They were at a tense stalemate — inching closer to each other as they spoke, harnessing the palpable hostility in the air, trying to keep the conversation neutral when the primal parts of all three of their brains were screaming, *Don't waste time! Fucking do it!*

But King really didn't want to do this. He preferred when the morality was black and white.

He hated the grey zone.

He wasn't sure if they deserved to die.

He figured there were a myriad of reasons they were out here — disillusioned by authority, traumatised by war, or just plain psychotic.

Any of the above.

But then he realised he'd been out of the game too long, and that in the end it always became black and white.

When someone tried to kill him, he tried to kill them, too.

Simple.

'What are your names?' King said.

'Why?'

'When I'm done here, I want to look you up. See what you both did during your time in service. I want to know what led to this.'

'This isn't a therapy session.'

'Humour me.'

The tall guy said, 'Rodgers.'

The short guy said, 'Fisher.'

'I'm King.'

'We don't care.'

'Please just walk away,' King said. 'Get out of here. The fairytale's over. Your house is destroyed. All your boss's resources are crippled. Chalk it up to a mid-life crisis and go do something worthwhile.'

'You don't know our boss,' Rodgers said. 'He'll rebuild like *that.*'

The man snapped his fingers.

As he snapped them, King stepped in and smashed a kick into the side of his knee.

Then he darted back out of range.

Rodgers grimaced, and sweat sprung from the top of his

forehead, and he stamped his foot into the earth once or twice to test the stability of his leg.

He came away satisfied.

He said, 'Big fucking mistake.'

King said, 'You think?'

'My boss told me about you.'

'Did he?'

'I want you to know something. Before this starts.'

King said, 'Okay.'

'Black Force came to me five years ago and screened me. Because of my reaction speed. I refused. By that point I was fed up with the government, and I got out before they psychologically scarred me. But I got the offer.'

King didn't respond.

Rodgers said, 'How well will you do when you're on a level playing field with your foe?'

King thought of a quiet road in Hungary, where he'd come up against Will Slater. Slater had manhandled him.

Got his back, taken him down, locked in the choke, and forced him to tap.

Like clockwork.

King told himself he'd been angry.

He'd been overly emotional.

If it was a fair, calm, measured fight, he would have won.

Is that true?

He didn't know.

And the fear of the unknown threatened to cripple him.

But all he'd ever known was a fight.

So he stepped in and thundered a fist into Fisher's gut, then pivoted into a spinning backward elbow that crashed off the side of his skull, and as Fisher was going down into a horrifying unconsciousness King stabbed out with a front kick and caught the angry little man in the face, breaking his nose and jaw at the same time.

Fisher hit the dirt.

He hit it so hard that King feared for his life.

The man lay still.

Rodgers watched from a distance, almost bemused.

'Fisher didn't get the offer,' Rodgers said. 'I did.'

King squared up to him.

Rodgers said, 'You think you can win?'

'We'll find out.'

Rodgers burst forward and tackled him into the churned earth.

71

I n the morose silence, Slater let the scalpel fall from between his teeth.

It served no purpose anymore. The true Ali Hawk stood six feet away, well out of reach.

If the man wanted to, he could saunter into one of the other rooms and come back with a loaded firearm. It would take him perhaps a minute, tops, and then he could snuff out Slater's life like it had never meant anything in the first place.

So there was no use holding onto the scalpel.

It would only serve to antagonise.

Utterly demoralised, Slater considered pleading for mercy for the first time in his life.

Quinn — no, not Quinn, *Hawk* — spoke up. 'George, never even think about disobeying me like that again. I told you all what roles you were to play, and you almost went off-script.'

'I'm sorry,' George said, and Slater could tell he meant it.

'We're moving forward with the surgery right now. You and Eddie can start your prep. You don't need Renae — you never did. She was brilliant, but so are you two. The three of you worked fine together, but we've refined the process now. Now the pair of you can do it on your own.'

'Where is Eddie?' George said.

Slater remembered the last remaining neuroscientist — it had been a four-person team before everything had gone to hell.

Well, three, he thought.

One of them had been Ali Hawk in disguise all along.

'I might kill him,' George muttered. 'I can't stop shaking.'

'That's his loss, then,' Hawk said.

Slater grimaced and closed his eyes.

This can't be happening.

'Get everything sterilised,' Hawk said. 'I want this over quick.'

'We can't do it quick.'

'We're getting faster and faster each time. We'll make it happen. We don't have time for a lengthy procedure.'

'Why not?'

Hawk pressed two fingers into his eyeballs, frustrated by how rapidly the tide had shifted, and said, 'Because now Fisher and Rodgers aren't answering their phones.'

'Aren't they up there?'

'They were. But I've heard no word from anyone I sent after King. They've all gone radio silent on me, which shouldn't happen *ever.* So they're dead. And now Fisher's probably dead. I don't know if King can get past Rodgers, but if he does...'

King made it, Slater thought. *He actually made it.*

Holy shit.

'That's it, then?' George said, and gulped.

'They'd called in an excavator. They were working on getting us out of here. I don't know what the progress is. But if King takes over the rescue effort in the absence of *my entire fucking army,* then he'll be down here in no time at all.'

George looked like he might start to cry.

Hawk jabbed a finger at Slater and said, 'Unless we turn his genetic rival against him. We need him on our side.'

Slater saw George go deep in his own head, inching steadily toward a drop.

He thought about it a moment more, pondering.

Then he metaphorically leapt over the edge.

The fear shrank away, replaced by intense passion. There was no nerves left. George seemed to realise it was counterproductive to be scared. Now he was *relishing* the adversity, devoting himself completely to Hawk's ideas. It was the only way he could see himself walking out of this nightmare alive.

And Slater suddenly knew he'd lost his one and only lifeline down here.

George had no doubts anymore.

If King didn't make it down to the basement, he was as good as done for.

Hawk and George called Eddie — a dull unimpressive man in his late forties — into the room, and the trio started prepping for surgery.

Slater sat back in bed and forced himself not to hyperventilate.

72

King hadn't been expecting a takedown.

He'd been priming himself for the sort of visceral, no-holds-barred street fight that often rose up in situations like these.

He'd expected a wild flurry of strikes — punches, kicks, knees — which would figure out the winner in the space of a few seconds.

In fact, he'd been counting on it.

He had more muscle than the tall, lanky Rodgers, and he figured his best shot at winning early was to throw caution to the wind and enter a wild brawl. So he'd been preparing to throw a colossal haymaker, his knuckles searching for Rodgers' chin, when the man ducked low and came in with the speed and grace of an Olympic wrestler.

Rodgers plucked King's leg off the ground by wrapping both arms around his knee and lifting.

The fabled single-leg.

King hopped once, and threw a desperate punch which glanced off the back of Rodgers' head. It did nothing to deter the man.

Rodgers stepped in and sliced his lanky calf behind the leg King was using to support all his weight. He utilised momentum and technique and threw him off-balance, sending him crashing down into the dirt. The earth was soft after the quake — the tremors had shaken and loosened the dirt. King copped a mouthful of the stuff, and found himself temporarily blinded.

Temporarily meaning a quarter of a second.

But that was the game they played.

Two Black Force-calibre combatants with similar reflexes and technique. Therefore, the edge came down to the near imperceptible gaps in time that the ordinary civilian could barely comprehend. To a bystander, the fight would have looked mad — two men fighting in a space the size of a phone booth. A wild tangle of limbs and rapid, jerky movements.

But they each were aware of the gravity of a mistake.

And King had made one by failing to anticipate the takedown.

Now he reeled and wiped dirt out of his eyes, and in that moment Rodgers leapt onto his back and wrapped his legs around King's mid-section in a picture-perfect body triangle. He used the back of his knee like a socket and looped his other foot around to rest in between, preventing King from being able to shake the long lanky man off his back. Then Rodgers went straight for the choke, and King's heart rate skyrocketed. He had nauseous flashbacks to Slater executing the same movement, and for a moment he thought, *That's it. You're done. Just like you thought would happen.*

Then Rodgers slipped, ever so slightly. The man shimmied a couple of inches down King's back. He adjusted the body triangle and locked it in even tighter, crushing King's abdomen between his bony lower legs.

But there had been enough of a delay for King to clear his mind and focus on what he could control.

He wasn't giving up yet.

Rodgers sunk the choke in. He looped his arm around King's neck and squeezed tight and found the right place to lock it up. He wrenched hard, and King felt the horrific sensation of his air being cut off, and then, on top of that, Rodgers continuing to squeeze until his face turned crimson and he was drowning, literally drowning, fading rapidly, fading, fading, fading...

And then he took five strides toward the porch and launched into a full somersault.

He outweighed Rodgers by close to thirty pounds, and he was supercharged with adrenalin, aware that if this didn't work Rodgers would ride out the impact and keep the choke locked in, and then King would fade into unconsciousness, followed quickly by death.

So this *had* to work.

Which meant he put everything into it.

Every ounce of his soul.

All the blood, sweat and tears he'd expunged from his body over a decade of training. It would all be meaningless if he didn't get Rodgers off him.

He leapt off the ground and pivoted in the air, carrying the lanky man on his back, and he came down on the edge of the porch, which was nothing but a massive granite slab dropped in front of the ruined mansion.

Rodgers came down on the corner of the slab, and then all two hundred and twenty pounds of King's mass came down on top of *him*. Rodgers landed on the small of his back, and King heard a vicious, barbaric *crunch* and knew that it was his adversary's spine snapping.

One of the most repulsive sounds on the planet.

Rodgers' grip slackened instantaneously and his legs came away from King's mid-section. They both bounced off the edge of the porch in unison and spilled into the dirt...

...but King was the only one who got to his feet in the aftermath.

Rodgers lay helplessly on his back, his face white as a ghost, his eyes bulging, his mouth flapping. The man knew immediately he was paralysed. King had pinpointed the impact zone and aimed for it as best he could, and he'd succeeded.

He'd cracked Rodgers' back like it was made of plastic.

Now King stood over the lanky man and gasped for breath, letting the blood drain out of his face. His cheeks were the colour of beetroot, and the veins pulsed and throbbed in his neck.

He knew how close he'd come to passing out, and he didn't even want to think about what might have happened if he had.

To put the Black Force candidate out of his miserable new existence, King stomped down on his throat three times, destroying all the soft tissue and sending Rodgers to a quick grave. He averted his eyes from the aftermath, and when he was finished he rolled the corpse onto its stomach so he didn't have to look at the damage he'd inflicted.

When he stepped away from the body, he found the man behind the wheel of the excavator watching in wide-eyed horror.

'Please don't run,' King said, walking toward the machine.

The worker — a big, burly man with hairy forearms and a bushy beard — had no colour in his face. He slipped out of the hard plastic seat and dropped to the ground in front of the mansion. He turned to run for the front perimeter fence.

King could tell the guy wanted to be anywhere but here.

King took one look at the mansion, debris strewn everywhere, lying in ruin, and knew if he wanted any hope of uncovering Slater from the wreckage, he'd need the worker alive.

And something told him he needed to act damn fast.

He reached out and grabbed the back of the guy's shirt, stopping him in his tracks.

The worker leapt on the spot like he'd been touched by a ghost, and spun around with his fist cocked.

Before he could even throw the punch, King caught it, wrapping a giant meaty hand around the closed fist and holding it in place with brute strength.

He said, 'You need to calm down, and we need to talk.'

The worker's mouth creased into a hard line, and he wrestled desperately to break free of King's iron grip.

King wrenched his fist down to waist level, so he couldn't throw a punch in a hurry even if he got the limb free.

King said, 'Please.'

Terror spread over the worker's face. 'You just killed that guy.'

'Yes.'

'Let me out of here, bro. Please just let me out of here. I don't want any part of this. I'll give you anything.'

'You were willing to help them, and they're a hell of a lot worse than I am. You don't know the sort of suffering they cause, but you were still going to take their money. And now you're going to take mine.'

'Yours?'

'Whatever they were paying you, I'll double it. I just need you to do exactly the same work.'

'No, man,' the worker pleaded. 'There's people who need help in Tapanui. I wasn't okay with coming out here in the first place. I only did it cause I thought you were decent folk.'

'I'm not with them.'

'You just stomped one of them to death.'

'You must have missed the part where he tried to kill me first.'

'I—'

'Are you going to help me or not?'

The guy didn't respond.

King said, 'I'm going to stand here and you're going to keep doing the job you were doing. I've got a friend down there who *badly* needs my help.'

'Down in the basement?'

King paused. 'Is that what you were clearing a path to?'

'Yes. There's an emergency stairwell blocked by rubble. You didn't know that?'

'I told you — I'm not with them.'

'Why should I stay? You're not armed.'

'And still I caught you. And now I'm holding you here against your will and there's not a damn thing you can do about it. If you turn and try to run, I'll catch you. I'm faster. And then I'll do to you what I did to the last guy. You don't want that, do you?'

The worker gulped and shook his head.

'Thought not,' King said. 'Get to work. And hurry.'

73

Ali Hawk — it still felt strange to address him by his true name — advanced toward Slater with a hypodermic needle between his fingers.

'What's that?' Slater said, icy with fear.

'Just a little something to make sure you don't go anywhere when we take the restraints off. And then we'll put you under. We'll electrically stimulate your neural tissue. We'll put state-of-the-art electrodes in your head.'

Slater remained mute.

Hawk said, 'When you wake up, you'll be mine.'

Slater kept his mouth shut.

Hawk said, 'Whatever I tell you to do, you'll do it. You won't be the same person. You'll have no control over your impulses. And it's irreversible. I'll make sure they're all attached permanently. You'll never be the same.'

George was hard at work restoring the overturned trolleys to their original positions and going through the process of sanitising the surgical instruments that had spilled onto the floor during the quake. He was single-minded in his determination, and Slater found it hard to believe how the man had descended so quickly into an anarchic state of mind.

George seemed to have concluded that his options were slim and decided to press forward with the best available outcome.

Slater wondered if things would have turned out differently had King not materialised as a threat.

With a rogue agent upstairs working on freeing Slater, George might have considered the more humane options. But now *he* was being threatened, and that changed things significantly. He was no longer concerned with the morally righteous decision.

He was focused on self-preservation.

And that involved turning Slater into an automaton.

'This is just a numbing agent,' Hawk said. 'To allow us to get you into position. The good stuff comes later.'

'Why are you telling me all this?'

'Because I want you to know what's about to happen to you. Makes it more exciting.'

Claustrophobia weighed heavy on Slater's insides.

He was fine with dying — he figured if it came on the battlefield, it would come quick. But the knowledge that some parts of him would still remain and some would be snuffed out terrified him.

Would he still be conscious in this new life, but unable to control his own decisions? Or would he be a new person entirely, forged out of altered parts of his brain?

Would the old Slater be wiped out completely?

All these thoughts ran through his head and he suppressed a stifling panic attack as Hawk slid the hypodermic needle into a vein on the side of his neck.

Hawk removed the needle, and fifteen minutes passed in uncomfortable silence.

It began with a soft tingling, followed swiftly by a numbness in all his limbs at once. Hawk stood back patiently and observed the results, and only when he was sure Slater wouldn't lunge off the bed did he undo the leather straps around his ankles and unlock the last remaining handcuff on his left wrist.

Slater was free.

But so far from free at the same time.

He lay motionless in a seated position on the metal bed, and Hawk reclined it back down to a horizontal plane. Hawk wandered over to the side, and Slater got a good look at him. He scrutinised the man's features for what seemed like the first time.

The true Ali Hawk was more physically flawed than the decoy. Slater understood why he'd used such a charming, attractive double. Hawk had the cunning personality of his dead counterpart — of course he would; the decoy had a mirror image of Hawk's personality — but his receding hairline was flecked with grey, and his eyes were large and spaced a little too far apart. He had a short squashed nose and chapped lips. His skin was mottled, seemingly from years of stress.

And when he looked at Slater with those dead grey eyes, Slater saw no humanity whatsoever.

The decoy — Quinn — had elicited some sort of sinister charm. With his thick black hair swept back off his forehead and bright brilliant eyes, the decoy had evoked memories of a cunning, dashing supervillain — perhaps precisely what Ali Hawk had been going for.

The real man was more bitter, more disillusioned with the world. There was none of the intoxicating passion of the decoy.

That had been invented — a fake ideal designed to impress.

And as Slater thought of what the decoy had told him, it began to add up.

Ali Hawk was a deeply troubled man.

Slater could still talk — just. Over the course of perhaps twenty minutes, he'd lost most of the feeling in his body, but his lips still moved.

He said, 'Ordinary life wasn't enough, was it?'

Hawk frowned down at him. 'What are you trying to achieve here?'

'I'm trying to get to the bottom of this.'

'It doesn't matter whether you get to the bottom of it. This procedure is going to happen to you regardless.'

'You're a brilliant man who got everything he ever wanted early in life,' Slater said. 'You figured it all out. You bought and sold companies and got rich beyond your wildest dreams. And then you realised it didn't make you happy, so you decided to go all-out in the hunt for power. You started playing around with the human mind, and you realised technological advances in the twenty-first century could allow you to physically control the brain. And now you think that's going to put everything in place. You think that's going to make you happy. But it won't. You can keep going on this path for as long as you want, but the quest for more control and more assets is going to reach its limit. And then you'll realise you never sorted your life out, no matter how brilliant you think you are. And that's going to be a bitch of a pill to swallow. You might even commit suicide when you get to the end of the line. I hope you find some sort of redemption before then.'

Hawk could have shut him up at any point during the spiel, but the ugly little man narrowed his eyes and let scorn creep over his face. And in that moment, Slater knew he was right. No matter what happened, he could die satisfied. He'd dedicated the majority of his life to a noble cause, and that was enough to take him to the grave in a semi-blissful state.

The fear shrank away.

The unease fell aside.

His mind opened up, and accepted where he was and where he'd come from and what he'd done.

And he closed his eyes with a smile, because if this was the end of the road then it had been a worthwhile journey.

Whereas Hawk stood over him, hunched and cold, brimming with rage.

Hawk rolled him onto his front, impatient to get on with the operation, and said, 'Are we ready?'

Someone — either George or Eddie — said, 'Good to go.'

'Doesn't matter what he thinks,' Hawk mumbled to himself, but Slater heard it all. 'He's my prisoner. Doesn't matter. He's wrong. He's a dead man walking. I'm right. I'm the pioneer. I'm the high achiever. I'm who will be remembered. Yes. That's it. That's right.'

'But you won't be,' Slater said, his chin pressed against the cold metal. 'No-one will remember you before long, no matter what you achieve. You should sort yourself out before you tear the rest of the world apart. Or don't. Like I said, we both know how you feel, deep down. All of this is overcompensating. Don't die as miserable as you've lived most of your life.'

Hawk said nothing. He simply slipped a needle into the vein just below the crook of Slater's elbow and injected a general anaesthetic into his bloodstream.

Slater said, 'I'm going happy.'

Hawk didn't respond.

Slater said, 'I'm going satisfied.'

Hawk didn't respond.

Slater said, 'I'm going...'

Then he drifted into the darkness.

Perhaps forever.

74

K ing had never experienced such an anxiety-
ridden wait in all his life.

Each pile of rubble cleared by the excavator
sent a fresh pang of tension through his chest. Something
was plaguing him the entire time. A gnawing feeling of
discontent.

He had the sensation that there was *something*
happening down there in that basement.

Something horrifying.

Something that would leave Slater a broken wreck.

King replayed the events of the last twenty-four hours in
his mind — the electronic safeties on the guns, the implants
in heads, the unexplainable deaths. It all rattled him, and he
thought he was piecing together what Ali Hawk wanted
from the pair of them.

He had a rough outline mapped out.

And it horrified him beyond description.

The guy in the excavator worked diligently, as if he
suddenly understood that King's fear wasn't unfounded. He
seemed to get it. The shock of the murder wore off, and the

guy was beginning to realise that whoever owned this mansion might truly be a bad, bad man.

King could be convincing when he needed to.

In any case, the man didn't seem to be in the mood to flee. He was committed to clearing the rubble. Perhaps he'd decided that the situation was too complicated to decipher, and figured he would simply do his job and then get the hell out of there as fast as possible. Without the harrowing consequences of the earthquake, he might not have stayed. The death of a man right in front of him would have rattled him more. It wouldn't have seemed as inconsequential amongst such rampant devastation.

At some point, Fisher picked himself up out of the dirt. King turned and watched him, but didn't react. The guy's face was a swollen, incomprehensible mess. King had been accurate in his initial assessment. Fisher's jaw was broken, and so was his nose. The guy spun in a semi-circle, barely aware of his surroundings. Through swollen puffy eyes he noticed King, and visibly flinched.

King didn't react.

He simply watched.

Then he pointed at the front gate.

A command.

Fisher saw Rodgers' body, then turned back to King and nodded gratefully. Thanking him for sparing his life.

He stumbled off in the direction of the road. His legs wobbled as he walked, and a bystander might have thought the earthquake was still in full effect.

King stood solemnly amidst the ruined landscape and let the guy wander away.

He'd killed enough people for a lifetime.

But he knew it wasn't done. There was *someone* below ground with Slater. Most definitely Hawk. Maybe others.

Those who had survived the initial tremors. Maybe some guards on the top floor had made it down to the safety of the basement before the rest of the house had come down.

It took thirty minutes for the excavator to get the job done.

When it was done, the worker spilled out of the cabin and sat down in the ruins of the house. His face was pale, and his breathing was laboured. Shock was setting in. He'd just seen King beat a man to death with his bare hands, and now he was doing *work* for that same man.

It shocked him. Flabbergasted him. Like a betrayal of his own morals.

King frankly didn't have time to convince him otherwise.

He said, 'Point me in the right direction.'

The worker lifted a shaking finger and pointed to a flat stretch of dusty concrete he'd cleared out in a corner of the mansion.

'There,' he said.

With a hammering heart King ran over to the space and swept aside some of the finer debris. He found the outline of a trap door, barely perceptible after the cracks were filled with dust, and he motioned to it.

The worker nodded, still resting on his haunches.

King said, 'Wait here. I'll be back up soon. Then I'll organise a wire transfer.'

'Keep your blood money,' the worker said.

He got in his excavator, turned it around, and trundled back toward an empty trailer bed attached to a pick-up truck near the front entrance. King had missed it on his way in. He shrugged it off and turned back to the square in the ground.

This was it.

The culmination of the havoc he'd received and dished

out since running into Slater in the ruin bar in Budapest.

He didn't dare give himself the once-over physically. He knew he was in bad shape, running on fumes, and as usual he wouldn't find out how bad the damage was until the dust had settled and the mission was completed. Adrenalin was keeping him going, but it was finite, and if he stopped to assess his injuries he'd deplete himself of the vital momentum he needed to keep going.

And besides, the end was in sight.

One final hurdle.

One last-ditch effort.

Or not.

Or he'd stumble down to the basement and find a monster there waiting for him.

Because that was his grand conspiracy. That was what he suspected Ali Hawk was trying to do. To *change* Slater into something new.

Something different.

Something terrifying.

'Change his brain, man. Like he did to me.'

He shivered.

He bent down and lifted the trap door.

Then immediately sprung aside.

Because he knew, if there was anyone down there with two brain cells to rub together, they'd station a guard directly underneath the entry point.

But no gunshot rose up to greet him.

There wasn't even a panicked reaction.

Just silence.

Cold wind howled through the ruins.

King stared down into the dark abyss, and made out a circular concrete stairwell spiralling ever downward.

He took a deep breath and plunged into the dark.

75

With each step down, King picked up speed.

The stairwell was dark and dank and smelled musty. Like it hadn't been used in years. It remained silent all the way down.

At the bottom of the concrete stairs, a faint shimmer of light floated up to meet the dawn light spilling down from the open trap door.

He found himself thinking, *If they were going to ambush me, they would have done it already.*

Which means they're all focusing on something.

Something that doesn't involve me.

His thoughts flitted to the scene of an operation. He pictured them dissecting Slater's brain, taking it apart and putting it back together *different*. But in reality he knew that was nothing but an old wives' tale. In all likelihood it would be a rapid procedure, over in a couple of hours maximum, with some sort of technological wizardry in the form of a microchip placed in the correct section of the brain. Connections would be made — perhaps hardwired in —

and synced to one of the many electronic devices King had seen on his journey across New Zealand.

A world you know nothing about.

He quickened his pace. His mind started to float to the likeliest possibility.

Which was, *It's already too late.*

They've already done it.

Slater is down here.

In the shadows.

Waiting for you to arrive...

He almost froze in paralysis. Something rustled in an alcove by his shoulder. He darted out of the way as silently as he could, hands coming up to protect himself, fear compounding.

But there was nothing there.

'Are you down here?' he whispered under his breath, inaudible to anyone but himself.

It reassured him slightly. Hearing the sound of his own voice. It was so dark down here. So impossibly dark.

Was Slater watching him as he moved?

Was it the same Slater?

He saw a silhouette, dead ahead.

Muscular.

Standing tall.

Eyes fixed on him.

He blinked, and it was gone.

An apparition.

A trick of the mind.

Or something else?

He covered the last few steps and came out at a crouch in a long rock corridor strewn with debris. There were wooden support beams smashed and discarded everywhere, and parts of the ceiling had caved in. It restricted his line of sight in either direction. He sensed endless pairs of eyes on him. The faint light he'd seen earlier came from gaps in the rubble. White artificial light spilled through, but they barely illuminated the stairwell King had come from. They only served to lengthen and stretch the shadows.

King stood perfectly still, and listened hard for any sign of activity.

He found it.

Somewhere close by.

He heard murmuring, and the rustling of instruments, and metal clinking against metal, and his heart leapt into his throat.

It was the sounds of an operation.

Or the preparation for one.

He couldn't know for sure. He didn't know where it was coming from, or how far they were into the process.

But the coldness of the sounds harrowed him.

Is it too late, Slater?

Are you still in there?

He listened for only a second longer, and then some sort of primal instinct activated in his brain.

He shifted his entire mental state in a heartbeat. He was no longer the safe tactician. He no longer cared about his own personal safety. There could be an army of Hawk's minions standing guard between King and the operating theatre, and it wouldn't have affected him in the slightest.

He'd rather go down in a blaze of glory than hesitate for a second too long and allow his brother-in-arms to become a monster.

So he exploded out of his crouched position. He didn't care how much noise he made. He ran flat out for the source — weaving around rubble, leapfrogging fallen beams.

He dodged an object that looked eerily like a woman's

corpse, half-buried under rubble, but he had no time to slow down and check.

He rounded a corner, spotted an open doorway gleaming with light, and threw himself into it without a moment's hesitation.

His intuition paid off. There was no-one standing guard. The three occupants of the room had heard him coming, but all three had been wrapped up in the surgical procedure.

And for good reason.

Brain surgery had no room for error. The tiniest twitch one way or the other could result in disaster, and it seemed that Hawk wasn't willing to risk it with such a prized possession as Slater.

But Hawk was nowhere to be found.

He wasn't any of the three scientists. One was grey and balding, an entirely unimpressive man, squared away in the corner of the room with a meek expression of fear on his face.

The other two men were equally as bland, but they were the ones performing the operation.

Slater was on his stomach on a metal operating table.

Passed out.

There was a knife in the back of his skull.

King didn't even think about his next move. He just burst off the mark — despite the two surgeons wielding scalpels in self-defence. He'd never been more enraged. He'd come to this godforsaken island for vengeance and ended up falling into the scheme of a goddamn lunatic. He wasn't about to let them get a moment further in their process.

But where's Hawk?

Then King saw him. Ali Hawk was lying on his back on the cold floor, staring up at the ceiling with glassy dead eyes.

His throat was cut.

So perhaps Slater had managed some preliminary revenge after all.

Before he charged at the surgeons, King flashed a glance at Slater and deduced that the operation had just begun. They'd been in the early stages of making the first incision in the back of his head. They'd shaved away the remnants of his buzzcut and drawn lines signifying where a portion of his skull had to be lifted away.

Not yet.

It hasn't happened yet.

He's not a monster.

He's still the same man you knew.

You know if he wanted to, he could come off that table with his teeth bared and tear you limb from limb.

But he won't.

Thank God.

Because King knew Slater could manhandle him effortlessly. That was the way it had always been.

He put his own feelings of inferiority on the back-burner as he made it to the operating table.

He maintained a full sprint and lunged forward with a push kick, catching the first man square in the chest. The guy was slim and frail and in no way prepared for a fight, and he tumbled off his feet with a wild outcry of despair. King heard a vicious *clang* on the way down and realised the guy had knocked the back of his skull against the operating table.

He collapsed to the floor, out cold.

King turned immediately to the second man, who lunged at him with a scalpel in his hand. King caught a glint of the blade whizzing through the air under the harsh fluorescent lights and jerked out of the way at the last moment. But he had nowhere to go, pinned between the operating table and a row of metal trolleys. So he vaulted over Slater's unconscious body and tumbled down into the fine debris on the other side of the ruined room.

The surgeon followed him around the table, slashing wildly.

King got to his feet and kicked out, but he didn't dare put his full weight into it. The reality of a knife fight is nothing like the movies — especially when one party is armed and the other isn't.

King had all the training and natural talent in the world, and the neuroscientist was small and squared away and looked like he'd never been in a fight in his life, but that did nothing to combat the simple truth.

The scientist had a knife, and King didn't.

It was next to impossible to disarm a frenzied, manic knife-wielder. There was simply too much room for error. The slightest miss on King's part would result in a slash across one of his limbs, perhaps bone-deep.

Perhaps severing an artery.

Then he'd be useless.

The scientist came at him fast, skirting around the operating table, and King picked up one of the metal trolleys and brought it down on the guy's head.

A trolley weighs at least a hundred pounds, and King brought it down hard. With the veins in his forearms pumping he aimed for the top of the guy's forehead and slammed it home with all the desperation he could muster. There was a brutal *crunch* and for a moment King thought he'd killed the man in a single blow.

The scientist's legs gave out and the knife spilled from

his hands and he folded at the waist and crumpled to the floor.

Dust particles puffed out in all directions from the impact zone.

King grunted and lifted the trolley up again, and slammed it into the small of the man's back.

The guy cried out and lay still, helpless, possibly permanently disabled by the blow.

King didn't care.

If he'd been a moment later, they would have removed a portion of Slater's skull and changed his mind forever.

King frankly didn't care whether the scientists lived or died.

He dropped the trolley, panting, before remembering there'd been a third man cowering in the corner when he'd walked in.

A man he'd never seen before.

He started to turn around and locate the target when a hypodermic needle plunged into his neck.

76

Everything happened in the blink of an eye.

Three separate actions, unfolding in a smooth chain of frantic movement.

Bang-bang-bang.

First, King reached up desperately in a wild panic, supercharged with fright, keenly aware of the foreign object embedded in his throat. He could feel the acute sensation of the needle worming around under the skin. He found the hands clutching the needle and latched onto them.

Second, the man holding the needle depressed the plunger. King felt hot liquid flow into his neck and panic seized him.

Third, he ripped the syringe out of his neck and shoved the unknown enemy away, opting to put space between himself and the man before figuring out his own predicament.

He stumbled a couple of steps. Worry seized hold of him. He'd just been injected with something. What was it? Who'd done it?

He found the answers shortly.

It was the third man. The man with the grey hair and the squashed ugly face. He stood panting for breath a few feet from King. Manic glee spread across his face. His features lit up like a Christmas tree.

He said, 'Well, that's it, then.'

King said, 'What?'

'I win.'

'Do you?'

'You'll start feeling your body go numb soon. Shouldn't take long.'

'You're weaponless. Defenceless.'

'But I'm a lot smaller. I can outrun you.'

King lunged forward before the man finished the sentence, hands outstretched, trying to snatch hold of his clothing.

The man darted back like a whip cracking, and in an instant he overturned a medical trolley across their path.

King leapt over it, but when he landed his right ankle slipped out from underneath him.

He inhaled sharply.

Then he noticed the tingling in the back of his neck.

The ugly man smiled, still panting for breath, invigorated by his success. He was eight feet from King, over by the doorway. He was poised like a coiled spring.

King said, 'What'd you do to me?'

'It's a numbing agent. I gave you triple the regular dose.'

'Why didn't you just shoot me?'

'I don't have a gun.'

'You injected Slater with that before the surgery?'

'Yes. It was all I had available. I had to think on the spot.'

'Smart.'

King kept his voice measured, but inside he was falling apart.

His surroundings had started to blur, and he experienced the uncanny sensation that he wasn't in control of his body. When he told his arms and legs to move, they responded late.

There was a delay.

And it was only getting worse and worse with each passing second.

The scientist seemed to sense it. He smiled wider, and said, 'How did you run through all my forces and then lose to me?'

'Your forces?'

'Oh,' the man said, and wagged a finger in King's direction. 'You don't know, do you?'

'What?'

'Did you meet Ali Hawk at any point in the last two days?'

'No. I think I saw him from a distance.'

'Do you see him now?'

King jabbed a finger over his shoulder. 'What's left of him.'

'That's a decoy.'

'Oh.'

'How much do you know about what I've been doing here?'

'You?'

'I'm Hawk.'

'You're—'

But King couldn't finish the sentence. He couldn't put a coherent thought together. His mind slipped, and his surroundings started to *shimmer*.

The overhead lights grew brighter and brighter, and he began to descend into some sort of fantasy world. Like a strong dose of hallucinogens, kicking in all at once.

He said, 'Fuck.'

'That's right.'

'Why are you still standing there?'

'Because I want to watch the most feared man on the planet succumb to a liquid I jabbed in his neck. That's personally satisfying, to say the least.'

'I—'

'Let's make this fun,' Hawk snarled. 'I'm going to go get my gun from the other room. You stay here if you wish. I don't care what you do. I know you're probably still too dangerous to approach, so I'm not going to risk it. Good luck.'

Then he left, disappearing into the ruined corridor outside.

The darkness swallowed him whole.

King stood rooted to the spot, unable to do anything but let his hands drop by his sides and his fingers twitch intermittently. He thought his legs were set in concrete casts, cemented to the floor. He lifted a hand to wipe sweat off his forehead, and then a voice in the back of his head began to scream at him.

Why did you talk to him for so long?

Why didn't you try to get a hold of him?

Are you insane?

Have you given up already?

He had no answers for his subconscious. Whatever the numbing agent was doing to him, it was also dragging him down into the pit of paralysis. He couldn't think straight. He couldn't prioritise. He was losing a grip on where he was. He figured the man — Hawk? Ali Hawk? — had administered an outrageous dose.

Which made him realise he'd be unable to function in a few minutes.

And that kicked him into gear.

Because Jason King, if he was anything, was not a quitter.

He powered forward, heading through the doorway into the darkness. Rubble and ruin rose up to greet him, and before long he realised he was moving at a snail's pace.

Moving through quicksand.

The air was quicksand.

The atmosphere was mud. It was dragging him down, crushing his throat and his chest and his internal organs. Lethargy fell over him in thick, crashing waves. He gasped for breath, but he was merely shuffling through the shadows.

He came to another room, and paused by the edge of the door frame.

His head swam.

His world swam.

He clawed for breath.

He slowly, gently rounded the corner.

A muzzle flash lit up his vision, and the bullet passed right by him. It was fired from shaky hands, and he made out the hunched silhouette of Ali Hawk at the back of the small office, and he realised in that moment the man was *scared*.

Hawk — the real Hawk — had missed a shot from nearly point blank range. He'd relied for years on hired help to do all his dirty work. He was the master of delegation, but he was far from the master of his own reality.

King stumbled and lurched back behind cover, plunging out into the ruined corridor once more.

But now he was invigorated.

Now he knew he stood a chance.

And then the truth hit him. It didn't matter where his

energy levels were. He was rapidly fading irrespective of his motivation, and if Ali Hawk camped out in the back of that room he would win by simply waiting it out.

Hawk wouldn't miss the next shot.

He'd panicked at first, surprised that King had mustered the awareness to make it to his office.

It probably seemed like he was being stalked by a predator.

But now the brutal truth was hammering home, and the momentum was seeping back in Hawk's direction.

King saw shimmering light in a ring around his vision. But it wasn't coming from external sources. It was in his own head, and the walls were closing.

One last chance.

Make it count.

This was all he had.

Another minute, and he'd pass out.

Another fifty seconds, and he was gone.

Another forty…

He was still waiting.

Go, his brain screamed.

His limbs twitched.

He fought hard through the endless quicksand. He felt the heaviness of the air. His brain sunk down in his head — or, at least, it felt like it. He couldn't comprehend anything. Panic bubbled below the surface of his consciousness, threatening to seize him and lock his limbs in place.

Then it was all over.

All over…

All…

Now.

He bent down, picked up a giant slab of rock like it weighed nothing, and sprinted into the room.

77

He wasn't sure what came over him.

He would never be able to pinpoint it.

If the concept of a second wind was scientifically accurate, then he used the mother of all second winds. Truth is, he was too delirious to even know what happened.

But a sharp *click* in his brain had spurred him into action, forcing all the side effects aside, replacing them with sheer barbaric determination.

So he picked up the boulder that had fallen from the ceiling with a grunt and a heave. Perspiration ran in sheets down his chest and back and arms but he didn't dare let it compromise his grip. He ran as best he could, taking three bounding steps into the doorway, and he kept the boulder in front of his chest and face. He wondered if Hawk would have the wherewithal to adjust his aim to King's stomach in the vital seconds he had, but he knew the man wouldn't.

He bounded forward.

The boulder jolted once, twice, three times.

Three shots.

Cracking the rock. Deafening in the enclosed space.

King flinched.

But he kept moving.

And he stayed alive.

And then it was over.

King hurled the boulder with every ounce of strength in his body — it weighed well north of three hundred pounds, and it required an animalistic intensity he was only able to tap into every so often.

It wrenched all the strength from his bones, and sapped all the willpower from his mind, and he knew the second he let go of the boulder it would be the final action he carried out before he passed out.

As the boulder was in the air, King fell to his knees.

He could barely keep his eyes open.

But he fought to stay conscious for a single second longer, because he needed to see the result.

He needed to see whether he would wake up from the ensuing sleep, or stay under forever with a bullet lodged in his brain.

The rock crushed Hawk against the far wall.

It broke his skull like a watermelon.

It cracked his chest.

It tore his ribs apart.

It popped his stomach like a balloon.

King didn't hear the sound the impact made, because he only had access to one or two senses — the rest were rapidly fading. But he saw the aftermath when gravity finally caught the boulder and discarded it onto the office floor.

Ali Hawk stayed standing for a few seconds.

Perhaps he was still alive, somewhere inside that broken bloody mess of a human.

Perhaps not.

But he was dead when he collapsed, and by that point King was already unconscious.

He knew he'd won.

He slipped into the deepest sleep on earth, sprawled out on his stomach on the office floor.

The carnage reached its apex, and then there was nothing but quiet.

78

S later opened his eyes.

How much time had elapsed?

Where was everyone?

More importantly — was he still the same man?

Well, he was certainly *something*. He had the same body, and as far as he could tell, the same brain. He rolled onto his back on the operating table, and a sharp pain resonated through the back of his skull as it scraped across the metal. He reached back and touched a finger to the source of the agony, and felt dried blood there.

So they did it.

I'm not the same.

Deep anxiety took hold. He started to hyperventilate, his breath coming in ragged gasps. He lay still on his back and tried to control himself. But for how long? When would it kick in? When would he lose the ability to think and feel independently? Would it be a laborious process? A slow build?

He lay on his back, with no sense of how much time had passed. But when his gaze drifted around the room, he realised the two scientists — George and Eddie — were right there beside him. George was dead. That was immediately apparent. He was lying face-down with a vicious dent in the back of his head. It matched the side of the operating table, which sported a few scuff marks. Eddie was alive, but barely. He lay in semi-conscious delirium, groaning in pain. Every couple of seconds, his legs twitched, but it seemed he had no control of them.

Then Slater noticed Eddie's shirt had been lifted up around his mid-section.

There was a dark, ugly, purple bruise across the entirety of his lower back.

And a damaged medical trolley rested beside him.

Betrayal?

Had Hawk given up on the plan at the last second?

Unlikely.

Where is Ali Hawk?

Slater tried to get up, but he couldn't. He was delirious and detached at the same time. And no wonder. The general anaesthetic was wearing off, but it was the equivalent of waking up from a lengthy procedure at a hospital. He was light-headed and dizzy and didn't have a proper grasp on reality.

He sat still on the operating table, his headspace muddied, and he decided not to try and think about anything. Coming out of a general anaesthetic in a hostile environment was a recipe for permanent psychological scarring.

He knew his mind was weak.

Patients in hospitals are gently coaxed out of their delirium and coddled for the first few hours after they wake up. Slater had none of those benefits.

He was surrounded by death and destruction. He was

unsure whether the surgery had been performed or not. He had no idea where King was, or if the man had even survived the journey to Tapanui.

So he sat there and thought about nothing at all.

His mind drifted, but he fought to bring it back to stillness.

And slowly, moment by moment, the anaesthetic wore off, unwrapping its tendrils from his brain.

He swung his legs off the table and put them down on solid ground. He stood up, and wobbled, and went straight back down into a seated position. He stayed there for a beat, and tried again.

This time, it worked.

He stumbled through the devastation, refusing to pay attention to much of it. He knew his mental state was too fragile. He treaded carefully, skirting around overturned trolleys and destroyed CPUs and the odd corpse that cropped up amidst the wreckage.

Still no sign of Hawk.

But Slater knew he was defenceless if the man showed up. His outer extremities were numb — he could barely feel his hands and feet. Gripping a weapon, let alone finding one, would be futile. He stepped out into the outer corridor — strewn with rubble and bodies, each discarded without mercy — and stumbled around in the dark for what seemed like a year.

Then he came to ... an opening.

A darker section of the darkness.

Black as night.

He went into it.

His foot nudged something.

A stair.

Could it be?

He didn't know. But he was sure as hell going to find out.

He went upward.

One stair, then two, then three.

And then he had momentum. With each step, the lingering effects of the anaesthetic ebbed out of his system. He could feel it shrinking away, reducing the numbness, bringing back feeling.

He saw light above.

He almost broke down in tears.

He imagined a sick game Ali Hawk was playing with him. Giving him hope, only to hold him at gunpoint as soon as he reached the top of the stairs.

But he forced that thought out of his mind, and kept climbing.

He came out in the ruins of Hawk's mansion.

It was late afternoon. He'd been out for eight or nine hours, he figured. His head swam as he gazed at the setting sun, and the endless farmland surrounding the compound, entirely empty. There was no-one in sight. If the earthquake had been as severe as he thought, they'd all be in Tapanui helping the injured.

He sat down in the wreckage.

He couldn't think of anything else to do.

His perception of the world had changed. His life had changed. It had all changed. He didn't know where Hawk or King were, and he didn't want to think about it. It was the first time he'd been alone since he'd run into King in Budapest. It was his first chance to digest, compartmentalise, decipher, be still...

As dusk settled over the ruins, he thought about all that had happened and wondered how on earth he'd come out the other side in one piece.

79

K ing had no dreams.

He had no premonitions.

He was dead to the world.

When he resurfaced, he had no clue how much time had passed. He sat up groggily, sporting a pounding headache and a dry mouth. He worked his gums left and right, felt the pain all throughout his body, and took a moment to compose himself before getting to his feet.

When he stood up, he almost passed out as the blood rushed out of his head.

He lowered his head between his knees, counted to ten, and tried again.

There we go.

He scrutinised the corpse of Ali Hawk. The man had come so close to holding the entire world in the palm of his hand. He would have been the pioneer of a psychocivilised society.

And perhaps he would have succeeded if he hadn't deemed it necessary to bring two of the most dangerous men on the planet into the fray. Now here he was, his body and face broken beyond repair, his features unrecognisable.

'Shame,' King said. 'You were brilliant. You almost had it.'

He figured that was enough of a funeral sermon, so he left the room.

He found the stairwell without incident and began to climb. Was it nighttime? Was it daytime?

Had he been asleep for one day?

Two?

Three?

No way to know down here in this underworld.

He took the stairs slowly. There was no need to rush. The fight was over. Everyone was dead or crippled. There would likely be an investigation on what had happened here, but the devastation of the earthquake would over-shadow any progress the authorities made. They'd probably come to some murky conclusions about what had unfolded.

By then, King would be a ghost.

He knew Slater was still probably face-down on the operating table, but he could stay there for a little while. First, King needed air. He needed to taste something other than artificiality. He needed to alleviate the tightness in his chest, a tightness that he knew didn't come from injury. It came from the ludicrousness of the situation. It was anxiety in its purest form. He needed to wind down from what had almost happened to himself, and to Slater.

They weren't automatons.

They'd kept their sanity.

They'd kept their minds.

He stepped out to find a setting sun bleeding into the horizon. The wind had picked up, and the ruins were cast in an orange hue.

Slater was sitting in the middle of them.

He was lost in thought, watching dusk fall, wrapped up deep in his own mind.

King walked over and sat down next to him.

Slater looked over and said, 'There you are.'

'Here I am.'

'Where's Hawk?'

'Crushed to death.'

'Good.'

'Yeah.'

Then they both lapsed into silence.

Thinking about what could have been.

80

I t was a long time before King spoke.

Slater let him think. He'd had his quiet time, and now he knew King needed it. They'd both been uniquely tested in ways they hadn't considered possible. They'd both been stretched to their limits.

Slater thought long and hard about the fate that would have been in store for them.

King said, 'I'm sorry I got you wrapped up in all this.'

Slater shrugged. 'It's fine. I'm fine.'

'You almost weren't.'

'How close was it?'

'When I made it down there, they were cutting into the back of your head.'

'Shit.'

'Another few minutes and you might have been beyond repair.'

'Imagine you were a few minutes late,' Slater said. 'Even if you killed them, my skull would have been hanging open. You're not a doctor. You wouldn't have been able to fix me back up. I would have woken up to...'

'Don't think about that,' King said. 'No use considering hypotheticals.'

'True. We both would have gone insane a long time ago if we did that.'

'But I get it. Sometimes it's hard not to.'

Slater said, 'Where the hell do we go from here?'

'I don't know.'

'Did you find the vengeance you were looking for?'

'No.'

Slater stayed quiet.

King said, 'I wish I never went looking. It feels like we opened a can of worms we know nothing about.'

'Maybe it's best we interfered. Without us, Hawk would have pulled it off without a hitch.'

'I still can't believe he wanted us. He knew about us. He killed my life partner just to lure us here.'

'There's always going to be people like that out there.'

'I don't know whether that motivates me to continue, or crushes me enough to just give up.'

'When have you ever given up?'

'I tried to. I tried retirement. Look where it got me.'

'That was voluntary. You achieve whatever you put in your field of view. So decide what to achieve, right now, and then we'll do it.'

'We?'

Slater said, 'No matter how ugly this game gets, no matter how bad the potential consequences become, I'm not leaving it. Because it'd be a hell of a lot worse without me in it. I realised that in Zimbabwe. I don't know what conclusion you're going to come to, but that's mine.'

'Even after you almost become something wretched?'

'Especially because of that. What if it was someone else on the operating table?'

King said, 'I don't know what I'm going to do. This wasn't the resolution I was looking for.'

'What were you looking for?'

'Something you could tie up with a ribbon, I guess.'

'That's not how life works.'

'I know. I guess in this case, I thought it would be.'

'Hawk was the one who gave the orders to kill Klara. He's dead. I'd say that ties it up with a ribbon.'

'Not like this.'

'What's changed?'

'Everything.'

And Slater knew it. He could deny it all he wanted, but that was the truth.

Slater said, 'Do you think someone else will be able to achieve physical control of the mind soon?'

King said, 'If Hawk did it, then it's probably possible. Which is downright terrifying.'

'We're not built for this world.'

'You saying we should both get out?'

'I told you — I'm staying in it, no matter what. But I can't shake the feeling that time is slowly passing us by. We'll be dinosaurs in this game before long.'

King said, 'We beat Hawk. And he was supposed to be the new breed.'

'Would we have been able to do it without the earthquake?'

Silence.

A long, pondering silence.

Slater said, 'A blessing or a curse?'

'It can be both at the same time.'

'Did you see the aftermath?'

King nodded. 'There'll be a significant body count when the dust settles. I can tell you that much.'

'We should go help out. Where we can.'

'You think that's safe?'

'Sometimes it's less about our own wellbeing and more about everyone else's.'

'You're right. I guess that's why we signed up to Black Force in the first place.'

'It's only about ourselves to an extent. And don't get me wrong, there's something satisfying about the self-discipline and self-control it brought out in us. We can apply that to any area of our life. But you can't do a job like that without wanting to help.'

'Which is why the world won't pass us by,' King said. 'There'll always be people in need of our help.'

'Does that mean you're back?'

Out of the corner of his eye, Slater saw King gaze around the wreckage.

He let King think.

Then King said, 'I don't know.'

'You'd better decide.'

'I will.'

'Then what are you waiting for?'

'I can't stop thinking about what almost happened.'

Slater didn't respond.

King said, 'If I didn't show up in time, what do you think you would have become?'

'We'll never know.'

'Does it scare you?'

'I'm sure it'll haunt my sleep for years to come. Right now, I couldn't care less. Right now I'm alive. And happy to be here.'

King bowed his head. 'Hawk put a hit out on Klara just to lure me here.'

'Yeah.'

'It was my fault.'

'It was Hawk's fault.'

'I told her early on that she shouldn't be with me. I told her something would happen. I shouldn't have let it slide so easily.'

'I should have done a lot of things, too,' Slater said. 'You think you're the only one who didn't manage to save someone? Everyone in Black Force has blood on their hands. Simply because we're genetic anomalies, which means every second we spend refusing to help people is directly contributing to their deaths. I mean, if you look at it that way, we're all monsters. But you can't look at it that way. We're just doing our best.'

'That's why you vowed to do this until the day you die?'

'Exactly.'

'I got the same feelings when I was retired.'

'Then I think we both know the answer to that question,' Slater said. 'There'll be another Ali Hawk. There'll be dozens of him. There's no limit to the depravity of certain individuals. All we can do is try our best to keep up. And if we fall short, then at least we tried.'

King looked across at Slater, their features shrouded by the darkening sky. 'Is that what this is now? A recruitment mission?'

'You tell me.'

King surveyed the landscape.

He took a deep breath.

He let it out.

He said, 'I think I'm back.'

Slater nodded, and let the ramifications of the statement sink in.

Slater said, 'I mean, really, what else would we do?'

King smiled. 'You're right. I think I've been neglecting what I do best.'

'What we both do best.'

'Seems you do it slightly better than me.'

Slater thought of the fight between them in rural Hungary. He remembered avoiding King's hardest punch with ease, slicing around behind him, locking in the choke, forcing him to tap.

He understood how drastically that could demoralise someone widely considered the best warrior on the planet.

Slater said, 'You single-handedly did all of this. You got through all Hawk's men. I was strapped to a bed the whole time. I was useless.'

'If the roles were reversed, you would have done it even easier.'

'That wasn't a fair fight,' Slater said. 'Back in Hungary.'

'It was enough.'

'You were angry. And irrational.'

'Remember when we first met?' King said. 'You beat the shit out of me in an airport.'

'I got the jump on you there, too.'

'Can't be luck if it keeps happening the same way.'

'We've never fought a fair fight. Not yet.'

King raised an eyebrow. 'Are you suggesting something?'

Slater smirked. 'While we're both semi-conscious and beat to hell? I don't think so.'

'But maybe one day.'

'Maybe. We'll see.'

'So what happens now?'

'You're back, but that could mean many things. Now you need to narrow it down.'

King sighed. 'This wasn't the way I wanted it to go, Slater.'

'Why?'

'I expected more closure. Now I'm stuck in limbo. I don't know where to go from here.'

'But you know you need to go back to helping people.'

'Helping people is a funny way of putting it. Really, it means sacrificing our health and our lives, eventually.'

'I'm doing it forever,' Slater said. 'You can go down your own path, or we can stick together.'

King stared at him. 'I know you like your solitude. What would you prefer?'

'It's not my decision to make.'

'It is, partly.'

'You decide whatever you'd like.'

King sighed again.

Then he went through the same motions.

Deep breath in.

Deep breath out.

He said, 'Let's do it.'

Slater said, 'Brothers in arms?'

'Brothers in arms.'

There was little else to be said. They hadn't discussed specifics, but they didn't need to. The resolution was enough. They were born and bred to do this. There was endless suffering everywhere, and they'd never be able to tackle all of it, and the consequences would likely ruin their lives at some point — either when their bodies broke down or they were caught in the heat of combat. But despite all the misery around them, and the losses they'd both taken over the last few months, at that moment all was right in the world.

King and Slater got up and walked out of the ruined mansion.

They reached the side of the highway in a few minutes,

stuck their thumbs out, and were picked up by a farmer heading into town to lend assistance to the injured and try to help clean up the mess. They didn't speak on the drive in. They looked out at the scenery, trying to digest what they'd been through.

Slater knew he was failing to grasp the big picture. He was only happy to be alive. Perhaps King was more morose after learning what could be done to the brain, but Slater didn't think he could take any further tension right now.

The farmer asked them if they were okay, and they both nodded.

They were bloodied.

Bruised.

But the earthquake made an effective cover story.

They made it to Tapanui, and climbed out of the car, and looked once at each other. There were a million unanswered questions lingering there in the silence.

What would they do moving forward?

How would they operate?

Were they a unit?

An army of two?

There was no clear answer.

Not yet.

For now, they were simply blood brothers.

So they nodded to each other, and surveyed the damage all around them, and got to work doing what they did best.

Helping people.

Together.

MORE KING & SLATER THRILLERS COMING SOON...

Visit amazon.com/author/mattrogers23 and press **"Follow"** to be automatically notified of my future releases.

If you enjoyed the hard-hitting adventure, make sure to leave a review! Your feedback means everything to me, and encourages me to deliver more novels as soon as I can.

Stay tuned.

Join the Reader's Group and get a free 200-page book by Matt Rogers!

Sign up for a free copy of '**HARD IMPACT**'.
Meet Jason King — another member of Black Force.

Experience King's most dangerous mission — action-packed insanity in the heart of the Amazon Rainforest.

No spam guaranteed.

Just click here.

BOOKS BY MATT ROGERS

THE JASON KING SERIES

Isolated (Book 1)

Imprisoned (Book 2)

Reloaded (Book 3)

Betrayed (Book 4)

Corrupted (Book 5)

Hunted (Book 6)

THE JASON KING FILES

Cartel (Book 1)

Warrior (Book 2)

Savages (Book 3)

THE WILL SLATER SERIES

Wolf (Book 1)

Lion (Book 2)

Bear (Book 3)

Lynx (Book 4)

Bull (Book 5)

Hawk (Book 6)

BLACK FORCE SHORTS

The Victor (Book 1)

ABOUT THE AUTHOR

Matt Rogers grew up in Melbourne, Australia as a voracious reader, relentlessly devouring thrillers and mysteries in his spare time. Now, he writes full-time. His novels are action-packed and fast-paced. Dive into the Jason King Series to get started with his collection.

Visit his website:

www.mattrogersbooks.com

Visit his Amazon page:

amazon.com/author/mattrogers23

Made in the USA
San Bernardino, CA
21 November 2019

60226677R00287